PRESS DIE TO CONTINUE

RAMY VANCE

MICHAEL ANDERLE

PRESS DIE TO CONTINUE

THE PRESS DIE TO CONTINUE TEAM

Thanks to our Beta Reader

Rachel Beckford, John Ashmore, Larry Omans

Thanks to the JIT Readers

Dorothy Lloyd
Zacc Pelter
Diane L. Smith
Deb Mader
Veronica Stephan-Miller
Peter Manis
Angel LaVey

If we've missed anyone, please let us know!

Editor
The Skyhunter Editing Team

Copyright © 2021 by LMBPN Publishing
Cover Art by Jake @ J Caleb Design
http://jcalebdesign.com / jcalebdesign@gmail.com
Cover copyright © LMBPN Publishing
A Michael Anderle Production

LMBPN Publishing
PMB 196, 2540 South Maryland Pkwy
Las Vegas, NV 89109

Version 1.00, December 2021
ISBN (ebook) 978-1-68500-638-9
ISBN (paperback) 978-1-68500-639-6

DEDICATION

Rocks in Your Pocket

—Ramy Vance

*To Family, Friends and
Those Who Love
to Read.
May We All Enjoy Grace
to Live the Life We Are
Called.*

— Michael

CHAPTER ONE

"Look, you mean bastards. Just do me a favor and shoot me?"

The stern-eyed boss man didn't look at the intruder sitting on the floor. Although the weird-talking trespasser looked strong and capable, seven of the boss man's thugs surrounded him. All sported ripped jeans, black shirts, gold necklaces, and other bling. They all brandished semi-automatic pistols at him. Instead, the boss man turned to the skinny thug standing outside the ring.

"Carl, what do you mean he just 'walked' in?"

The skinny thug shrugged, accidentally pointing his pistol at the boss man as he did. "I have no friggin' clue."

"Hey. Watch where the hell you point that gun. What do you mean you don't know? We've got guards posted throughout the building." Turning suddenly from the skinny man to face the competent-looking man on the floor—the crazy man asking for them to shoot him—the boss man said, "Who the hell are you?"

The man sitting on the floor between the boss man and Carl cleared his throat. "My name is Z." He wore combat boots, jeans, and a black muscle shirt that displayed his thick, muscular arms and trim physique. A thin gold necklace resembling those around him glinted at his neck. He looked prison-fit, and the pencil-thin scar on one half of his face only supported that idea. "Now can one of you shoot me already?"

"Shut up!" the boss man spat. In one hand, he gripped a briefcase. Z studied it. It was his mission, after all. It was why he was here.

"Yeah, shut up," Carl echoed with a tough guy shrug, inadvertently tilting his gun at his boss.

The boss man lanced Carl with a stern look. "What did I say about pointing that fucking gun in my direction?"

"Sorry. Sorry." The skinny thug lowered his gun and continued. "About twenty seconds ago, I was standing by the side of the door, filling my water cup from the jug when this prick waltzed in. Instinct took over, and I knocked the gun out of his hand and pistol-whipped him in the head." He angled his gun at the man on the floor and Z's suppressor-equipped pistol that lay off to the side.

Carl looked proud although it came off a bit comical with his bookish appearance, nasally voice, and a roll of packaging tape hanging from one hip.

One of the thugs muttered, "Well, ain't you a black belt, Carl."

The scarred, tough-looking man sitting on the floor—Z—scoffed. "Black belt? You caught me unawares. Your mom's a black belt."

All the thugs squinted at him. Finally, the boss man wiped his forehead. "Shit. Not only do we have a goddamned Houdini on our hands. He's a fuckin' wackadoo to boot."

Wackadoo? Then Z realized what the boss man meant. Yo mama jokes didn't come around until the nineteen-nineties, and unfortunately, he was in the eighties for this mission. *Goddamn time travel.*

"So," the boss man continued, addressing Carl again, "he just shows up out of the blue? Why?" He spun again to Z sitting on the floor with all the guns pointing at him. His briefcase jiggled on its handle with the tight maneuver. "You know about the bioweapon?"

Z considered his words as he eyed the briefcase containing the bioweapon he was supposed to obtain. "If I say yes, are you finally going to shoot me?"

Exasperated, the boss man closed his eyes and threw his hands up, accidentally knocking himself in the head with the briefcase. "Fucking wackadoodle," he muttered.

Two analog stopwatches, one on each of Z's wrists, continued to tick downward, one from three minutes, the other from two hours. He'd set the three-minute stopwatch right before entering the foyer.

After catching his breath, the boss man crouched and moved closer to Z. Z smelled the man's pungent sweat.

"What are those wrist timers for? You got bombs strapped to you? Huh?"

Bombs. That was the language that these criminals spoke. Z deflected, wrinkling his nose. "Whew. You ever heard of a shower? The eighties had showers, right?"

The boss man frowned. "You trying to piss me off?"

"Actually, yeah. I'm trying to piss you motherfuckers off so you shoot me, and I can warp back in time—"

"Oh shit, boss." It was Carl who had interrupted Z.

The boss man spun to him. "What?"

Carl held up his radio. "I called Jerry. He ain't answering."

The boss man's eyes widened in fury. He crouch-walked up to Z again. "What did you do to Jerry?"

Z glanced at his suppressor-equipped pistol lying out of reach.

"Motherfucker," the boss man snarled. "Why'd you kill him?"

Z rolled his eyes. "Your briefcase contains a biological weapon with the ability to destroy the entire multiverse if it gets out. I got sent here to make sure that doesn't happen. Some or all of you are probably going to have to die to do that. The more, the merrier, I say."

"Multiverse?" the boss man said. "Someone slap some box tape on this wackadoo's mouth until we can figure out what's going on here."

Carl tucked his pistol into his pants and grabbed a roll of packaging tape hanging at his side. When Carl stepped in close, he noticed the odd tattoos on Z, one on the underside of each forearm.

"Whoa." The skinny man jumped back a step. "What are these for? You in a cult?"

Z raised both arms and glanced down at the boxy tattoos. Unintelligible shorthand filled the boxes with strings of letters and numbers. A couple had lines drawn through them. "What? My tattoos? They help me keep track of the wrongs I'm trying to right."

"Wrongs you're trying to right?" the boss man repeated. "You like a…" He laughed. "A fuckin' crusader or something?"

Z let that idea bounce around his head. *Intergalactic Time Crusader.* Nah. Too cheesy.

"Man, those are some ugly tattoos," one of the thugs remarked.

Z sighed. "I did them myself. Me being righthanded, the tattoo on my left side is a little neater. If you squint at it from the right angle."

"Why you put them in some kind of code then? All the numbers and letters. I can't make shit out of them."

"That's because I've got to keep track of which parallel Earth the mistakes are in and what year and date and month and...it's all rather complicated for your thick skulls."

"You fucking making fun of me?" the boss man said from inches away from Z's face. "I get the sense that you don't have too many friends."

"Oh, I do have one. He's a little guy... Like you."

"Why, you sonofa—"

Z lurched forward and headbutted the bridge of the boss man's nose. Blood instantly splatted both men as he pulled back.

All of the guns surrounding him *clacked*.

That's it. Shoot me. Shoot me in the head. He was running out of time.

The boss man stood and stepped back a step. Then he raised a handkerchief from his back pocket and wiped his nose. "You must really want us to kill you. Why?"

Z shook his head once. "You wouldn't believe me."

"I'm a rather open-minded individual. Try me."

Z stole a glance at his wristwatch, the one that was counting down from three minutes. He now had less than forty seconds.

"Okay, fine," he said, glancing up at the boss man. "I have this unique ability. I can warp back in time up to three minutes into the past."

"So you're a time traveler?"

"Yeah, you could say that."

Carl scratched his chin. "So you want to warp back to before we caught you?"

Z nodded, stealing another glance at his watch. "Carl, you catch on quick. I think you should be the boss."

"Then why don't you warp back then?" the boss man said.

"Because he can't," Carl said. "Unless he dies. That must be the trigger."

Z whistled.

The boss man turned his gaze back at Z. "That is the craziest shit I've ever heard. Wackadoo. Tape his mouth shut." He winced. "I'm going to wash my nose out in the sink."

The stopwatch on Z's wrist showed only twenty seconds left. If he didn't warp back now, his mission would be exponentially harder—they greatly outnumbered him.

Time for my backup plan.

"Germ," he said. "Do your thing."

Carl slapped some tape across Z's mouth. Then Carl's eyes widened as one of Z's pockets bulged. He and the rest of the armed thugs watched in uneasy silence as a small black octopus-like blob with two beady black eyes climbed out from Z's pocket and hopped up onto Z's waist. It stretched a couple of tentacles backward and launched itself up Z's elbow in a great leap, then up to his shoulder, and finally onto Z's head.

The tiny black octopus raised one tentacle, and it morphed into a miniature human-shaped fist. The middle finger flipped up at the men.

"The hell…"

"What is that thing?" The men started shouting.

Come on boys, Z kept thinking. *Put a bullet in my head. It's not that hard.* His stopwatch said seven seconds.

"Maybe it's friendly," Carl said with a dopey grin as he leaned in and extended his hand like he was about to pet a puppy dog. "Hey there, little guy—"

Germ, the tiny black octopus thing, suddenly opened its

seamless jaw beneath his black eyes and chomped down on the man's hand.

"Ahh kill it!" Carl screamed.

As Z's stopwatch hit three seconds, the ring of guns spat bullets.

Then Z got his wish.

He died.

CHAPTER TWO

(Three Minutes Earlier)

Z opened the door and quickly shot to the side. There Carl stood, about to fill a paper cup from a water jug. Carl's eyes went wide. Before he could react, Z lunged forward with a two-fingered jab to the side of the man's neck.

Carl dropped to the floor like a limp doll, his head smacking the base of the water jug stand. It made a surprisingly loud *thudding* sound.

"Ouch," Z muttered.

Nice technique, Germ mentally projected into Z's head.

"Thanks." It was interesting how some things changed on each of the parallel Earths. This mission was already going much differently than on the other Earths. When he'd executed this mission on them, a man with a giant bowie knife stood in the foyer instead of Carl.

The funny thing was, Carl had been a bigger challenge than the knife guy.

Getting back to the task at hand, Z quickly surveyed the

room. There wasn't much to see, only a bare open foyer. He had been here before, warping back in time, so he was already familiar with the layout. He'd entered one door and another was off to the side where the seven thugs and the boss man were. With Carl incapacitated, he wouldn't be calling them in for backup any time soon.

Z's gaze locked on the side door. It had a tall glass rectangular window set into the top portion of it. The boss man, and more importantly the briefcase dangling by his hand, were in that room. That's where he needed to be. He needed to make sure he could attack them and not the other way around this time.

"Yo, Carl. You all right?" a man's voice called from the side room.

It appears that they heard Carl's body hit the floor.

"Yup," Z muttered to Germ, speaking out loud from habit, then cupped a hand to his mouth to muffle his next words. "Uh, yeah, I uh, tripped and fell."

Tripped and fell? Germ sounded rather incredulous for a black oozy mass that preferred to take the form of a tiny octopus.

Z kept his voice low as he responded to the bulge in his pocket. "Cut me some goddamned slack. You know I'm better with my fists than my mouth."

True. True.

The man's voice came louder from the side doorway. "You tripped? On what?"

Z knew he had to dispel the doubt in the man's voice before he or another of the thugs came to investigate. He needed to put things in his favor, not that of the goons. He cupped a hand over his mouth again as he surveyed the room for something plausible that could have caused Carl to fall. It was completely bare. No fucking thing to trip over. "Um…my damn shoelaces caught me."

During the pause that followed, Z briefly wondered if Carl was clumsy. He certainly had a bookish look to him.

The man's voice came back even louder this time. More mistrustful. "Carl, you idiot. Your shoes don't have shoelaces."

Z tilted his head down and over at Carl's prone body. Sure enough, the man was wearing Velcro tennis shoes instead of ordinary lace-up sneakers.

It is the eighties on this Earth, Germ added unhelpfully.

Frantic footsteps suddenly sounded from the doorway on the side.

Goddamnit.

Z raised his suppressed pistol, but this wasn't the way he wanted things to go. This man was going to alert the rest of the men. Then he'd be outnumbered again and unable to complete his mission of obtaining the bioweapon.

A moment later, a man in a jean jacket with gold bling around his neck rushed into the room, leveling his pistol at Z. Behind him, the rest of the seven thugs trundled in, all lifting their pistols as they saw Z standing over Carl's unconscious form.

Not wanting to repeat the first incident, Z lowered his head and charged toward them with a furious war cry.

All of their guns started firing, and bullets riddled his body.

He died.

(Thirty Seconds Earlier)

Z's two-finger jab to the neck dropped Carl like a limp

doll. This time, before the man's head hit something, Z caught the man under the arm and eased the flaccid body silently to the floor. While his head didn't hit anything, his hand smacked the floor with a soft *click*—probably the man's wedding ring striking the surface.

Very considerate of you, Germ said.

"Thanks," Z muttered as he rose to his feet and looked at the side door where the seven thugs and the boss man had rushed in the past two times. They wouldn't rush through the doorway this time though—

"Yo, Carl," a man's voice called from the other room. It was a different voice than the one that had called to him before warping back the last time.

Shit. How the hell had they heard him this time? Had they heard the man's ring click against the floor? It had hardly made a sound.

Z placed a hand over his mouth to muffle his words. "Uh, yeah?"

There was a pause. Carl's voice was nasally and unsure and easily replicable. Surely they had bought his impression...

Patience, Germ said.

Then the man's voice sounded again from the doorway. "You got the time?"

"Time?" Z muttered.

Clock, Germ said. *He wants to know what time it is.*

Z exhaled silently. Patience wasn't his strong suit.

He glanced down at both of his stopwatches, at their hands softly ticking backward. Neither showed him the current time.

He glanced up at the walls of the wide-open foyer, but they were as sparse as the floor, There was no clock anywhere.

"Uh. Carl? You still breathing?" An uneasy chuckle followed the man's words through the doorway.

Z was starting to ponder how he'd get to die this time around when a thought hit him. Why would the man ask Carl for the time if there was no clock in the room? Answer: Carl had to have a watch on him.

Z crouched and inspected Carl's body. The man's right wrist was bare, but his left wrist—

"Carl?" the man's voice called from the other room.

Z leaned over Carl and lifted the man's left wrist, which bore a Rolex watch that looked much too expensive for his paygrade. He twisted the wrist so he could read the time. A large hairline crack marred the glass surface from where the watch had impacted the floor. So it hadn't been a ring that had made that clicking sound but his watch.

The watch had broken.

For fuck's sake.

Wait. If the watch had broken when it struck the floor, it had to be accurate still, right?

Z tilted Carl's wrist a little farther, straining to read the time through the cracked glass. "Eight-thirty-two," he called in his muffled imitation-Carl voice.

"A.m. or p.m.?" the man called.

Z's hand unconsciously curled into a fist. "A.m., you jerk."

"Geez," the man called from the other room. "Just messing with you. Chill. Don't have to snap on us, Carl."

Z glanced back at Carl lying unconscious on the floor. He couldn't imagine a guy so puny as him ever snapping on someone.

It's the quiet ones you got to watch out for. Z smirked. He was glad he hadn't had to kill Carl. He was probably a decent enough guy, criminal resume notwithstanding.

Turning his attention back to the matter at hand, Z crept up to the side room's door. He peeked through the rectangular glass window.

Inside was a medium-sized room with a few long tables set up. They contained piles of stripped-down gun parts. The seven thugs were taking their time assembling weapons, mostly assault rifles. At the opposite side of the room, the boss man paced back and forth with the briefcase dangling from his hand. Behind the boss man was another door, this one more reinforced than the one Z currently peered through.

The same as when he'd completed this mission on several other parallel Earths, Z needed to obtain the bioweapon before the boss man could carry it through the reinforced door. If not, the boss man might escape the warehouse build-ing, which was bad because the man planned to demonstrate the weapon's capabilities during rush hour traffic within the hour. That meant Z had to act now.

There were seven armed thugs in the room with the boss man. As much as Z loved the thrill of rushing into any given situation guns ablaze, he had only a suppressor-equipped pistol and knew those were terrible odds, even for a Repeater who could warp back in time when he died.

He had to act.

As he scanned the room a final time, he spotted a small canister resting on the end of the nearest weapons table.

"Hey Germ," he whispered, "You think I can use what's in the canister to attack those men?"

Let me take a closer look. Germ climbed out from Z's pocket and jumped up to perch on Z's shoulder. As the little guy peered through the window, his cute beady eyes extended in length like a pair of miniature binoculars. There was a pause.

Oh. Most certainly. I can read the label. That's a deadly but quick-dispersing nerve gas.

"Sweet," Z muttered. That would do. That would do nicely. "It pays to have a tiny MacGyver in my pocket."

What is a MacGyver?

"It's not important. Now let's get ready to spring our trap."

CHAPTER THREE

Z was preparing to crack open the door and shoot the nerve gas canister when one of the seven thugs turned toward the door. Z managed to pull back just in time.

"Hey Carl, you idiot. Bring me a beer."

That's it, Z thought. He was tired of these assholes giving Carl shit.

Carl wasn't one of the line items tattooed on either of Z's arms, but dammit, he was going to stand up for the man.

With a sudden burst of speed, he threw open the door and targeted the nerve gas canister. He fired once, his gun making a rasping cough sound, and the canister skittered off the table. Gas spewed into the air.

Z shut the door and wedged his boot against the bottom of the door to reinforce it.

That was rather cold. Was it necessary?

As the seven thugs and the boss man shouted and scrambled toward the door, Z glanced at his shoulder and met Germ's beady but cute black eyes. "Necessary? Are you asking me if it's necessary to make things go boom? Or in this case, hiss?" Before waiting for a response from the little octopus, Z said, "No. I like making things go boom. That and punching people. I like that too."

Judging by the way Germ stared back at him, the octopus didn't buy his bravado. *This is about something else. Human emotion, is it not?*

Z checked to make sure he'd placed his boot firmly against the door where it met the floor. The metal door tried to open as one of the thugs threw themselves at it, but Z held it shut.

He turned to Germ. "Look, you don't know jack shit about human emotions. I can't let them detonate the bioweapon in the city so I triggered a canister of nerve gas to kill them first. This has nothing to do with human emotion—"

Gunfire sounded from the other side of the door, shattering its window. Glass sprinkled onto Z's shoulder, and he shook it off. A hand shot through the door's window, frantically pawing at the door handle, not that it would do the poor bastard any good—Z's boot was still firmly planted against the door's bottom. The man on the other side didn't know that. Blood trailed down the door as the jagged glass shards lining the window frame cut open his arm.

Z shook his head and pistol-whipped the man's prying hand. Shrieking, the man tried to withdraw his hand back through the window, but Z had already tucked his gun into his holster and gripped the man's bleeding wrist. While keeping his boot pressed against the door to prevent it from opening, Z jerked the man's wrist, hauling the man's upper torso through the door's window to block it.

With his free hand, Z rammed his fist against the man's nose. Blood exploded outward as the man slumped unconscious partly through the door with an exhausted sigh. A bit of nerve gas trailed upward through the window and Z made sure to stay leaning away from the door. He'd gotten a quick look through the window before he'd moved out of the way. It looked like the gas was starting to dissipate.

I've got it, Germ said. *You're attacking these men to stop the bioweapon from being detonated but also to defend the honor of the man named Carl. May I ask why you're defending the honor of the man named Carl?*

Z's face flushed. "What? That's the stupidest thing I've ever heard."

Your elevated facial temperature suggests that you're telling a fib.

Grunting, Z thought, *What the hell.* "Fine. Yeah. I'm a dick because they were treating Carl like shit. It wasn't right. Someone needed to teach them a lesson."

Why?

Z considered lying or trying to change the subject, but what did it matter? "Carl reminds me of someone I used to be —er, know."

I am confused.

"Cheer up, little buddy. Like I've said, humans are a confusing animal to try to understand."

And females are the more confusing gender, correct?

"We're not going to have that talk again right here, okay—"

Gunfire exploded from the other side of the door, and slugs blasted into the metal door all around where the passed-out man's body hung. While some shots penetrated the door, the others looked like nails driving through to his side. When a bullet struck the man stuck in the window, the thug gave a wild-eyed grunt and passed out again.

Inside, the remaining thugs were still shouting and firing their guns.

"Jesus," Z said. "I figured they'd have all been dead by now…"

Perhaps you feel guilt for killing these men?

"Guilt? Hell no. These motherfuckers have already killed me twice. Don't you forget that."

I cannot help but think this is another one of those 'human emotion' issues.

"Open the hell up," a thug coughed from the other side. "Or we're going to…going to…" The man's words devolved into violent coughs. There was a *thud* on the other side of the door.

Z kept his boot against the door for nearly a minute after. When there was no further noise on the other side, he eased his foot away from the door and bent to massage his leg.

"Shit, I think I might've pulled a hammy."

Should've stretched first.

Z shook his head at the notion. On his home Earth, Earth-Z, his best friend and genius Buzz Lugger had scientifically proven that stretching could do more harm than good. The best way to prepare for a mission was breathing exercises.

"I'm fine. Can you tell if the nerve gas is all gone now?"

Yes. It should be safe for you now.

He took hold of the door handle and carefully cracked open the door, cringing at the sound of the shoes of the man stuck in the door window scraping against the floor. *Maybe he had used excessive force…*

Then, *Nah.*

He stepped inside, searching the floor for the boss man and the briefcase he was carrying. He only counted six bodies lying in the gassed room. The reinforced door at the opposite side of the room was closed.

"Shit."

It would appear that the man with the briefcase has escaped.

"No shit, Sherlock. At least I took care of all the other thugs, though—"

"Hey, you maniac!"

The voice had come from directly behind him, from out in the foyer. It had a faint nasally sound to it.

"You've got to be shitting me," Z muttered as he slowly turned to face Carl's gun pointed straight at his face.

Carl pulled the trigger.

Z died.

(Five Seconds Earlier)

Z spun, his gun already gripped tight in his extended arm, tracking Carl as he groggily picked himself up off the floor and raised his pistol.

Z's first shot struck Carl in the fingers gripping his gun. Blood splatted and Carl's gun clattered to the floor.

"I stood up for you." Z shook his head. "This is how you treat me?"

Snarling, Carl glanced from his bleeding hand to his gun lying on the floor in front of him. One of his severed fingers twitched eerily next to it.

Carl glared at Z, then eyed his gun.

"Don't do it, bud."

Carl did it.

Z put a round through the man's head as he lunged for his gun. Cocking his elbow and raising his pistol, Z blew his gun's smoking barrel. "A headshot for a headshot. Guess we're even now—"

Not really, Germ interrupted. *He can't Repeat like you. He's dead.*

"Yeah. Sucks for him. He shot me first, and I gave him a chance." He sighed. "Let's go finish the mission now, shall we?" Upon glancing at his stopwatch, the one ticking down from two hours, he added, "So I can right another wrong from my list before time is up."

CHAPTER FOUR

With the gas cleared out of the room, Z entered and stepped over the bodies of the dead thugs. He only briefly glanced at the tables containing what the men were working on, mostly guns in various stages of being stripped down and assembled. Cardboard boxes sat on one table for the guns to be loaded into, probably what Carl needed his packaging tape for. On one table was a baggie of some kind of white powder—cocaine by the look of it.

These weren't nice people. Whether they'd chosen this life of crime or it had chosen them, it had claimed their lives.

Do you feel the human emotion 'guilt' for ending these men's lives?

Z shook his head. "They would've killed me. Before I warped back in time, they *did* kill me. If we don't stop the bioweapon from being detonated, a whole lot of civilians are going to die. Puppies too."

I do not understand humans' fascination with puppies. They eat their poop, correct?

Z stepped over the last of the sprawled-out men and reached the reinforced door on the other side of the room. "We overlook the faults of those we love." He gazed through the window set in the reinforced door. It must have been bullet-resistant glass because it was spider-webbed from the seven thugs trying to get through, to chase after the boss man who had left them to their fate. In the corridor on the other side of the door was a dribbling blood trail on the floor.

The boss man must have gotten wounded in the scuffle.

Z realized then that Germ, perched upon his shoulder, was peering through the glass as well.

How are you going to open this door when these other humans failed to open it?

Z smirked. "These fools didn't have explosives on them."

You do like things that go boom.

"That I do." Z took the small clay-like pellets from his pocket and wasted no time inserting them onto the door frame where the hinges would be on the other side. Then he calmly took a few steps away and, with his back to the door, raised a small flat rectangular remote from his pocket. "You ready for this, little guy?"

I am always rea—

Z's thumb struck the button, and three soft but sharp bursts pierced the room. The door shivered on its hinges but remained in place.

Perhaps your explosives were not up to the task?

"I'll show you 'up to the task.'" Z turned and strode up to the door. He gripped the door handle and stepped to the side. With a quick jerk of the wrist, the door fell outward, flat onto the space he had been standing on, smashing the leg of one of the dead thugs.

"Man, I love explosives," Z exclaimed as he confidently

rushed through the doorway.

Bare ceiling bulbs placed at long intervals lit the corridor beyond. Some of them flickered, giving the place an eerie feel. He'd been in worse bad guy shitholes, but this was pretty bad.

Of course, he couldn't shake the persistent feeling that something was wrong with the mission on this Earth. He'd undergone this same mission on several parallel Earths before —ah, the pitfalls of parallel threats on parallel Earths and one man with a space and time capsule tasked with de-escalating all of them so that the multiverse could continue to function…

Never had things gone this roughly. On all the other Earths, he hardly had to Repeat at all. Not that he was complaining. He liked using his powers, even if it killed him.

Also, another disturbing thing about this Earth was that there was no guy with a giant bowie knife. On all the other Earths during this mission, there had been a crazed man with a bowie knife waiting for him in the foyer. Instead, on this Earth, he'd been confronted by a…Carl.

The brainiac that invented the time machine and the ability to jump to parallel Earths theorized that every timeline was basically the same with minor amendments. *The ninety-eight percent rule.* Everything was ninety-eight percent the same, but that two percent was a doozy of differences.

Z didn't buy it. His theory was that the two percent difference was all about him and not that the worlds differed. On Earth-T, he was a second faster entering the room, a second slower punching a bad guy.

That second accounted for the differences. Not the two percent variances…that was bullshit devised by a scientist who only ever did one jump.

Then there was the big bad. That asshole could also hop to

other Earths and fuck up timelines, although how he did it without a space and time capsule, they hadn't figured out yet.

That said, the parallel Earths did have differences...like Earth-D, the worst place ever. That place sucked.

All these ninety-eight percent rules and two percent variances and him being slower or faster theories gave him a headache. All Z wanted to do was punch someone's face in.

There were plenty of bad guys left on this Earth to punch.

A corner was approaching, and Z slowed his pace to creep up to it. With his finger resting against his gun's trigger, he peered around the corner. When he saw no one there, he rounded it and continued down another corridor.

He didn't mind too much about his current intergalactic job. It meant that he got to punch a lot of bad guys and blow shit up. What better perks could a job offer? Plus, he had a lot to atone for. Cue the tattooed list on each of his arms.

He sure had a lot of wrongs to right, and being a Repeater who could warp back in time up to three minutes—not to mention that he had a space and time capsule at his disposal—meant that he had a lot of time.

He glanced at his two-hour stopwatch. Figuratively speaking, of course. He needed to wrap this mission up so that he could get to fixing his shit.

Five yards ahead was another bend in the corridor. Other than the sound of his boot strikes, the place was silent. The boss man with his briefcase must have already made it to the next room. That had never happened on the other Earths. Z picked up his pace. He was running out of time to be overly cautious.

As he rounded this corner, a shape jumped out at him.

He could afford the recklessness—if the figure meant him harm, Z would simply warp back up to three minutes with the knowledge of what lay around the corner. Then he'd deal with the threat.

There in front of him lay a big threat.

The thug with the bowie knife he'd yet to see on this Earth.

"Yeeeaaaa motherfucker!" the man with the bowie knife screamed as he lunged. He was high on something—maybe the cocaine back in the weapons room.

Z managed to throw up a forearm. The knife man's arm struck Z's and the man's eyes enlarged in fury as he raised his arm to strike again. Z strafed to the side, keeping his eyes on the wild-eyed, drug-addled man with the terrifyingly long knife. It was probably big enough to be considered a damn sword.

The air before Z whistled as the man hacked at him. Z backstepped, his back connecting with the wall behind him in the tight corridor. Off to the side, in the flickering ceiling light, Z saw a door at the end, which most likely led to a giant warehouse room and a back exit.

Z mentally scoffed. A petty criminal organization like this in possession of a bioweapon? And not any bioweapon—a bomb containing a variant of the time virus that had originally infected Z, thus giving him his warping powers. From his experience, exposure to the time virus killed the vast majority of any biological lifeform it touched. Z was an anomaly.

As the ceiling lights flickered off, he realized that he was also a dead man. He tried to jump out of the way, but the knife guy had already shoved the big ass knife right into Z's chest, scraping ribs as it rendered his heart to a bloody pulp.

Z fell to the corridor floor in the dark.

He died.

. . .

(Twenty Seconds Earlier)

That certainly looked painful, Germ said.

"You're telling me," Z scoffed. "You ever get a knife jabbed through you?"

I do recall you using a knife against me once—

"All in the past, okay? Now, look sharp. I might need your help up here."

Ooh, the macho man requires help?

Z was quickly approaching the corner where the knife guy was hiding behind. "Don't let it get to your head, you little octopus."

The corner was upon him.

Z could've pulled up in an abrupt stop and waited for the knife guy to lunge out, thus providing him with the perfect opportunity to dispatch him more safely from a short distance. That wasn't the "Z way."

Instead, Z lowered his left shoulder and charged around the corner with his pistol gripped in his right hand. He blind fired into the dark humanoid shape in front of him at the same time that his left arm and shoulder connected with the knife guy's bulky body. The man was more solid and compact than he had previously thought. The man didn't budge.

His bullets had struck the knife guy, though. Z still heard the slapping sounds echoing in his ears.

The knife guy growled as he stiff-armed Z across the chest, sending Z flying back against the wall.

"Yeeeaaaa! I kill you!"

With a grunt, Z thought, *Not this time.* Then he said, "Germ, blind him."

The knife guy was preparing to swipe his blade up at the

nearest ceiling light to douse the immediate area in relative darkness. As the man did so, Germ tensed against Z's body and flung himself out at the knife guy.

The little black octopus connected with the man's face with a *splat*.

The knife guy's swipe at the ceiling light missed, and he turned his attention to getting the oozy black thing off his face. He blindly reached a hand up to his face, and Germ slapped it away with one of his tentacles.

"Yeeeaaaa! Alien! Monster!"

Z stood back and smirked as he placed his fists upon his hips and watched. "He's no alien. But he's a little monster, all right."

As the knife guy spun and slashed out blindly with his enormous knife, he resembled a blindfolded person swinging a bat at a pinata he couldn't see. Poor bastard. Germ was no stuffed pinata. He was a sentient weaponized blob from the future.

Only a few moments had passed since Germ had launched himself at the knife guy, but Z remembered that they were running out of time to stop the bioweapon exchange on the other side of the door at the end of the hall.

"Okay, Germ, bite him."

With a bobbing nod of its tiny octopus head, Germ shot from the man's face and onto the knife guy's knife-hand. Opening wide, the little guy chomped down on the drugged-out man's wrist.

The man dropped his big knife, shrieking and howling.

Z strode up, bent, and picked up the bowie knife. He nodded at Germ, who gracefully leapt back to his shoulder.

"Hey," Z called to his attacker, who was grasping his bleeding wrist with a look of confused terror on his face.

"Like a damn deer in the headlights," Z muttered with a smirk as he swung the blade at the man's muscled neck.

28

CHAPTER FIVE

Z set the timer on his three-minute stopwatch.

Flinging open the final door, Z found himself in an expansive warehouse-type room with several stacks of wooden crates littered throughout. Z's eyes locked in on the boss man leaning over the open briefcase resting on a sturdy oak desk. Even from a distance, Z could see the metal canister inside the case.

The bioweapon.

Was he thinking about detonating it here inside the warehouse instead of out on the city streets?

The boss man's focus was solely on the contents of the sturdy oak table. When Z rushed in through the doorway, he twisted his head back and glared.

"Kill him!" the boss man suddenly shouted as he slammed the briefcase shut and limped away from the desk.

That's when Z noticed the four men at each side of the warehouse. He sent his eyes back to the boss man, limping toward an emergency exit at the back, trying to escape.

Not if Z had anything to say about it. The man was bad

and had a bioweapon in his possession. Z was going to take him out as well as recover the bioweapon, per his mission.

With two men rushing toward him from both the left and right, it meant that Z was probably going to have to die to get this right.

Which was fine by him…

The closest man on the left carried a double-barreled sawed-off shotgun, and the thug behind him had a handgun. A quick jerk of his head to the right revealed that those two men had compact machine gun pistols.

From his glance at the start, he'd noticed a revolver at the boss man's side.

Time seemed to freeze as Z wrapped up his initial scan of the environment and committed all the important details of the layout and hazards to memory. Then he proceeded with commencing his death wish.

He zigzagged and bolted for the man with the sawed-off shotgun. At this distance, the man couldn't miss, and Z was counting on it.

Boom. Kaboom.

Both blasts of the man's shotgun struck Z full-on, the first blast shoving him back like a mad fist to the left pec while the second blast took off part of his shoulder.

Goddamnit.

Ouch, Germ said. *You okay there?*

As Z slipped and fell backward to the floor, he heard the boss man's voice boom through the interior as he stopped before the back exit. "I've changed my mind. Don't kill him if possible—I want to know what he knows."

"You sure, boss?" one of the thugs said.

"I'll pay you all triple for him alive."

Z scoffed. Surely these thugs would finish the job and kill

him so that he could warp back in time, thus enabling him to kick all their asses with his foreknowledge. They were dumb, trigger-happy hitmen, right?

"Triple pay?" the one with the shotgun said with wide eyes as he shoved two more shells into his weapon.

Another thug chimed in. "That could buy me a new TV."

"Or a hot rod," another said excitedly.

Are you kidding me? Z glanced at his three-minute watch. He'd have to do the job himself.

As the four armed thugs stood over him, assessing his gaping wounds, Z grunted as he gripped his gun and turned it upward on himself.

I hate this part. Germ turned his tiny octopus head away.

Z fired once, and his head snapped back.

He died.

(Twenty Seconds Earlier)

Z flung open the door to the warehouse, immediately darting to the left as the boss man was inspecting the bioweapon on the desk in the open briefcase.

As the shotgun thug raised his weapon, Z fired one round through the man's skull. Lining a shot up over the man's slack shoulder, Z took out the second armed man on the left. With each of his two shots, his suppressor-equipped pistol emitted two rasping coughs.

"Kill him!" the boss man screamed as he slammed the briefcase shut and limped for the back door.

Z barely ducked behind a stack of crates in time before the two thugs on the right unloaded their guns at him. Splinters and chunks of wood flew into the air, dousing Z's shoulder and hair.

Peeking out from his pocket, Germ spat out a mouthful of sawdust.

Z waited for the approach of frantic footsteps before calmly raising his arm to the side of the crates and firing once into the center of the oncoming thug's chest. The man's legs shot out in front of him, and he slammed backward onto his back and head with a *crunch*.

"Might want to see a chiropractor about that," Z muttered as he rose in a half-crouch in preparation to take out the fourth and final thug.

And a heart specialist, Germ said.

Z smirked down at the little guy. "Nice one." He waited until he heard the final thug's gun click empty, then coolly rose and shot him once in the face. "Now him, he's gonna need a facelift."

Without pausing to relish his joke, Z spun toward the back door where the boss man had hobbled up to. The boss man was reaching for the doorknob when he turned and fired his revolver at Z.

The shot went wide, and Z fired his last bullet in return. It struck the man in his good leg. He collapsed with an anguished wail.

Z holstered his suppressed pistol without skipping a beat and retrieved the dropped shotgun from the ground beside him. Then he rose and strode toward the back door and the boss man cursing and gripping his injured legs.

When the boss man saw his shooter approaching him, he hurriedly reached out for the revolver he'd dropped. Z's first shotgun blast struck the concrete right in front of the gun, sending up a cloud of debris. The injured boss man abandoned his briefcase and sat up with a grimace. Then, with a quick motion, he reached a hand to his boot and came up with a second, much smaller gun. Z's second shotgun blast took him in the chest, throwing him back against the floor with his arms stretched to either side.

"Good riddance, I say." Z dropped the emptied shotgun to the floor and scooped up the briefcase containing the bioweapon. With his free hand, he opened the door.

He passed through into the streaming light of day.

Drawing in a deep breath of fresh air and closing the door behind him, he set down the briefcase and adjusted his black muscle tee. It was bad guy blood-free except for a few specks that the black fabric mostly hid. He didn't have any injuries that might give rise to suspicion to those he passed on the street. He'd done well.

Before starting, he reached up and yanked the imitation gold necklace from his neck, and cast it off into the gutter beside him.

Mission successful, Germ said.

"Damn right. Now let's send the contents of this briefcase off-world to Buzz."

He was only the muscle, not the brains of this intergalactic *Mission: Impossible* operation. He'd finished his part. Now it was time for Buzz Lugger on a different Earth to sort through and communicate his findings with the rest of the Buzzes spread throughout the multiverse. Yes, Z took his orders from a Council of Buzzes newly formed to protect the multiverse. He couldn't give the bioweapon to the Buzz on this Earth because, it being the nineteen-eighties, Buzz hadn't been born yet. Neither had Z.

Once he sent Buzz the bioweapon via his space and time capsule, they would give Z his next assignment, most likely on a different Earth. He just hoped it wasn't Earth-D.

Earth-D was the worst.

He glanced back at the warehouse's backside. The good thing about operating in a parallel Earth back in the 1980s was that there were no pesky surveillance cameras to catch him in the act. Plus, everyone who had seen him was dead.

He drew another deep breath and picked up the briefcase. Then he walked toward the sounds of the city. "You know what I think we should do to celebrate another successful mission?"

Grab some donuts?

Z smirked. "You know me too well."

CHAPTER SIX

Germ stared at Z.

"You got something to say, little guy?"

Just pondering how unhealthy jelly-filled glazed donuts are for you. So much sugar.

"Hey. I work it off, okay? I train. I kick bad-guy ass. I get donuts to celebrate. It's what I do." Z was now wearing a light jacket he'd picked up after sending the bioweapon off-world to Buzz.

They were sitting outside under the hot noon sun on a patio outside of Caleb's Ice Cream Emporium fast-food restaurant. Numerous other people sat at the umbrella-covered tables, most of them happy young families. At least, that's what all their smiles said.

Z knew that under those confident smiles were layers of doubt and fears. Like "Am I giving my kids the best life I can?" and "What if something happens to my kids when I'm not there?"

He recalled his thoughts back when he had a family of his

own. He had to admit, raising kids was harder than any mission he'd ever undertaken.

Z grimaced. Children made you soft, and that was okay. Of course, he didn't have any kids anymore. He made a fist under the table.

You okay? Germ asked.

He'd had a family of his own, and he'd loved them with his entire being. All up until Nunez's time virus took them away from him. After that, he'd gone a little crazy. Had done some things he wasn't proud of on many parallel Earths throughout the multiverse. Of course, the virus had messed up his brain a bit at the time. Not that that was an acceptable excuse.

Now he had Buzz's space and time capsule to combat new time virus threats throughout the multiverse and right some of his wrongs.

Hellooo?

Z shook his head. He realized that Germ was still sitting on his lap out of view of other people, but the little octopus was waving a tentacle up at him to snag his attention.

"Yeah?"

You're reminiscing about all your past failures again. Aren't you?

"Uh, no. I don't know what you're talking about."

The tiny octopus thing cocked its head up at him. *Oh really? Then what are you thinking about?*

"Oh, the usual things. Beer. Guns. Women. Tough guy things."

Germ stared at him. *I thought you came here to right a wrong.*

Z glanced at his watch, the one ticking down from two hours, and back at his box of jelly-filled glazed donuts.

"We have a few minutes yet." He selected a donut and held it down to Germ in his lap. "Here, want one to pass the time?"

You know I only eat organic life matter. That collection of fried, sugary carbs is most definitely dead.

Z winced, no longer hungry for donuts. "You sure are a buzzkill."

Germ shrugged.

"I know I probably should know this by now, but do you ever eat anything? I've never seen you do it." As he said it, he wondered if he might regret hearing the answer.

Germ smiled up at him with its beady black eyes. *Of course I eat.*

"What do you eat then? Cows? Ducks? Kids?"

Grass. I eat grass. And other vegetables. I don't eat meat anymore. Germ gave him a quizzical look. *You have a messed-up mind.*

Leaning back in his seat, Z said, "Why, thank you." His watch said it was about time. He scanned the people around them who were busy enjoying being with their families and eating the greasy and sugary food. The great thing about Caleb's Ice Cream Emporium was that they served burgers, fries, ice cream, and donuts, among other things. It was cheap too.

He pushed the box away from him on the table, glad for the umbrella above him that blocked out the hot sun. It also had the added benefit of concealing him from others somewhat.

Upon instinct, he surreptitiously scanned the crowd for anyone watching him as he feigned a yawn, his sunglasses masking his eyes. As expected, there was no one watching him. He was the one doing the watching. He couldn't help but note that this heavily crowded public spot was a pickpocket's dream. All those wallets and purses. Everyone's attention on their food and their families...

Care to let me in on who you're watching for? I could help you look.

"No. I have to right my wrongs. Ah, there they are."

Who? Who? I cannot see. Germ hopped up from Z's lap and tentatively peered over the table's top in a manner that didn't make him visible to the other customers.

Z's focus was on the outdoor serving window of the restaurant. His eyes locked in on the little girl and her father now walking away. The father had a donut in one hand and held his daughter's hand in the other. She held a waffle ice cream cone in her other hand, gleefully licking her strawberry-vanilla ice cream.

Them? Germ said. *Who are they to you? Do you know them?*

Without taking his eyes from them, Z whispered, "Sometimes you ask too many questions. You know what, you're kind of like my kid. Heh."

Germ pinched Z's arm. *At least I eat my green beans.*

Z frowned and glanced down at the little octopus's cheesy grin. He chuckled and shook his head, then turned back to the matter at hand.

So what's the mission? Did you wrong this man and girl when you were a crazy, bad man?

"I was never crazy."

You tried to start a war.

Ugh. "Just watch and be quiet. Okay?"

The tiny octopus made a lip-zipping gesture with one tentacle across its mouth.

Z watched as the father and daughter walked up and stopped near him, searching for an empty table. There didn't appear to be any.

Z smiled up at the father and gestured at the other side of his table.

The man must have seen the pencil-thin scar on one side of Z's face because he gripped his daughter's hand and tugged her away. The girl, meanwhile, smiled back at Z and waved at him.

Z didn't blame the man. Most people saw a stereotypical movie villain when they saw a person with a scarred face. Oh well.

He was still going to help them.

The father and daughter duo had weaved past a couple of tables farther down, still searching. With a frustrated look, he apologized to his daughter. Stress lines worried his face.

Here was the man's story in a nutshell. Within the next few minutes, a pickpocket would steal his wallet. That meant he'd be late to a courtroom appearance to maintain part-time custody of his daughter. If he were late to the courtroom, he'd end up losing his case, and he would commit suicide the next day since he could no longer legally see his daughter.

Z shook his head. The world had enough tragedy in it already. It didn't need this one too.

Z glanced down at his watch again. The pickpocket should be there at any moment.

He was about to rise and confront the father when something horrible happened.

The daughter took another gleeful lick at her ice cream cone only for the hot sun overhead to have melted the side of it. The girl's ice cream splatted to the hot baking concrete.

The girl cried.

"Well, shit..." Z muttered.

Time to die? Germ said with much confusion.

Z didn't answer, only bent and drew a knife hidden in his boot and turned its point to face his chest. After finding a space between his ribs that afforded him a clean shot at his heart, he punched the blade home with the meat of his palm.

As blood leaked from his chest and dribbled out the corner of his mouth, he fell backward out of his seat to the hot baking concrete. His eyes sighted along the ground to the melting scoop of ice cream at the girl's feet.

He was only vaguely aware of people starting to shout and scream from all around his body. The concrete was burning his cheek.

Then he died.

CHAPTER SEVEN

(A Minute and a Half Earlier)

A little extreme, do you not think?

Z had warped back to the point in time where the father and daughter were stepping away from the restaurant's serving window. The father anxiously searched the crowd for a place to sit as he gripped his daughter's hand.

Already Z could see why the ice cream had toppled over the side of the girl's cone. The restaurant employee had poorly stacked it, and the sun was accelerating the ice cream's demise.

Z watched as a rivulet of melted ice cream ran down the side of the cone, unnoticed by the girl cheerfully licking the cone from the other side, speeding up its inevitable spillage.

It's only ice cream. Why did you warp back? Germ asked.

"It's not only ice cream. It's that little girl's heart on the line."

Is this about the daughter you do not get to see anymore?

"Yeah," Z muttered. "Something like that." He rose from his table and backed away, ducking out from under the table's umbrella. As the father and daughter approached him, he turned slightly to the side to hide his face scar from them.

"This table taken?" the father asked.

Z grinned. "All yours."

The father nodded his gratitude and motioned for his daughter to sit. As she did, he gave Z a careful look.

I think he finds you suspicious, Germ said.

"Yes?" the girl's father said when Z didn't leave. "Can I help you?"

That's when Z finally saw the pickpocket, a few tables back over the father's shoulder. He only caught fleeting glimpses of him as he passed between the umbrellas, but it was him: a boy in his late teens, wearing jeans and a tee and a backward-facing ballcap. He didn't look out of place. In fact, he fit right in. Also, he seemed completely harmless. Certainly not a seasoned pickpocket.

"Excuse me." Z turned away from the father. "I'm looking for someone."

The girl's father shrugged as he sat at the table next to his daughter. Z couldn't help but notice the man's billfold protruding from his back pocket as he leaned over the table to eat his donut and talk to his daughter.

Z only had to wait a minute, the whole time his eyes tracking the pickpocket as he sauntered up toward the girl's father from behind, his hands casually thrust into his pockets.

The pickpocket was nearly to the girl's father, preparing to "bump" into him. He swept up behind the father, his hand leaving his pocket as he prepared to lift the man's wallet from his back pocket.

Z seamlessly set his hand upon the pickpocket's wrist, and like a set of talons, lifted it and angled the boy around, and guided him out in front of him through the tables and umbrellas.

"Ah, found him," Z said cheerfully so as not to cause a scene.

"Hey, you creep—" the boy started.

"Hush it, thief," Z said in a harsh whisper as he guided the boy toward the end of the densely packed tables.

The boy shut his mouth. Z meanwhile flashed onlookers a grin as if he was taking his delinquent son out to give him a stern talk.

When they got outside the tables, Z guided the boy under a tree. They were in a small park. "I want you to straighten up your act. You hear?"

The pickpocket took one glance at the scar on Z's face and gulped. Then defiance lit his face. "Why should I?"

Z glanced over his shoulder at the tables to make sure no one was watching their interaction too closely. He turned back to the boy. "Because you stealing shit from people can have bad effects."

"Oh yeah?"

"Your actions can ruin lives."

"Look, man, I'm not scared of you."

Ensuring that he kept his back to the people at the tables, Z flicked his knife up from his boot and angled the blade at the thief's face.

The boy's hands shot up. "Shit, okay, okay. I get it. I'll stop plying my trade here."

Z scoffed. "I know you're gonna keep at it. Just take it someplace else, will ya? Any place that isn't Caleb's Ice Cream Emporium. Maybe go to the mall like any self-respecting pickpocket?"

The boy's bulging eyes stayed glued to the knife. He

nodded. "Of course. Yes. You're…you're not going to kill me. Are you?"

Z pretended to consider it. "Nah." He returned the knife to his boot and shrugged as if they'd had a heart-to-heart, father to son. He slapped the boy's shoulder a bit harder than necessary. "Good talk, son," he called, louder than necessary for the benefit of anyone who might be trying to eavesdrop. "See you after dinner."

The boy turned and bolted away.

Z smirked. "Well, that was too easy."

People do seem to take your threats seriously, Germ said.

"Gee. Wonder why," Z muttered as he turned and made his way back to check on the father and daughter from a distance.

They were both sitting there enjoying their ice creams. Z suddenly recalled that he had never done this with his daughter in his original timeline on Earth-Z. He had never had ice cream, only him and his daughter. There were a lot of things he'd never done with her that he should have. His wife always took care of those things. The notion saddened him.

He'd done his best as a father. Still, he'd been far from perfect. That was part of the reason for his list of wrongs to right.

He'd been watching the father and daughter a couple of minutes when, to his anguish, the top half of her ice cream fell off and plopped to the ground.

You going to warp back again? Germ asked.

Z drew in a breath and let it out as a sigh. The girl was already starting to cry.

He took out his knife again and jabbed it into his heart.

He died.

· · ·

(Two Minutes Earlier)

Z warped back to after his talk with the pickpocket under the trees. After watching the pickpocket hurry off in the opposite direction, he immediately strode up to the restaurant's serving window and purchased a strawberry-vanilla ice cream.

Once the employee handed him the waffle cone, he immediately walked toward the father and daughter's table. The girl's ice cream fell to the ground right as he reached their table. The girl looked about to cry, and her father was about to console her.

That's when Z stepped in. "Here, take mine. I haven't eaten any of it yet."

The girl's eyes lit up in appreciation. She took the treat from him.

"Thanks again, sir," the father said, squinting at Z. "Do I know you or something?"

"No." Z paused reflectively. "Although I guess you can think of me as your guardian angel."

The man reached into his back pocket and grabbed his wallet. "Here. Let me pay you for it."

Z placed a hand on the man's shoulder. "I don't want the money—just paying it forward. The butterfly effect is all I'm concerned with. You have a good day now." He removed his hand.

The man swallowed. "I hope I do. Got a courtroom appearance today…" He flashed a look down at his daughter, who was too busy enjoying her ice cream to notice the discussion her father was having with this stranger. "It's a long story. I don't even know why I'm telling you."

Z winked. "I think you'll do fine. As long as you get there on time. Know what I mean?"

The girl's father nodded, his face warm with appreciation.

Z left them and walked back to the restaurant's serving window, where he bought another donut.

Another one? Germ said.

Z wasn't in the mood for arguing. "I've got to have some happiness in my life. Let me enjoy it. Okay?"

He walked until he found a park bench all by itself. He sat, ate his donut, and closed his eyes.

Eventually, his pager beeped, and he checked it. Buzz was letting him know to stop by the newspaper place to pick up his next assignment.

He hoped it didn't involve going to Earth-D. He licked a couple of donut crumbs from his fingers.

Yep, Earth-D was seriously the worst.

CHAPTER EIGHT

"The big man returns," the tallest of the three newsmen called from the second story of the building when Z finally reached the news office. He was leaning over the rail and smoking something in a pipe. It was the eighties, so who knew what it was. Above the scrawny newsman was a sign on the building that said *Paper Warriors—NYC's alternative news publication.*

Luckily for Z, a restaurant was located on the first floor of the building below the newspaper office. The smell of Korean barbecue wafted out from its door and windows, covering the odor of the newsman's pipe. He could stand there basking in the delicious smells for hours if he wanted. The restaurant's food was even better than it smelled. He wasn't here to eat, though.

Z glanced up at the scrawny young man contently smoking his pipe while leaning over the rail. The sun had gone behind some clouds, and it had been drizzling on him for most of the walk here. Z raised a hand over his eyes to see better. "I'm expecting a new paper to print. You see it yet?"

The young man shook his head. "I got a call from an

eyewitness account in upstate New York says he saw Sasquatch. I'm typing out the story right now. Taking a break of course to recharge my brain. This is going to be a big hit with the readers. *Paper Warriors'* breakout news story of the year. Gonna put us on the map. Get us tons of new subscribers. Make us rich."

"Sure." Z approached the metal stairs leading up to the second-story newspaper office. He could only hope that the alt science publication never gained that kind of notoriety. He'd have to find a new, lower-key office then.

The newsman called down again. "Oh, and we're making kombucha up here so it might smell when you get in."

Z groaned. Again? Oh well, it was always something. *Home sweet home.* Or as close to one as he was going to get. He was a man without an Earth to call his home.

Aside from the three nerdy newsmen who worked here, it didn't make a bad office for him on all the parallel Earths he traveled to. It was a good center of operations for him, and he had a comfortable chair that he could lean back in and sleep with his boots up on his desk.

The multi-versal *Paper Warriors* office was an arrangement that the Buzzes had worked out. Also, rent was free, so that was a bonus since he never knew which Earth he'd be spending time on during any given week of the year. The only bad thing was that the smell of Korean barbecue from the first floor reminded him of his wife, Aki.

Maybe that was a good thing. It was good not to forget where you came from and all that shit.

When he reached the second floor and stepped into the printing press, the sweet-sour smell of fermentation nearly took his breath away. He immediately saw the three newsmen off to the side leaning over five-gallon buckets of kombucha.

"Did you tell him?" the medium-sized newsman said.

"Yes," the tallest one said.

The shortest one wiped his forehead with the back of his hand. "Good. Good. Don't want him thinking we're weird or something."

"He's the weird one," the middle one said.

"I can hear you," Z called as he slid out of his jacket and hung it on the hall tree. Raindrops dribbled off it to the floor below.

"He is, though," the middle one squeaked. "Always going into his office and disappearing for weeks on end. Then he shows up like no time has passed and goes about his business. He's always mumbling about time travel and parallel Earths and the butterfly effect and stuff."

The tallest one left his other two associates and headed over to his typewriter. "Dudes. Seriously. This Sasquatch story is going to be the best ever."

Chuckling, Z left the foyer and headed away from the three newsmen and toward the back of the office, which housed an expansive and elaborate-looking printing press. It was large and wooden with a bunch of metal struts and ink reservoirs and hoses. Since it was in the 1980s on Earth-G, the printing press looked much more archaic than in the more futuristic Earths.

On each Earth, though, the *Paper Warriors* printing press played an important part in Z's and Buzz's multiverse protection operation. Buzz had developed a transdimensional pager. Other than that, the intergalactic printing press was his only means to communicate with the Buzzes on the other Earths, and with Z. It was cumbersome, having to reply via newspapers, but it was all they had. It sure beat intergalactic carrier pigeon messages.

The best part was that the intergalactic printing press was developed and originally used by Nunez, their enemy, who now threatened the worlds with his time virus schemes. At least some good came out of it.

Z walked along the machine, sliding a palm against its polished side rail. It was quiet and still. He leaned back against it as he waited for a message from Buzz to arrive.

What would be his next mission? He was getting tired of hopping to other Earths to obtain the bioweapon in the warehouse before someone deployed it in the city. It was getting boring, even with all the minute differences that he attributed to his timing on each Earth.

Maybe there was some new threat. Perhaps it was on a beach somewhere. Or some sunny paradise that wasn't New York. Someplace full of babes in bikinis...

He started when the printing press at his back stirred. Standing to his full height and turning, he saw the inner workings humming to life. He stood back as the feed pulled a large sheet of paper into it. Then the press's top portion descended and hid the sheet as the internal mechanisms applied the ink to the paper's front cover.

Gasps escaped the three newsmen off to the side. "It's finally printing something!"

When the printing press opened and relinquished the hot paper, Z scooped it up, realizing that the three newsmen were standing next to him, trying to peer at it. Z jerked it back away from them.

"This paper is for me, boys." Z turned and headed for his office.

"He's doing it again," one of the newsmen said. "He's going to go into his office and disappear."

"What does he do in there?" another newsman wondered

aloud.

"Let your imagination run wild, boys." Z smirked as he unlocked the door to his office. He flicked his gaze back at them. "Like Sasquatch. Get it? Run wild…" Then he left the three newsmen staring at the closing door.

The interior smelled of dust and was slightly musty. It comforted him.

"Ah, finally some privacy," he muttered as he sighted his dusty desk. He leaned over it, brushed off a clean space, and tossed the newspaper onto it.

Then he walked around the desk. As he did so, he regarded his office's empty walls. The place was barren, but it was all his. Against one wall was a large, long, smooth object under a sheet. He'd probably need that later.

Once behind his desk, he plopped down into the leather swivel chair, his weight wrinkling the cracked leather.

He knew he ought to look at the newspaper now and get it over with, see if his assignment was to a tropical paradise or…that other place. First, he needed to enjoy the moment of not having to worry about anything. He lowered his elbows to his knees and balanced his chin in his upraised hands as he stared out the office's sole window.

The mini blinds were closed, but the gaps between the slats afforded him a slivered view of the city beyond. The neon marquee outside the window advertising the Korean barbeque place beneath his office glowed through no matter how tight he cranked the shades.

Ah. This was the life, wasn't it? Nothing to tie him down. Saving the worlds—plural. Helping right some of his past wrongs in his free time. What could he possibly be missing?

My wife… My friends… My old life…

He sighed. He had a new life now. Plus a tiny octopus thing as a friend. He had everything he needed.

With his moping out of the way, he kicked his boots up onto the desk and plucked the newspaper from its dusty top.

"Come on," he said aloud. "Buzz, be nice to me. Give me a good assignment."

He read the newspaper's headline: **You Are Hereby Re-Assigned To Earth-D.**

Z flung the paper back to the desk.

"Fuck."

CHAPTER NINE

He continued reading the article beneath the newspaper's headline.

Dr. Eduardo Nunez from Earth-Z spotted on Earth-D. No other details at this time. Your mission, if you choose to accept, is to go to Earth-D and await further directions via the Paper Warriors press. See below the exact time and coordinates for Earth-D.

Since I know you will accept, you should also know that my algorithms have detected the time virus bioweapon on Earth-D and it's already in the thugs' possession. You must obtain it from them before they deploy it in the city. So, you have two missions.

I have calculated the best time to complete the "warehouse mission" on Earth-D. Once you arrive on Earth-D, you will have only a few hours until the time you need to be in position to complete the mission.

In the meantime, be ready. Stay vigilant. Say hello to the ladies for me. -B

Z inhaled. While the last thing he wanted was to spend any

amount of time on Earth-D, if he could finally get his hands on the scientist who had engineered the time virus on Earth-Z that had wrecked his life and taken his family from him, he was going to take it.

The good doctor, as he'd taken to referring to the mad scientist, was going to pay if he had anything to say about it. His pursuit of science had taken too much from Z.

"About time," Z muttered, flexing his fist in anticipation of finally confronting the man. He was ready for some payback.

I thought you didn't want to go to Earth-D, Germ said.

"What have I told you about the 'R' of my life's mission?"

Revenge?

"No. Redemption. I can't keep chasing down weaponized versions of the virus on all of the Earths. I have to eventually confront the man behind it all and stop all this. I have to redeem myself for all the bad shit I did after his virus messed with my head."

With new energy coursing through him, Z popped up from behind his desk and walked over to the other side of the cramped office. It was cramped because of the large, long, smooth object beneath the sheet against the wall.

Z gripped the sheet in both hands and, with a quick jerk, ripped it off the sleek form of his space and time capsule. Its metal and glass contours gleamed in the light of the neon sign outside the window, lending it a cyberpunk feel even though they were in the nineteen-eighties. Not that the space and time capsule was from that time—it was from the twenty-forties.

That wasn't important. What was, was that this Superman-esque spacecraft device allowed him to hop to parallel Earths. It could also jump backward or forward in time once he was on an Earth.

Z unlatched the glass lid and climbed inside.

Ready to leave already? Germ said. *I thought you hated Earth-D.*

"I'm not wasting any time. It's Nunez. I'm gonna nail the bastard. He's not ruining anyone else's life."

Earth-D

When the space and time capsule stopped vibrating, Z checked the time and coordinates on the center console to make sure he was on the right planet at the right time and place.

The place was easy. He had programmed the space and time capsule to take him to his office in the *Paper Warriors* news office on Earth-D. He'd input the exact date and time that Buzz had provided him in the newspaper. This Earth's version of the printing press was on the second story above a Korean restaurant too. The same three hippy newsmen also ran it as in most of the Earths. Z loved messing with them.

Before he did anything, he set one of his stopwatches to start counting down three hours until he had to undertake the warehouse mission on this Earth.

Another day. Another mission, he thought.

Z unlatched the space and time capsule's lid and climbed outside into an office identical to the one on Earth-G. It even had the same type of desk, covered in a thick patina of dust, and the walls were equally as bare. Outside the room's sole window, the Korean barbeque sign glowed. It looked like the sun was starting to rise on this Earth.

He was about to leave his office and check on the printing press to see if Buzz had sent him any further information on the Eduardo Nunez sighting. Then he realized the space and time capsule was resting there, parked neatly along the sidewall, exposed for prying eyes.

Not that he made it easy for eyes to pry. The second-story window had no fire escape outside. So only Spiderman would be peeking inside that way. Also, the specially-designed window could withstand the impact of a rocket-propelled grenade blast—not that he'd ever had cause to test that feature out. The door leading into his office was equally reinforced. Nothing short of an elephant was going to knock that door down. He equipped the door with a special lock plate that made it easy to tell if anyone ever tried to pick it.

While he didn't have any fear that the three newsmen would try—let alone succeed—in sneaking into his office and seeing the futuristic device, Z knew it was best to play it safe. Buzz had said to be careful in his latest communication. No one on this Earth except Z would ever know that time travel or parallel Earth hopping was possible.

Z went behind his desk and rummaged through the drawers until he found a large wadded-up bed sheet—he was never one for making his bed. He pulled it out, unfolded it, and draped it over the sleek space and time capsule so that it resembled a covered abstract sculpture instead of a rocket-shaped world-hopping device.

As he was about to open the office door leading into the newsroom, he tried to recall if the abstract art period was before or after the nineteen-eighties. It didn't matter. For all he knew, Earth-D never had one.

So far, Germ said, *this Earth-D looks the same as Earth-G.*

Z shook his head as if he'd lost a close friend to some horrible disease. "Just you wait and see. It's awful. This world is—"

He opened the door, and a tall busty brunette woman nearly fell into his arms.

Z steadied her by the shoulders and helped her stand upright. She gave him a sexy grin.

"Gorgeous," Z gasped.

Gorgeous didn't begin to describe her. She had bronze legs that seemed to go on forever up to the nearly thigh-high bright blue dress that hugged her natural curves and bosom. Her face was stern but playful with high cheekbones, and she had long blonde hair falling in curls back over her shoulders.

Speaking of shoulders. Her dress had puffed-up shoulder pads built into the shoulders. Z flinched. They were so… weird. Damn the eighties and their bizarre fashion trends. Aside from the shoulder pads though, the woman oozed sex appeal like honey on a hot day. She'd slung her blue purse casually over her shoulder.

Z fluffed his shirt collar as he glanced past her to ensure he was still in the *Paper Warriors* news office and not some model agency. Behind the woman, the three red-faced newsmen stood arguing with each other and pointing at the woman's back.

"Hey?" Z said at last.

The woman flashed him a businesslike smile. "Mr. Z?"

"Please. Just Z. And you are?"

Now it was the woman's turn to size him up. "Alice."

He glanced past the woman with a questioning look at the three newsmen.

"She's been coming in here and looking for you every day for the past two weeks," the tallest one said.

The middle newsman shuffled his feet. "Yeah, she waits by your door in the morning."

"You're a lucky man," the shortest man said with a gulp. "I think."

Z turned to the woman blocking his way. "This true?"

She nodded.

He leaned against the door frame. While he didn't mind gorgeous women falling into his lap, he couldn't help but notice the oddness of the situation. He rarely showed his face here on Earth-D. Yet she somehow knew to look for him? Here in the news office?

He stood admiring her sexy curves. She seemed to appreciate his attention.

Feeling a growing sense of attraction to her, he cleared his throat. "Why exactly have you been looking for me?"

Alice struck a confident pose. "I need your help."

CHAPTER TEN

"Help? What kind of help?"

Alice flashed him a sexy grin and leaned forward a bit. "If I'm not mistaken, you have a reputation of being a fixer."

"A fixer?" Z was equally intrigued and surprised. Again, he didn't exactly frequent Earth-D, and he hadn't righted any wrongs yet on this Earth. So how did she know him?

Her sexiness made him almost hate himself for what he was about to say next. Still, he was technically on a mission and couldn't afford to get distracted. "Maybe you're mistaken."

He tried to walk through the doorway into the newsroom, but she blocked his way with a hand upon his chest. He stopped, and her palm and fingers felt up his muscles.

He narrowed his eyes at her.

"Oh, I don't think I'm mistaken," she said.

"Then how do you know me?"

She cocked her head. "Really? You don't trust me?"

"It's not every day a stunning woman walks into my office."

She raised a hand to her mouth, feigning coyness. "You think I'm stunning?" She angled her body and leaned a hip closer to him.

Z smirked. A very forward woman, she was certainly his type. Maybe Earth-D wasn't as bad as he'd once given it credit for. Besides, Buzz had instructed him to say hello to the ladies for him…

"Oh, that?" Z winked. "I tell that to every dame I meet."

She gave him a playful smile as if glad to know they were both on the same page. Finally, she placed a hand on her hip. "Well, you going to invite me in?"

He wanted to. He really did.

However, there was the issue of the bedsheet-covered space and time capsule along one wall. With a hand on her shoulder, he guided her away from the doorway as he closed his office door behind him, jiggling the knob to make sure it locked. Nope, he did not want to deflect any questions she might have about the space and time capsule.

"Seriously," he said, as he walked her over toward the printing press in the office. "How did you hear about me?"

She looked at him. "Isn't it obvious? I'm a big fan of the *Paper Warriors* publication. When I discovered that I needed help, I placed an ad in the latest issue. These three gentlemen called me and said they had someone in mind." She turned and batted her luscious eyelashes at the three geeky newsmen.

The three men looked ready to faint at her acknowledgment.

"Is this true?" Z called.

"Y-yes," the tallest one answered.

That made Z feel a little more at ease. Upon consulting his stopwatch, he saw that he still had nearly three hours until the warehouse mission. The Earth-D printing press hadn't printed any further news about the Eduardo Nunez sighting on this Earth. He had some time to get to know this fine mama.

"How about we go for a walk then," he suggested to her.

"Fine by me."

The three newsmen flashed Z jealous looks as the two of them headed downstairs. On the way, Z grabbed his jacket off the hall tree. He usually kept at least one jacket in the newspaper office on each world for when he returned to them.

As they were descending the steps to the ground floor, Z admired the woman's backside. She saw this and seemed to take pleasure in him watching her. He led her outside. It wasn't raining on this Earth.

"You know," he said, "you don't look like a person who subscribes to alt magazines. No offense."

She didn't even try to refute it. "None taken."

"So you believe in aliens too?"

They reached the sidewalk, and Alice straightened her short dress. "The truth is out there."

Z chuckled. She'd inadvertently quoted the X-Files, a TV show that didn't come out until the nineties. Also, he couldn't believe a woman as fine as her believed in aliens. Sure, time travel and parallel Earths were a thing, but aliens? He hooked her with his gaze. "You're a surprising woman."

She eyed him back in turn. As her eyes followed the arc of his pencil-thin scar, she licked her lips. "I need help, and I think you might be able to provide it."

Z started walking and motioned for her to keep up. "What kind of help?"

"It's my sister."

As he nodded for her to continue, he realized the genuine look of fear that had suddenly crept over her face. She was scared about something. That much was for sure. He reached over and grabbed her hand.

She pulled a white handkerchief from her purse with her free hand and wiped her eyes. "My sister. She...she's gone missing."

Z paused. He knew he should try to be more sensitive. "What happened to her?"

After dabbing her eyes again, she continued. "Police are saying that she might have skipped town. Happens all the time in a place as big as New York."

Z reached up and stroked a tear from Alice's cheek. "It's okay. It's okay."

She met his eyes and blinked to try to gain some strength.

"Let me guess. You know her better than the police do, and you know she didn't skip town?"

"Yes. Mel and I are close. She would've told me if she was going to up and leave the city. She makes good money. Why would she have just left? It makes no sense. Something happened to her. Something bad. It's the only thing that makes sense."

He silently took in her words. When he didn't say anything, she smiled weakly.

"You think I'm a crazy person. Don't you?"

"No."

"You think because I read tabloids and wacky world news stories that I'm a screwball. Like the police. Is that it?" Her crying was starting to make her makeup go all drippy, which made her look a bit crazy. He kept that to himself.

"I didn't say any of that."

She pulled away from him, and Z caught her by the wrist and shoulder. He pulled her in close to him. "I believe you. Okay? But I'm going to need more than that to help you."

She wiped her nose with her handkerchief. Then she held up her purse and peered inside. After a bit of digging, she found her wallet and pulled a small photo from it. The image showed an attractive, petite woman wearing a pink sunhat smiling for the camera. She was standing in a field with a bunch of people all around her. There was a stage in the background.

"This is her." Alice met his eyes. "I took it the night she disappeared."

"Mel's last name?"

Alice was now looking back at the photo. "Phoenix. Mel Phoenix. I'm Alice Phoenix." She offered him the photo with a weak smile.

Z took the photo from Alice, turning over the last name Phoenix in his head. It was a badass last name. He hoped he could make Alice's missing sister return the same as the bird of legend.

He scrutinized the photo. After memorizing Mel's face and features, he handed it back to her. "Where was this taken?"

"She and I attended a Music Under the Stars event in upstate New York with some friends. You know, bring your blanket and picnic basket and listen to bands play music at night under the stars. She was there with us one minute, and the next she was just…gone."

Z arched his eyebrows. "Gone?"

She nodded. "There were a lot of people there. It was dark. She got separated from us. When it was time to pack up, and everyone left, she was nowhere around. I can't help but blame myself. She only came because I begged her to." Alice folded her hands together pleadingly, a sheen of tears glazing her eyes as she looked up at him. "Z, you have to help me. You're my only hope."

Z glanced at his watch to check how much time he had left until he had to undertake this Earth's mission at the warehouse to get the bioweapon from the thugs.

Alice batted her eyes. "Please?" She bobbed toward him, her bosom jiggling and her tanned thighs reflecting the overcast morning sun.

They were legs a newly single man like him couldn't turn down.

"Of course. I'll take the case—"

She threw her arms around his chest, squeezing and catching him off guard for a second. "Thank you, oh thank you." She hugged him tight and rested her cheek against his chest.

It felt good.

Such elevated hormones, Germ said. *I have never seen you so... aroused like this.*

"How would you know?" Z muttered.

Because I am in your pants pocket, remember?

"What?" Alice said, tilting her head up at him.

"Oh. Um, nothing. Just talking to myself. I know where to begin my investigation."

Her eyes widened with surprised joy. "You do?"

He nodded. "I have a friend on the police force."

CHAPTER ELEVEN

The short walk through the streets of NYC to the police precinct gave Z some time to think. He wasn't exactly a thinking man who sat around deliberating. He did his thinking while on the go. Whenever they passed a coffee shop, Z scowled.

You sure you have time to follow up on this woman's case? Germ said. *Should you not be scoping out the warehouse on this Earth for your upcoming mission?*

Z scoffed down at his pocket as he passed another café. "Don't take this the wrong way, Germ. You know nothing about women."

I admit I do not. Still, I do not see how that is relevant—

"Those legs," Z said simply.

There was a pause. *And?*

Z threw up his hands, causing an old lady powerwalking on the sidewalk to give him a confused stare.

Fine. Fine. I will drop the subject.

They passed yet another coffee shop. Z all but snorted in disgust.

You speak as if this is the worst Earth in the multiverse, but I still fail to see how it is any different than the rest of the Earths. There are people. There are shops. There is food—

Z's finger shot into the air to make a point. "That, little buddy, is where you're wrong."

Germ peeked out from Z's pocket and peered up at him. "What do you mean?"

"Oh," Z scoffed. "Let me show you then."

When he came to the next coffee shop, he ducked inside. Surprisingly, there were only a couple of people in line, and he quickly reached the café's counter.

A portly woman wearing a hairnet said, "Hun, what can I get for you today?"

"One coffee, black, with two donuts."

The woman smiled as her hand hovered over the blocky keys of an old-fashioned cash register. "One coffee, black," she repeated, punching out the price for one cup. "And..." She glanced up at him. "I'm sorry, what else did you say you wanted, hon?"

Z stood there patiently at the counter, trying to hide his irritation. He gave a polite smile. "Two donuts. Please."

The woman turned back to her cash register, looking to punch the number keys. Her smile faded as her brain interpreted what Z had said. "Come again?"

Z changed his voice as if talking to a small child. "Dough. Nuts. Two of 'em."

She regarded him over the cash register as if he'd ordered in a foreign language. "Donuts? I'm...sorry. I've never heard of a 'donut' before." She was starting to look a bit agitated. The line behind Z was growing, and he was holding it up. "Hun, maybe you're new to America. This is a café. We sell coffee—

hot black liquid with caffeine in it. As well as cookies, brownies, and scones."

He didn't want a goddamned scone; he wanted a donut.

"What about bagels?" Z asked. He didn't give a shit about bagels, but in all the other Earths, this city was like the bagel capital of the world.

"Come again?"

Z raised his hands so that the woman could see them over the cash register. He formed both hands into circles with his fingers to look like he was holding up two O's. "Yeah. Donuts. Bagels. Round rings of dough. You fry donuts and put icing on them and jelly inside them."

The woman and several customers in line behind him gave him disgusted looks.

"You cook bagels in boiling water, then brown them in the oven. People eat them with coffee."

The woman glared at his hand circles as if they were some obscene gesture. "Do you want anything or not?" she said sternly.

The woman's fiery gaze looked like it could melt butter.

Z's shoulders sagged. "Just the coffee, please."

He paid for it and humbly accepted the warm beverage.

As he left the establishment with his coffee, he said, "Germ, now can you see why I hate Earth-D?"

I do not understand. Why are there no donuts here?

Z sighed. "From what I can tell, the people here on Earth-D are evil dicks."

Germ scrunched up his tiny octopus face as he peeked up at Z. *The humans on Earth-D are penises?*

"It's a figure of speech."

Oh. So no one has ever tried to make donuts here?

"Oh, I've tried putting the idea in people's ears every time I come to this shithole Earth. Everyone is like, 'Ew. That sounds disgusting.' Once, I managed to convince a baker to try a recipe I brought from another Earth."

What happened?

"The donuts turned out delicious. When the baker tried them, and when he let his customers try them too, they all spat them out like they were allergic or some shit. Have you ever heard of that before? Allergic to donuts?"

Could be a gluten intolerance, I suppose.

Z laughed incredulously. "That's a bullshit reason if I ever heard of one."

You are very defensive of donuts.

Z sipped his coffee. "Someone's got to defend their delicious honor. They're inanimate objects. And God's gift to mankind. Donuts sum up everything it is to be an American. This Earth sucks."

If you say so.

"I do."

A few minutes later, they reached the police precinct Z was looking for. From the outside, it looked the same as those on most of the other Earths. On the inside...

There were no donut boxes. Anywhere.

Z glumly shook his head.

The precinct was a big place, and it took him a few minutes to locate who he was looking for. The young beat cop stood arguing with a short man in an expensive tan suit.

Z stepped closer.

"It's not going to hold up in court," the man in the tan suit said.

The young cop stood his ground. "The perp is obviously guilty. His alibi doesn't check out. We have eyewitnesses who can place him there an hour before. He's guilty, and you know he's guilty."

The suit sneered and raised his hands as if he was extracting himself from the situation. "That's the law system we have. Your evidence is not admissible in court. It's Law 101..." The man in the suit paused as he noticed Z standing a few feet away from them. "Y-yes?" He studied the scar on one half of Z's face.

Z cocked his head. "Some kind of trouble here?"

The suit sneered. "Oh, only a gross violation of the law. My client—"

"Your client is guilty as hell," the cop said.

"My client has rights."

Neither man looked like he was going to back down. Until Z took another step forward and literally inserted himself between the two men. He fluffed the jacket over his black muscle shirt, standing so that his scar faced the man in the suit.

"You the defendant's attorney?" he asked.

The suit nodded indignantly.

Z didn't say anything, merely stood there for a moment with his hands in his pockets.

"Well," the attorney finally said. "Just who the hell are you?"

Z feigned hurt surprise. "You probably don't know me, but I'm the judge's friend. We go...way back. We're poker buddies."

The suit stared incredulously at him. "Really? You know the judge? I didn't know she played poker."

She? Z thought. Oh well. No one out-bullshitted him.

"Yeah. She's a real vicious player."

The suit shook his head as if to clear a horrible mental

image from it. Then he turned and pointed at a framed photograph on the precinct wall. In it was a female judge wearing a black robe. She had a sweet, placid face. "This judge. She plays poker?"

Z shrugged, already committed to the story. "I know. I know. You wouldn't think so, right? But she'll take your money. She's like a shark." Out of the corner of his eye, Z checked the attorney's face to see if he was buying it.

The man crossed his arms over his chest. "So, what if she does play poker? What's that got to do with anything?"

"I've got her ear. She owes me. So maybe you should drop this bullshit case?"

"This is…this is ridiculous—"

Z leaned forward and tilted his head a bit so that the ceiling light hit his scar just right.

"I'll, uh." The attorney shuffled his feet. "I forgot I had something I need to do. I'll be seeing you."

He turned and exited the room, leaving only Z and the officer.

"Well, I'll be danged," the officer said.

Z frowned at the language.

The officer extended a hand to him. "Name's Officer Marshall Peet. And yours?"

Z took the offered hand. "My friends call me Z."

I thought you don't have any friends, Germ said.

Officer Marshall Peet nodded as he absorbed the strange name. "I'm glad you stepped in when you did. I was about to punch that guy. That prick is really busting my balls."

Z smirked. "No problem, Dad."

The young cop did a double-take. "What did you say?"

CHAPTER TWELVE

"Excuse me?" Z said.

Officer Marshall Pete stared at him. "What did you say?"

Shit. "What did it sound like I said?"

"Sounded like you called me 'dad.'"

Z chewed his lip as he debated how to proceed. Then he laughed. "That's because I did call you dad. Where I come from, everyone says that to everyone."

The cop narrowed his eyes at Z. "Where exactly do you come from?"

He wasn't about to explain that he came from a parallel Earth. "Someplace like this. But different. So different, you could almost say it's a whole different world."

The cop scratched under his chin. "So you're from New Jersey?" Finally, his face started to lighten up. He chuckled.

Z smacked Marshall's shoulder. He gave a fake cheesy grin. "You got me."

"Why didn't you say so? I'm from Jersey. Say, were you looking for me or something?" The officer leaned over his desk to arrange some papers.

"As a matter of fact, yes. I need your help with something."

Marshall fumbled with the papers he was shuffling. "Me? I'm only a beat cop."

"You're not only a beat cop. I asked around. You've got quite the reputation for your diligence and eye for detail. You ask me; you're a natural. Ought to be promoted to detective."

Marshall fidgeted. "I don't know about all that…"

"I've got this case I was hoping to run by you. Maybe you're even familiar with it."

Marshall glanced up at a wall clock. "You helped me out with that attorney. My midnight shift is almost up, but sure. I can see what I can do for you. I haven't seen you around before. You a PI?"

Z wasn't exactly a private investigator. He was more like a fixer. But those legs… Today he was a PI.

"Something like that. The case involves a missing woman."

Marshall nodded glumly. "Too many of those in this city if you ask me. I remember back when the world was safer. What's this lady's name?"

"Mel. Mel Phoenix."

"Phoenix. Phoenix…" The officer appeared to be tasting the last name in his mouth. His eyes lit up. "I think I remember that case. With a name like that, hard to forget. Mythical firebird that rises from the ashes, right?"

"Something like that." Z nodded as he leaned forward for a better look at Marshall's desk.

Meanwhile, Marshall walked over to a filing cabinet and selected a drawer. He pulled it out, and a few moments later he lifted a folder. "We don't have the actual file. Another precinct handled the missing person report. We received the rundown back when it happened in case we came across anything. Let me check the notes real quick. Can't exactly turn it over to a civilian to look at, if you know what I mean."

Z pretended that he did. It wouldn't do to make a scene, and he didn't need the notes anyway. He needed to check out the scene of the crime.

"Don't get me wrong," Marshall said as he scanned the file. "You look like a tough character who knows how to take and deal some punches. I bet you have some real-world experience."

Z recalled the days when he and his team used to take down global threats on Earth-Z. "I'm experienced."

Marshall looked up from the file. "Anything world-ending?"

"Just the usual." If his father from another Earth only knew…

"Ah yes," Marshall said. "Now I remember. Lady disappeared from an outdoor concert. Some kind of Woodstock wannabe event. Dang hippies."

Z frowned at the officer's clean words. The Marshall he knew—his dad on Earth-Z—was quite foul-mouthed, to put it lightly. "I take it you don't like weed much?"

"Heck no. I see what it does to people. Erodes the mind."

Z winced. "Maybe take it easy on your kids if you have any one day and you find them with a joint. Okay?"

Marshall made a face. "You trying to give me parenting advice? I don't have any kids."

Z shrugged. "Eh, give it a few years. Just try to take it easy on them, okay? Especially if you have a boy."

Marshall grunted. "They do say boys are the hardest… here. I think I might have found something. According to the notes, Miss Phoenix's friends said she was wearing a pink sunhat the night of the event. The morning after, a pink sunhat was found in some weeds about half a mile away near an old black-painted barn. A warrant enabled local authorities to search the barn, but there was only farm equipment inside." He stopped abruptly. "Hey, are you okay?"

Marshall's mention of a black-painted barn sent a cold chill through Z. Surely, it wasn't the same barn…

"You said there was only farm equipment inside?" Z asked.

Marshall thought about it. He nodded. "Farming implements. A lot of straw. The usual. Why?"

Z chewed that over. Maybe it was a coincidence. All the same, he needed to see the barn in person to confirm. It was probably an ordinary barn. Probably.

"You got an address for it?"

"Sure. Got it right here." Marshall glanced at the clock again. "Let me guess. You want to go take a look?"

"You read my mind."

Officer Marshall returned the file to the cabinet and sized up Z. "Then I'm going with you."

He hadn't expected that. "Don't you have a beat?"

Marshall stifled a yawn. "Didn't you hear me? My shift just ended. This case intrigues me. I do hate missing women reports. I want to help you. Let me call my wife Carolyn first and let her know I'll be home a bit late."

Carolyn. Z's mother, on another Earth.

As Marshall lifted the bulky landline phone sitting on his desk and prepared to dial, he caught Z's eye. "You married too?"

Z's smile faltered. "I was."

The phone was ringing on the other line. "Sorry to hear that," Marshall said. "How about I drive?"

The fields and trees were calming to look at as they passed Marshall's car's passenger window. The officer was off-duty so they took his fire engine red coupe.

The drive was pleasant, and the car was a joy to ride in. Since Z knew his father from another Earth, he had plenty of conversation topics to talk about, and there was a good rapport between them. That is until Z asked, "What's your favorite food?"

"No doubt about it, my wife Carolyn's hash browns. Oh, and her homemade chocolate chip cookies are a close second."

"Sounds...good," Z said, fondly recalling those warm gooey cookies from his childhood. Anytime he smelled cookies baking brought him back to those days

"What's yours?" Marshall asked as he kept his eyes on the road. He stifled another yawn due to his midnight shift, but he was an alert driver.

"Donuts." The word was out of his mouth before he even realized he'd said it.

Marshall made a face. "Donuts? What's a donut?"

Not to stereotype, but it seemed absurd that a policeman didn't know what a donut was. Of course, this was Earth-D...

"It's dough batter that's fried and glazed. Sometimes they have jelly inside."

"Yuck. That sounds disgusting."

"Does it though?" Z pressed.

"Yeah. What kind of disgusting pastries are they baking in New Jersey these days? Ugh. I feel like I ought to wash my mouth out for imagining that. I mean, jelly inside a fried piece of dough?"

"With icing on top," Z added helpfully.

Marshall shook his head. "I'll pretend I didn't hear any of that."

Z knew he ought to stop defending his favorite food, but damnit, he had to. "They're really good. Where I'm from, the best places to get donuts are Krispy Kreme and Dunkin'. Even gas stations sell them."

Marshall flicked Z a mistrusting look. "Now you're bull-crapping me. I've never heard of this Krispy Kreme or Dunkin'."

"That's what's wrong with this place," Z said.

Marshall's head whipped around. "You disrespecting my city?"

That escalated fast, Germ said rather unhelpfully.

"You know, this is a nice car," Z said, changing the subject.

Marshall nodded. "Thanks. It's a smooth ride."

They drove in silence for a few minutes. Then Marshall pointed at the windshield. "See that field there? That's where the Music Under the Stars concert was. From what I hear, the whole place was full of people. Some officers were present, but it wasn't my precinct so I don't know the details."

Z nodded as he surveyed the fields. They were empty now —just grass. The event had cleaned up well afterward.

"That strange black barn mentioned in the report should be coming up soon. Just over that little rise."

Surely it wasn't a Buzz Barn. Those were barns that Buzz had sent out to all the Earths throughout the multiverse back during the time virus crisis.

Z shook his head at the memory of his darker days.

The officers who'd investigated it had reported finding only farming equipment and straw inside—and not futuristic Buzz tech. So it couldn't be a Buzz Barn.

Right?

The red coupe was approaching the sloping hill. He would find out in a minute.

They crested the small hill.

"Yep, there it is," Marshall said.

From a distance, the dark paint job sure looked like a Buzz Barn.

Z couldn't believe it. "Shit."

CHAPTER THIRTEEN

Marshall gave Z a worried look. "Everything okay?"

Z shifted uncomfortably in his seat. What was he going to say? Then he had it. "I remembered I left my stove on. Again."

Marshall started braking. "Want me to turn around?"

Z waved toward the road. "Nah. Just keep going. Pull up to the barn. Shouldn't take long for me to investigate."

"I can try to find a farmhouse nearby. See if you can borrow their telephone."

Thank God for no cell phones in the eighties, Z thought.

"No. It's fine. Seriously. It's a safe kitchen. Not the first time I've forgotten to turn off the stove."

Marshall scrutinized Z. "That's not something I'd be telling a police officer. It's a dang public safety concern. What if you burn down your home?"

Z smirked at the thought of the *Paper Warriors* news office burning to the ground. It wouldn't be a literary shame. However, it would be a crime for the Korean barbecue place on the first floor to burn down.

Z shook his head. "It's well ventilated. It'll be fine. I'll take a quick look up here. Then we'll head back. Trust me."

At that moment, he didn't think Marshall looked like he trusted him.

When Marshall pulled up to the barn and parked outside, he hesitated. "Are you sure you don't want to—"

"This case is important to me, okay. We're good. For all I know, I did remember to turn my stove off. I shouldn't have said anything."

"House fires are huge deals," Marshall said, but Z already had the car door open and was climbing out of the vehicle.

Z closed the door and immediately surveyed the barn before him. It was wooden, and the thick coat of glossy black paint gave it an eerie aura.

However, Buzz Barns were made of metal and had high-tech security options. This was a regular barn painted black.

Relief flooded through Z as he proceeded to inspect the building.

Tall weeds grew up unchecked along the wall he was facing. That must have been where they'd found the pink sunhat. Turning to face the way he'd come from, he judged that the wind could've blown the hat over here across the grassy fields from the outdoor concert. Maybe Mel Phoenix had been abducted from the event, and this barn had nothing to do with her disappearance.

Then again, when was there any such thing as coincidences?

"Hey," Marshall called as he started getting out of the car. "Are you sure you don't want to—"

Z edged around the corner to check out the barn's other side.

He spotted an oversized barn door and inspected it. It was locked.

When he heard Marshall saying something from around the corner, coming closer, he pulled bolt cutters from his jacket pocket. Z never knew when he might need the tool on missions and it was one of the reasons he always liked to wear a jacket. He quickly snipped the shank, took it off, and stuffed the lock and bolt cutters into his pocket. Then with a silent grunt, he heaved the door open a crack.

Marshall appeared around the corner.

Z glanced at the man. "You said they locked this place? Looks open to me. Hold on. I think I see something pink inside."

Before Marshall could protest, Z slipped inside the dark barn. He drew a small flashlight from his jacket. He switched it on and raised it to get a look at the interior.

Sure enough, the barn contained tractor parts, bales of straw, and some other farm supplies. He stepped deeper into the gloom for a better look.

"You can't just go in there, man," Marshall was saying from somewhere outside the barn. "You're trespassing."

Z placed a hand in front of his mouth to muffle his voice. "Can't hear you." He knocked down some cobwebs in front of him. The air was musty. Dust particles sprinkled down in places. If there was ever a place to hide a kidnapped or dead body, this would be it.

He continued searching. Finding no light switches or ceiling lights, he kept using his flashlight. Before he'd started hopping to parallel Earths, Buzz had instructed him on the importance of not bringing future tech back to the past. So unfortunately, it being the nineteen-eighties, his flashlight was a real piece of crap and didn't illuminate too much of the barn's interior at a time.

He didn't spot anything out of the ordinary on the ground floor. Then he saw the wooden ladder leading up to the hayloft.

"Hey," Marshall yelled into the barn from outside the doorway. "What the heck are you doing? This is trespassing—"

"I think I hear something up in the loft," Z whispered back. "Sounds like a woman struggling…"

"You what—oh crap. I'll go call for backup."

"Let me check it out first real quick. It might be nothing."

As Z crept toward the wooden ladder, he suddenly had the eerie feeling that someone or something was watching him.

It's only Marshall, he told himself, but his intuition said it was something else.

He put his hands on the ladder's rungs and started climbing. Before he reached the top rung, he paused, drew a deep breath, and climbed another rung. He peered into the darkness with his flashlight.

A sudden high-pitched screech and a flutter of movement nearly caused him to fall backward off the ladder. He clung to the wood as he raised one hand to ward his face.

Then he realized it was a couple of bats. The creatures flapped past both sides of his head and exited the barn via the open door.

Z heaved in a breath and climbed into the hayloft. Crouching, he played the weak flashlight over the loft. Footprints coated the dusty floor that showed through the patches of loose straw. Was someone up here?

Most likely the footprints were due to the police officers who had investigated the barn.

There was still the bothersome feeling that someone was watching him…

"You okay up there?" Marshall yelled inside.

Z wiped some sweat trickling from his forehead. "I'm good."

There was only one place a person could be hiding and watching him from up here: an old wooden wardrobe with a tall vertical door on the front. There were small cracks in the sides of the cabinet so it was possible that someone was inside and watching him.

It seemed highly unlikely.

Marshall yelled again. "See any signs of anyone?"

Again Z's eyes were drawn to the giant wardrobe. It was certainly big enough to hide a body in.

"No." He stood and slowly started moving in the direction of the wardrobe. Straw crunched under his boots like twigs. The closer he got, the more the feeling of being watched intensified.

There couldn't be someone inside there watching him. It made no sense. They would be trapped.

"You better come on out then." Marshall cleared his throat outside. "We need to get going. I'm not going to be an accomplice to trespassing. You hear?"

Z blocked out the rest of what Marshall was saying as he closed the distance to the wardrobe. He stopped right when he reached it and twisted around, playing his flashlight over the rest of the loft. This was the only place a person could be hiding.

Again, why would a person hide in there? They would be trapped.

He glared at the wardrobe, a few inches away from him.

You are scared, Germ said.

"Am not."

Your elevated heart rate suggests that you are.

"Goddamnit, I'm not scared," Z said as he set his hand to the knob on the wardrobe's door and tore it open.

A man in a black tuxedo stood facing him, his long arms hanging limply at his sides. Dark sunglasses concealed his eyes, but he was clearly an older man. The skin seemed tight around his cheekbones. He had black hair slicked back over his scalp. He looked like a dead man.

"Who the fuck are—"

The man's arms shot up. Both of his broad hands enclosed around Z's throat, his gangly fingers wrapping around the back of his neck.

Before Z could react, the older, tuxedoed man wrenched his hands, cracking Z's neck.

Hm. Guess you did have something to be scared about, Germ said calmly.

I'm not scared, you motherfucking octopus... Z thought.

He died.

CHAPTER FOURTEEN

(Three Minutes Earlier)

Z warped back as far as he could. He was standing outside the barn with the bolt cutters in his hand, about to cut through the lock.

Who the fuck was that guy? How did he get inside if the barn door was locked? Was there another way in?

From his brief inspection before cutting the lock, this was the only door leading inside. So what the hell?

Marshall's voice came closer around the barn's corner. He was coming Z's way.

Z cut the lock and pushed open the door. Then he tucked the bolt cutters and padlock in his pocket. He already had his flashlight in hand as he stepped inside. He played its beam over the dark interior, the weak light illuminating cobwebs and farm implements.

This is like that horror movie we watched the other night, Germ said.

"Shut up," Z said gruffly.

Suddenly a creak came from the other side of the barn. It

sounded like it had come from the direction of the wooden ladder. Z held up his flashlight, but the light wasn't strong enough to light up the ladder.

Was the tuxedo man climbing up the ladder? Z took a step toward it.

"You all right in there?" Marshall yelled inside.

"Yeah, fine—"

There was a blur behind Z, and as he turned, he caught a glimpse of the man in the black tuxedo lunging for him in the darkness. Broad gangly hands clamped onto Z's head and, with a violent jerk, tore Z's head from his body.

"Gross. What was that? You sure you're good?" Marshall said.

Nope. Germ smirked.

Z died.

(Twenty Seconds Earlier)

Z was back at the barn door. He felt his head and neck with both hands.

Fuck, that hurt...

He had to go back inside and see what the hell was going on in here.

He cut the lock, pocketed it and the bolt cutters, and stepped inside. He played the flashlight upon the floor all around him, closer instead of farther away so that he could see worth a damn.

You sure this is a good idea? Germ said. *If the past is any indication of the future, you are about to get your ass handed to you again.*

Z grunted. "I know I sort of lost my head the last time..."

That pun was so bad it was good, Germ said.

"Thanks," Z muttered. "Now help me try to keep it this time. Keep your beady little eyes peeled." He cleared his throat before addressing the darkness. "I know you're in here." Silence. "Who are you?" More silence.

Marshall peeked inside the barn. "Hey, what the heck? What are you doing in there? You're trespassing."

Z kept his mouth closed. He surveyed the darkness in front of him. "You need to stay outside. It's not safe in here."

"You need to come out too. You're trespassing."

"A bad man is hiding inside here. I need you to stay back."

Marshall screwed up his face. "How do you know?"

With a glance over his shoulder, Z said, "Intuition."

"I don't like this. I'm going to go call for backup."

"We don't need back—"

A whistling sound interrupted Z. As he realized it was the sound of an object hurtling at him, a pitchfork caught him square in the chest and he pitched backward out into the open barn doorway. The grass felt soft beneath his head. Above him, Marshall towered, wide-eyed.

Marshall gasped. "What the fuck?"

Z clutched the pitchfork protruding from his chest with one hand and gave Marshall a thumbs-up with the other.

Then he died.

(Twenty Seconds Earlier)

Z cut the lock and opened the door.

You're seriously going to go back inside?

Z pulled out his flashlight. "I'm the only person on this Earth who can Repeat."

And?

"So who the hell is this guy in there? Is he another Repeater?"

Maybe.

"It's like he knows where I'm going to be each time."

Maybe he can see in the dark. You do have a shitty flashlight.

"I do," Z conceded. "Still, he always gets the jump on me. I think I need to contact Buzz about this."

Germ peeked out of Z's pocket and nodded at the door. *Well, you've already cut the lock. Might as well try one more time.*

Marshall trotted around the corner. "Hey. What are you doing? Did you cut that lock?"

As Marshall was walking the rest of the way up to him, Z had an idea. He turned to face Marshall when he was right behind him. Then Z two-finger jabbed Marshall in the side of the neck. He dropped to the grass, unconscious.

Z smirked. "It's so hard to focus when you're always yelling at me, Dad."

I did not have a father, Germ said, *but I can understand how that might be annoying.*

After straightening his jacket, Z raised his flashlight and stepped inside the dark barn. He couldn't afford to waste any time. If he died again, it would be nice to be able to warp back to the entrance.

So he did something he hadn't tried yet. With the flashlight beam focused out in front of him, he took off at a jog throughout the dark interior, being careful not to trip or impale himself on any of the sharp tools scattered around.

When he'd completed a full loop of the ground floor, he grimaced.

Must be in the loft again, Germ said.

Z quickly scaled the ladder. When the bats flew screeching

from their roost in the rafters, he simply ducked. They parted on both sides of him.

Then, while keeping the wardrobe in his peripheral vision, he quickly checked the loft. When he found nothing, he knew that the tuxedoed man was again hiding inside the cabinet.

If the man was a Repeater, why was he hiding in there again? Didn't he know that Z was prepared this time?

Should I close my eyes? Germ said as Z cautiously approached the wardrobe.

Moving in a slow semi-crouch, Z drew the knife from his boot. Then he raised to his full height, preparing to attack. "Nah. You've seen more gratuitous violence than I'm about to do to this creepy bastard."

His free hand found the doorknob. On the count of three, he'd throw it open.

He gripped his knife in a downward offensive stance.

One. Two. Three—

He threw open the door, his knife stabbing the air on its descent.

It thudded into the wardrobe's wooden back.

"What the hell?" he muttered.

Wasn't expecting that, Germ said.

The floor creaked behind him. Z spun, kicking out with his boot, striking only air. There, on the floor, a mouse stood on its hind legs nibbling on something shiny. It dropped the object and darted off into the straw bales.

Still on high alert, Z lowered himself into a defensive stance as he scanned the darkness for any threat, whether the tuxedoed man himself or a flying pitchfork.

About thirty seconds passed in total silence and darkness.

Then Z crept up to where the mouse had been standing. He bent and picked up the shiny piece that the mouse had been chewing on. It was hard to tell exactly what it was in the dark, but it resembled a piece of a metal earpiece. Except it looked futuristic. As in possibly more futuristic than his timeline on Earth-Z. This wasn't any kind of tech any of the Buzzes had ever developed.

Buzz would need to know about this. It might connect to the man in the tuxedo. The creepy bastard. Where had he gone?

"Germ, keep your eyes open. Okay?"

Always, Germ said. *Try not to fuck this up, you big lug.*

Z couldn't help but scoff. He'd taught the little octopus thing well.

He played his flashlight beam down the ladder, the multi-shadowed rungs dancing all over the straw-strewn floor. The entrance was only about fifteen yards away from the ladder's base.

So close and yet so far... That tuxedoed creep could be anywhere down there, lurking, waiting to decapitate him or something.

What are you waiting for? Germ said. *Scared like a pussy cat?*

Okay. Maybe he needed to watch what he was teaching the little guy.

He grunted. "I'm not scared."

With that, he climbed down the ladder and sprinted for the light at the end of the barn. No broad gangly hands reached for him or launched any deadly projectiles at him.

Once outside, Z closed the door, fished the lock from his pocket, and dropped the severed shank in place. From the outside, it would hold if someone inside tried to force their way out.

Of course, the tuxedoed man had been strong enough to rip his head off...

Z stepped to the side of the door and put his back against the wall. He breathed and wiped the sweat from his forehead. Then he glanced down at Marshall. His father from another Earth lay unmoving on the grass. Then he saw Marshall's chest rising and falling as he breathed, and Z relaxed.

He half-expected pitchfork tines or a scythe blade to punch through the barn's wall from the inside. Such an attack never came.

He had an idea. Even though it was cloudy outside, it afforded much better light to inspect the metal earpiece again. He pulled it from his pocket.

It was definitely from the future, and it looked broken. Where had it come from? Had the tuxedoed man dropped it? Who the hell was he? Was he a Repeater? He didn't seem like one. How else would he know how to evade Z and how to kill him so efficiently multiple times?

Whoever the tuxedoed man was, he was trouble.

CHAPTER FIFTEEN

Still leaning against the barn's outer wall, Z checked his watch. It showed that he had only an hour until the optimum "go time" as determined by Buzz.

"Damnit. Time to do the warehouse mission on this Earth. Whoopie," he said unenthusiastically. All this fixing the Earths of the multiverse was draining.

This Earth had no donuts, which was even more draining.

Think of this way, Germ said. *With as many Earths as you've already completed it on, this time should be what you humans call a cakewalk.*

That was true. His last run-through of the warehouse on Earth-G had come with its share of hiccups. Namely, Carl being at the water cooler instead of with the other thugs. Plus, the crazy thug with the bowie knife hiding in the hallway.

He mentally ran through that mission in fast forward. The hiccups had probably resulted from him not getting there the exact time Buzz had calculated for that Earth. On this Earth, he'd make sure to show up on time. As in, he'd be at the front door before his stopwatch reached zero.

On the ground in front of him, Marshall stirred. With his eyes still closed, he twitched his nose.

For Z to get to the warehouse, he had to have a set of wheels to take him there.

His gaze fell back on Marshall. Around the corner was a shiny red coupe that fit the bill—it would enable him to hit his weapons cache on this Earth and scope out the warehouse before mission time.

Marshall wouldn't miss the car, would he? Depending on how long he was out, it wasn't out of the question for Z to be able to finish the warehouse mission, then come back and pick Marshall up. He could make up some bullshit about Marshall falling and hitting his head or falling asleep due to his midnight shift. "You should go see a doctor about that," he could say.

"Nah. Can't do it," Z muttered.

The man was his father after all, not on this Earth yet, but it still counted in Z's book.

He decided to wake the man up and try to persuade him to let him use his car. Also, he needed to get word to Buzz via the *Paper Warriors* printing press.

He thought about that for a second. Maybe he could knock out two birds with one stone.

Once he figured out what he was going to say, he bent and roused Marshall.

"Huh, what, who?" Marshall blinked up at Z. "What happened to me?"

Z stared Marshall straight in the face. "You passed out. If I hadn't caught you at the last moment, you'd have probably bashed open your head against the barn. Probably saved your life."

"What? Seriously?"

Z nodded. "You could be dead now."

"What? That doesn't…"

Z could all but see and hear the gears turning in Marshall's head as he tried to figure out what had happened. "I guess those midnight shifts are wearing on you."

Marshall considered it. "I have been working a lot of late hours."

"What if you had had a little fender-bender? What would your wife say if you fell asleep behind the wheel? I mean, you're an officer of the law. Wouldn't look too good."

Marshall drew his keys from his pocket and looked at them. He stifled a yawn and then made a frustrated face at the involuntary reflex. "Maybe it might be better if you drove us back to the city?"

Z feigned surprise at the notion. He had convinced Marshall that it had been his idea and not Z's. Still, Z had an even better idea. He draped an arm around Marshall's shoulders and turned him around and walked him back to the red coupe. "Buddy, there are two important things I remembered when you were out cold. One, I need to get back home to turn off my stove. Two, I need to get an urgent message to a certain newspaper office as soon as possible."

After massaging his forehead, Marshall nodded. "Let's go then."

"Hold up," Z said. "Here's the deal. I live a good ways away. Can I take your car and go shut off the stove?"

"Absolutely. I thought I suggested that you drive—"

Z held up a hand. "Aw hell. Here's the thing. I'm not supposed to tell anyone this, but I'm…" He shot a furtive glance left and then right. "Well, I'm not a private investigator. I'm an undercover government operative, and I have an important mission about to go down in the city." He twisted his wrist so Marshall could see the ticking countdown on the stopwatch's face. "This is a matter of national security."

Marshall had on his serious thinking face. "The stove..."

"There is no stove. Shit. I think you might've hit your head harder than I thought. I was calling the mission the stove because I forgot all about it when we came out to investigate this place. I didn't realize it was so far out in the countryside. Understand?" He paused. "No one can know about the mission. You can't even tell your wife."

"I-I don't even know what the mission is," Marshall stammered.

Z patted his shoulder. "It's better that you don't. I've got to scram if I'm to get equipped for it and get in position."

Z stepped up to the driver's side door and held his hand up for the keys. Marshall tossed them.

"How about I wait out in the car while you do your mission," Marshall said. "Since you don't have a stove that needs turning off."

As Z inserted the key into the car door, he shook his head. "As I said, this is a matter of national security. Plus, I need you to carry out a mission of your own for me."

Marshall leaned a hand against his car.

Z reached inside his jacket for a pen and a piece of paper. He jotted down a quick note, ensuring that he wrote down the correct date, time, and Earth. He needed this message to reach the right Buzz. Then he folded the note, sealed it with some chewed bubble gum, and handed it to Marshall.

He gave Marshall the address to the *Paper Warriors* office and told him not to open the note.

Z continued. "Those three geeks will tell you that I have strictly forbidden them from touching the printing press. I have. Tell them that this is the exception. If they do exactly what my note says, I'll…be in their debt."

He hoped that wouldn't come back to bite him in the rear. What was the worst that those newsmen could ask for? A life?

Marshall stared down at the note, then at his car, the keys to which he had tossed to Z.

"Don't take this the wrong way, but I don't even know you."

Z shrugged. "I saved your life, remember?" He pointed at his head and the barn. "Since when do strangers do that? What would your wife say if you had hit your head and died?"

"Well, I…"

"This is all for national security. If you help me, you'll be doing this country a service."

"Can I see a badge?"

"No." Z patted his jacket over the heart where a badge might ordinarily be. "I'm undercover, remember?"

"How am I to get this note to the newspaper office if you take my car?"

With a weak grin, Z held up a thumb. "Hitchhike?"

Finally, Marshall relented. He patted his car's fender lovingly. "Take care of her. Okay? Don't hurt my baby."

Z climbed behind the wheel. "Wouldn't dream of it."

Now Z was flying down the backcountry roads toward his weapons cache. Then it would be onto the warehouse mission to recover the bioweapon. Then it was time to right a major wrong on this Earth.

He glanced down at his stopwatch. He had plenty of time.

What could go wrong?

CHAPTER SIXTEEN

Stopping by the weapons cache was the easy part of the mission. Infiltrating the warehouse would be the hard part.

Of course, Germ kept reminding him that this should be a cakewalk. He'd only done this mission on how many other Earths? Seventeen? Maybe it was eighteen.

Regardless, he knew how many guards to expect patrolling out front and how many were inside. Even if things did go a bit bumpy like the last mission—where he had shown up a few minutes later than Buzz had calculated—he knew the end game: obtain the bioweapon from the boss man's briefcase. All the thugs he got to fight along the way were a bonus.

The morning sky had grown overcast, and it looked like it might rain at any second.

Z easily found the warehouse. It was a good-looking building in a bad part of town. It was multiple stories tall, but Z had only ever needed to explore the first floor as he executed the mission.

As Z pulled Marshall's red coupe up behind the warehouse in the alley, within a short sprint of the back door he had exited the prior time he'd completed this mission, he glanced up through the windshield at the warehouse's bleak exterior. Gray paint that wasn't peeling like the other nearest buildings. Windows that were clear and transparent versus the grimy opaque windows of its neighbors.

Who would ever think this building was a front for guns and now a bioweapon? That its occupants were a bunch of thugs with ambitions of power and fortune?

Maybe that's how local police overlooked it for so long on all the Earths. Not that the police had the necessary resources to deal with the threat inside. These guys were well-numbered, well-armed, and knew what they were doing. There was a reason their smuggling ring had gone undetected for so long.

Although the low-level thugs didn't have a brain to spare between them, their boss man had things all planned out. He had a brain. He also had their muscle—and copious guns.

Raindrops splatted against Z's windshield.

The million-dollar question was, how were they getting the bioweapon in the first place? Not even Buzz with all his genius brainpower and supercomputer algorithms could figure it out.

The bioweapon in question contained raw elements of the time virus developed by Eduardo Nunez. Not good.

Which reminded Z, what had come of the Nunez spotting on this Earth? It was why Buzz had reassigned him to this Earth in the first place. Then the missing woman case had fallen into his lap, and now he had to complete the warehouse mission on this Earth. Not to mention tackle righting some wrongs he wanted to fix on this Earth while he was here.

Leave the thinking to the geniuses and the computers, Z

reminded himself. He was a fighter. A get-er-done character. Give him a mission. He got it done.

Z got out of the car. After he slammed the door, he checked his appearance in the driver's side window's reflection.

He was wearing his black shades and a gaudy gold chain around his neck. Jeans and combat boots covered his lower half, and the black muscle shirt beneath his jacket had already seen this mission through on Earth-G and was starting to stink of sweat. He'd need a wardrobe change after this mission. Who knew? Maybe he could talk Alice into celebrating with him. She had slipped him her number before he had left for the police precinct. His heart rate hiked at the thought.

Head focused on the mission, he reminded himself.

He locked the car, popped the collar of his jacket, and sauntered down the alley alongside the warehouse to reach the front door. Along the way, he passed a dumpster and a first-floor window that looked in on a storage room containing cleaning supplies. The rain was falling in large scattered drops now.

Once he was ready to start the mission, he'd set his three-minute stopwatch as usual. That would let him know how much time he had at his disposal if he needed to warp back to before stepping into a danger zone. It was a good system, and so far, it had always paid off.

His only real concern was ensuring he didn't get caught in a situation where warping back three minutes didn't get him out of danger. He couldn't chain multiple warps together to go back farther than three minutes like he once could.

He came around the corner of the warehouse and spotted its front entrance. The asphalt out front held stacked metal shipping containers, and he knew from experience that multiple guards were patrolling there, although he was too far away now to spot them.

He shaded his eyes to better see through the scattered rain. As silly as it might seem, Buzz had calculated that his best chance of infiltrating the warehouse was to go through the front door instead of trying to enter through a side door or window.

It had always worked in the past. So that would be the way in today as well.

He leaned back away from the corner to shield him from any of the guards patrolling out front behind the metal shipping containers.

Before he started the mission, he quickly checked his weapons: his suppressor-equipped pistol, his knife tucked into his boot, and his "special weapon" he had tucked safely in an inside jacket pocket. He probably wouldn't need it, but it was always good to be prepared.

With his weapons check done, he glanced down at his pocket. Germ peeked his octopus head out and winked at him.

Z set his stopwatch timer for three minutes. "Let's get this party started."

As Z approached the warehouse's entrance, his suppressed pistol within easy reach inside his jacket, something felt wrong.

His normal play was to stroll up and take a look at the guard patrols. If he felt confident, he'd attempt to dispatch them right then and there, whether covertly or by direct force. If he didn't like any aspect of the confrontation, he'd simply turn his gun on himself, warp back to before he'd walked up, and repeat the fight with his knowledge gained. It was like shooting fish in a barrel. Except the fish were thugs with guns.

This time though, his gut was telling him something was off. He jogged up past the metal shipping containers and surveyed the entrance from side to side.

Where are all the guards? Germ asked.

He was right. No thugs patrolled the entrance.

He checked his stopwatch to make sure he was on time. He was. He had started when his stopwatch had hit zero.

"This is all wrong," Z muttered.

He stepped up to the double doors of the warehouse's entrance. They were metal with no windows he could look through to see what was on the other side.

After patting his jacket again to make sure his gun was easily accessible in its holster, Z put his hand to the door handle.

He threw it open.

At least ten gun barrels stared him down like metal alien eyes. They were right in front of him. The thugs wielding them had been expecting him.

Z cracked a smile. "Hey guys, I'm the repairman. I heard the A/C was on the fritz—"

All ten guns fired.

Z's body was carried backward by the multiple impacts, zigzagging like a dropped puppet.

He collapsed in a bleeding heap upon his back.

He died.

(One Minute Earlier)

Z was peering around the warehouse's corner one last time before he began his assault, his fingers ready to set the three-minute stopwatch.

"One thing's for sure. This isn't a damn cakewalk. It's a fucking bloodbath. How the hell did they know I was coming?"

Germ shrugged.

"Seriously. How could Buzz have been this wrong about this mission?" He peeked through the scattered rain at the entrance forty yards away. He sighted the double doors and the ten gunmen waiting behind them, ready to blow his guts out his back.

Perhaps we should enter by a different means? Germ said.

Z nodded. "That's what I was thinking." He drew his gun in case he needed it quicker than he could draw. Then he quickly searched for an alternate way in.

He remembered that around the back was a lone window that looked in on a storage room of some sort. It was on the ground floor. It would be easy. All he had to do was break the glass and climb over the sill.

He started back that way.

When he came to the window, he peered in to make sure the room was empty. It held only a couple of mop buckets and some other cleaning supplies. He set his three-minute stop-watch. He wasted no time positioning his back to the window and elbowed the glass with a quick jab.

He could've used a brick or even the butt of his gun, but where was the drama in that?

The glass shattered inward with more sound than he would have liked but who was there to hear it? The armed welcoming committee was waiting for him at the front door, not in this lone storage room on the other side of the building.

As the glass still skipped and hopped on the floor inside, Z quickly scraped the windowsill free of any remaining jagged shards.

He climbed inside, taking care while stepping on the glass.

Other than the window, the metal door directly in front of him was the only way in and out of the storage room.

Z confidently crept up to it and eased open the door.

Five men with guns stood blocking the way with sneers on their faces.

Before Z could react, they fired their guns.

He died.

CHAPTER SEVENTEEN

(Two Minutes Earlier)

They cleaned your clock. Get it? Germ said. *You died in a storage room full of cleaning supplies—*

"Yes, yes, I get it," Z huffed as he pulled back from around the corner that overlooked the front entrance.

Where was the best place to enter? Not the front door. Not the side window...

He spotted a window above a dumpster in the alleyway he was currently in. He climbed onto the dumpster and was about to peer through the window when a thug toting a shotgun on the inside let loose.

The discharge nearly took his head off, and he fell to the alley below.

He died.

(Thirty Seconds Earlier)

Z ran around the building to search for another point of entry.

Before he got twenty steps, a sniper on the roof sent a bullet through his back.

Z toppled forward onto his chest, his chin splashing in a puddle.

He died.

(Fifteen Seconds Earlier)

This time, Z ran blindly in the other direction.

The unseen sniper sent a bullet through the base of his skull.

He died.

(Five Seconds Earlier)

What the hell is going on? It was like these thugs knew where he was going to be each time. Or there were so many inside that they could cover each possible entrance.

That was the most probable of the two scenarios. The sniper only fired when he broke into a run. There was no way the soldiers could be reading his mind. They certainly weren't Repeaters. Z was the only Repeater on this Earth. He considered if maybe that creepy old guy in the black suit was involved. Was it possible he was a Repeater too?

More disturbingly, why was this all happening on Earth-D of all places?

It didn't take Buzz's genius brain to put together that it might have had something to do with the Nunez sighting on this Earth. Was that the answer? The mad doctor himself was somehow involved in this?

What are you going to do? Germ asked.

Z already had a working plan in his mind.

Maybe you should abort the mission and contact Buzz, Germ said.

That was an idea. However, he wasn't a runner—he was a fighter.

"I'm doing this my way."

This time, instead of blindly running either way, Z eyed the dumpster along the alley wall. He flicked his eyes up at the window above it. While he couldn't see the thug with the shotgun on the other side, he knew he was up there. Waiting.

"Fuck it," Z muttered, slowly walking up to the dumpster. Then he spun and hoisted himself on top of it. If the sniper or snipers on the roof were watching him, he didn't have much time.

He rose to a crouch and had his silenced pistol in his hands as he stood. He fired three times as he came up. The glass shattered inward and the man with the shotgun grunted as he fell backward, clutching his chest.

Z clambered through the window onto the warehouse's second floor. The discharge of a sniper rifle thundered outside in the rainy alley, and a bullet *pinged* as it struck the dumpster.

As Z got his bearings in the small room he now found himself in, a door ten feet in front of him opened. Z leveled his pistol at the opening door and fired when he saw several gun-toting thugs trying to get in.

Z's first shot took the lead thug in the face. His arms raised as his body slumped backward. Z's second shot found the next thug in the shoulder. The thug fell back a step, and Z put another round in the man's chest. He fell backward in a heap.

The third thug fired a submachine gun as the door was still opening. Z flattened himself to the floor as he tilted his gun upward. He fired a few rounds in quick succession.

For a moment, Z didn't know who had shot who. Maybe they were both wounded in the exchange. When he glanced down at himself and then at the bullet holes in the wall beside him, he realized that the barrage of bullets had missed him, but he hadn't missed the thug who'd fired them. With unseeing eyes staring forward at Z, the third man dropped unceremoniously beside his other two fallen thugs.

Nice shooting, Germ said.

Z ejected an empty magazine and inserted a fresh one into his pistol. He racked the gun to load a round into the chamber, then scooped up the gun lying in front of him. It was a pump-action shotgun. He holstered his pistol, moving fluidly as any well-trained operative should.

He edged up to the doorway, careful not to step on any of the three bodies and lose his footing. Then he peered out into the hallway beyond.

There were two doorways in the hallway facing each other on opposite sides about midway down the hall. A door at the far end had a sign with some stairs on it. Most likely that's where he needed to go to intercept the boss man and his briefcase with the bioweapon in it.

Those two doors leading up to it concerned him. Not the doors themselves but the potential armed thugs inside the rooms.

Eena meena munka moe, which door contains your foe? Germ said.

Z set his three-minute stopwatch. "You're a damn poet, and you don't even know it."

Oh, I know it, Germ said.

Z drew a deep breath. There was one way he knew of that ought to flush out the enemy. "Hold on." Then he tucked his head and charged down the hallway with a brutal cry that

Hercules or Conan the Barbarian might give as they rushed into battle.

A rifle barrel protruded from the door on the left.

Z fired the shotgun, taking the man in the throat. Another gun barrel poked out from the doorway on the right. Z pumped the shotgun and fired again. Pumped. Fired again. There was a startled cry.

Another thug with a gun jumped out into the hallway from the left doorway with a shotgun in his hands. Z pulled his trigger first.

Click.

That's not good, Germ said.

"No shit, Sherlock," Z yelled as he slammed his shoulder up against the opposite wall in a desperate attempt to avoid the thug's gun blast.

The shotgunner fired, tearing through the opposite wall where Z had been standing.

Out of ammo, and only a few steps away from his opponent, Z took a step forward while simultaneously flipping the shotgun around in his hands. Then, with its long reach, he clubbed his attacker with the butt of the weapon.

The man's gun discharged, the fire blasting out of the barrel singeing Z's cheek. With the barrel of his weapon, Z batted the other man's shotgun out of the way and shoved the butt into the man's face. He fell backward with a grunt. As he fell, Z dropped his shotgun, stripped the other man's shotgun from his hands, and turned it on the man who was already reaching for a pistol holstered at his belt.

"Hasta la vista, you sonofabitch." Z beat him to the trigger.

With the man dispatched, Z stepped inside the room on the left as it afforded a better tactical advantage than waiting out in the hallway.

The room looked empty of further threats. Just some boxes full of guns and gun parts stacked throughout. Upon second glance, there were a lot of boxes. He quickly checked behind them all to make sure there wasn't anyone else in the room. Then he turned toward the doorway.

He paused, listening for any activity out in the hallway. He didn't hear anything. He was amazed at how he hadn't had to Repeat once during that heroic charge. It was a feat worthy of celebrating after this was all over. He'd relive it as one of the greatest glory days of his Repeating career.

Uh, Z... Germ said.

"Hold on a sec. I'm savoring the memory of that glorious gunfight."

Really, that maneuver had been the thing of legends. Rarely in life did one charge down a hallway with an indeterminate number of armed foes on either side and not die.

Z, really, there's— Germ said.

Hollywood ought to make a movie about his exploits. Well, not *his* exploits. Some fictional special agent that had infinite lives.

Z! Germ shouted.

Finally, Z turned, miffed at being interrupted when the room was obviously a safe zone.

That's when he saw the wild-eyed thug with the bowie knife rise from one of the nearest boxes like a silent sadistic jack-in-the-box hyped up on cocaine.

Z had no time to react.

"Oh for f—"

The bowie knife tore out his throat in a vicious horizontal slash that nearly severed his head from his body.

Z closed his eyes in disgust as he fell backward.

He died.

. . .

(Ten Seconds Earlier)

Uh, Z... Germ said.

Z spun and unloaded his shotgun into the cardboard box the knife guy was hiding in like some sort of demented contortionist.

The torn-open box tipped over and the knife guy's body sprawled out onto the floor.

Z placidly regarded the dead body. Then he drew a deep breath, his shoulders rising and falling with the inhalation. "Ah. I feel better now. I've needed a jaunt like this for a long time. It's good to test one's abilities. Know what I mean?"

Who are you talking to? Germ said.

"Hmph. I guess myself." He wiped the sweat from his forehead. "Now, let's relieve these bastards of that bioweapon."

CHAPTER EIGHTEEN

The question was, where was the bioweapon?

On all of the other Earths, he'd battled his way through a bunch of thugs to the boss man with the briefcase containing the bioweapon. In all but the last mission, he had obtained it rather cleanly before the boss man could run off with it through the building. The boss man always had the bioweapon.

So the goal right now was to find the boss man with the briefcase.

Z regarded all the dead thugs lying in the hallway. After trading his shotgun for a semiautomatic rifle, he stepped over them and cleared the room on the opposite side of the hallway. It likewise contained boxes of guns and gun parts, not surprising since this building belonged to an arms smuggling ring.

Z liked the feel of the rifle in his hands. He had stepped back out into the hallway when he heard the door to the stairwell crack open. There in the partially opened doorway stood the stern-eyed boss man, the briefcase dangling from his hand.

The man shouted, his voice carrying quite well down the length of the hallway. "Just who the hell do you think you are? Killing my men."

"Your men are trying to kill me," Z answered. "I'm returning the favor." He took a step forward and stopped as the man raised a revolver.

"That's close enough."

"What?" Z said. "You going to shoot me?"

"If I must. You alone?"

Z studied the man's facial expressions from about twenty yards away. "You think I would tell you that? How stupid do you think I am?"

Perhaps he is stalling for time? Germ said.

That's what Z was thinking.

That's why he jerked up his rifle while backing inside the side room. He wasn't a moment too soon. A hail of gunfire tore into the doorway from both ends of the hallway.

"I will kill you!" the boss man shouted from the far end.

"We'll get him, boss," several thugs called from the opposite end of the hallway.

"The ol' flanking maneuver," Z muttered as he checked his rifle. He scoffed. Not a bad plan, except they were dealing with a Repeater. Poor schmucks. There was no way they could know what they were up against.

He would show them a move they'd never seen before.

He tensed into a semi crouch inside the doorway. When there was a lull in the gunfire, Z dove out through the hallway with his rifle aimed down at the three newly arrived thugs. As his body sailed through the air, Z pulled off some shots. Just before his body landed on the floor in the opposite side room, he saw one of the thugs go down.

"Suckers…" He picked himself up and edged up to the doorway. From there, he was able to pick off the other two thugs with careful peeks. From the other end of the hall, still standing in the stairwell doorway, the boss man howled in rage.

Z ducked back barely in time to avoid his bullets.

Blam, blam, blam. Click.

Time for the boss man to reload…

Z poked back out into the hallway and fired. The stern-eyed boss man fell back a step in the stairwell as blood burst from the side of his upper arm.

"You bastard!" the man shouted. The briefcase dropped and banged against his knee, then the floor. As Z lined up his next shot, the man snatched up the briefcase and started down the stairs, out of sight.

Z smirked. "I do love a good chase scene."

Before rushing after the boss man and the bioweapon, he picked up a submachine gun from one of the fallen thugs and slung its strap over his shoulder. He kept the rifle gripped in his hands. One could never have too many guns.

A few seconds later, he was at the top of the staircase. Below him, the boss man threw himself through the doorway leading to the ground floor. Z fired off a shot, clipping the back of the boss man's shoes. The man cursed as he stumbled. Again, the briefcase slammed against his knees, but he kept hold of it.

Z hurried down the stairs after him. "Do you even know what kind of weapon you have in that briefcase?"

"The world's most dangerous superweapon," the man called back over his shoulder.

Z stepped up to the doorway and pulled back right before a revolver round tore into the doorway.

"The world will finally take this organization seriously."

Z didn't even know what the name of this little organization of thugs was. It didn't matter. Once he was through with them, their weapons smuggling days were over. Sure, a rival organization would take over their turf, but at least the bioweapon would be out of play.

"Where'd you get the bioweapon?" Z called from behind the doorway.

"I'll never tell."

Z had a feeling the man might if he could separate the gun from his hand and properly interrogate him.

"How long have you had it? How did you get it?"

"Screw you!" the boss man called as he fired two more rounds into the stairwell doorway. He was crouched behind a large crate of ammo and appeared ready to turn and sprint down the hallway and out of Z's reach. Z couldn't have that.

Z dashed out of the stairwell, blind firing as he dove to the side. The boss man was only about ten yards away, still hunkered behind the ammo crate.

The boss man fired, and Z threw himself behind a metal crate. "You're going to die!" The boss man fired twice more, each bullet *pinging* against the metal.

The man was starting to piss Z off. He patted the bulge in his jacket to make sure he had his special backup weapon. Maybe he would have to use it after all. Part of him hoped he would have to.

"How'd you get the bioweapon?" Z called from behind his cover. "We've been surveilling your operation for days. We never see the briefcase come in."

"We?" the boss man said. "You're bluffing. You know nothing about my operation."

"One of your right-hand men is named Carl. Dorky little guy."

"Shit." The boss man wiped his brow with the back of his hand. His injured arm was still bleeding. "How many of you are out there?"

The man was clearly rattled. That much was for sure. Maybe he could rattle him further. Z called, "We know you got the bioweapon from Nunez."

"Huh? What? How?"

"We're just that good," Z said. "Go ahead and make a run for it. I promise not to put a bullet in your back."

Z saw the man glance over his shoulder.

"Where are all your men now?" Z asked.

"Shut up."

"How'd you know I was coming? How'd you know to place them at all the entry points?"

"I ain't telling you nothing!"

Z smirked. The guy was about to make a run for it. The quaver in his voice gave it away.

Z fired, purposefully missing the crate of ammo. The boss man hunkered back down, deterred from running.

The briefcase looked fairly well-protected so Z decided to bring out his special weapon. He wasn't stupid. With as many thugs as this organization had, they were probably right around the corner.

All Z had to do was kill this bastard, pick up the briefcase, and drive off in Marshall's red coupe.

No more playing games. He reached into his jacket and pulled out the grenade. "Last chance to tell me something useful."

"Ha! You're going to have to make me."

"I'd like to but, well…time." Z bit down on the grenade's pin and pulled it clear. He waited for a second and lobbed it over the ammo crate.

The boss man shrieked. "You mother—"

The grenade went off with a *bang*. Then the box of ammo went off with an even bigger *bang*.

The blast rocked the floor, shook the walls, knocked dust from the ceiling. The lights all went out in the hallway.

"Holy shit. That was awesome," Z muttered. He wiped the dust from his sweaty forehead, then brushed the dust off his pants.

In the low light, he could barely make out the form of the boss man sprawled out on the debris-strewn floor. What was left of him, at least.

There, lying against the wall, was the briefcase.

Z picked himself up from his position behind the metal crate and started walking toward the briefcase.

Footsteps sounded from the darkness beyond the brief-case. Z gripped his rifle, prepared to fire.

The footsteps grew louder as a new form appeared in the darkened hallway. He was tall and sharply dressed, and he didn't appear to have any weapons on him.

Then the figure stepped into better view, stopping right beside the briefcase.

"Aw shit."

It was the creepy man in the black tuxedo.

CHAPTER NINETEEN

The man's grim lips curled up into a smile beneath his sunglasses. His slicked-back black hair gleamed under the scant light in the hallway.

"Who the hell are you?" Z readied his rifle. At this distance, it would be impossible to miss.

The older, tuxedoed man smiled, his sunglasses hiding his eyes. He took a step closer to Z.

Z gripped his rifle tight, pressing the stock against his shoulder. "Don't take another step, you murdering bastard."

The man again moved forward.

He took another step, Germ said unhelpfully.

Z sighted down the rifle's barrel. "What do you want with me?"

Instead of replying, the tuxedoed man lurched forward and charged at Z.

Z fired.

The bullets struck the charging man but didn't seem to faze him. The impacts drove him back a half step each time, but he kept on coming. Z couldn't see how badly the man must be bleeding due to the low light, but with the number of rounds he was putting in the guy, he had to be losing a lot of blood.

I thought I was masochistic when I charged blindly down hallways to flush out the bad guys. This guy was taking it to a whole new level. As far as Z knew, the man wasn't a Repeater. He was a normal man.

Impossibly, the tuxedoed man closed the distance and now pulled up right before Z. He threw his long arms up, catching Z by the throat and shoulder with his wide, gangly hands.

"Oh shit," Z grunted and dropped the rifle.

With the strength this guy possessed, he wasn't a normal human. He couldn't be. Plus, he'd absorbed all those bullets as if they hadn't even hurt him.

Z expected the tuxedoed man to finish him quickly. Instead, he was slowly choking the life out of him. *Switching things up.* Z recalled his deaths in the barn.

Then he had another thought. What if the tuxedoed man knew he was a Repeater and was trying to render him unconscious to take him somewhere for some purpose?

Aside from his three-minute warp time limit, being knocked unconscious was another weakness of Z's. If he passed out and woke up in a holding cell where he couldn't kill himself, that would be very bad news. He could be experimented on for the rest of his life, trapped like a lab rat.

Maybe he was getting ahead of himself.

"Do you know who I am, asshole?" Z asked.

The tuxedoed man smirked beneath his sunglasses. "Repeater."

He knows who he's dealing with, Germ said.

Anxiety crept in as his vision faded. He couldn't let the man knock him out despite being outmatched. He had to figure out what was going on here and get away. And he had to take the bioweapon in the briefcase with him. Couldn't let this monster have it.

Those long gangly fingers were choking the life from him.

Z fought back as he dangled in the man's grasp. He kicked the man in the crotch.

The man didn't flinch.

Z tried to claw out and reach the man's throat, but he was being held too far out of range.

Then he remembered that while he'd dropped his rifle, he still had the silenced pistol under his coat and a submachine gun strapped to his back.

As his consciousness began to fade, he fished his good hand under his jacket and found the pistol. He angled it up at the man's face and fired a few times.

The first two bullets impacted harmlessly into the man's cheek. The final bullet exploded the tuxedoed man's sunglasses.

The man grunted.

Z meanwhile felt his stomach upend. The tuxedo man had bright glowing red eyes that looked demonic in the darkness.

I think you are combatting a robot, Germ said.

"No shit, Sherlock," Z muttered as he fired two more headshots.

Finally, his opponent's grasp on his throat and shoulder relaxed and Z wrenched himself free. He fell to the dark floor.

Barely having any time to catch his breath, he scrambled around the man's legs and lunged for the briefcase containing the bioweapon. He scooped it up and sprinted through the debris toward a corridor on the other side of the room.

Z didn't know where he was in the building so he followed

the neon glow of an Exit sign. It wasn't far away. When he threw himself against the door, it didn't budge.

"You shall not pass." The tuxedoed man spoke his first complete sentence to Z. His words were grim and hard. "Hand over the briefcase, and I will release you for the moment."

Z spun, pressing his back against the emergency escape that wouldn't open. He stared at the tuxedoed-robot man's glowing red eyes as they slowly approached through the gloom.

With his free hand, Z pulled his weak flashlight from his pocket. He played it to both sides revealing a debris-strewn floor and dust still falling from the ceiling and the blasts. The air was so thick with the acrid smell of discharged powder that it irritated his eyes and burned his throat.

The tuxedoed man stepped closer and Z shined the light on him, starting at the legs and working his way up.

The tuxedoed man-robot appeared fine from the waist down. From there up, he was a mess of bullet holes that tore the fabric of his expensive tuxedo and the white button-down shirt beneath it. There was no blood anywhere.

Not surprising since the man was a killer robot-for-hire. Still, this was the friggin' nineteen-eighties. The robots of this time were far from human and were probably mostly found in factories and science labs.

So how did a robot from the future get here?

Z realized it at the same time Germ did.

"Nunez," he muttered.

Nunez, Germ said.

Z played the flashlight over the tuxedoed robot's face. The parts of it torn away from his bullets revealed a hard plastic-looking element beneath it. The skin surrounding one of the eye sockets was gone, and the glowing red eye illuminated the "plastic skull."

The robot was five yards away and closing.

"You're an ugly one. You know that?" Z reached behind his back for the submachine gun.

"You are weak and made of flesh while I—"

"Am getting another dose of lead!" Z shouted as he traded his flashlight for the submachine gun and unloaded the entire magazine into the oncoming robot.

He'd learned his lesson not to shoot at the robot's center of mass. It didn't do anything. Instead, he tilted the barrel up at the robot's face, which had seemed to stun it earlier.

The robot stopped abruptly, throwing its hands to its head.

After picking up the briefcase, Z took his opportunity and darted around the side of his opponent.

The robot reached one gangly hand out at him as he passed. "I will find you."

Z didn't waste a breath on the reply. He'd stunned the robot again, but the thing was a total killing machine.

He saw sunlight off to the side and darted toward it. He passed through an open, reinforced metal door into a medium-sized warehouse room with a skylight set in the high ceiling. Immediately, he shut and locked the metal door behind him to buy himself some time. Not that he was going to be staying in this new room long. He had to find a back door leading out of the building.

The glowing Exit door sign on the far wall caught his attention and Z rushed over to it and tried it.

Locked.

He threw his weight against it. It didn't budge.

Shit. Maybe he was going to be in this room for a little longer than expected.

He quickly inspected the door. Someone had soldered the metal door to the metal doorframe.

Smart.

The warehouse mission on this Earth appeared to be a complete setup for him. Not only had the thugs already been waiting for him at all the entry points with guns, but they'd sealed some of the doors.

At least the tuxedo man wasn't a Repeater. He was thankful for that. But possibly worse, he appeared to be an unstoppable robot.

No. He shook his head. Not unstoppable. He needed a bigger weapon and a better plan for dealing with the robot.

He checked his guns and realized that both his pistol and submachine gun were empty and he was all out of ammo.

That meant all he had for weapons at the moment was a knife.

He grunted. He'd been in worse situations. He just needed a way out of here.

The reinforced door behind him would keep the robot man out for only a short time.

CHAPTER TWENTY

Z played his flashlight along the metal shelving, crates of gun parts and ammo, and pallets stacked on one wall. The lights were still off due to the power outage caused when he'd blown up the ammo crate back when he was fighting the boss man who had the briefcase.

"Any ideas?" Z asked.

Climb the shelves to get to the skylight? Germ said.

Z had already thought of that and quickly dismissed the idea. While he was physically able to climb the metal shelving, he would still be too short to reach the skylight above. Even if he had a grapnel and rope, it would be a stretch for getting out before the robot came crashing in.

"I'm not Batman, you know."

Germ snickered. *Yet 'Batman' is the password to your online banking account on that one Earth—*

"Shut up. I'm a superhero. Basically."

Batman didn't kill that many people. You are basically a one-man killing machine—

"Cut the moral talk. Since my cure from the virus

madness, I've never killed anyone who didn't deserve it. It's called self-defense." He inspected the wall on the other side of some shelving.

Sometimes you kill them before they shoot at you...

"Yeah, because they killed me or tried to kill me before a warp."

Germ peeked out from Z's pocket and scratched his head with one tiny tentacle. *I don't understand the concept of human morality. It seems to differ from one individual to another.*

"Hey, Dr. Phil. How about we stay focused?"

That's when Z heard the *click* of a gun cocking from somewhere behind one of the shelves.

"Hello?" he called.

"St-stay where you are," a nasal voice called from the darkness. "I've got a gun."

The voice seemed familiar. Where had he heard it before?

Although both of his guns were empty, the man in the shadows didn't know that. Z needed to get one of them into his hands to even out the odds so they could have a friendly chat. Maybe the man would know if there was a way out of this room.

There was a metal shelf directly to Z's left. It was full of all sorts of items that would stop a bullet. It would provide good cover since Z knew roughly where the man was hiding somewhere in front of him.

"Look," Z said calmly. "How about we—"

He dove to the left, behind the metal shelving. A pistol fired, and bullets immediately ricocheted off the shelving and its contents. After the gunfire had stopped, Z waved his silenced pistol so the other man could easily see it in the light of the skylight.

"I have a gun too, but I don't want to use it. I grossly outmatch you."

"Oh yeah?" the nasal voice said.

Shit. Z remembered where he'd heard that voice before. "Carl?"

"Huh? What? How'd you know my name?"

Z could now see Carl's form, half-crouching behind a different section of metal shelving. The man was fidgeting badly.

Carl jabbed the air with his pistol. "How do you know my name?"

Z smirked. "You wouldn't believe me if I told you."

"Try me."

"Okay. I infiltrated this same warehouse on a parallel Earth to steal the bioweapon, and in the process, I met a parallel you there."

Carl spat, "I don't believe you."

Z glanced down at his pocket. "They never do."

Germ shook his tiny head in agreement.

Z peeked out of cover to face Carl. "You don't have to. I don't want to have to hurt you—"

A loud thud sounded against the reinforced door to the warehouse room. The tuxedoed robot man was trying to get in.

"—but I'm running out of time, and I need a way out of here."

Carl paused, then his face grew defiant. "There's another way out of here, but I'll never help you. I'm loyal to my boss. And my crew."

Z tapped the barrel of his pistol against a strut of the metal shelving in frustration. "Your boss is dead." He raised the briefcase so Carl could see it. "So are a bunch of your 'crew.'

Real outstanding guys. They make fun of you behind your back, you know."

"No, they don't. Shut up."

He'd obviously hit a nerve. Time to keep hitting it. "They laugh at your Velcro shoes."

Carl glanced down and back at Z. "Velcro shoes are the next big thing!"

"Sorry to burst your bubble, but I've been to a lot of other Earths, and they aren't. They fade to obscurity, except they're quite popular with baby shoes—"

"You're a crazy liar!"

Z thought back to everything he could remember about Carl on Earth-G. The only thing that stood out was that the guy was loyal to his crew regardless of how they treated him. "You're a smart guy. How about this? If you help me get out of here, I'll let you work for me. I'll be your new boss."

"Why would I—"

"Look, Carl, I've already killed a lot of your buddies. With your boss out of the way, this organization is probably going to fall apart quickly. Another organization will come in and wipe out the rest of you. I'm giving you a way out."

There was a louder pounding on the reinforced door. The robot man was starting to weaken it.

Z could tell by the furtive glance Carl flashed at the door that he was worried about whatever was out there too.

"What the hell is that thing?" Carl asked.

"You wouldn't believe me if I told you."

Carl swallowed. "Okay. Don't tell me. Fine. I'll help you. There's a door up on the catwalk. I'll show you to the stairwell."

Z nodded, and Carl tucked his gun into his waistband. Z holstered his weapon but was ready to act if need be. His gun was empty, but his body was still a deadly weapon. As Carl led, Z made sure to keep a few feet behind him in case he tried to pull something on him as he did on Earth-G.

With the pounding growing louder against the reinforced door, Carl led Z through the congested metal shelving to a metal stairwell tucked away in the corner. It led up to a grated catwalk directly overhead along one wall.

Once they were at the top, Carl stopped and pointed at a metal door at the end of the catwalk. "That door leads into a corridor that will take you to a warehouse room like this one only bigger. There's an emergency exit on the back wall. It's not sealed shut like this one is. It should lead you out to the back of the warehouse."

Where Marshall's red coupe is waiting. Perfect. Part of him was surprised it had been so easy to escape the room. He wasn't particularly looking forward to fighting the tuxedo man robot with only a knife.

"Thanks, Carl. I don't care what they say about you. You're one of the good guys—"

The muzzle of Carl's gun pressed into the small of his back. Z was fast, but Carl's gun was faster. The bullet exploded out of the gun's barrel. Z's kidney didn't stand a chance.

As Z toppled forward to the catwalk's grating, clutching at his mortal wound, Carl fired again at point-blank range, blowing apart Z's skull from behind.

He died.

(Ten Seconds Earlier)

Z and Carl were standing side-by-side on the grated

catwalk. A muted *thud* came from the reinforced door down below leading into the warehouse.

Before Carl could betray him, Z backhanded Carl across the mouth. Carl had already been reaching for his gun and wasn't expecting it. It caught him off-guard, toppling him backward against the catwalk's railing. Carl uttered a cry as he backflipped over it, then crashed to the floor with a *thud* and a sick, slicing sound.

Z glanced down at Carl's body, impaled on a thick piece of iron rebar sticking out of a box.

Ouch, Germ said.

"Fucking Carl," Z muttered as he stared at the body, recalling how Carl had shot him in the back on Earth-G during the last run of this warehouse mission. "You're a back-stabbing bastard on all the Earths, I guess." He observed it impersonally as if maybe watching a cat eating a mouse.

Then another *thud* came from the reinforced door leading into the warehouse room, and he snapped back to reality. The door sounded like it was about to give way.

He needed to get out of here.

Z opened the door at the end of the catwalk and started down the corridor beyond, ready to escape through to the back exit Carl had proposed, presuming that the man told the truth.

CHAPTER TWENTY-ONE

Z sprinted across the corridor to yet another metal door. When he tried the handle, it was locked, but at least it wasn't sealed shut like the exit doors. According to Carl, the room on the other side contained a back exit that would lead him right to his getaway car.

He had to get this door open first.

As he dug in his jacket pocket for his lockpicking set, he strained to hear any sound of the tuxedoed robot man ascending the metal staircase and stomping across the grated catwalk. So far, he didn't hear anything. Maybe it had given up on trying to get in?

Z leaned toward the lock as he attempted to pick it.

There was no way that robot was going to stop now. It had said that it was after the briefcase. So why hadn't it broken through into the room yet?

The lock *clicked,* and he slid his tools back into his jacket pocket. He amusedly noted how very "PI" of him it was to carry a lockpicking kit, which reminded him of the case he was working for Alice.

One thing at a time.

He eased open the door and peered inside the new room. It was the same as the one on Earth-G in the previous warehouse mission, although he'd never paid much attention to the catwalk that ran along one side of the room.

The elevated walkway ended at the far wall next to a window that overlooked the warehouse's backside. A metal stairwell beside the window led down to the ground floor. The back door was farther down in the wall.

The rest looked the same too. A sturdy desk sat near the center of the room and stacks of crates lay scattered around the room.

Z started across the catwalk along the side of the room. He was almost halfway when the *clacking* of guns down below caused him to stop abruptly. A glance down over the catwalk's railing revealed a dozen guards armed with shotguns and rifles and handguns.

"Well, this ain't good," Z muttered. All he had was a combat knife.

"Stay where you are," one of the thugs called from below. "We'll come up and take the briefcase."

"Like hell…" Z softly said as he reset his three-minute stopwatch. This would probably take more than a few Repeats to make it out of this one alive.

While one of the thugs trotted toward the metal stairwell at the far wall, the others kept their guns trained on Z.

Z was usually one to escape a gritty situation with violence. He glanced down at the knife in his boot. Could he possibly leap down upon the thugs like Rambo knifing a wild boar in *First Blood*? His chances of surviving didn't seem too good. They outnumbered him twelve to one.

Maybe he would have better success with words?

He called, "Better not shoot me or I might drop the brief-case, and the bioweapon could leak out."

It wasn't the strongest of arguments. It was a very sturdy briefcase. It did seem to deter all of the thugs on the floor from shooting at him.

The thug who'd spoken earlier was now ascending the metal stairs to the catwalk when a door opened and closed somewhere below Z.

The remaining thugs on the floor turned to face whoever had arrived. Footsteps sounded. They grew louder.

One of the thugs went to meet the newcomer. "Now who the hell are you—gah!"

There was a tearing sound, then a *flop* and a *thud* as the man's head and body struck the floor. The man in the tuxedo stood calmly beside his handiwork.

"I have come for the briefcase. Stay out of my way."

Judging by all the thugs' shocked faces, Z thought they might simply step aside and let the robot man pass. Then horror and anger settled into their faces. "Kill him!" one of them shouted. Others yelled their agreement.

They opened fire on the tuxedoed man.

They had to have seen the glowing red eyes and the peeled-back face. They had to have known that it wasn't a man.

Oh well. It was their loss.

The tuxedoed robot stopped and stood its ground as the ten men loosed a barrage of bullets at it. When they were done and were reloading, the robot sneered and strode confi-dently toward them.

They didn't stand a chance. Its wide gangly hands mangled them terribly. All of their anger turned back to horror and to shock as it cut them down, one and two at a time with broad sweeps of its arms.

When the sole remaining thug on the catwalk fired at the robot, the robot wrenched a pistol from a dead man's hand, raised it, and fired one shot that entered the thug's forehead. With a dull moan, the man fell over the side of the catwalk railing to the ground floor.

Yikes... Germ said. Then, *Good luck.*

Z didn't even consider trying to hop over the catwalk railing to the floor below and sprint for the back door. Even if he managed not to break or twist an ankle upon the landing, the robot was down there and would surely catch him.

He decided to run down the catwalk toward the window and stairwell and hope for the best. He'd react to whatever the robot did next.

What the robot did next was pick up one of the thug's bodies and launch it up at Z.

The feat shouldn't have been possible. However, the robot had superhuman strength. The body landed on Z, striking his shoulders and knocking him flat on his chest.

As Z climbed out from under the body, another one fell on top of the first, and now Z had two bodies to extract himself from. Meanwhile, the robot planted its feet and jumped.

Jump might not be the correct term, but the robot landed on the catwalk as Z pulled himself free and rose to his feet with the briefcase in his hand.

With a hard shove, the robot man threw Z back against the catwalk's rail. Z's back popped, but it didn't snap. Worse, the robot wrenched the briefcase containing the bioweapon from Z's hand.

Z's first thought was to finish himself off with his knife so he could warp back and redo this. Before he could, the robot fell on top of him, holding his chest in place against the rail at his back. It thrust its deformed face in front of Z's, its red eyes boring right through him.

"Repeat if you dare. I will still find a way to beat you. And finish my objective." It hefted the briefcase as it backed away.

"How? How can you beat me if you can't warp?"

The robot's eyes gleamed. "Because my algorithm is superior to yours."

With that, the robot spun and turned to face the rest of the grated catwalk and the window beyond. Then it tucked its head and sprinted down the catwalk as if the walkway were a runway and the robot was a plane. When it reached the catwalk's end, it leapt deftly onto the rail and threw itself forward against the window. The glass shattered outward in a magnificent blast as its body disappeared. A crunching *thud* came a moment later, followed by the receding sound of running footsteps.

Z collapsed to the catwalk in defeat. He clutched his lower back. The robot had done a number on him. He wasn't crippled, but he'd need a hot soak in a shower or a deep tissue massage to feel right again.

"Germ, fix my back, will ya?"

You want happy ending? Germ said.

Shit. He'd taught this octopus thing too much. "No. A massage, you perv."

One quick massage, coming right up.

Z flipped over onto his chest while Germ climbed out of his pocket and made his way onto Z's lower back. He slithered under Z's jacket and shirt and began to knead Z's lower back with his suction-cupped tentacles. Who knew that octopi were such great masseuses?

"Your tentacles are so cold," Z muttered.

I could stop...

"No, no. Go on. Continue. I feel like a truck hit me."

A couple of minutes later, Z felt able to walk again, and Germ climbed back into his pocket. Z shook his head at how the tuxedoed robot had handed his ass to him. Even worse, it had taken the bioweapon.

He needed to regroup. Figure out the robot's weakness and where it had taken the bioweapon. Also, how was it related to Nunez being on this planet?

This wasn't the first super-robot Z had faced. Man, they sucked to fight, especially on your own. Their superhuman reflexes coupled with their superhuman strength and super-computer minds made them nearly invincible.

Oh well. A man as stubborn and doggedly persistent as he was would find a way to defeat the robot. Now it was time to clear out of this place before any more thugs barged in to exact their revenge on him.

Before he did, he walked the rest of the way down the catwalk to glance out of the window the robot had leapt through.

He almost wished he hadn't.

"You've got to be shitting me," he muttered when he saw what the tuxedoed robot had landed on when it had fallen to the ground.

There, parked outside the warehouse was Marshall's red coupe. It now had a giant dent in the roof.

Z put a palm to his forehead. This wasn't going to be a fun conversation with his parallel Earth dad.

Maybe he should've tried to warp back after all.

He consulted his secondary stopwatch. Not only did it keep track of Buzz's missions, but it also helped him keep track of his quests. He'd completely forgotten all about a wrong he needed to right. It was a big one to him, and he had only a half-hour to get there to fix it.

He didn't have much time. The chat with Marshall and breaking the news to Buzz that he'd failed to recover the bioweapon would have to wait until after that.

CHAPTER TWENTY-TWO

At least the car still runs. Z cruised down the highway. He was on the road leading upstate.

He drummed the meat of his palm against the steering wheel. "Come on. Come on. Don't tell me I'm late."

He couldn't remember exactly where the accident occurred. Hopefully, with his intervention, there wouldn't be an accident. He peered through the windshield down the highway. Miraculously, the windshield hadn't cracked when the robot man fell on it. However, even with a clean windshield, Z still didn't see what he was looking for: a green car pulled over on the shoulder.

"Germ, can you do your thing and look into the distance?" He was driving way over the speed limit to try to make up lost time. If the warehouse job had only gone according to plan—hell, at least halfway according to plan—he wouldn't have had to worry about rushing.

Now, he was lucky a police officer hadn't pulled him over for speeding.

Germ had been sitting on the passenger seat, and he now

launched himself up onto the dashboard so he could peer through the windshield. A moment later, Germ's beady black eyes elongated like a pair of binoculars.

Green car. Side of the road? Germ asked.

"Yeah. You see it?"

Nope.

Z gritted his teeth. Maybe the accident had already happened, but he hadn't seen anything yet.

He had to keep driving…

Then he saw it in the rearview mirrors. Flashing blue and red lights.

"Gimme a damn break."

Germ turned away from the windshield and sighted the flashing lights through the rear window. *You're not going to kill them, are you?*

Z scowled. "What the hell kind of question is that? I only kill bad guys."

They may prevent you from righting your wrong. Are they not bad guys in this situation?

Dropping his head, Z said, "You really don't understand human morality, do you? I'm on the same side as the police. We're both the good guys."

Aha!

Z's eyes were on the flashing lights growing closer in his rearview mirror. He started to slow the car. "You finally figure out human morality?"

No. It is the green car. I can see it up ahead. A shame you must stop…

Z had an idea. Maybe he didn't need to stop. Perhaps he could try something.

He lifted his foot from the brake and increased his speed. The police car sped up to match him. Then, when the green car on the side of the road came closer, Z flipped on his turn signal and pulled off the road behind it.

He hopped out and rushed over to the green car. A man crouched beside the rear tire facing the highway.

"Hey, need some help?" Z called, waving in an overly friendly manner as he approached, his boots crunching the gravel beneath his feet.

Behind Z, the police car had stopped. The door was thrown open, and an officer stepped out with his service revolver drawn. In a booming voice, he called, "Stop where you are, sir! Hands where I can see them."

Z threw his hands up. He twisted his head back at the officer. "Just a big misunderstanding is all, officer."

The officer didn't look convinced. "It always is. It always is. Hands against the car."

Z turned slowly toward the red coupe. "Officer, I need to help this man. He's trying to change a tire, and this is a dangerous stretch of highway—"

"Hands against the car."

Z hesitated. If he did as instructed, the officer would pat him down and find Germ in his pocket and the knife in his boot. He could two-finger-jab the officer and knock him unconscious, but that could cause more problems when he woke up and put out an APB on him.

With his hands still raised, Z cleared his throat. "Officer Marshall Peet sent me. This is his car."

The officer stared down the barrel of his gun. "I don't know who that is nor do I care." His eyes narrowed suspiciously on the big dent in the roof.

Z slowly turned and faced the officer. "If you don't let me go right now, that man changing his tire is going to die. I can't let that happen."

The officer scoffed. "Who the hell are you? A psychic? This is your last warning."

Over the officer's shoulder, Z saw a semi-truck quickly approaching. He noted the gentle swerve of the semi's trajectory as it neared the green car up ahead.

With a burst of air that buffeted Z and the officer, the semi rushed past and went off the road, scraping against the green car's side.

All that remained of the man changing the tire was…well, it wasn't pretty.

As for the semi, the trucker tried to correct and ran off the road, flipping on its side. Sparks tore up into the air as its metal sides scraped along the asphalt.

"Ho-ly shit," the officer breathed, panic creeping onto his face as he watched the horror unfolding before him. "Mister, you really are psychic."

Z smirked. "Nope. I'm dead."

"Dead?" The officer whipped his head back to Z. His eyes nearly bulged out of their sockets as Z turned his knife toward himself and plunged it into his chest.

The officer leaned over Z as he lay upon the ground, staring along the asphalt to the remains of the green car and semi, but there was nothing he could do.

As his strength faded, Z caught the officer's wrist and met his eyes. "Even though you won't remember this, I'll…make this…right."

He died.

(Three Minutes Earlier)

When Z blinked, he was cruising along the highway in Marshall's red coupe. He'd warped back as far as he could. He still couldn't see the green car up ahead so he had to be close. Also, the flashing lights hadn't started behind him.

He slowed down so he wouldn't be pulled over for speeding.

Eventually, he made it to the green car pulled off to the side of the road. Its driver knelt, changing a flat tire.

Z unstrapped his seatbelt. He didn't have much time to save the man before the semi barreled up and killed him.

He climbed out of the coupe and jogged up to the man changing the green car's flat tire. The man looked up at Z and scratched his head. "Who are you?"

Z bent and grabbed the man's arm. He tried wrenching him to his feet, but for all his muscle, he didn't have good leverage. "Hey, stop it! Who the hell are you?"

"Doesn't matter," Z said. "I need you to get up so you don't die."

"Die?"

Z shook his head. "The butterfly effect."

"Butterfly effect? You crazy, man?"

Z didn't have time for this. Normally he didn't have to explain himself when he was righting wrongs. "If you die, then you don't catch a drug smuggler at the airport, and in turn…some bad stuff happens. I can't let you die."

Uh Z, Germ said.

Irritated, Z glanced down. "What?"

Behind you, Germ said.

The semi came out of nowhere. It didn't even sound its horn. It struck Z and the other driver, crushing them both against the green car. Then the semi flipped.

Z cursed.

Then he died.

· · ·

(Three Minutes Earlier)

Now whatcha gonna do? Germ asked.

His use of slang startled Z, who was cruising along in Marshall's red coupe. He needed to figure out this situation. What was the best way to avoid getting arrested and save the green car's driver from getting killed? He didn't have enough time to warn the driver whether he sped or followed the speed limit.

He didn't blame the green car's driver. If some guy with a facial scar pulled up and started talking about the butterfly effect, he probably wouldn't believe him either.

He tapped the wheel as he thought about the solution. The problem, he knew, was the semi driver, a tired man who'd been driving for eighteen hours straight. No wonder he couldn't keep his semi in between the lines. So how could he get the green car's driver out of the way?

Perhaps a different line of thinking is called for? Germ said.

Hm. Maybe Germ was right. Perhaps he needed a different way to reach the solution. If he couldn't get to the green car's driver in time to get him out of the way, maybe the answer lay in getting the semi driver to change course.

An idea came to him. This red coupe was the off-duty car of a police officer. That meant there was probably a police radio in here.

His eyes shot down below the car stereo, and the police radio clipped there. He hadn't even noticed it until now. It hadn't made any sound so Marshall must have turned it off. He reached down and pressed a button, and it came to life.

While keeping the coupe on a straight course, Z plucked up the police radio and depressed the button on the side. "All squads, there's a semi swerving on…" A highway sign came up on the right, and he read off the name and latest mile marker over the radio. "Exert caution. Driver is sleep-deprived."

There was a pause, and the police radio crackled. "I'm in the area," replied the police officer who had pulled Z over earlier. "Who the hell is this?"

Z didn't know how to respond to that so he hung the police radio back up and drove at normal speed up to the green car. He pulled off to the side and casually got out of the car. He walked up to the man changing his tire.

Z did his best to keep the scarred part of his face angled away from the man as he approached. "Flat tire, eh? Need any help?"

The green car's driver didn't even glance up at him as he worked on the tire. "Nah. I've almost got it. Thanks for stopping, though."

Z inserted his hands into his pockets and turned to face the highway back the way he had come. The semi was approaching. Would his plan work in time though?

The driver continued, "In fact, if I'm lucky, I should be able to make it to work on time. Out at the airport."

Z held a hand to his eyes and watched as the semi grew closer. It was almost on them now. The semi started to swerve toward the green car.

It looked like he would have to Repeat. Then police lights flashed behind the semi, and a siren began to whoop.

The trucker corrected, and the semi's front bumper scraped past Z's chest with only an inch of clearance between them. The resulting wind blast whipped at Z's face and chest, flapping his clothes against his body.

The semi proceeded to pull off onto the shoulder without crashing or flipping.

"By God," the green car's driver gasped with wide eyes as he wiped his forehead. "You're the lucky one…"

Z shrugged, his veins still coursing with adrenaline from the close scrape with death. "All in a day's work." He headed back to Marshall's red coupe. Then he climbed in and drove off.

CHAPTER TWENTY-THREE

When Z pulled up to the *Paper Warriors* news office building, Marshall waited outside the first-floor Korean restaurant on the sidewalk. He was so deep in thought that he didn't realize his red coupe had pulled up beside him.

Z could've called but instead he honked the coupe's horn. Marshall snapped to attention with a start. Then he saw it was Z and his features relaxed. He began to yawn and then he saw the giant dent in the coupe's roof.

"My car! What the hell happened?"

Z shut the car off and hopped out. He tossed Marshall the car keys over the hood as he joined him.

"It looks a bit worse than it is."

"Are you messing with me?" Marshall was starting to freak out now. "I entrusted you with my car, and you wrecked it."

"Technically a robot fell on it."

Marshall's eyes bulged. "What?"

"I said I think you're hungry." Z nodded at the Korean restaurant beside them. "How about we grab some food? I'll make everything right. I swear. I'll pay for all the damages. The main thing is that the car still runs."

Marshall looked about to be in shock at the sight of his car. Z took him by the shoulder and guided him inside the restaurant.

Z ordered the beef bulgogi.

"What would you like to eat, sir?" the server asked Marshall.

It was nearly lunchtime so it was difficult to hear. Hungry patrons occupied most of the booths and tables crammed into the small restaurant. The dining area was dim because its lighting came from light bulbs hanging from the ceiling, covered by paper lanterns.

Marshall glanced uneasily down at the menu on the table and back up at the server. "Do you have any meat and potato dishes?"

The server beamed. "Yes."

Marshall nodded. Beneath the table, his foot tapped against the floor. "Give me one. Any one. I...trust your judgment."

"Very well." The server took their menus and headed for the kitchen.

Z couldn't help but notice Marshall's nervousness. "You okay?"

Marshall eyed the paper lantern ceiling lights. "How has this place not burned down? Those have to be fire hazards."

Z smirked. "This restaurant has been around for years, or so I've heard. It's not going to burn down anytime soon."

"Also, it doesn't take a fire marshal to see that this place is filled past maximum capacity. I ought to write a citation…"

Z snapped his fingers in front of Marshall. "Relax. You're off the clock. Let's enjoy a meal together, father and son—I mean, you remind me of my father. Not that you are my father."

Marshall stopped tapping his foot as he studied Z. "I've got two things for you, Mr. 'Z.' One, a cop is never 'off the clock.' Crime never sleeps in a city this size. Two, I think you might be as wacky as those damn newsmen upstairs. Clicking away at their typewriters, writing stories about Sasquatch. Gimme a break." He started laughing softly.

Z joined him in laughing, then the two of them were chuckling hard.

"They are some odd ones," Z said.

"Tell me about it." Marshall made a sweeping gesture with his hands. "While I was researching that missing person's case, they kept on talking and talking about aliens and zombies and contagions in the city water. In fact—"

"Hold on. You were researching while you were waiting for me to get back?"

Marshall nodded. "After I delivered your message to those three newsmen with your instructions, I called the precinct where the disappearance happened. They provided me with a few more details than were in the notes we had back at the station." He crossed his arms over his chest and leaned back proudly in his booth. "Got us a lead."

Z whistled. "No shit?"

"Yes sir."

He hadn't considered what his next move would be with Alice's missing sister case and now Marshall was just about to drop the next clue into his lap.

"Well, go on." He waved for Marshall to continue.

There was a glint of proud excitement in Marshall's eyes as he started. "As it turns out, Miss Mel Phoenix isn't a Miss but a Mrs."

Z leaned forward over the table. "You're saying that Mel Phoenix is married? Alice never mentioned that."

"Yep. She got married a couple of years ago, a low-key secret Vegas thing. Eloped. The sister probably didn't even know."

It had certainly seemed like Alice was close to her sister when she had cried on his shoulder after she had told him about the case. Something wasn't adding up here. "Are you sure? What's her husband's name?"

Marshall dug a scrap of paper from his pocket. "A guy by the name of Ray Garcia."

That name didn't sound familiar to Z. "Did you run his name through the precinct's database—er, I mean, you know. Check with police records?" He had to remind himself that this was the nineteen-eighties and there were no such things as internet databases.

Marshall cracked a smile. "Of course I did. You think I'm an amateur?" Now he leaned forward over the table so that he was inches from Z's face. "He's clean. No records." He licked his lips.

"And?" Z said.

"I got us an address. We can check it out after we eat."

Working a case with his parallel Earth dad? Z found the idea intriguing. "But you're off duty."

"A cop is never off duty."

"Shouldn't you call your wife, Carolyn?"

"I did at the news office. Plus, I'll go home as soon as we

stop by Mel Phoenix's place and have a chat with her husband." He shook his head. "Poor man must be beside himself. I don't know what I'd do if my wife ever disappeared. That's why we've got to find this Mrs. Phoenix and get her back."

Z hoped the missing woman was still able to be saved. He wasn't naïve. He knew how badly missing persons cases could end if the cops didn't locate the victim within the first twenty-four to forty-eight hours. Mel had been missing for a lot longer than that.

Z thought about his father helping him. It would be good to have someone with Marshall's experience and instinct on the case. He might pick up on something Z didn't.

He reached across the table, and Marshall shook his hand. "You know, now I get why you do what you do. This detective work stuff feels good."

When he saw Marshall eyeing him strangely, Z said, "You got me. I'm a bit crazy. Hey, I think I see our food coming..."

Marshall wiped his mouth with a napkin. "That was pretty good. Now, you said something about you footing the bill?"

"Of course." Z slapped some cash onto the check lying on the table and got up. He straightened his jacket and shirt underneath.

"Hey, is that blood?" Marshall said.

Glancing down at his black muscle shirt under his jacket, Z saw a fleck of bad guy blood from the first warehouse mission. He forced a smile. "Nah. Just some strawberry jelly from a donut I had for breakfast."

Marshall frowned.

You're on Earth-D, remember, stupid? Germ said.

Z smacked his forehead. "Did I say donut? I meant cherry cobbler. I'm a dessert for breakfast kind of guy."

"Uh-huh…" Marshall didn't look like he bought it. Damn Earth-D and its lack of donuts.

Before Marshall could say anything else, Z said, "How about you get the car started? I need to check on something upstairs in the news office before we leave. Won't take but a sec."

"Sure. I'm never handing over my keys to you ever again."

"I said I'm going to pay you for the damage." Z turned and found a back stairwell in the cramped restaurant that led directly up to the news office. Dust coated the steps. Z was probably the only person who used the stairwell, but it came in handy when he ate here, which was a lot.

Once inside the *Paper Warriors* news office, he went straight to the intergalactic printing press. The office was empty. The three newsmen must have been out to lunch. Checking the printing press, he still didn't see anything further from Buzz. He checked to make sure that the three newsmen had sent the contents of the letter he had Marshall deliver earlier. They had, he was relieved to see.

His message had contained three major items for Buzz to address. One, did he know anything about the tuxedoed robot man? Two, FYI—he'd recovered a futuristic earpiece from the black barn, which turned out not to be a Buzz Barn and to be on the lookout for it. Three, was Eduardo Nunez on this Earth or not?

Thinking about that last item prompted Z to withdraw his wallet from his back pocket and pull out a piece of printer paper that had been folded down into a small square and tucked inside the wallet. Unfolding it, he stared at his enemy's face.

It was an age-simulated composite sketch—Dr. Nunez had disappeared decades ago on Z's original Earth—but Buzz assured him it would at least closely resemble the man. Z had already committed the features to memory.

High forehead. Thick bushy gray eyebrows and a mustache that wrapped down around his mouth and chin. Slightly hooked nose. Wavy grey hair.

He kind of resembled a Mexican Colonel Sanders.

"I'm going to get you, you bastard. You took everything from me…"

Z gritted his teeth, folded his enemy's sketch back up, and reinserted it into his wallet.

Then he walked over to his office door to send the earpiece fragment. Before he opened the door, he crouched and inspected the lock plate to see if anyone had attempted to break inside.

Maybe it was just him, but it looked like there was a tiny scratch on it. Hm. He rubbed a thumb over it to make sure it wasn't a trick of the light.

Maybe it had been there for a while. He didn't have time to think about it at the moment. Closing the door behind him, he went immediately to the space and time capsule. He opened a small compartment in the center console and inserted the futuristic earpiece. Then he closed it and tapped the controls that would send the object to Buzz on his Earth so he could inspect it. Something told Z that the earpiece had something to do with the tuxedoed robot man and possibly even Nunez himself.

With that done, Z rose and headed back toward the door.

Your dad seems nice, Germ said.

He reached for the door. "He's not my dad. Not on this Earth."

Must be nice to have a dad.

"It is what it is." Z opened the door and locked it behind him. "Now let's go before he gets anxious and leaves without us."

CHAPTER TWENTY-FOUR

Traffic was horrible, but Mel Phoenix's house wasn't far from the *Paper Warriors* news office.

Marshall parked his red coupe at the sidewalk curb, and for a few moments, the two of them studied the building through the windshield.

It was a modest one-story building. A couple of hedges out front. Shutters on the windows. A cracked sidewalk leading to the front door. They could see through one of the windows. A young man was sitting at a table with his back to them.

While still appraising the house outside the car, Z asked, "So how do we want to approach this? I question the husband while you ask to use the restroom and search for clues?"

He was excited about this. The thrill of the mystery, he guessed.

There was a *click,* and he felt something on his wrist. He turned in time to see Marshall *click* a handcuff onto the coupe's steering wheel. The thin chain trailing down from it connected to the handcuff on Z's wrist.

"What the hell?" Z said.

Marshall bit his lip. Then he pulled the keys out of the ignition and opened his car door.

"The thing is, I don't trust you. Something's off about this whole case. The way you acted at that barn? If I didn't know any better, I'd say you somehow knocked me out. Sure, I may be tired, but I'm not one to fall asleep on the job—and I'm always on the job."

Z couldn't believe it.

Marshall continued. "I called the precinct from a pay phone while you were up in your office. You hiding something up there? Dead body, maybe?"

"What the fuck? No, I'm not."

You've got a space and time capsule up there, though, Germ said.

"You bastard," Z said. "This is my case."

"Go cry on it."

"I hate you."

"What was that?"

Z shook his head. How low had he sunk? Resorting to teenager-to-parent insults. It had slipped out.

"I didn't do anything wrong," Z said.

Marshall shrugged. "Additional cops are on the way. I gave them this address over the pay phone. Maybe you're innocent after all. I've seen my share of blood, and that is not strawberry jam on your shirt. So you're a liar either way, Mr. Government Secret Agent."

Marshall got out and slammed the door before heading for the front door.

Now that was unexpected, Germ said.

Z let out a deep breath. "You don't know my dad. He's very competent and intuitive. I shoulda seen this coming."

Outside the house, Marshall was now knocking on the

front door. The man who had been sitting inside opened the door for him, and they stepped inside. As Marshall did so, he flicked a serious look back at the car.

Z fake-smiled back, waiting until the front door closed. Then he reached inside his jacket and retrieved his lock-picking kit. He was out of the cuffs in no time at all.

What are you going to do now? Germ said. *Marshall said the police were on their way.*

Flashing Germ a look, Z said, "I'm going to get some information about my case. I'll worry about the police later."

He climbed out of the red coupe and headed around the side of the house, keeping low so they didn't see him from inside. Luckily there were no guard dogs, and he found the back door unlocked. Not that a locked door would've impeded him.

He opened it silently and crept inside the house.

Yellow wallpaper with white lilies covered the walls. The floor was linoleum. *Gotta love the eighties,* Z thought.

He was in a small dining room nook. Marshall's calm and authoritative voice came from the kitchen on the other side of the wall.

"You said she disappeared two weeks ago?"

"That's right," said the man who had to be Mel's husband, Ray. There was a sad quiver in his voice, and he spoke with a slight Spanish accent.

"You don't know where she could've gone?" Marshall asked.

"Gone? Gone? I've looked everywhere for her. She didn't go anywhere. Someone had to have taken her!"

As Marshall tried to calm the man down, Z crept around the dining room, searching for anything the police might've missed. On a cupboard, he found some framed photos of Mel and her husband, Ray.

Mel had a million-dollar smile, dark hair, and a petite body. Ray was thin, had tanned skin, and must like tan Panama hats. He wore one in almost every photo.

One was a wedding picture—there was a Las Vegas-style chapel in the background. Another picture showed Mel and Ray hugging each other in front of what appeared to be Niagara Falls. The couple looked so happy together. Another photo showed them kissing in front of a school building.

Z glanced around the rest of the dining room. The only other thing of note was that the man certainly appeared to be living alone. There was only one chair at the dinner table.

In the kitchen, Marshall was still trying to comfort the man. He was explaining that he was an officer and he was on the case. Ray, in turn, explained how he'd already spoken to the cops and they didn't have any leads.

While the two of them were speaking with their backs to him, Z saw his chance to sneak through the dining room doorway to a hallway containing three doors. He slipped silently into the hallway.

The first door was a bathroom. Nothing in there.

The second door led to the master bedroom. Z peeked. Only one side of the bed had been disturbed, and the man's aloneness at night reminded Z of his aloneness and missing his wife.

He shook his head and moved on to the third door.

Ray had converted it into a small office with a window. There was a desk and on one wall was a bookcase. There were a few hardback books on it but what was intriguing were the glass test tube sets and flasks resting on the shelves.

Who was this guy?

From out in the kitchen, Marshall asked what Ray did for a living.

"I'm a college chemistry teacher."

Z took a step closer to the bookcase and realized that the hardback books were chemistry textbooks. Nothing out of the ordinary in this room either. Maybe the husband was in the clear regarding his wife's disappearance. He hadn't thought it was likely, but he had to check all the boxes.

Marshall continued. "What can you tell me about Mel's sister, Alice?"

"Sister?" Ray stammered. "Mel doesn't have a sister. Not one that she ever told me about. This makes no sense."

Z had to agree. He knew that some families had internal disagreements and spats but wouldn't Alice have known if her sister was married? Why hadn't she told him when she offered him the case?

Things weren't adding up.

Z snuck back toward the kitchen.

"Your wife," Marshall said. "Did she say anything to you the night she went to the outdoor concert with her friends?"

"Nothing out of the ordinary."

"Why didn't you go with her?"

There was a tense pause. "Are you accusing me? Am I a suspect?"

"Just doing my job, sir. It's a valid question."

Ray scoffed. "You're like the other officers. You think because I'm an immigrant that I'm a suspect?"

Z crept up to the end of the hallway and peered past a refrigerator next to the opening. Marshall and Ray stood ten feet away. Their backs were to him. Ray was wearing chinos, a polyester shirt, and a tan Panama hat.

"No," Marshall said. "That's not what I'm saying."

"Then what are you saying? Why can't anyone find my wife? Some lunatic probably kidnapped her."

"Why would someone want to kidnap your wife? Did she have any enemies?"

Ray started to sob.

Marshall asked, "Do you have any enemies?"

Z hung back against the hallway, hoping neither of them would walk his way.

"Sir, do you have any enemies? Someone you think may have taken your wife?"

"No. No," Ray said. "It's not that. It's just that I feel responsible for her disappearing. If I'd gone to the concert with her instead of working late at the college—"

There was a knock at the front door.

Ray stiffened.

Marshall said calmly, "It's okay. That's probably the police."

"Police?" Ray asked. There was alarm in his voice. "I didn't do it. I didn't have anything to do with my wife's disappearance. I love my wife. I'd do anything to get her back. Anything."

"Look," Marshall said. "They're not here for you. I have…a suspect out in my car. I called them here because this is where I was heading."

Z peeked out of the hallway past the refrigerator. Marshall headed toward the front door, but Ray stopped him with a hand on his arm. "I'll get it."

Marshall hung back in the kitchen while Ray went to the front door. When Ray opened it, Z's veins iced over.

Standing on the front stoop was the tuxedoed man with sunglasses. His face was unmarred, and his clothes were crisp and new. There was absolutely no trace of the violence at the warehouse earlier that morning.

Z unconsciously made a fist at his side, his stomach twisting into a hard knot.

In the robot man's hands was a Tommy gun.

"Who are you? What is the meaning of this?" Ray said.

The robot man karate chopped the man in the neck, and Ray slumped unconscious to the floor. Then, with Ray out of the way, the tuxedoed robot turned his gun toward Marshall.

CHAPTER TWENTY-FIVE

Z dove toward Marshall, catching him with one arm and taking him down to the kitchen floor as the Tommy gun's spray peppered the kitchen's walls and cabinets. Dust smothered the room. Z managed to flip over the kitchen table so that it shielded them from the gunman's view.

"You followed me? You plastic-headed bastard!" Z yelled as he scampered behind the overturned table, dragging a coughing Marshall with him.

The tuxedoed robot replied with another burst from the Tommy gun that chewed angrily through the table's defense. Z pressed himself and Marshall down. When the gunfire stopped, a large chunk of the table fell off and landed upon their backs.

"You know this murderer?" Marshall gasped as he drew his service revolver.

Z shrugged. "Eh. We got into a little scuffle earlier today. He's the one that dented the roof of your car."

Marshall stared at him as dust and gun smoke wafted past them. "You're joking. Right?"

"Wish I was."

From the way Marshall positioned his body, Z knew he was about to peer over the top of the table and open fire on their attacker. Z also knew that it would do no good against a killer robot machine. They had to get out of here and now.

Why had the robot come here in the first place? Was he tracking Z? Or had he come to kidnap Ray? Part of him considered warping back in time to get Ray to safety but based on his last confrontation with the robot, warping in its presence usually didn't give him much of an advantage. It was time to run.

As Marshall peeked over the remains of their table barricade, Z rushed past him, hooking him around the upper arm.

"The hell?" Marshall said as Z tugged him off his feet toward the hallway.

The Tommy gun opened up again, barely missing Z and Marshall, most of its bullets embedding themselves into the refrigerator.

Marshall resisted. "What are you doing? We have to stand and fight. Ray's still back there—"

"You wouldn't stand a chance," Z breathed into his ear as he prepared to tug him farther down the hall. "We have to get the fuck out of here."

"I'm no coward."

"Don't make me knock you out again."

Marshall's eyes narrowed at him.

"Get in the office room," Z said, pointing at the third door in the hallway. "There's a sturdy desk in there you can use as a barricade. Also a window to escape through if things turn bad." He turned back toward the kitchen toward the sound of the robot's growing footsteps.

"Where are you going?" Marshall said.

"To try to buy us some time." There must have been something in his grim face that made Marshall decide to follow his directions. When he saw Marshall sprinting for the office room, Z said, "Germ, get out there and do your thing."

Certainly, Germ said.

Germ shot out from Z's pocket and danced across the linoleum on his tiny tentacles. The robot grunted and started firing at Germ with his Tommy gun.

This is fun! Germ said.

"Don't have too much fun," Z called from his position behind the refrigerator. When Germ leapt up onto the wall and began to dash around the room using his suction cups, the tuxedoed robot spun and fired, tracing an arc of destruction along the walls after Germ.

The robot fired until it ran out of ammo. As the robot inserted another magazine into his gun, Germ launched himself at the robot's head. Upon landing, he jettisoned a blob of blackish goo on the robot's face, then hopped off and landed on Z's shoulder.

"That's gross." Z watched as the robot took a step backward toward the fridge.

Z grabbed the refrigerator door and swung it wide. The metal door smacked into the robot's front as it tried to orient itself, and the Tommy gun clattered to the floor. Z swung the refrigerator door at the robot a second time. This time, the robot's wide gangly hands caught it. Its fingers dug into the door like metal claws. A *screech* followed as it tore the door from the refrigerator.

Time to run, Germ said.

Before he did, Z scooped up the Tommy gun and dashed around the corner into the hallway.

Duck! Germ said.

Z dove forward into the hall as the robot heaved the refrigerator door with such force that it embedded itself into the hallway wall.

Geez. The robot was strong.

Z sprinted down the hall and clambered sideways into the office. Marshall had repositioned the heavy desk in the center of the room, facing the door with the window at its back. Marshall crouched behind it with his revolver pointing at Z's chest.

"What the hell is happening out there?" he yelled.

Z ran up to the desk, put a palm on top of it, and vaulted over it to join Marshall on the other side. "Oh, you know. Just another scuffle."

"Scuffle? If I'm not mistaken, I heard a refrigerator door tear off its hinges."

"Yep," Z said. "Now help me overturn this desk."

The desk was heavy, but with both of them lifting from the backside, they managed to upend it so the flat side was facing the door. As it crashed to the floor with a thunderous *boom*, the tuxedoed robot appeared in the doorway.

In its hands were dual pistols.

"Seriously?" Z said.

He and Marshall ducked as the pistol shots tore into the far wall, then the sturdy desk.

It seemed odd that the robot was taking its time with them. Why wouldn't it rush them and tear them to shreds with its hands like the thugs back at the warehouse?

The robot fired until both guns *clicked* empty. Then Z turned to Marshall.

"Now it's our turn." His fingers wrapped around the Tommy gun in a death grip. Z rose over the desk and opened fire. "Take that motherfucker!"

The stream of bullets ate into the robot's tuxedo, knocking him back a few steps into the hallway.

Wide-eyed, Marshall also rose and fired his revolver.

Together, they fired until they'd pinned the robot against the opposite wall of the hallway. Its body had crushed in the wall so that it had to extricate itself with the crack of splintered drywall.

After it had freed itself, it calmly reloaded both pistols.

Z tugged an incredulous Marshall back under their desk barricade.

"H-how the h-hell is that f-fucking possible," Marshall said. "That thing's n-not—"

"Not human. Yup. I already told you. It's a robot."

"But. But…"

Z clapped a hand to Marshall's shoulder to calm him amid the tearing impacts of bullets against the wood desk. "I know. It's a lot to take in. Get ready. We're going to have to make our move in a few seconds, and if we time it right, we might make it out of here in one piece."

"Wh-what?"

Z waited for the telltale *click* that signaled the robot's pistols were both empty. Then he rose and turned the Tommy gun toward the office room window. He shattered it with a short barrage.

"Go! Go! Go!"

Marshall didn't have to hear it again. He rose and made for the window. Some shards remained at the bottom of the window frame. He batted them out of the way with the butt of his revolver. Then he was through and outside.

On the other side of the desk, the robot had nearly finished reloading. Z got a running start, jumped, and threw himself through the window. He landed amid a sprinkling of glass in the small grassy back yard. He rolled and popped up to his feet.

"N-nice landing," Marshall stuttered.

"Thanks, Dad—I mean, Marshall."

Marshall was still too stunned to notice that Z had called him Dad again. He looked like a traumatized statue.

Z grabbed his arm and led him away from the house. The robot would be coming out the window at any time…

The *whoop* of police sirens from the front of the house made Z stop and reconsider.

Moments later, the cops kicked in the front door. There were shouts of, "Freeze! Police!"

Z smirked at the idea of how the police coming to arrest him would provide the distraction necessary for him to get away.

He half-carried Marshall around the front of the house as a shootout began inside the house. He thought about leaving him on the sidewalk but then thought better of it. After helping a bewildered Marshall into the passenger seat, Z climbed behind the wheel.

Too bad the keys were still in Marshall's pocket.

Gunfire flashed in the window inside the house.

Z snapped his fingers in front of Marshall's face. The man was staring blindly into the space in front of him.

"Hey. Keys."

In his peripheral vision, Z glimpsed the robot fleeing the house with Ray in his arms.

Without blinking or even looking to see what he was doing, Marshall obeyed and tossed over the keys.

Z caught them and shoved them into the ignition. The engine fired up, and they were gone.

CHAPTER TWENTY-SIX

As Z drove up to the playground, he checked to make sure he read the sign out front correctly. Yep, this was the place. He parked the red coupe on the curb next to a merry-go-round.

Beside him in the passenger seat, Marshall had passed out, probably from a combination of exhaustion and shock at fighting an unkillable super robot.

Z considered waking the man but instead let him sleep it off.

Z wasn't a patient man. He waited for twenty minutes and still no one had shown up. He consulted the tattoos under his arms to recheck the time.

Shit. He'd misread his inking and was early.

"Enough of this sitting. I gotta stretch my legs," he muttered as he climbed out of the car.

He thrust his hands in his pocket and walked across the playground. There was a teeter-totter, a slide, and one of those metal spiderweb-type contraptions you could either climb on or swing from beneath.

There were other types of playground equipment scattered around, but he no longer saw them. In his mind, he was mentally replaying the scene of his daughter having fun at a playground a few years ago back on his Earth.

That day, he hadn't been watching her too closely because Buzz was busy triangulating the position of a war criminal who had flown into the city. Z's eyes had been on his phone instead of on his daughter. He'd been waiting for Buzz's text with the bad guy's coordinates. Then he would hand his daughter off to her nanny.

In those days, there always seemed to be no shortage of bad guys to catch or stop and not enough time to spend with family. He now knew that it was his fault for not prioritizing family.

At the time, he was all about his job. Always after the bad guys. Until somewhere along that way, he became a bad guy himself.

No thanks to Nunez.

"Daddy. Hey Daddy. Look at me!" his daughter had said. But he hadn't looked. "Daddy," she said, her words insistent and all spoken in one rushed breath. "Come on, look real quick. I can't hold this position for long ahh—"

He had finally looked then, had seen his daughter fall off the monkey bars. A *thud* followed, and she had started to cry.

Cursing to himself, he had hurried over to her and picked her up. He'd kissed her on the forehead and apologized. He should have been watching—it was all his fault.

She had been fighting back her tears, trying to be brave for him.

At that moment, Z had wanted to kill himself for being a bad parent. He'd let his child down.

When he inspected her leg, he discovered she had sprained her ankle. It was only a sprain, and she would be fine in a few days if she stayed off it, but he knew what he had to do.

He had set her gently upon the soft playground mulch beside the monkey bars. He crouched beside her. "Everything is going to be all right. I'm going to fix this."

He had taken her hand in his then and kissed it. "I'll be right back, okay?"

She had smiled up at him. There was a gap between her teeth from where she had lost a baby tooth a few days earlier. Her smile warmed him. It was a smile he would kill to protect. "Okay, Daddy. I'll wait right here."

He had kissed her forehead one more time and her sore ankle.

"Daddy, you're embarrassing me in front of all the other kids."

He had placed a palm on her head and tousled her hair a little. "Sorry." He rose and walked behind some nearby bushes.

"Daddy, are you peeing?"

Z's throat caught as he pulled his knife from his boot. He twisted his head backward. "No, honey. Be back soon."

Then he'd plunged the knife into his chest.

He'd died.

After dying, he'd warped back and made sure to watch his daughter crossing the monkey bars. Since he was watching that time, she continued across instead of hanging near the middle and waiting for him to look at her. She hadn't fallen that time.

"You're the best, Daddy," she said when she reached the other side, beaming with pride.

He thought he would've learned from that experience—to

cherish all the time he had with his family—but he hadn't. He'd still been a bad father after that.

With a shake of his head, his thoughts returned to the present day.

He was still walking through the playground, but now there were finally some people coming his way. Four kids.

Perfect, he thought. *Go time.*

The four kids were arguing next to a swing set.

They were all boys, and one of them was several inches shorter than the others. They were maybe thirteen or fourteen years old.

"Tattletale. Tattletale," the biggest of them was saying to the smaller boy.

Another one of them joined in. "Yeah, nobody likes tattletales, you big fat tattletale."

"Tattletales eat dirt," said the third bully. "So we're gonna make you eat dirt."

"Oh yeah?" the smallest boy said. "You can try."

The first bully planted his hands on his hips. "Hear that, guys? He says we can try."

"'We can try,'" the second bully mimed.

"Go ahead. Take your best shot, dirt-eater," the third one said.

The smallest boy stepped forward, cocked his fist back, and tried to punch the third bully. The bully smacked the fist away before it could connect. When the small boy threw another punch, a jab to the belly, the bully scoffed.

"Pathetic," the third bully said.

The second bully sneered. "Pathetic."

"Guys," the first bully said. "Make this pipsqueak eat dirt."

The second and third bullies threw themselves at the small

kid and wrestled him to the ground. When they had him pinned down, they shoved his face into the dirt.

Z stood back and watched with his arms folded over his chest, slowly shaking his head.

"Eat dirt. Eat dirt. Eat dirt," the bullies chanted.

Fast footsteps sounded behind Z, and he turned as Marshall came running up. "What the heck is going on here? Break it up, boys, break it up."

"Make us," one of the bullies said.

"I am an officer of the law—" Marshall started, but Z cut him off and pulled him aside.

"Easy there."

"Easy? Those punks are beating that poor kid half to death. I have to help him."

Marshall made to rush forward, but Z caught his arm. "There are other ways of helping people."

Marshall looked incredulous. "You call standing around and watching helping? You're an accomplice to this crime. In a few years, these bullies are probably going to be in juvie. For assault and battery."

"Maybe," Z said. "Give me a minute to work things out my way?"

With fire in his eyes, Marshall relented.

The smallest boy grunted in pain.

"Say uncle," one of the bullies said.

"Uncle."

The three boys lifted their hands from him. "See, he's a whiny tattletale dirt-eater." With a glance in Z's and Marshall's direction, they walked away.

Z walked up to the smallest boy and crouched beside him. "You're Jimmy, right?"

The boy nodded. "How'd you know?"

"Um…friend of your father's," Z said.

"Oh. What's your name?" Jimmy asked.

"You can call me Z."

"For real? Your name is a letter?"

Z nodded.

"That's badass!"

"Watch your language, son. Now, I was watching your technique, and while I admire your bravery, you're not going to win any fights like that. Throwing punches they can see coming from a mile away."

The boy flashed him a look that said, *Go on.*

"Now, I could kick their butts for you. Or my friend can arrest them. That will probably make them madder at you."

He had Jimmy's full attention. "Then what do I do? I just want them to stop picking on me."

Z grinned. "Here's what you need to do…"

Z stepped back from Jimmy and joined Marshall.

"What did you tell the kid?" Marshall asked.

Z grinned. "Watch and learn."

Jimmy cupped his hands over his mouth and addressed the three bullies still walking away from him. "Hey, you three stooges, come back here."

The bullies stopped and turned.

"Did he call us stooges?" the first bully said.

The second bully nodded.

"What's a stooge?" the third one asked.

"Say that again," the first one said. "I dare you."

With his hands still cupped over his mouth, Jimmy called even louder. "Come and get me, you stooges!"

The three bullies rushed him as one.

Since Jimmy was smaller and quicker, he was able to dodge out of the way. Then he ran up behind the first bully and kicked him behind the knee.

"Hey—ow!" The first bully toppled over, embarrassed.

When the second bully reached for Jimmy, he dove between the boy's legs and popped up behind him. Gripping the boy's belt, he yanked the bully's pants down.

"You little twerp!" The bully bent over to pull his pants back up, and Jimmy tackled him from behind, sending the second bully sprawling on top of the first one.

The third bully barreled up to Jimmy and flattened him backward to the ground. The playground mulch softened his fall, and Jimmy quickly popped back up with one hand closed in a fist.

"I'm gonna make you eat dirt!" the third bully spat.

Jimmy threw his fist forward. He opened his fingers, and mulch and bits of dirt sprayed at the bully's face. While the bully swatted the air in front of him, trying to see, Jimmy sauntered up to the bully and kicked him in the crotch.

The bully went down.

Jimmy stood over the three downed bullies and planted his fists on his hips. "Are we good now?"

"Yes. Yes!" they shouted. "Just stop hurting us."

Z turned back to Marshall. "See? All is right with the world again."

As Marshall thought that over, Z tossed him the car keys. "About time you woke up. You care to drive me back to the *Paper Warriors* news office? Then you can finally go home to your wife. The woman is probably missing you and family is important, right?"

Marshall turned the car keys over in his hand. "Family is the most important thing."

As they walked to the car, Z stopped and took one last glance back at the playground.

"Fucking monkey bars," he muttered softly and followed Marshall.

CHAPTER TWENTY-SEVEN

When Marshall dropped Z off at the *Paper Warriors* office, he still looked a little dumbstruck. On the drive back, they had heard over the police radio that the tuxedoed man had escaped with a hostage—the homeowner Ray Garcia. An officer was wounded, but at least no one had died. The police were saying that the tuxedoed man must've been high on drugs…

"Drugs?" Marshall said. "How am I supposed to go to work every day now knowing that there are killer robots out on the streets?"

Z unstrapped his seatbelt. "Take it one day at a time. There's more crazy stuff than killer robots out in the world."

"What do you mean?" Marshall said.

"Oh, you know. Time and space manipulation. Butterfly effects."

"I was right, wasn't I? You're one of those wackos who believe in aliens and stuff."

Z leaned forward in his seat and angled his head up at the

second-story alternative news office. "Gee, what gave it away?" He smirked, and Marshall chuckled.

"You're all right in my book," Marshall said. "I think. I'll clear everything up at the station regarding you possibly being a suspect. Something tells me that you really are some kind of black ops government agent, and I don't want to know more."

"Fair enough." Z got out of the car.

Marshall cleared his throat. "Let's hope this is the last time we run into each other. Okay? After the day I've had, I'm going to need a damn shrink to get my head straight."

Z held up a hand. "Stay right here for a moment. I'll be right back."

While Marshall kept the red coupe running in front of the Korean restaurant, Z dashed up the stairwell to the news office. A minute later, he came back down to Marshall and tossed a stack of hundred-dollar bills inside the red coupe's window.

"That's for the damage to your car. Should be enough."

Marshall's mouth dropped open.

Z raised a hand. "Don't worry. It's not dirty money."

"D-don't you have insurance like regular people do?"

Z scoffed. "A guy with my ability doesn't need insurance."

Marshall frowned and looked ready to ask why, but then he shook his head. "All right. Look, I'll back off your missing persons case, okay? I don't want any more trouble. You'll get the job done, right?"

Z nodded. "I won't stop 'til I get to the truth."

"Good. Now I'm going to go home and pass out in the recliner for a few hours until I've got to go in for my shift tonight."

"A cop is never off duty," Z said.

"A cop is never off duty," Marshall repeated and drove off. Z stood there and watched.

You two hit it off well in the end. I think, Germ said.

"Yeah, it was good getting to know him on this Earth. He's a good guy." He turned and headed back up to the news office.

When he returned to the printing press, Z was relieved to see a stack of newspaper correspondences from Buzz. Finally, some answers.

He scooped one up and started to read the headline.

He didn't scare easily, but he nearly jumped when he realized one of the three newsmen was lurking right behind him.

With an embarrassed smile, the newsman finger-waved at him.

"Uh, hello?" Z said.

"Hi." The newsman stood there.

"Do you need something?"

The newsman twiddled his thumbs in front of him. "Umm."

"Come on, what is it? I'm busy."

"It's just that…you owe us a favor for sending that message to your friend through the printing press."

Z groaned. He had said that. Now it was going to bite him in the ass. "Go on."

"Well…" The newsman glanced over his shoulder at the other two newsmen busily typing away on their typewriters. Both of them paused and held thumbs up for him to continue.

"The thing is, times have been tough here at *Paper Warriors*. We're losing subscribers. They're complaining about the quality of our stories. They call them, and I quote, 'Lacking originality.'"

Z stared at the man. "So? They're kinda right. How many stories about Bigfoot do you think people want to read?"

The newsman's stance went rigid. "How dare you!"

Z raised his hands to calm the man. "Look, sometimes I say hurtful things from a place of caring," he bullshitted. "You have to branch out, or readers will get bored. Report on other…phenomena than Ol' Sasquatch."

One of the newsmen sitting at his typewriter suddenly stood. "For your information, Bigfoot is a completely different entity than Sasquatch!"

With fire in his eyes, the other scrawny newsman sitting at his typewriter picked up a No. 2 pencil and snapped it in two.

Shit, Z thought with a chuckle. *If I don't calm these nerds down soon, they might try to kill me.*

"I have a suggestion," he said. "Maybe poll your readers in the next issue about what they want to read about."

"That's stupid," the newsman standing in front of him said. "Readers don't tell us what they want to hear—we tell them what they need to hear. That's why we're cashing in our favor that you owe us, now."

Z straightened the newspaper he was holding. "Um, okay."

The newsman smacked the newspaper out of his hands.

"What is this favor?" Z repressed his anger.

The newsman beamed. "You seem like you've lived an interesting life. You've seen the world or world*s*. We want you to find us our next big story."

"What? How am I…" Z turned so he had some space to think. Ten seconds later, when he turned back, the three newsmen were standing shoulder-to-shoulder right in front of him.

"Tell us a story," they said rather creepily.

"A good one," one of them said.

Z rubbed his forehead. Shit. He was all out of ideas. Now maybe if he had a donut, he'd be able to think…

Donut.

Grinning from ear to ear, Z reached out and put a hand on the outer shoulders of the three bunched-up newsmen. "Boys, have I got a story for you. One that will turn your newspaper into a big hit."

Their faces looked rabid and hungry for more details.

"What is it? What is it?" one of them said.

Z stood a little straighter and adjusted his jacket. "You're correct. I have seen many worlds. I do have a big story for you. If presented correctly, it could be a huge gamechanger on this Earth."

"What is it? What is it?"

"Tell us!"

Z smirked and inclined forward. "A little something that I like to call the Great Donut Conspiracy…"

With the three newsmen frantically typing away at their keyboards, looking at the notes they'd taken, Z headed to his office with Buzz's newspapers tucked under his arm.

Maybe Earth-D would get donuts after all. He doubted it, though.

He entered his office and closed the door behind him. Then he sat behind his desk. The space and time capsule rested against the wall, a sheet draping its sleek form.

He started reading the newspapers Buzz had sent him.

Tuxedo man is not a man, the first article read. He already knew that, though. He continued reading.

Tuxedo man is one of my robots. I call him Ozzy. While still a prototype, he will be the gold standard in my upcoming butler and bodyguard line of robots. Nunez must have stolen him from one of my storage facilities and reprogramed him to do his bidding. The man is smart, and he's keeping tabs on us.

Z rubbed his jaw. At least now he knew why the robot was so good at fighting and killing. Although he would've named the robot line Alfred.

Weaknesses include, well, I didn't build any faults into Ozzy. He has very high computational powers and high strength, agility, etc. I don't envy you having to face one all on your own. Ozzy doesn't bleed, but as with most things in life, excessive force can destroy him. Good luck.

Z grunted. Then he read the next article.

I received what you described as a "futuristic earpiece," and you are correct. This is beyond what I can build at this time. My best guess is that it's how Eduardo Nunez keeps in contact with his robot.

The design of it is incredible. Buddy, I'll spare you the scientific jargon and say that this technology would probably allow Nunez to communicate with the robot from other worlds and through time. Not even I can do that yet, hence the reason why we're using such archaic methods of communicating, such as an intergalactic printing press—which Nunez built, may I remind you. The earpiece is like printing press version 2.0.

I shall keep analyzing it. Maybe I can find a way to replicate the technology to talk to each other when you're on different Earths and times.

That would be nice. Without having Germ to talk to, Z might've already gone crazy. Of course, Germ was a tiny octopus-sized sentient bioweapon, so…yeah. Maybe he already had.

As for if I was able to ascertain whether or not Nunez is on Earth-D…I have not. He's a slippery old bastard. For all I know, he could be traipsing about on Earth-D while wearing a disguise. See page A4 for some recent surveillance photos of him that I was lucky enough to capture on several different Earths.

I'm not sure how, but he has the means to hop to parallel Earths. He just can't jump back in time like you can in the space and time capsule. Earth-D's timeline is in the 1980s, so he wouldn't need to warp back.

Since he doesn't have the Repeater gene, he's only getting older with each linear parallel Earth hop. After we foiled his last plan to reverse time, he's probably getting desperate to figure out a solution before he dies of old age. Or heart disease.

Again, check out the latest photos of him on page A4.

Let me know if I can be of further service.

-B

P.S.: Women's shoulder pads were a big fashion trend in the eighties. See any? Heh. So bizarre.

Z flipped to page A4. *Indeed they are.* That reminded him of Alice, and he dug out her phone number from his pocket. He needed to sync up with her and figure out what she knew about Mel's husband. Had the killer robot kidnapped Mel too?

If so, how were they connected to Nunez, who might or might not be on this Earth?

With the newspaper open to page A4, Z glossed over Buzz's latest photos of Eduardo Nunez. There was a photo of old Nunez wearing a pinstripe suit, standing on a street corner. Another showed Nunez with his hair pulled back into a ponytail and sunglasses on his face. He was sitting at a restaurant.

A third photo depicted Nunez about to get into a taxi. The tan Panama hat that hid his high forehead obscured his wavy gray hair.

Z set the paper on his desk and stared at it.

That hat. He'd seen it before…

Where was it?

Ray.

Ray had been wearing a hat just like it. Ray—Mel Phoenix's husband.

Why? How? Was it a coincidence?

You constipated again? Germ said.

"No. Why?"

That face you're making.

Z shook his head. "No. I think I figured something out, but I don't know what it means yet."

What?

"Oh shit. I've got it." Z drew a deep breath. "Brace yourself. I think Ray Garcia is a young Eduardo Nunez."

While Z was still trying to process the latest piece of information, he read the last newspaper article Buzz had sent.

By the way, how'd the warehouse mission go on Earth-D? You haven't sent the bioweapon to me in the space and time capsule yet. I'm sure everything went smoothly as long as you got to the warehouse at the optimal time I specified. You are the best at what you do.

*   -B*

Yeah…about that bioweapon. Ozzy the robot had taken it as well as young Eduardo Nunez.

Shit.

Z got up and left his office. He went straight to the printing press to send his reply to Buzz. He hated failure.

He typed out the following reply.

The warehouse mission was a disaster. I mean a total FUBAR. They knew I was coming. Ozzy took the bioweapon in the briefcase. Not sure why. I think old Nunez is here. He can't warp back in time, but as you said, Earth-D's timeline is in the 1980s so technically he could hop here.

Also, I'm working on a missing persons case. A real gumshoe operation. Might be connected. Stumbled upon a young Eduardo Nunez. He was going by the name Ray Garcia. Ozzy took him too.

What is going on? What am I missing? Why would old Nunez kidnap his younger self? Am I going crazy? Maybe you can figure out what's going on.

Also, I teamed up with Marshall on this Earth. It's been good working with him.

I'm going to get hold of my female contact now and question her. I think she knows something.

I'll make this right.

-Z

He adjusted the Earth, date, and time dials on the printing press so the newspaper would print on Buzz's Earth. Then he punched the button to start the transmission.

He didn't know how the hell the contraption worked, but he had a hologram cube that he carried at all times in his jacket no matter what Earth he was on in case something happened to the printing press. It contained detailed instructions on every working aspect of the printing press in case it ever malfunctioned, but it was all mumbo-jumbo to him. He'd probably never need it.

If things ever got really bad, he could get in the space and time capsule and hop to another Earth. Ah, simplicity.

He glanced over at the three newsmen. They were still busy typing away on their typewriters. He reflected on how excited they'd been when he'd given them the story that on all the other Earths, donuts were one of the most delicious breakfast foods and desserts ever devised by man. They had eaten the story up—pun intended—which was a good thing because it was a true story, dammit.

With all the thinking about donuts, he didn't realize his heart rate had started to hike.

Are you thinking about sex again? Germ asked.

Z straightened his shirt collar and coughed. "What? No."

Then why are you getting excited?

"I was…thinking about donuts."

Oh. Right. That fried dead food you so love.

"Damn right."

One of the newsmen glanced up at him and happened to catch his eye. He gave Z a big thumbs up and got back to his typewriter.

Z returned to his office. Then he picked up Alice's phone number and dialed her up on the bulky landline telephone sitting on his desk. He half-expected her not to answer.

On the seventh ring, he was about to hang up when the ringing stopped.

Silence.

Z frowned, trying to decide if he should say something or wait for the person on the other line. Eventually, he said, "Hello? Alice?"

More silence.

"Alice?" he repeated.

"Z. Hi." It was Alice. She clipped her words. Like she was scared.

"Are you okay? Are you safe?" The words came out of his mouth.

"I'm…yes. I'm okay."

Z frowned. "Someone's not holding a gun to your head,

are they?" He meant it as a sort of joke, but he didn't know how it came across.

"No. No gun." She laughed softly. Then he realized she was crying or had been crying.

"Then what's wrong? Are you hurt?"

A choked sob escaped her throat. "I…"

"Alice."

"It was a lie," she blurted. "I lied to you. He…he made me."

Z was gripping the phone so hard his knuckles were white. "Who?"

"I can't tell you over the phone."

Shit. "Where are you?"

"Uh…a friend's house. You can't come here."

"I need to talk to you. Where can we meet? What's close?" Z grabbed a notepad and a pen, preparing to jot down an address.

"Central Park in ten minutes?" she said.

"Okay. Where at? It's a big park—"

The line clicked dead.

Z ran a hand back through his hair. That wasn't good. He considered dialing her back up but instead hung up the phone.

He'd planned to change shirts before meeting her next, but with a deadline of ten minutes, he didn't have enough time for that. He didn't even have time to hail a taxi—it would take too long with the street traffic.

He'd have to run, and maybe he would make it to Central Park in time.

After setting one of his stopwatches for ten minutes, he dashed out of his office, slamming the door closed behind him.

The three newsmen glanced up at him over their type-writers.

"I'll be back," he called. Then he was out the front door and descending the outside stairwell as fast as he could without tripping himself up.

When he reached the sidewalk, he broke into a sprint, picking his way toward Central Park. For the most part, people got out of the way, and when he came to streets he had to cross, he ran across without looking.

If he died, he'd warp back to before crossing with the fore-knowledge of how to dodge the cars.

However, he was skilled at reading the environment and didn't come to any bodily harm along the way.

It was a good thing he was in such good shape. When he reached Central Park, he kept to the main sidewalk path and wound his way through the green grass and trees tucked away at the heart of the city.

Sweat ran off both sides of his forehead in rivulets when he finally spotted her, sitting alone on a park bench.

He drew a deep breath and wiped the sweat off his head with the back of his hand. Then he straightened his jacket and approached the park bench. His stopwatch said he still had twenty seconds left.

"Alice?" he softly said as he approached her from behind. She was still wearing the blue cut-off dress with built-in shoulder pads, her hair resting along the back of her neck. Her purse sat beside her on the bench.

She didn't move.

Fearing the worst, Z rounded the park bench and crouched next to her.

Her eyes flicked up to his, and she sprang up and threw her hands around his neck. "You...you came."

Z held her close against him as she heaved in breaths. When she pulled away from him, he saw the streaky marks of tears down her face. What the hell had her so frightened?

He placed his palms gently on each of her shoulders. "It's okay now. I'm here to protect you. What's wrong? What happened?"

She looked at him like she didn't know where to begin.

Z tore his eyes off her long bare legs and moved them back to her face. "You said someone made you do something?"

Alice swallowed, then bobbed her head in agreement. "I lied to you. None of this is real."

"What isn't real?" Z asked.

"I'm not who you think I am. I'm not Mel's sister."

Z nodded for her to go on. He'd surmised as much.

"I was paid to impersonate this missing woman's sister by a guy."

Z gently shook her shoulders. "Who?"

Her head turned back and forth. "I don't know his name."

"What did he look like?"

"You'll think I'm crazy."

His words were insistent. "I won't."

"He was a crazy-looking old man with wavy hair. He had bushy gray eyebrows and a gray mustache and beard."

"Holy shit," Z breathed. "Nunez. He set you up to meet with me at the *Paper Warriors* office?"

She nodded.

"Why?"

"I-I don't know."

Z removed his hands from her shoulders and wiped a palm over his face. "Have you seen him since?"

"No. But..."

He placed a finger beneath her chin and tilted her face up at his. "But what?"

She swallowed again. Then, with one hand, she brushed back her hair on one side of her face, revealing her ear. A shiny futuristic-looking earpiece rested inside her ear.

Z's eyes narrowed on the device. Here in front of him was a direct link to his enemy.

He sucked in an excited breath. This was the big break he needed. He could send this piece of tech to Buzz in the space and time capsule. Buzz could analyze it and then use it to track Nunez's location down for Z to confront and end his antics.

Lost in his thoughts, he didn't realize the shift in Alice's face.

"I'm sorry," she said flatly, pulling her white handkerchief from her purse.

"What—"

That's all he got out as she pressed the handkerchief against his face. The harsh chemical smell of a knockout solution stung his eyes and entered his nostrils.

Then Z slumped to the grass and blacked out.

CHAPTER TWENTY-NINE

Humans are so difficult to read, Germ said.

Z didn't know where he was. The world was black, and there was a faint rhythmic *hum.* There was also a low growling sound. At intervals, he felt his body jostle up and down.

He realized his eyes were closed, but his eyelids seemed too heavy to lift.

Germ continued, *You should not feel too bad. She fooled me as well. I now understand what you said about human relationships being 'complicated.'*

What the hell was Germ talking about? Since Z couldn't open his eyes, maybe he could open his mouth and respond to Germ. Ask him what had happened.

He tried to open his mouth, but the action felt weird as if someone had sewed shut his lips or gums.

Please do not open your mouth to talk. They will know you are awake.

They? Z thought. *Where the hell was he and what had happened to him?*

Staying as still as he could, he felt feeling creep slowly into parts of his body. It was a trippy sensation as if he'd been numb all over, but now he was recovering his senses. Judging by the pressure against his wrists and ankles, they'd strapped him down to some sort of hospital bed.

The bed jostled up and down again.

He was on a bed, and he was moving. He could still hear that far-off *hum* and a low growl.

He thought back to the last thing he remembered. A park. He was in Central Park. He was talking to a gorgeous woman. Those legs... What was her name?

He searched his mind.

Alice.

That was it. Now the memory of her white handkerchief pressing against his face popped into his mind. A handkerchief laced with a knockout solution.

So that's what Germ had been talking about.

Alice had double-crossed him. Had set him up for Nunez.

I should have known.

Now he was in a room that was moving with people watching him.

More feeling came into his face, and he now knew that he could open his eyes if he wanted to. With the slightest movement, he cracked one eyelid open.

He was in a small rectangular metal room. Two guards armed with combat shotguns were seated at each side in front of him along the walls.

The room jostled up and down again, and he eased his eye closed.

He knew where he was.

Rubber tires were making the humming sound. The low growl belonged to a large truck or armored vehicle.

They were transporting him somewhere.

Shit.

The guards began to talk amongst themselves. "Think the poor bastard will ever wake up?"

"What do you mean?"

"I read the label on the IV. That's enough shit to knock out a pack of elephants for a week."

"Herd, you idiot."

"Huh?"

"It's not a pack of elephants. It's called a herd of elephants."

"Oh—"

"Shut up, you two, okay? And stay alert."

"We can do whatever we want. He's knocked out cold. Will be until we get to the destination and place him in the containment cell."

"We're getting paid good money to stay alert. To do our job. So do it."

I disabled your IV shortly after they inserted the needle into your skin, Germ said. *You starting to feel good now? If so, twitch your right pinkie.*

Z did so. It was a subtle movement; the guards weren't paying attention to him and shouldn't have seen it.

"I know. A shit ton of money. After this job, I can retire. Maybe buy a golf course and play golf the rest of my life."

"You've never played a game of golf in your life."

Also, I have already taken the liberty of cutting your wrist and ankle restraints. Only a thread holding them all together for the sake of appearance. Understand?

Z twitched his pinkie again to signal his understanding.

"Never too late to learn to play golf."

"Wonder what the bastard did and who's paying us to do this to him."

"Don't wonder. It'll get you killed."

You may need to use deadly force soon. You think you are strong enough?

Again, Z twitched his pinkie.

"Hey—"

"What?"

"I think I saw him move."

Z held his breath.

"Impossible. Elephant tranquilizer, remember?"

"Check him out. Maybe there's something wrong with the IV."

"Bullshit. I inserted that needle myself."

"I said check it, goddammit."

"Me, check him out? Why can't you check him out? Afraid he's going to snap your neck or something? He's in a damn coma."

"Rock, paper, scissors you for it?"

"Yeah, what the hell."

With his eyes still closed, Z listened to the sound of two of the guards playing rock, paper, scissors. After three rounds, one of the guards sighed.

"Fuck you. Fine. I'll go check him out."

Z heard one of the guards stand and walk toward him.

Get ready, Germ said. *Three, two, one...*

The guard stopped at the side of Z's bed. Z felt the man's shadow on him. The guard paused, then leaned over him and grabbed the IV stuck into Z's wrist. As he did so, Z's wrist came free from its restraint with a loud *rip.*

Z flicked both eyes open.

Before the guard could utter a sound, Z had both of his arms wrapped around the man's neck. He wrenched sideways, and the man's neck snapped.

"What the—" one of the guards said.

"Oh fuck—" another said as Z stripped the dead guard's shotgun and rotated it around to face the back of the cargo area.

Two shotgun blasts later, two more of the guards were dead, their brains decorating the interior.

That left Z and the most sensible-sounding of the four guards. Plus the dead guard that Z held in front of him as a human shield. He jerked the shotgun's barrel at the last remaining guard, a few feet away from him. The guard also had his shotgun trained on Z—or rather, his human shield.

"Who the hell paid you to do this to me?" Z demanded.

"I'm not going to tell you shit—"

Z pulled the trigger, blowing out part of the guard's leg. With a cry, the guard had also fired his shotgun, tearing off the dead guard's arm. Z fired again, decimating the man's wrist. His shotgun clattered to the floor.

Seizing the opportunity, Z let his human shield drop to the side and moved to the wounded, last remaining guard, kicking the fallen shotgun to the side. Moving in quickly, he jabbed the barrel under the man's jaw. Flesh sizzled around the muzzle.

"I'm not messing around," Z said.

"I don't know. I don't know! It was an anonymous employer. Offering too good of a payday to turn down."

"You should have turned it down, I guess."

The guard nodded, cradling his wounded wrist and trying not to put any weight on his leg.

"Where were you taking me?"

"Some cold storage facility in Maine. We were to hook you up to food and saline IV lines and lock you up so you couldn't get away. Fucked up if you ask me."

"I didn't ask you."

The guard shut up.

"You pick me up from Central Park?"

"Yes."

"Was there a woman with me when you scooped me up?"

"No. You were slumped over in the grass like you were drunk and sleeping it off. There was a white handkerchief over your face. Soaked in a knockout solution. We carried you out to the vehicle without causing a scene."

Z thought it all over.

You going to kill him now? Germ asked.

"He's defenseless."

"Huh?" the wounded guard said.

Z chuckled, removing his shotgun muzzle from under the man's jaw and moving back a step. "Oh, just talking to Germ."

"Germ? What's that?"

Me! Germ peeked out from under the hospital bed and waved a tiny tentacle at the guard.

The guard's eyes shot wide. "What the hell is that?"

Z said matter-of-factly, "That's Germ. Ah, crap."

The guard went for his sidearm, his eyes terrified at the sight of Germ.

Z pulled the trigger one last time, and the guard sat still on the floor. "Germ, we're going to have to work on your stage presence. They always seem to want to kill you."

Germ hopped onto his shoulder. *I am so misunderstood.*

"Yeah, yeah." He surveyed the carnage in the back of the armored transport vehicle. The tires were still humming, carrying him down the road so the driver must either not have heard the commotion or had strict orders to keep driving to the destination regardless of what happened back there.

On one side of the area was a bulging duffel bag. He unzipped it and found it brimming with stacks of hundred-dollar bills. "Yahtzee," he said as he stuffed some of the guards' payment inside his jacket. That might come in handy down the line. You never knew when you might need to bribe someone.

He drew a deep breath.

Now he needed a way out of the armored vehicle. The back end of the interior had a lock on it so that was going to be it. He edged up to it and prepared to throw the lock. Before he did, he glanced at Germ.

"How did the guards not find you when they abducted me from the park?"

I hid.

"No shit, Sherlock. Where at?"

Germ fidgeted. *I hid in one of your orifices when the woman named Alice knocked you out.*

"Which orifice?" Z made a face. "Wait, I don't want to know."

He turned his attention back to the vehicle's back door and threw the lock. Then he shoved open the door.

He held up a hand to block out the sun. It was mid-afternoon, and the highway flew by below them as Z studied the ground outside. It was all open road and fields to either side. There were no other cars in sight. "How fast do you think we're going?"

I would estimate sixty-one-point-five miles per hour, Germ said.

"Okay, wise ass."

They were going much too fast for him to expect not to get hurt from hopping out the back. Also, the vehicle was raised pretty high, so that was another variable to consider if he jumped. Still, he was confident he could pull it off. He might have to die a few times to get it right.

He didn't want to waste any more time. He needed to get back to the *Paper Warriors* office and plan his next move. First on the list was to contact Buzz. Then he was going to track down Alice and get some actual truth from her.

So? Are you going to jump or are you scared? Germ said.

"Shaddup."

Before he jumped, he gathered up a couple of the dead guards' pistols and secured them in his waistband under his jacket. Then he peered out.

"Geronimo, motherfucker."

He died.

CHAPTER THIRTY

(Five Seconds Earlier)

He was back in the armored vehicle. He jumped.

This time he managed to tuck his shoulder and roll when he struck the road, but the angle was slightly off, and his neck snapped under his weight.

He died.

(Five Seconds Earlier)

He was back in the armored vehicle. He jumped.

He fell forward too fast this time, tripping on his ankle, and collapsing in a rolling sprawl when he impacted with the ground. With a groan, he realized he was on the side of the road.

He had survived the fall, but had sprained his ankle. That wasn't good. How was he going to get around with an injured leg?

Reaching into his jacket, he raised a pistol to his head and pulled the trigger.

He died.

(Fifteen Seconds Earlier)

He was back in the armored vehicle.

Sweep the legs, Germ said.

"This isn't easy, you know."

It would be if I got on your back and fluffed myself out like a parachute behind you.

Z stared at the little octopus. "You can do that?"

Germ looked back at him with cute beady eyes. *Sure.* He climbed onto Z's back, and Z jumped out of the moving vehicle.

He fell flat on his face.

He died.

(Five Seconds Earlier)

He was back in the armored vehicle.

"Where was the goddamned parachute?"

I was joshing you. I am so little, and you are so big. How do you expect me to keep all two hundred pounds of you up in the air?

"You cheeky little bastard."

He shook his head. Then he jumped.

Using every bit of knowledge and experience gained from his prior jumps, he used a diagonal trajectory off to the side of the road. The ground was a little softer, not that it would matter much—the vehicle was roaring forward at over sixty miles per hour.

He managed to throw himself into a successful roll upon connecting with the ground, and then his body tumbled sideways a few times like a rolling barrel of muscle and bone.

The stacks of money inside his jacket provided some padding. When he stopped a few yards away, he held his breath.

He picked himself up and checked himself. His ankle had been slightly irritated in the fall, but he hadn't sprained it. He could walk on it. Cuts and scrapes littered his face, arms, and knees, but they were all superficial.

He patted the dust off himself. Behind him, the armored transport vehicle continued down the road until it became a speck on the horizon.

Z pumped his fist. He'd done it.

"Now, time to hitch a ride back to civilization."

About ten minutes later, as he walked on the graveled shoulder, Z spotted a candy apple red Corvette speeding his way. This was the nineteen-eighties. People were more likely to give you a ride. He hoped this was his. He held up his thumb.

When the sports car slowed, he peered through its windshield at the driver, a stunning blonde wearing movie star sunglasses. This was his lucky day. His heart began to beat harder.

The Corvette stopped beside him. Both of the car's windows were down, and the woman lowered her sunglasses far enough to appraise him over their rims.

Z grinned. "Am I glad to see you." He noticed then that he still had a piece of hospital bed restraint dangling from his wrist.

She flicked her gaze from his wrist up to his facial scar and crazy hair. "You just escape a prison bus or something?"

"Um, no."

The woman pushed her sunglasses back up. "See ya, psycho." Then she floored it, spitting pea gravel in Z's face.

Germ peeked out from Z's pocket and glanced up at Z's disheveled appearance. *You do sort of look like a serial killer.*

Z drew one of his pistols and pulled the trigger.

He died.

(Twenty Seconds Earlier)

Standing on the shoulder of the road, he saw the Corvette coming.

This time he tore off the wrist restraint and combed his hair back with his hand. He couldn't do anything about the tears in his jacket and pants or the scrapes on his face, though. He'd have to play up the bravado.

His heart started to race as she slowed. When she stopped, she looked as stunning as the first time, maybe even more so.

She lowered her sunglasses and smiled at him. She even had a movie star smile. "Where ya headed, stranger?"

He smiled back at her and leaned forward onto the open passenger window. "The Big Apple, babe."

She continued smiling for a moment. "Ooh, a facial scar. Are you a bad boy?"

He shrugged. "Maybe."

Then her nose twitched, and her demeanor completely changed. "Ew, you stink. Get lost, loser."

Then she floored it, spitting pea gravel in Z's face.

That was awfully rude, Germ said.

Z drew one of his pistols and pulled the trigger.

He died.

. . .

(Twenty Seconds Earlier)

Standing on the shoulder of the road, he saw the Corvette coming.

He was going to try this one last time…

This time when she stopped, he kept his distance from the car and returned her smile.

"Where ya headed, stranger?"

He scratched behind his ear. "Nowhere, at the moment. My car ran off the road a few miles down."

Worry etched her beautiful face. "Need a ride?"

Z sighed. "That would be great. Although I gotta apologize in advance for my sweat." He chuckled. "It's hot out today."

She nodded. Then her smile faltered as her gaze dropped down his front.

"Something wrong?" He stepped up to the passenger window.

She bit her lip. "Either that's a roll of quarters in your pocket, or you must be really happy to see me."

Z glanced down at his pants. There was a bulge where Germ had bunched up in his pocket.

"That's not—I can explain."

"Sorry. I better get going," the woman said. She pushed up her sunglasses and drove off.

Germ peeked out from his pocket. *Perhaps she is out of your league?*

Z grunted.

Like you said, human relationships are hard. At least she did not peel out like the last two times.

He shoved his hands in his pockets. "You're right. Love is hard." He started walking down the road.

A couple of minutes had passed when the next car passed. It didn't slow.

Later, two pickup trucks and a van passed. None stopped. One of their drivers flipped him off.

"Shit," Z muttered. "You know you have it bad when it's easier to escape a moving armored transport vehicle under the watch of four guards than it is to catch a ride."

Truth, Germ said.

He walked onward, moving incrementally closer to New York as he did so. "You know, sometimes I feel like the universe is conspiring against me. For what crime?"

Germ peeked out. *Didn't you say you tried to start a world war on that one Earth?*

Z scoffed. "I was in a bad place, okay? Like you're one to judge. You're a sentient bioweapon—hey, I think that car is stopping."

Behind him, a vehicle was slowing as it approached him. When he was able to see it better, he grimaced. It was a piece of shit jalopy with a rusted paint job.

"Beggars can't be choosers," he muttered.

It rolled to a stop beside him.

A weaselly man with beard stubble and shifty eyes looked him up and down. "Hey, neighbor."

The smell of weed rolled out from the car's open windows.

Z was tired. Instead of talking to the man, he drew one of his pistols and waved it at the car.

"I'm going to need this vehicle. You...might not see it again."

The man's eyes bulged. "Y-you can't do this. You can't just r-rob me of my car."

Z reached into his jacket, pulled out some stacks of money, and handed them through the car window. "Here's five thousand dollars."

The driver threw open the car and sprinted down the highway with the money. "It's yours!"

Z stared at the car for a moment. It was small, and he wondered how he was going to fit in it. It had two spare tires in use, a cracked rear windshield, and part of the steering wheel was simply gone.

He shook his head and approached the open driver's side door. He had to duck his head to climb inside. When he put the car in gear, it backfired and lurched forward.

It was far from a smooth ride, but it was better than nothing.

CHAPTER THIRTY-ONE

The sun was setting when he drove into the city. What had been Alice's part in this mess? Yes, she'd been working a job—him. Still, it hadn't been to simply hand him over to those guards to lock him up at an offsite facility. She must've had another objective. So what was her angle?

He had a feeling that he needed to find out fast before she skipped town for the next job.

Traffic was as bad as he'd expected it to be, and it was getting dark by the time he pulled up outside the Korean restaurant below the *Paper Warriors* news office.

When he got out of the car, several bystanders gave him, and his car, odd looks.

Yeah, yeah. He stank like repeatedly dried sweat, he'd torn his clothing, and scrapes covered his face. He could clean up once he got upstairs and put on a fresh change of clothes. Once he'd sent word to Buzz about what had happened, that was.

Although his eyes traveled up the outside stairwell leading

to the *Paper Warriors* office, his legs carried him toward the Korean restaurant.

Your office is that way, Germ said.

His stomach growled. He realized he hadn't eaten since lunch with Marshall. A lot had happened between then and now. "Yeah, but first, food."

A line of people waited outside the restaurant, but Z edged his way past them and sidled up to the bar. There was one seat available, and he took it.

"To drink?" the bartender said.

"A beer. Any beer."

The bartender nodded and turned away.

Z placed his elbows up on the bar top and cradled his face in his palms.

What a day.

He sat that way for a time with his eyes closed. While he waited, he mentally reviewed the events of the day. The warehouse mission. Saving the life of the man changing his tire. Visiting Mel's house. Showing the boy Jimmy how to stand up in a fight against bullies. Getting betrayed and breaking out of the armored transport vehicle.

He was vaguely aware of Germ poking him in the leg.

At the moment, Z was too tired to care.

Z, wake up, Germ said.

"What? Is it beer time?" Z mumbled, opening his eyes and expecting to see his beer sitting in front of him or maybe the bartender trying to get his attention over the bar.

What he saw was neither.

What he saw was an older man in a tuxedo and black sunglasses standing across the bar in front of him.

"No beer for you," the tuxedoed man rasped.

Before Z could push away from the bar, the robot man had

already grabbed him by the jacket collar and jerked him face-first over the bar.

Z tried to resist, but the robot was damn strong. It hauled him up in front of its sunglasses-covered face. "You shouldn't be here."

Luckily, being a robot, its breath didn't smell bad.

"I shouldn't be here?" Z choked out. "You shouldn't be here."

"You are a wildcard. Were supposed to be out of the picture. Computing new course of action."

Z chopped his hands up and knocked the robot's wide gangly hands off his jacket collar. "Compute away, asshole."

From behind Z, several people gasped. A woman screamed.

As the robot recovered, Z threw a fist across its jaw, staggering it back a step. He tried picking himself up off the bar top, but then the tuxedoed robot gripped him by the scruff of his jacket and shoved him down along the length of the bar like a human bar rag. With arms held out in front of him to guard his head, Z knocked drinks to the side like a bowling ball striking pins.

Glasses crashed to the floor. People shouted. Z rode the slick bar top to the end and toppled to the floor. He picked himself up and wiped alcohol off his face.

He licked his lips. "Hey, rum—"

He ducked as the robot swung at him. He caught the robot's next swing and socked him across the jaw again. The robot stumbled back a step.

Maybe they weren't so indestructible. Their heads certainly seemed somewhat vulnerable. He recalled from his previous adventures how shooting it in the head seemed to slow it down as well.

All around Z, people were shouting and running around. Z's focus wasn't on them, though. It was on his opponent. He saw a glass water pitcher in his peripheral vision. He grabbed it and, as the robot lunged at him, smashed it over its head. Glass exploded outward, and water drenched the robot's tuxedo coat.

The robot swiped out at Z with its hands, but he backstepped, bumping into an attractive redhead.

"Hello, lovely," he said.

She smacked him hard across the cheek and ran out of the room.

"Ow—" Z complained, then knifed over as the robot swung a doubled-up fist into his gut. "Ow!" He fell to his hands and knees.

He was vaguely aware that his eyes stung. Pausing to think, he smelled smoke. From the kitchen?

Above him, the robot lifted one polished black loafer to stomp down on Z's back. Z rolled out of the way, his shoulder *thudding* against a table, which wobbled. He quickly scooted out from under it as the robot slammed both fists down on the wood, snapping the sturdy tabletop as if it was particleboard.

It didn't make sense to Z why the robot was here. If he was supposed to be out of the picture, what was its objective?

He dodged another swipe of the robot's hands that would have taken off his face. "Why are you here? What's your mission?"

The robot sent a quick kick up into Z's chest that sent him sprawling backward on top of a booth table. As he picked himself up off the surface, he saw the fire.

The restaurant's entire back wall was aflame. That's where the smoke was coming from.

"You're burning the restaurant down?" Z said. Aside from this being his favorite restaurant in the city, his office was above the restaurant.

The robot fell forward with a punch. Z dodged it, and the fist crashed through the wall, sending up a cloud of plaster.

"You bastard! Why?" Z asked. He circled the robot and kicked it behind the knee. It barely fazed the tuxedo-clad form. As the robot turned to face him, Z bumped up against a table set for eight and started launching partially empty glasses at the robot's face. It used its wide hands to swat them aside, but some of the glasses got through and crashed against its head.

"No one burns down my office!"

He noticed a bulging glass fishbowl on a nearby table. He picked it up and threw it at the robot. It struck its head, and the robot stumbled sideways as it tried to recover.

Z turned and started toward the restaurant's back stairs that led up to the newspaper office. The spreading fire was about to reach it. The situation was out of hand.

Maybe if he warped back a full three minutes, he could stop it. But how had the robot lit the fires? There had been no smoke when he'd gotten there. And he had been fighting the robot ever since they'd spotted each other.

Did it have an accomplice?

"We meet again." The voice was raspy and came from behind him.

Z spun and found himself face-to-face with the tuxedoed robot. Except now the robot's face was distorted as if someone had shot it several times. Gunfire had shredded its tuxedo.

Z did a doubletake and glanced back at the tuxedoed robot

picking itself up from the floor. When he turned again, there was still a robot standing before him.

There are two of them! Germ said.

"Fuck," Z gasped. Before he could get out of the way, the robot standing before him threw a right hook across his jaw.

Z slumped to the floor.

He was vaguely aware of a tiny voice in his head.

Get up! Get up!

Z blinked.

He was looking at the floor of the Korean restaurant. Tables lay overturned. Food and broken plates and glass shards lay everywhere.

An inferno raged, about to engulf him.

Beside him on the floor, Germ coughed and repeatedly blinked his tiny eyes.

"I'm up. I'm up." Z pushed himself up. His body ached like a son of a bitch. "How long was I out for?"

A couple of minutes.

Shit. Not enough time to warp back to stop the fire.

He was trying to figure out what to do when he heard a little girl crying out amid the smoke choking the restaurant's interior.

"Help! Help me. I'm—" she coughed, "—trapped."

The image of his daughter flashed through his mind. "I've got to help that girl," Z muttered as he tried to get his bearings. Heat burned his skin, and the smoke assaulted his eyes.

Raising his sweaty muscle shirt over his mouth as a makeshift mask, Z stumbled around the debris, looking for the trapped girl.

He found her off to the side of the front doors, trapped under a couple of overhead beams that had fallen. "I'm here. I'm here."

He bent and grabbed one of the beams. It was hot to the touch, and it started to burn his skin. He managed to lift it and push it to the side. He took the girl's hand, pulled her out, and carried her out of the restaurant.

"You're going to be fine," he said as he crossed the threshold and fresh air hit his sooty face.

Then the restaurant gave an angry groan, and the building caved in behind him. The force of the draft billowing out through the front door shoved him forward to his knees, but he managed to hold on to the little girl.

A woman rushed up to him, crying, and took the girl from his arms.

Behind him, the building creaked and shifted.

It was now a burning rubble pile.

There was no more Korean restaurant.

No more *Paper Warriors* news office.

Gone was his only way off this Earth—the space and time capsule. As well as his means of communicating off-world— the intergalactic printing press.

He dropped his gaze and cursed.

CHAPTER THIRTY-TWO

When Z was a boy, he'd lost his dog. A car on the street outside his house had hit it. His parents had said that it wasn't his fault, but he'd known that was bullshit.

If he'd only called his dog back away from the road instead of letting it run free and have fun that day...

Staring at the smoking remains of the Korean barbecue place and the *Paper Warriors* news office on the second floor, he kind of felt the same way he did back then. He could've been more careful. Buzz had warned him, had said that Nunez was probably keeping tabs on him.

Looking back, it only made sense that Nunez would eventually send his robot goons to destroy the intergalactic printing press that Z and the Buzzes had taken control of and used for their purposes. To Nunez, it must've been like a slap in the face, Z using the news offices as his home base, offices that Nunez had built on the parallel Earths so he could use them. Nunez was only returning the slap.

It had been a long time coming.

Now, circumstances had trapped Z on this Earth without a means of communicating with Buzz or getting off this planet.

Wait, the space and time capsule...

He cursed, suddenly realizing what was going on here. Sure, he could buy the fact that Nunez would torch the printing press. But the space and time capsule? He wouldn't do that.

The man was a genius who'd found a way to hop Earths, but he still couldn't travel back in time as Z could. Nunez wouldn't have destroyed the space and time capsule—he would've taken it for himself.

He'd sent not one but two superhuman robots to do the job: steal the space and time capsule and torch the place to cover their tracks and trap Z here. Had that been their plan all along? Had they succeeded in stealing the space and time capsule?

The only way to find out would be to climb through the wreckage and look for its scorched remains himself.

Z moved toward the still-smoldering building, but a beefy fireman caught his arm. "Sir, you can't go back in. It's still too hot. And the smoke. Whole thing could come toppling down at any moment."

The second story was still standing, for the most part, at least the section where his office was. The Korean barbeque marquee was still perched outside his blackened office window, although not lit up.

At first, Z thought to fight past the fireman, but then an even bigger fireman walked up and looked down his nose at Z. It wasn't worth hurting the good guys to check on the space and time capsule. He could do that later when things had calmed and cooled down.

He wasn't going anywhere.

He was stuck in this godforsaken donut-less shithole of an Earth.

It wouldn't be due to do something stupid he'd regret. He remembered Buzz's advice concerning breathing exercises and drew a few deep breaths.

Turning, he saw the three *Paper Warriors* newsmen sitting on the sidewalk, their chins tucked over their upraised knees that they were gripping against their chests.

You should talk to them, Germ said.

"Why? I have shit to plan."

By the looks on their faces, they are grieving, the same as you.

Z took a closer look at the newsmen. All three were either sobbing or had tear streaks on their cheeks. "So?"

Are not all humans equal? Are they not all supposed to care for each other? Morals?

Z shook his head. "Believe me. They didn't lose as much as I did in that fire."

How do you know? You have not talked to them.

"Why the hell do you want me to talk to them?"

Because...it is the right thing to do. Is it not?

Z chuckled, shrugging off his jadedness. "For a germy blob, you're wise beyond your years."

Why thank you. It should not come as much of a surprise, though, considering with my accelerated genetic evolution, I am the equivalent of millions of years old.

Z scratched behind his ear. "So, what? You're like a dinosaur?"

I think we are both like dinosaurs. Too old for this world that wants to move on without us.

Shit. This was getting too philosophical. "Fine. Fine. I'll

talk to the scrawny schmucks. And I'll try to be less... dinosaur-like."

When Z trudged over to them, the three newsmen's eyes lit up. They wiped their tears away.

"Z," the tallest one said. "Thank the nature goddess that you made it out alive."

The newsmen hopped up and embraced Z, who awkwardly stood there with limp arms as they crushed in on him.

It looks like you do have friends, Germ said.

When it seemed like the newsmen weren't going to let go of him, Z cleared his throat and lifted his arms to separate them from him. "All right. All right. I'm glad you guys made it out safely too."

The middle newsman sighed. "It's...almost too big a tragedy to fathom."

"What?" Z asked.

"That someone started the fire on purpose. It's what people are saying. That someone burned down the office."

The shortest newsman threw his arms up. "Why? It's so senseless. Someone could have died."

"Maybe one of us has an enemy," Z offered, feeling a little guilty.

The tallest newsman crossed his arms. "We wouldn't hurt a fly."

Z smirked. That was the truth of it. "At least you guys made it out."

The middle newsman cast a forlorn look down at the sidewalk. "Our soon-to-be award-winning newspaper article didn't."

"Huh? Oh. The Great Donut Conspiracy article you guys were working on?"

They all nodded.

"You didn't save your progress to the cloud?" Z asked.

The newsmen glanced up at the sky. "Huh?" the shortest one said. "How is a cloud going to help us?"

Z smacked his head. "Right. How could I have forgotten? It's the nineteen-eighties."

The tallest newsman suddenly looked about to cry. "We worked so hard on it. Now all our work is gone. Reduced to so much ash on the wind..."

The middle newsman wiped his eyes on his shirt sleeve. "Even our typewriters are toast."

"It's not so bad," Z said. Typewriters were replaceable. Intergalactic printing presses and space and time capsules... not so much. "You can always buy new typewriters and start fresh."

The shortest newsman jumped in. "They were Royal Custom IVs. You know how much those cost? How are we ever going to be able to afford that and start over?"

Z shrugged.

You could help them, Germ said.

Z chewed over the idea for a few moments. Then he reached inside his tattered jacket and pulled out a stack of hundred-dollar bills from the armored transport vehicle duffle bag. "Here's a couple of thousand bucks. It'll cover a few typewriters."

At first, he thought maybe they hadn't heard him. Then he saw their bulging eyes and wide-open mouths.

The tallest one was the first to speak. "With that, we could rent a whole new building."

The middle one said, "Heck, we could probably put a down payment on a new building."

The shortest one wiped back a fresh tear. "Well, boys,

looks like all is not lost." He grinned. "But it's going to take some time to find a new place. What do we do in the meantime? We'll go crazy if we don't find something to do with our hands. Typewriting is addicting. My hands need to move."

"Me too!" the tallest and middle newsmen said.

They all turned to Z to see if he had a suggestion.

Shit, he thought. *Who do they think I am? Their sensei or something?*

"I'll…let me think on it. I'm sure I can find something for you to do. First, I need some alone time."

"Understandable," one of them said.

Z scratched the beard stubble on his chin. He needed to shave, but oh wait, he didn't have a newspaper office bathroom to shave in anymore. "Where will you be? I'll find you when I have a job for you."

The three newsmen glanced from Z to the money stack in their hands. "That's a no-brainer," the shortest one finally said. "We're going to the nearest McDonald's to celebrate the turning of a new page in our lives. Can you even imagine all the Big Macs this can buy?"

"I can't." Z lowered his voice. "Maybe not flaunt all that cash for everyone to see?"

The newsmen narrowed their eyes at him. "Why? Is it dirty?"

"So no one gets the idea to rob you." Z didn't know how some people could be so naïve. Give natural selection another century or two and these guys' offspring would be gone.

"Oh, good idea." The newsmen divided the cash and stuffed it into their pockets.

They started to walk away, a pep in their step when the tallest newsman turned back around. "Feel free to join us for a Big Mac if you want."

Z nodded. While a greasy double-stacked burger sounded great, he had other business to attend to.

Namely, tracking down the person who had betrayed him—Alice Phoenix.

Or whatever the hell her name was.

CHAPTER THIRTY-THREE

He hung low for a while as the evening wore on. NYC was a big city, and he had only one clue about how to get hold of her—the phone number in his pocket.

He could've called it. He didn't want to spook her if she was still in town. Instead, his play was to wait until Marshall's night shift started, call him, and have Marshall trace the call. Alice had said she was staying at a friend's place. Maybe that was true and maybe not. Wherever she'd been, a police trace would be able to find it for him.

Hopefully.

Knowing that it was going to be a long night, he found a quiet alley and threw himself down on the ground, wedging himself between the brick wall and a dumpster positioned at a slight angle away from the wall. Sitting up against the dumpster and the wall, he used a small trash bag as a makeshift pillow and closed his eyes.

"Wake me around ten p.m., will ya?"

But how will I know the time? Germ asked.

"Go peek into a window or something. Be creative."

Okay. Germ paused. *Maybe you should set the time on your stopwatches so you know the time.*

Z groaned. "What would be the use? I'd be constantly changing the time every time I hopped to a new Earth. It's hard to keep track of time when you go to parallel Earths—some of which are twenty or even forty years behind the time you're used to." He yawned. "Now shut up. I need sleep."

Z's eyes shot open when he felt a pinch on his arm.

Shhh! Germ said as Z prepared some witty quip.

Without moving, Z scanned the alley around him. Wedged behind the dumpster like he was, with some trash bags out front, he was well-hidden from view. Also, a streetlamp was farther behind him in the alley, and it cast him in the dumpster's shadow.

There, five yards in front of him, a man in a black trench coat paused to draw a deep breath. He couldn't see Z.

That man walked into the alley a few minutes ago. He might be a threat. Be ready.

Z was ready. The knife he hid in his boot was already in his hand. The trench coat man yawned and turned to face the shadows back behind the dumpster.

"Oh, I know you're there..." the man hummed out in a drunken melody as he stared glassy-eyed at the alley's brick wall. "...when I'm not around..."

The man yawned again and reached inside his trench coat.

Could be going for a weapon, Germ cautioned.

Z didn't say a word. He tensed, ready to spring out to meet the man if he needed to.

The man continued with his drunken melody. "You're always gone...in another man's hands..."

Get ready, Germ said.

A soft zipping sound ripped through the night.

Suddenly, Z eased up in his position in the shadows. The man wasn't reaching for a weapon. He was reaching for...

"In another man's...hands..." the man slurred as he began to urinate against the brick wall with a sigh.

Germ tensed on Z's shoulder. *Gross!*

At least he's not pissing on me, Z thought.

The trench-coated man twisted his torso, spraying a zigzag line along the brick wall and out into the shadows.

And across Z's unseen face.

"Fuck," Z grunted, simultaneously raising a hand to block the stream and rising to his feet.

The trench-coated man cried, "Holy shit, it's a trash monster!" and spun and ran off.

Z flicked his wrist, his fingers dripping hot urine. "You've got to be kidding me..." For a moment, he considered killing himself so he could warp back to before it had happened.

He sure gave you a mouthful, did he not? Germ said with a chuckle.

"That's not funny." Z spat, trying to rid his mouth of the awful taste that had trickled inside.

It is a bit funny.

"You're not the one who got pissed on."

I know. What a wake-up call.

Maybe it was the anger and frustration building from the *Paper Warriors* office burning down the issue of the printing press and the space and time capsule. But he was furious.

Germ saw it too. *Are you going to kill that man?*

That wasn't the worst idea he'd ever had.

So it's okay to kill someone if they urinate on you?

"What? No. It's..." He drew a deep breath. "I didn't mean it literally." Although part of him did. "Look, I probably deserved that, okay. Besides, it's not the first time someone's pissed on me. Unfortunately. Part of the job, I guess."

He wiped his face on his burnt and torn muscle shirt. He'd never been able to shower and put on a new shirt because of the fire. Oh well, he was getting used to the smell. He glanced up at the rectangle of night sky above the alleyway. "Is it time to wake up?"

Germ nodded. *That man entered the alley when I was about to wake you.*

"Good. Marshall is on duty by now. Time to find a damn payphone."

It was the eighties, and he was in New York—there were payphones everywhere scattered throughout the streets. He stepped up to the first one he came across, dug inside his jacket pocket for some quarters, and inserted a few into the slot. It seemed so archaic, as if he was offering some metal relics to a god for a sacrifice.

He went through the ritual of speaking to the operator, and he gave her the name of Marshall's precinct.

"Is this an emergency?" she said. "Perhaps you meant to dial 9-1-1?"

"No. I need to speak with Officer Marshall Peet. It's important, but not an emergency."

"Who is calling?"

"Huh? Oh...an informant," he lied.

"One moment, please," she said.

Z whistled while he waited. Germ whistled too, which was annoying since it was directly in Z's mind.

Finally, Marshall came on the line, his voice light and friendly enough. "Hello?"

"Marshall, it's me. Z."

There was a long pause. "Oh, great. To what do I owe the pleasure?" Marshall's voice dripped with disdain.

"Umm…yeah. Hey, I was calling to—"

"To what? Give me more parenting advice?"

"No—"

"Or to see if I'll give you the keys to my car again?"

"No, really, I—"

"You have some nerve calling me at work. Do you know how much crap I got from the boys when I pulled up tonight, and they saw that giant dent in my roof? I mean, how the hell do you explain a dent that big? A piano fell on it?" Marshall scoffed.

As frustrating as it was to be on the other end of his father's sarcasm—and after getting pissed on—he couldn't help but smirk at this new level of toughness Marshall had developed. He'd need it if he were to stay a cop. That much was for sure.

"This isn't about any of that, you asshole," Z said. "It's about the missing woman. Remember, Mel Phoenix?" It wasn't exactly a lie. Z strongly doubted that Alice was Mel's sister, but she was still messed up in it. Alice was working with Nunez, which made tracking down Alice killing two birds with one stone.

Marshall's voice stiffened. "Oh. Yeah, I remember her. You promised you'd see her case through to the end."

Z leaned up against the side of the phone booth on one

elbow. "I'm getting closer. But I need you to trace a phone number down for me. Can you do that?"

There was another pause. "That's all? Trace a phone number?"

"Yup. Promise." He waited. "Hello? Marshall? You still there?"

"Yeah, I'm here."

"Then what are you waiting for?" Z asked.

"I'm waiting for a goddamned 'please.'"

Germ snickered. Z flashed the tiny black octopus a dirty look. "Please, Marshall?" he said into the phone.

"That's Officer Peet."

For crying out loud. "Yes, please, Officer Peet?"

Z could imagine Marshall grinning in triumph on the other line.

"Okay, gimme the number, and I'll pass it on—"

"Bullshit. I need an address, and I need it now. ASAP. Or is that not an acronym on this shithole Earth yet?"

Marshall made a *clucking* sound with his tongue. "I'm not sure if you're on meds or out of your mind, but..." His voice grew softer. "If this is to help find that missing woman, I can rush the trace through. Gonna take an hour or two. Have to call up the phone company and wake them up. Then I'm going to have to get it signed off on and approved with my boss and..."

Z was no longer listening to the voice on the phone. His ear had perked at a woman's scream.

It sounded close.

CHAPTER THIRTY-FOUR

"Do what you got to do," Z said to Marshall. He gripped the phone in one hand as his eyes scanned the darkness of the alley. The scream had come from somewhere out there. He just wasn't sure where.

All he knew was that he was close.

Z put his mouth to the receiver. "Someone's in trouble. I'll call back soon." He hung up the phone and took off out of the phone booth.

"You hear where it came from?" Z asked. Germ had better eyesight and hearing than he did.

Sounded like it was one-point-two-five blocks away.

"Directions?" He jogged down the alley toward the street.

Turn left.

As Z was exiting the alley and entering the sidewalk, another scream cut through the night. It was closer.

The sidewalk was empty. For a city that never slept, this part of it sure did. Z whipped his head from side to side. "Which way?"

Keep going straight. Turn left again into the next alley.

Z did as instructed, his legs wildly pumping as he ran. If there was one thing in this world he hated, it was when someone hurt the weak. Or worse.

He came to the next alley opening and shot into it.

This alley wasn't as well-lit as the one he had previously been in, but it was light enough for him not to trip over the trash and debris littering it. He couldn't see them, but rats the size of hamburgers trundled about with harsh *squeaks*.

"Where—" Z started. Then he saw them.

Ten yards ahead, partially masked by the shadows, a woman fought to free herself from the assailant behind her with his arms wrapped around her. Z knew her assailant.

It was the drunk trench-coated man.

"…I know where you go at night…" he hum-sang in a slurring melody. When he saw Z approaching, his eyes and grip on the woman grew feral.

Z pulled up short to assess the situation. "Oh, I know where you're going, all right."

The trench-coated man snarled. "Get out of here, punk." His posture was too rigid for him to be too drunk to fight—he could be a dangerous foe if pressed.

Z drew a deep breath and made eye contact with the frightened woman who had stopped resisting. She was tall and angular and was wearing a purple dress. She had probably come from a bar.

"Are you okay?" Z asked calmly. "Has he hurt you?"

"I don't even know this freak! He grabbed me. Dragged me into the alley—"

"Shut your mouth!" the trench-coated man snapped. The assailant slapped her, and the woman whimpered.

Z made a fist. "Does he have a weapon?" he asked the woman.

Her assailant clapped his hand over her mouth. "Yeah, you punk. I got a gun. A big one."

Z sized him up. "I don't see one."

"It's under my coat, you asshole. Now get lost, and we all get to live happily ever after."

He needed to end this as soon as possible, Z knew. This woman was suffering and all because she was in the wrong place at the wrong time. That's often how bad things happened. Of course, the trench-coated man had brought this on himself.

Z took a step forward in the dimly lit alley. "I'm giving you one chance to let her go. One." He grounded the fisted knuckles of one hand into his palm. "Then I'm going to kick your ass so hard you're not going to be able to sit without remembering my scarred face."

The trench-coated man never took his eyes off Z. "Oh yeah? Go ahead and try."

Z sprang forward, cringing when he heard the bang of a handgun going off. A slight muzzle flash peeked out from a newly formed hole in the trench coat, and the woman gasped and collapsed forward.

Z was going to have to die and warp back now.

Setting his teeth together, Z said, "You're going to pay for that." As he closed in on the trench-coated man, he pulled up and raised a fist. The handgun fired again, and Z felt a searing pain in his chest. It staggered him, but he regained his footing and prepared to throw his punch. Two more gunshots sounded, and Z fell sideways back against the alley's brick wall.

Z gasped for breath. When he placed a hand to his chest,

warm blood dribbled over his fingers.

"Look what you made me do. Look what you made me do." The trench-coated man crouched over the woman he'd shot, his handgun lowered at his side. "I didn't mean to. I…I wanted us to…to be happy together."

Z wheezed as he sucked in a pained breath. It took all the concentration he could muster to push himself back up to a standing position. He was going to die and had to die—he knew that—but there was something he had to do first.

The trench-coated man was holding the woman's lifeless body in his arms now, tears starting to form in his glazed eyes. His handgun was resting on the dirty alley floor beside him. He left it there. He staggered forward, and a rat scurried off, but the drunk man didn't notice him approaching.

"Hey." Z swayed from the blood loss.

The trench-coated man tilted his head up and around to look at him. Z was already kicking out with his boot. It connected with the man's cheekbone.

Judging by the sound of the strike, the man was dead.

Smirking, Z collapsed to his knees and glanced down at his bloody chest. He'd lost a lot of blood, and he probably had a collapsed lung. How he was still conscious was a mystery. Yep, he'd be dying shortly.

He slumped forward onto his chest.

He died.

(Two Minutes Earlier)

Z now knew what he was up against as he ran along the empty sidewalk. When he reached the alley with the man and the woman in it, he slowed his pace to a brisk walk and started feigning a slight drunken limp as he headed toward them.

"Who, who are you?" the trench-coated man called to the darkness.

"Just a man looking for some hooch and cigarettes." Z walked closer. "Got any?" He tried to make his voice sound friendly enough, although what he had in store for the woman-battering man was anything but friendly.

"No. No, I don't. Now get lost."

Z bobbed his head as he continued making his way toward him. "I won't bother you. Just looking for some hooch. And cigarettes."

What is this hooch you speak of? Germ said.

"Alcohol," Z muttered under his breath.

"What?" the trench-coated man said.

"Umm, alcohol. Hooch. I sure do love it." He was almost right on top of the man, who was angling the woman away from Z as if to hide her from him.

"You crazy?"

Z shrugged. "I get that a lot." Then, moving fast in the dark, he brought his fist up and sent it crashing into the man's face.

The man released the woman, simultaneously grabbing his face with one hand, his other hand going for his gun under his coat.

Z deftly caught both of the man's hands and wrenched them back behind the man's back. Then he forced the man to his knees. While holding the two hands together, he grabbed a zip tie from his coat and wrapped the man's wrists together, making sure he wouldn't be escaping any time soon.

"Hey, you can't do this," the trench-coated man said. "I got rights."

Z jabbed him across the jaw, and the man slumped forward. Z dragged him back into a sitting position next to a dumpster and secured the man's bound wrists to the pipe. He wouldn't be going anywhere soon.

After flexing his hand to shake out the pain from punching the guy, Z turned to glance at the woman. She had already fled the scene.

Germ was peeking out from Z's pocket. Z glanced at him. "This is a thankless job. You know that?"

Z checked to make sure the trench-coated man was unconscious and not faking it. Then he went out to the sidewalk and found a payphone. He asked for Marshall's precinct again.

"Got that address?" Z said when Marshall answered.

"Not yet. But I'm working on it."

"Good," Z said. "In the meantime, I have a perp tied up next to a dumpster in the alley on..." he glanced at the street sign and gave its name to Marshall.

"What the hell? You can't go around beating up people and—"

"He grabbed a woman off the street and dragged her into the alley to...well, let's just say his intentions weren't pure. He's sleeping it off now."

Marshall paused. "You got a witness?"

"No. She ran off. I don't blame her."

"There's nothing I can do then," Marshall said.

"Maybe there's a warrant out for his arrest?" Z said. "Send an officer to go check. Anonymous tip."

Marshall cleared his throat. "I won't stand for vigilante justice in my city."

"Blah, blah. I saw a bad guy. I stopped the bad guy. I tied him up for the police. What you guys do from here on out is your business."

"Now wait a minute—"

"I'll call you again in an hour." Z hung the phone on the receiver.

What are you going to do now? Germ asked.

"I think a Big Mac is calling my name."

CHAPTER THIRTY-FIVE

With all the street lights and lit-up storefronts and signs, the city was nearly as bright as during the day. As he walked down the sidewalk, the big McDonald's sign was impossible to miss. It was the nearest hamburger joint to the *Paper Warriors* printing press, and it was where the three newsmen had said they would be.

It is interesting how you help people even when they are not on your list of wrongs to right, Germ said.

"What?" Z muttered. "Oh, that woman back there? She needed help. I had the means to help her. It was the right thing to do."

Germ raised his tiny octopus eyebrows. *You sure it didn't have anything to do with her long legs that go on forever? Whatever that means.*

"Shut up. I didn't do it for that reason. Well, a little bit. I hate seeing dames in distress. It's the reason Alice got the jump on me." He shook his head. Marshall had better come through with him for an address to run down. The longer she was in the wind, the worse his chances of ever finding her and getting answers out of her.

The McDonald's was right in front of him now. A few people were meandering outside, smoking and chatting, and a few of them eyed him suspiciously. Z stepped past them. Inside, the old-fashioned interior of the McDonald's greeted him. The smell of fry grease and freshly cooked hamburger hit his nostrils with a wallop, and before he knew it, he was standing in front of the cash register, ordering a Big Mac meal.

He paid for it, and when it was all ready, he carried a tray laden with a Big Mac, fries, and a Coke into the dining area. There he found the three newsmen slumped back in a booth, exhausted.

He set his food tray down on the table with as loud a noise he could without spilling his food. The three newsmen started, clutching their pockets and glancing frantically around them. One of them had a hundred-dollar bill poking out from his pocket.

Z slapped a palm on the tabletop. "You're a ripe target for a mugger, passed out in a booth with money sticking out of your pockets."

"Well, um—"

"You see—"

"We weren't passed out—"

Z unwrapped his Big Mac. "Hush it." He took a bite out of the burger. "Ah, there it is." He washed the food down with a sip of Coke.

The newsmen made faces at Z as he ate. When he finished with the burger, he crumpled up the wrapper and started squeezing ketchup on his fries. If Buzz were here, he'd be complaining about how nutritionally unhealthy this meal was.

Buzz wasn't here.

Earth-D might not have donuts, but it had Big Macs, and that was a small relief.

Z angled his eyes down at the crumpled burger wrappers already on the table. "You didn't squander all your money, now did you?"

"No," the tallest newsman said.

"Good." Z ate his fries, relishing every last hot greasy bit. He noticed how the newsmen fidgeted in the booth. They couldn't quite keep their hands still as they scratched behind their heads, twiddled their thumbs, and tapped on the table-top. "I promised I'd give you something to do to keep you occupied. I thought of something."

"Oh?" the middle newsman said.

Z sipped his drink. The caffeine would certainly be a plus tonight. He stood. "Follow me."

After throwing all their trash away, Z led the way toward the exit. On the way, he topped off his Coke and instructed the three newsmen to do the same. "We might be in for a bit of trouble. Follow me and stay out of the way, okay?"

The three newsmen exchanged nervous glances. "What kind of trouble? What's going on?"

Z smirked.

He pressed open the door and stepped out into the neon night. All the people who had been chatting had left. Now three unsavory-looking characters stood outside the door. They wore beat-up jackets and torn-up jeans. Gold rings adorned their fingers, and they had shaved haircuts.

"Hah," the biggest of the three said. "I believe you guys have something we want."

"Um, a news story?" the tallest newsman said.

The big man's reply was nearly a bark. "No. That money

sticking out of your pocket. How much dough you got on you?"

Z stepped between the big man and the newsmen. "I don't think you want to do this," Z said.

The big man placed his hands on his hips. "Oh really? What are you going to do about it?"

Z didn't say anything, only stood there holding his Coke.

"Hah. That's what I thought. Step aside, scar boy. Our business is with these scrawny—"

He didn't get to finish. Z popped off the soft drink's lid and shoved the cup at the big man's face. Carbonated beverage sloshed out, drenching the man's eyes.

"Now!" Z said to the newsmen. "Do the same."

The three newsmen shakily popped off their lids and threw their drinks at the remaining two thugs, managing to douse one of them in the face.

"You bastards are gonna pay!" the big man said, wiping dripping Coke from his face. "Get 'em!"

The thugs looked tough, but Z had a plan.

He let the big man throw a hard punch at him, easily ducking out of the way. Z effortlessly stepped behind the man, twisted his arm back at the wrist, and kicked him behind the knee. The man fell on his face with an agonized grunt.

Then Z turned to the thug the newsmen had managed to splash. Z came upon him from behind, gripped the back of his collar, and slammed him up against the side of a parked van. The man fell backward to the sidewalk, stunned.

The third thug ran up to Z and threw a fist, but Z shoved it to the side and rammed the meat of his palm against the man's nose.

"Aghh." The man fell backward to his ass, and Z patted his hands together as if knocking the dust from them.

"Are we done playing now?" he said.

The big man held his arm in a pained manner and nodded for his sidekicks to join him in a limping retreat.

When they had gone from sight, the newsmen stared proudly at Z. "That was amazing," the tall man said.

Z shrugged. The whole fight had lasted all of ten seconds, and neither Z nor any of the newsmen had suffered a scratch. Also, Z hadn't needed to Repeat.

Some things were too easy. Now, time to get back to the task at hand.

Z started down the sidewalk, and the three newsmen hurried up to catch up with him as they walked back toward the *Paper Warriors* news office.

"What is it you have for us to do?" the middle man asked when they were nearing the charred remains of the Korean barbeque restaurant and the *Paper Warriors* office.

The building was a blackened frame. It was pathetic to look at. In the white light of the street lamps, it looked like a cemetery of burned concrete blocks and timbers. He didn't know how the part of the second floor that was his office was still partially intact.

He eyed the window beside the marquee. There was nothing to climb. He wasn't getting in that way.

"Stay here," he told the three newsmen.

He started toward the ruined front door.

The tallest newsman held up a hand. "Are you sure you should be going in there?"

"If I die, I'll warp back." Z didn't look back at them.

The newsmen exchanged glances. "Warp back?" the middle one said.

The short one rubbed his chin. "Now, I bet that would make a great story."

Z found the entranceway mostly obscured by timbers and twisted metal and the caved-in second floor. Still, there was a passageway. He had to suck in his chest and squeeze through.

He had to go inside. He needed to find out what remained of the space and time capsule and the printing press. Maybe by some miracle, one or both might still be functional, but he doubted it.

He drew a deep breath and let it out. He wiggled through the gap, using his palms to help guide him. Once, halfway through the gap, he felt the surface on one side shudder, but then it stopped. He made it through and pulled out his flashlight from his jacket. The weak light cut a beam through the dust and ash mingling with the air.

With one hand, he pulled his shirt up to cover his mouth. It wouldn't do to survive this ordeal, only to develop lung cancer twenty years from now. Warping couldn't fix that shit.

In this fashion, he was able to proceed farther into the fire-stricken building. While there was a good bit of soot and dust in the air, the ruined interior was also wet from the fire department putting out the fire.

It was a mess, and his sweaty, torn-up clothes got even dirtier as he climbed over ruined tables, and in places, the collapsed second floor. In some areas, the city lights peered down through cracks in the patchy ceiling.

There came a point when the collapsed second floor formed a sort of ramp up to the news office. He didn't need the flashlight here. Carefully, he used both hands and clambered up to the burned-out second floor.

He barely recognized the *Paper Warriors* news office. He didn't see the intergalactic printing press, but he saw the remains of a desk and a melted typewriter on top, and one of the walls contained a framed and blackened newspaper with a headline about Sasquatch.

As he pushed his way toward his office, he caught his breath. Someone had torn its reinforced door from its hinges.

I do not think the fire did that, Germ said.

Z grimly shook his head in agreement. He carefully edged up to the open doorway, testing the floor for any weak points. There were a few creaks and groans, but the surface held his weight. He proceeded through the opening.

Through the room, he saw the marquee still hanging along the outer wall. The window—was gone.

"What the hell?" he muttered as he stepped into his office. Then his vision darted to the rest of the room. His desk. The open window. An empty spot along the wall where the space and time capsule was supposed to be resting.

A small part of him had hoped to find it in a blackened, damaged condition. As he'd concluded earlier, Nunez's robots must have stolen it.

He groaned. "That ain't good."

At that moment, the floor started to shake. An audible rumbling filled the room.

Neither is that, Germ said.

The entire second floor was about to collapse.

CHAPTER THIRTY-SIX

Think fast, Germ said.

Z was still reeling from not finding the space and time capsule in his office—where the hell had it gone?—so he simply reacted on pure instinct.

He felt the floor pitch. It started to drop behind him, and he threw his center of gravity forward into his office as the building roared behind him like a giant beast. He sprinted toward the open window.

You have some balls, Germ said as Z dove out the window. *Or a death wish...*

Z didn't fall to his death. Instead, he caught the sign and held on with his fingertips.

An angry commotion tore out the window into the night. Z winced as the building's exterior wall started to crack and crumble beside him. It would only be a moment before the wall fell and the sign with it.

With a grunt, Z pulled himself up so that he had one arm wrapped over the top of the marquee. Then he planted the soles of his boots against the sign's side so that he was kind of in a Spider-Man stance against it.

"Look!" one of the newsmen called from down below on the ground. "It's the Mothman!"

Z smirked.

Suddenly, the sign began to tear from the wall. It jerked beneath his grip, and he nearly fell but held on. Then the wall crumbled with an outward puff of dust and ash that blasted past him, and he gripped tightly as the wall and sign dropped to the ground floor.

Before it struck, Z pushed off, leaping away from the sign. He connected with the ground and executed a shoulder roll that sent him into a fire hydrant.

"My back," he muttered as he clutched it and clambered farther away from the crumbling building so the debris missed him.

Then he waited.

While he checked his lower back to make sure he wasn't too injured and didn't have to kill himself and warp back, multiple hands fell upon his shoulders.

On instinct, he reached up and threw someone over his shoulder and onto the sidewalk before him.

"Hey!" The tallest newsman picked himself up and rubbed his head. "That hurt."

Z glanced over his shoulder. The air was thick with dust, but the other two newsmen were standing behind him, looking down at him with a mix of awe and concern.

"Sorry." He gritted his teeth at the pain in his lower back. It wasn't serious, but he'd irritated it. The three newsmen stepped up to him and steadied him.

"That was so cool!" the middle one said.

The shortest newsman nodded. "The way you flew through the air…"

"…like a spider monkey," the tallest one finished.

Z patted the dust from his clothes. "Thanks. I think." He turned back to survey the ruined building. It looked odd without the partial second floor. Now its destruction seemed more final. He became aware of a hand on his shoulder.

The tallest newsman lifted his hand and pointed at the building's remains. "You said you had a job for us?" He looked doubtful.

Z scratched behind his forehead. "I did. I was going to ask you to help me carry out the space and time capsule."

Instead, Nunez's robots had already taken it. The building fire had been a distraction meant to give one of them time to carry the capsule out of the building.

Z recalled that he'd been unconscious for a couple of minutes. That would've provided the robots plenty of time to get the capsule out of the building. As big and heavy as it was, the robots had proven to be immensely strong and had probably carried it out through the second-story window.

It was a big opening, and they'd probably kicked the panes outward. The building architects had designed it to ward off entry from the outside but not the inside. It certainly hadn't come with a futuristic robot-proof guarantee.

One of those robots would've been able to survive a fall from the second floor. He shook his head. It didn't matter how they'd done it. They'd gotten away with the space and time capsule, and that was the main thing. They'd probably taken it to Nunez.

Z scoffed. Too bad for Nunez that only Z knew how to pilot it. The scientist could probably figure it out eventually, but it gave Z some time to recover it before that happened.

"Well?" the newsmen said as one.

Z snapped back to attention. While they couldn't help him with the space and time capsule, they could possibly help him with another matter.

The building and most of the ash cloud had settled, and Z made his way around the building's exterior, stopping at the point where he roughly figured the printing press should be inside. What shape it would be in after falling from the second floor, he didn't know.

A quick inspection of the wall yielded a weak spot, and he began to open a hole in the building's exterior wall with his hands. The newsmen excitedly watched as he tossed bricks aside. Soon he had a plate-sized hole through which he could see inside the building. He pulled out his flashlight and shone the light inside.

It reflected off the metal struts of the intergalactic printing press.

His hopes started to rise as he resumed enlarging the hole. He continued until it was large enough for him to climb through. He entered the building, creeping along the sides of the printing press and inspecting every angle of it with the flashlight. It was amazing how the fall from the second floor hadn't crushed it. In fact, it didn't seem damaged in any way.

"Holy shit..."

That printing press is well-constructed, Germ said.

Z nodded. "Definitely wasn't made in China. Can you tell what material it is?"

Germ hopped out of his pocket and scrutinized the press up close. Then he returned to Z. *Some kind of futuristic steel alloy. The wood is not real wood but a synthetic substance of incredible strength.*

Z thought that over. It wasn't out of the realm of possibility that he could use the press again. "What about its power source?"

Germ danced along the printing press's surface and inspected it further. As Z watched, he saw that some of the inner workings and interior parts were damaged, but a monkey could repair those if said monkey had good instructions—which Z did.

As he waited for Germ to return with his report on the power source, he reached inside his jacket and pulled out a holocube. Buzz had given it to him in case something damaged a printing press on any Earth. There were different models of printing presses, but they were all similar, and the holocube contained the schematics to each. Buzz had said the holocube could scan any model and highlight the part that needed fixing on the schematic.

Z had never thought he'd ever need to use the holocube, but he was glad he had it now.

He needed to report his findings and recent happenings to Buzz, and he needed a functional intergalactic printing press to do so. A plan was forming in his head.

While he tracked down Alice, he would task the three newsmen with having a moving crew transport the press to the closest available vacant office. Then they would use the holocube instructions to repair the machine. After Z found Alice, hopefully, the printing press would be functioning.

That was if the power source was still good.

Germ returned to Z. *A simple, grounded 120-volt electric cord is all it requires to run. The current wire is damaged, but an electrician could easily fix it.*

"Perfect," Z said. It looked like all the repairs would take was time and money. He had a lot of money in his jacket. Just not a lot of time.

He carefully exited the ruined building via the hole he'd made and turned to the three newsmen.

After explaining his plan to them, he handed them another couple of stacks of money. "I don't care how much it costs. You get this moved and functional as soon as possible. Okay?"

They nodded, enthused to have something to do.

"The fate of the multiverse could depend on it." It wasn't a stretch. If Eduardo Nunez figured out how to start and pilot the space and time capsule before Z recovered it, who only knew what the mad doctor would do.

"On it, sir."

"You can count on us."

The third newsman saluted. "We're the right guys for the job!"

Z hoped so. He gestured for them to start while he turned and headed for the nearest payphone.

He stepped inside the first phone booth on the sidewalk and called Marshall back.

"You got the address?" Z asked.

"Hello to you too, asshole," Marshall said.

Z smirked at his father's snark. "So, you got it or not?"

"I have it."

Z let out a sigh of relief.

Marshall gave him the street address. "Looks like a motel."

Z had a feeling Alice had been lying about staying at a friend's house.

"Is that it?" Marshall said. "I have to go."

"On your beat?" Z asked.

"No. We've been getting flooded by calls of a building collapse in the area of your news office. Know anything about that?"

Z chuckled as he raised a hand to hail a taxi from the phone booth. "No, sir. Not me."

CHAPTER THIRTY-SEVEN

"Is she staying here or not?"

The motel clerk winced. Z was facing him with both palms flat on the counter. The clerk was a twenty-something man with greasy hair. His thin slouching frame complemented the run-down interior of the motel's check-in room. Worn, faded carpet. Sagging, outdated wallpaper. Crooked windowsill.

It was certainly a low-key place for a person to disappear for a while.

Regaining his composure, the clerk raised both hands. "Like I said, hard to tell for sure. We get a lot of guests. Some come in late at night. Others during the day. It's hard to remember everyone's faces."

There was a gleam in the clerk's eyes that Z couldn't miss. He had information, but it wouldn't be free.

Z pulled away from the grimy countertop. He reached into his pants pocket and pulled out a single hundred-dollar bill he'd crumpled up and put there before stepping into the place. The rest of his money remained stashed inside his jacket, but its quantity was starting to run low after all his recent "expenditures." Besides, it wasn't wise to grab a stack of hundreds from your jacket in a place like this.

With a satisfied smirk, the clerk barely even glanced at the wadded up hundred-dollar bill on the counter, although he kept it in his peripheral vision as he sized up Z. He folded his arms. "Tell me again what she looked like."

Z did.

"Okay yeah. I'm starting to remember her, I think…" He flicked his eyes down at the wadded-up money. "But my memory is still a bit foggy."

Z slipped another wadded-up bill onto the counter.

The clerk nodded appreciatively. "You said she had long legs?"

"Yeah. Legs that went on forever."

The clerk snickered. "My paps said when I was growing up that there's no such thing as forever, that we're all destined to live and die, then nothing—"

Z slammed a fist onto the counter. "I don't give a damn what your paps told you as a kid. Is she staying here or not? Or do I have to kick in every door to find out myself?"

The clerk threw his hands up. "No, no. Um. Look. We don't need any of that. If she's who I think you're talking about, she's in Room 108."

Z turned to leave.

"But," the clerk continued, "she's not in right now."

"How do you know?"

"She left a few hours ago. I can see her room through the door window."

Z turned toward the front door to verify that he could see some of the motel units from the counter. He whipped back to the clerk. "What do you mean? She left the city?"

"I don't know, man. She had her purse with her when she

left. Didn't take her suitcase with her and she already paid for the night so she'll probably be back. She gets in real late some nights."

The clock on the wall said it was almost midnight.

"What does she do at night?" Z asked.

The clerk leaned forward on his elbows over the counter. "What do you think she does at night? A woman like that got to make money somehow…"

Z thought that over. He'd pegged Alice as a con artist—not an escort as the clerk was suggesting. Just because she hadn't taken her suitcase didn't mean she hadn't fled the city. He needed to check out her room.

Before leaving, he slipped the clerk a third hundred-dollar bill. "I was never here, okay?"

The clerk nodded.

"I never broke into her motel room either, okay?"

The clerk nodded again.

Z stared the man down, angling his face scar at him. That usually seemed to do the trick with people. "Good."

As Z exited the motel check-in lobby and walked along the sidewalk to Room 108, he reached inside his jacket and pulled out his lockpicking kit.

She came in a little after one in the morning, wearing her high-cut blue dress and high heels. One of her dress's shoulder pads was askew, revealing a snapped bra strap underneath.

Guess I know what she does for a living, Z thought.

He was reclining in the dark in the room's sole chair in the corner next to the bed, a faux leather chair with a cracked, sticky surface. Not seeing Z, Alice closed the door behind her and threw the lock bolt.

Alice's back was to him when she dropped her bag to the floor beside her suitcase and flipped on the lights. When she turned to face him in the corner, her eyes tightened on the silenced pistol in Z's outstretched hand.

"No sudden movements," Z ordered calmly. "This should go without saying, no screaming."

A mask of fear crossed her face. A tear started to form in one eye.

Z scoffed. "That trick won't work on me again. Sorry."

Alice eyed him closely, then dropped the act, her face hardening. "You going to kill me?"

Z pretended to think it over. "Not if you don't give me cause to."

"I swear I didn't know what that crazy old man was going to do with you."

"Don't care." Z shook his head. "This was all about the space and time capsule, wasn't it? You used me to scope out my office."

She pierced him with her eyes. "Does it work?"

When Z didn't respond, she bent slowly at the waist, turning her backside to him as she picked up her blue purse from the floor. She rose as slowly, then tossed the purse over onto the bed next to Z's chair. Eyeing his gun, she cocked a hip. "I'm so tired…" Her words were soft and silky. Seductive.

Z gritted his teeth. He wouldn't let the woman get the jump on him twice. "I need to know everything you know."

She smiled as she flicked off her high heels. "Can I please come over and sit on the bed? My feet are so tired."

Z wondered if she had a weapon on her. He stood and motioned her forward. When she was an arm's length away, he tucked his pistol into the small of his back and patted her down—not that she had many places to conceal a weapon in her high-cut blue dress. Except maybe those obnoxious '80s shoulder pads.

"You like that, don't you?" Alice said with a gleam in her eyes as he finished the pat-down.

Retrieving the pistol from his belt, Z took a step back and angled the gun barrel at the bed. Alice giggled and sat on the bed's edge. "You can join me. I don't bite. Hard."

Z wagged the gun barrel before him. "Start talking. Now."

She pouted. "You're no fun." She crossed her arms beneath her bosom. "Fine. I'll talk. But you've got to do something for me."

"You're in no position to barter."

"I want you to kill that crazy old man. Nunez, you called him."

For a moment, the gun quivered in Z's grip. "What?"

She flicked stray bangs from her eyes. "At first, I thought he was a lonely, crazy old man who had too much money on his hands. I thought he was after my...company, like most men. Which, for the right price, I don't care how old you are."

She blinked, her luscious eyelashes enthralling Z. "That's not what he wanted me for." She blinked at him again, observing his reaction.

When it was evident she wasn't going to continue, he jabbed the gun at her.

"Not until we have a deal," she said. With her arms still crossed, she arched her back and thrust her chest forward and her shoulders backward. She licked her lips.

"Shit," he muttered, trying not to fall for her spell again. He struggled to lift his gaze from her cleavage to her alluring eyes. "You're saying you'll help me if I kill the old man Nunez?"

She nodded. "Exactly."

"Why do you want me to kill him?"

She tugged at her snapped bra strap.

Are you okay? Germ said.

Z swallowed, trying to disregard the throbbing in his nether region.

Alice saw his arousal. Instead of slipping off her dress, she gently draped the strap back over her shoulder and straightened her dress's torn shoulder pad. "I want you to kill him," she paused, her features turning eagle-like, "because tonight he tried to kill me."

CHAPTER THIRTY-EIGHT

Z stiffened. "Nunez did that to you—tore your dress? You said he wasn't interested in your body."

Alice shook her head, her hair bobbing with the motion. "Not him. He sent an older gentleman in a tuxedo. Which normally I wouldn't have had an issue with." She hooked some hair over one ear. "He wouldn't remove those black sunglasses when I told him to. So creepy."

She drew in a breath. "Again, I told the tuxedo man to take them off. He wouldn't. He smirked. So I reached out and took them off." She lanced Z with her eyes. "He had red glowing eyes! Red fucking eyes!" She sighed in disgust and let herself fall backward on the bedspread.

Z tugged on his shirt collar. "What happened next?"

"I asked the man, 'What the fuck are you, some kind of robot?' He gave that creepy smile again and replaced his sunglasses over his eyes—"

Z held up a hand. "Wait, you had sex with an old robot man?"

She shot back up into a sitting stance on the bed. "Fuck

you. No! We never got to that point. And we never would have. I screamed, and he reached out super fast and went for my throat with his hands. He got my bra strap and my dress pad, but I ducked to the side and rolled off the bed out of the way."

"Shit," Z remarked. "It let you get away?"

"It didn't *let* me. I burst out through the door and nearly ran into a second tuxedoed man…robot…I don't know what the hell they were. The second one swiped out at me like it was trying to grab me or claw me, maybe. Its hand tore out part of the wall when it missed me.

"I managed to get around it and slip outside. Then I ran as fast as I could in my heels around the next street corner where I had my taxi waiting for me." She shook her head at the recollection. "The taxi is waiting outside this motel right now. I came here to gather my things so I could run for my life like some kind of fucking mob witness without witness protection. You know what I mean?"

Z didn't know if he could trust her or not. She had some details she could only know if she'd run into Nunez's robots. That didn't mean she wasn't in collusion with them and had devised a believable story for Z. The woman was a born actress and knew how to work her natural charm.

He drew a deep breath and sat again. He holstered his pistol under his jacket. "Don't take this the wrong way, but—"

"Oh my God, you don't believe me, do you?"

"It's…well, you've duped me twice before."

"Fucking unbelievable." She threw up her hands. "Some old crazy guy sends old robot dudes after me to kill me. I know I read alt science magazines, but I couldn't make this shit up."

Z chewed on his lower lip. "I know about the red-eyed robots."

"Then you know what they can do. They're killing machines. I need your help."

"Eh, seems like you're making out all right on your own. How do I know they didn't 'let' you go?"

She flipped him off. "Seriously? I. Am. Not. Involved. With. Them."

"And I'm not a bear. Saying something doesn't make it true, lady."

Your antics are sometimes bearish... Germ said.

Alice leaned forward on the edge of the bed so she was closer to Z. "They're planning to detonate a time bomb in Central Park at noon tomorrow," she blurted.

Z jolted upright in the chair so their faces were inches apart. "What did you say?"

"N-nothing. I uh—"

Z reached out and gripped her wrist. "That's their plan? How do you know?"

Alice tried to pull away, but Z had her held tight. "The robot man. He got a call when he came inside the hotel room I was supposed to meet him in. A call on some kind of...I don't know. Mobile phone, I guess."

"A cell phone?" Z released her wrist.

It's the eighties, remember? Germ said.

She looked at him as she felt at her wrist. "Cell phone? What's a cell phone?"

"Wait about twenty years, and everyone will have one."

"You would know that how?"

Z shrugged. "I'm from the future. What? I have a space and time capsule."

She rolled her eyes. "I walked into that one, didn't I?"

Z regained her attention. "So you overheard the robot talking?"

"To the man who hired me. Nunez. They must've figured it wouldn't matter if I heard since the robot was supposed to kill me. I'm a loose end, I guess." She massaged her temples. "Shit. What have I gotten myself into?"

"A big fat mess," Z said. "You're sure the robot mentioned a time bomb?"

"Yeah. What the hell is that?"

"You don't want to know."

This wasn't good. Nunez planned to detonate the bioweapon that Z had failed to secure from the warehouse mission on this Earth. Why? What was he trying to do?

On the bright side, at least he now knew where the bioweapon would be so he could take it out of the equation. That didn't mean it made any sense to him. By his reckoning, Nunez had gotten the bioweapon into the thugs' hands at the warehouse only to steal it back again during Z's warehouse mission. What angle didn't he see here?

"So you'll help me?" Worry creeping into Alice's hopeful voice.

Z gave her a resolute stare. "I'm stopping that bastard Nunez either way. Yeah. I'll help."

Alice sighed with relief.

"Do you know where the space and time capsule is now?"

She shook her head.

"Then start from the beginning," Z said. "What did Nunez pay you to do?"

"Initially, to wait for you to 'come to this Earth.' I thought this Nunez guy was crazy and meant you were coming to this city. He instructed me to contact *Paper Warriors* to look for you. He must have handpicked me because of my connection to the publication, me being a reader. The psycho.

"Then he gave me a rough sketch of a sleek rocket-ship-like capsule. He said that if the man with the face scar showed up on this Earth, he would have the capsule. Nunez said he needed that capsule but that I was only supposed to locate it—he'd take care of the transport."

Z nodded. "Did you have fun picking the lock on my office door?"

She smirked. "That lock was a bitch. You have good security." She paused. "Not good enough for me. I waited until those three newsmen went out for a snack and then slipped inside."

She brushed back her hair on one side of her head and pointed at her ear. "I spoke to Nunez via the metal piece he'd given me to wear in my ear. I told him I'd found it, and I wanted to meet him in person to share the location. He told me there was no need, but he had another job for me, and he would pay me double to do it."

"Let me guess, lure me to Central Park and knock me out with the inhalant?"

"You got it." She gave a nervous chuckle. "I'm glad he didn't kill you."

"He can't kill me. Not for good. I overpowered the armored transport guards and made my way back to the city right before those two robots torched my office."

Alice's gaze dropped to the floor. "I didn't know." She raised her eyes to him again. "I have a question that I probably don't want to know the answer to, but I'll ask anyway. Do you think those robots can somehow trace me with that earpiece Nunez gave me?"

Z considered it. "It's possible."

She smiled weakly. "Maybe it would be better in your possession then?"

"That would be good. I might be able to find a way to use it against Nunez."

With a swallow, she nervously eyed him. "It's in my purse. Is it okay if I go get it?"

He nodded, thinking about the broken futuristic earpiece he'd sent to Buzz earlier. Buzz had been doubtful that he could figure out anything from it anytime soon. Now that Z could pass on an intact earpiece, he could finally figure something out.

Of course, that all hinged on him getting the space and time capsule back first. Also, if he confronted Nunez and got the capsule back, he didn't need Buzz to analyze the earpiece, did he?

All this thinking was making his head hurt.

After rummaging in her purse for a few moments, Alice said, "Found it." She turned to him with a big grin. "So, we good?"

He rose from the chair. "For now—"

She fell into him, throwing her arms up around his neck. "Oh, thank you so much. I thought you were going to kill me and I'm so scared and—"

Z felt that something was wrong, but her warmth felt so good against his chest and neck. Surely he wasn't being played again.

A painful jolt entered his neck, and he collapsed backward into the faux leather chair.

In Alice's hand was a miniature Taser. "Sorry about that. I had to make sure I could get away. It's like you said, how can I take you at your word that you're not going to kill me? You can say anything—doesn't mean it's true."

"I'm going to…" Z breathed, but it was hard to talk. His body felt numb from the neck down.

"Some kind of stun device." Alice slipped the Taser back into her purse. "Nunez said I might have to use it against you when he hired me. I didn't know if it would work or not so I decided to go with a knockout drug the first time."

Alice pulled the futuristic earpiece from her purse and set it on the bed within his vision. "Kill that creep Nunez, okay? I'm keeping my word. Here's the earpiece."

She backed away toward the motel room door and picked up her suitcase. "It's been a pleasure working with you, but I have to go. If all goes according to plan, we'll never see each other again."

"It never does…go to plan," Z managed.

She opened the door and blew him a kiss from the doorway. "Remember. Time bomb. Central Park. Tomorrow at noon. See ya."

CHAPTER THIRTY-NINE

The futuristic Taser shock wore off a couple of minutes later, and Z could move again. Shit. She'd done it again. Had made him look like a fool. He never even had a chance to question her about the missing woman Mel and this Earth's younger Eduardo Nunez, who was going by the name Ray Garcia.

Women seem to hate you, Germ said.

The thing was, even though Alice had betrayed him—again—he didn't hold it against her. He felt like she and he were cut from the same cloth. Sure, a little rough around the edges, but confident and extremely capable in their ways. Z scratched behind his neck. "Little buddy, you probably didn't sense it because you're not human, but I think she likes me."

Germ shook his tiny octopus head. *I think you're crazy.*

"No, really. There was some chemistry between us." He couldn't get her alluring eyes out of his mind.

Dream on, lover boy.

He popped his neck. Luckily the effects of the shock had worn off, and now it was time to get back to work.

The clock on the wall said it was after 2:00 a.m. That

meant less than ten hours until he had to stop the bomb threat at Central Park.

Don't you have a right to wrong in the morning? Germ said.

Z inspected the tattoos under his arms. "Shit. You're right. 9:00 a.m. today at a Choice One Bank branch downtown. A robbery."

So you have to stop a bank robbery at nine. Then you have to stop the robots from detonating the time bomb bioweapon at Central Park at noon?

Yup. Too bad he didn't know where the two robots and Nunez were. If he did, he could end this all right now.

A yawn escaped him. Despite all the adrenaline rushing through him from his encounter with Alice—was that even her real name?—sleep was gnawing at him. He'd taken a nap in the alley earlier, but he couldn't remember the last time he'd slept in a bed. He'd been too busy hopping Earths and saving the multiverse.

He glanced at the motel bed.

She'd paid for it...

"Wake me up with the sun, will ya?" Z said.

Then he dropped onto the bed and fell asleep.

Germ woke him around 6:00 a.m. Z stumbled to the bathroom, where he splashed cold water on his face.

Less than three hours until you have to be at the Choice One Bank, Germ said.

Z splashed more water on his face, looked in the mirror, and studied the little black octopus perched on his shoulder. "Ugh. Don't remind me. I didn't even have any alcohol last night, and I feel like shit."

The human body can only endure so much. Humans are so weak and soft—

"Okay." Z raised his hand. "That's enough psychobabble from the resident germ blob." He shut the water faucet off and toweled off with the musty motel towel. "Hopefully, that gives us enough time to track down the new temporary *Paper Warriors* news office first. Any bets on whether or not those newsmen came through for me?"

Humans are quite unpredictable. I shall wager nothing.

Z left the motel with Alice's futuristic earpiece in his jacket pocket, waving at the check-in lobby in case the greasy clerk was still watching Alice's place. Then he hailed a taxi. He was going to have to rely on some old-fashioned detective work if he was going to find the new printing press office before the bank mission.

After half an hour of searching the streets surrounding the old *Paper Warriors* location with no luck, he decided to try a new approach and stepped into a phone booth. He flipped to the Moving and Transportation section of a phone book and started to call all the moving companies one by one.

Finally, he reached a moving company that said they'd moved an antique printing press for three guys in the middle of the night. They'd charged quadruple the normal rate for the job considering the time of night, the size of the printing press, and the fact that it was in a ruined building surrounded by yellow caution tape. They gave Z the address, and Z flagged down another taxi on the bustling New York streets.

It was already after 8:00 a.m. when he finally reached the

address the movers had given him, which meant less than one hour until the bank job.

Z paid his fare and climbed out of the taxi. Sizing up his destination, he saw a coffee shop in front of him. The strong aroma of coffee made him alert and hungry for donuts, which in turn made him angry since this Earth didn't have any.

He was about to go on a donut rant to Germ when the door to a small, abandoned shop opened with the jingle of a bell. It had a glass storefront with tinted windows so he couldn't see inside it, and shared a wall with the coffee shop.

"Big man!" The tallest newsman leaned out through the open doorway. "You found the new place. Come on in and see what you think."

The newsman's beaming pride gave Z hope. He followed the newsman inside the unmarked storefront.

At first, all Z could see were bright pink walls. "What the…hell?"

"It used to be a wedding cake shop," the tallest newsman said.

The middle newsman waved from the back of the room. "It went bankrupt."

"We got a real good deal on the place," the shortest newsman said. He stepped out from behind the intergalactic printing press, tucked away in the back corner. The tinted sunlight entering the glass front of the store glittered upon the press's metal struts.

Z rushed up to it. "I bet you did." He quickly inspected the machine. There were still some damaged internal parts, but the press might be in usable shape. He went to the back of the printing press and inspected the electric cord. "You got the cord replaced too?"

The tallest newsman stood with his hands on his hips.

"Electrician just left. Charged us triple for the rush job. We're gonna need more money."

Z absentmindedly reached inside his torn jacket and tossed a stack of hundred-dollar bills to the newsmen as he kept his eyes on the printing press. He tested the knobs and levers, and they all worked. The building fire had scorched off some of the dates and times. He could still read the ones he needed, though.

Wasting no time, he set up a reply to send to Buzz. He condensed all the major events that had happened to him on Earth-D as briefly as he could. There was quite a bit, and he was in a time crunch. When he finished, he pressed the big button that initiated the message transfer out to the other printing presses. The printing press *whirred* to life, and a small green light flashed on it. Then it went still.

The middle newsman twiddled his thumbs. "Did it...work?"

"I'm sure Buzz is anxious to hear from me since I haven't sent word in a while. We'll see in a few minutes if he's able to send a reply." Z surveyed the stark interior of the new office. "Place could use some furniture. And some signage."

The shortest newsman rubbed his fingertips together. "We could make it happen with some more money."

Z scratched the back of his head. "Shit. You guys are as bad as Congress." He glanced over all the espresso cups scattered across the floor. "You guys haven't slept all night, have you?"

They shook their heads.

"You said it was important," the tallest one said.

"It was. Thank you. I appreciate it. You guys came through."

The three newsmen shared looks, then rushed toward him

and threw their arms around him. "Bring it in, bring it in," they said. "We three are like family, and now you're one of us."

From Z's pocket, Germ snickered at Z's discomfort.

Z pushed himself out from under their group hug. "Well, uh. Thanks, but I'm uh, not a hugger."

You sure like hugging Alice, Germ taunted.

The middle newsman grinned at Z. "You big softie. You probably have the biggest heart out of any of us."

Z scratched his head again. "I don't know about that—"

Suddenly, the printing press hummed to life. The *crunching, clicking* sounds of stuck and broken gears made Z cringe as he made his way back over to it. He was considering powering it off to prevent even worse damage, but then a newspaper was sucked into the press, and the top half came down. Ink leaked out from beneath the press like black blood. There were more *crunches* and *clicks* and stutters. Eventually, the top half rose, and it spat the freshly printed newspaper out.

Z scooped it up.

The ink job was poor and spattered, but at least he could read most of Buzz's reply.

DO NOT LET NUNEZ DETONATE THE TIME BOMB!

Good job escaping that armored truck but way to get tricked by a woman, you dope. Don't tell me you were sleeping with the enemy. Actually, if so, please send all the juicy details.

Right, back to the matter at hand—it's critical that you stop the time bomb. You must also recover the space and time capsule before Nunez can figure out how to use it. If he does, it's game over. I haven't been able to crack the broken earpiece you sent. I think you may be right—that earpiece could contain GPS tracking software that would allow Nunez to track you. Too bad you can't send it to me. Glad the holocube instructions paid off.

Be careful. -B

P.S.: Stay away from the ladies!

Z smirked. Yes, he had to stop the two robots from detonating the time bomb at noon. First, he had less than half an hour to stop a bank robbery.

CHAPTER FORTY

Even though Z could warp back in time up to three minutes, he couldn't stop or slow time. As such, he didn't make it to the bank before 9:00 a.m. because, well.

NYC traffic.

When his taxi arrived, the robbery was already in progress. The police were on scene, conversing in a huddle in a small parking lot across from the bank that afforded a view of the bank's awning-covered façade. A police car barricade was set up in the street in front of the bank, blocking traffic.

This was going to take some thinking and probably a bunch of Repeats.

Z strode up to the police captain in charge of the scene in the side parking lot. "What kind of situation do we have?" Z asked.

The captain dismissed him with an irritated bark. "Hostage situation. Civilians stay back." The captain turned back to a few other officers he was speaking with.

Z didn't move. He cleared his throat. "I can help."

The captain turned. "I advise you to vacate the area. This is no place for civilians." He sniffed. "Maybe get cleaned up. You look like you haven't slept or showered in days."

"It's been Earths since I've done either," Z admitted. "I'm no civilian."

The captain scrutinized him. "Oh? Who the hell are you? And don't play the 'I'm FBI' bullshit. It's a criminal offense to impersonate a law officer."

Z was still trying to think of something to say when a red coupe pulled up into the side parking lot. The car had a giant dent in the roof.

Marshall leaned out through the open driver's window. "It's okay. He's with me." He got out of his car and flashed Z a dirty look that only Z could see.

The captain looked perplexed. "Who is he?"

"A contractor," Marshall replied. "He's done some under-cover work in the past. A black ops CIA kind of thing."

Straightening a bit, the captain regarded Z. "My apologies. Thanks for your service."

With a smug smirk, Z fluffed his dirty jacket collar. "So what are we up against?"

The police captain pointed at a blueprint of the bank building folded out on the hood of a squad car. Before making any explanations, he said, "Officer Peet, shouldn't you be off duty?"

"I was finishing up some paperwork when I heard the call. You know what they say…"

"A police officer is never off duty," several of the gathered officers said.

The captain looked Marshall in the eyes. "Don't you have a wife?"

Marshall nodded.

"Well, this is an all-hands on deck situation. I've heard

about your accomplishments on the night shift. If all goes well today, I'll see what I can do about getting you reassigned to the day shift. Join the rest of these fine officers."

"Wow, sir. I mean, let's resolve the situation."

"Right." The captain indicated the bank lobby on the map with his finger. "We've got three perps inside with shotguns. At least three bank employees. Four adult civilians. Three child civilians."

Z was familiar with this case. It was the kids he was the most concerned about.

"We have the place surrounded. One of the robbers leaned out through the front door and warned that they'll start shooting hostages if we try to breach."

"What's the plan?" one of the officers said.

As they exchanged glances, Z stepped forward. "Let me go in. I have experience with these kinds of situations."

The officers stared at him.

The captain set his jaw. "You got any weapons on you?"

Z pointed at his brain. Then he lifted the back of his jacket to show his pistol tucked into the small of his back, sans suppressor.

"No offense, but I don't think that'll work." The captain stroked his chin. He turned to a fellow officer observing the bank's entrance with a pair of binoculars. "Any activity?"

The officer shook his head.

Z stood his ground. "We don't have much time. I've done this countless times—off the record, of course. Negotiating with bad guys is like an art for me."

"Officer Peet." The captain glanced at his watch and wiped the sweat from his head. "We have the bank surrounded but SWAT is still inbound. I think this man is right. I don't think we can afford to wait any longer. Are you sure we can trust him?"

Z grinned at Marshall, who was probably considering how Z's actions might affect his promotion to day shift.

"He's the very best," Marshall said at last. "Although I don't always agree with his tactics, he knows things. I would trust him with my life."

Z made a crossing gesture over his heart. "I'll get the civilians back without a scratch."

"There are three shooters in there," the captain said.

"Hah. Three to one? I've been up against worse odds."

The captain made his decision. "All right. We'll do this your way, Mr.?"

"Z," Z said. "Just Z."

One of the officers muttered, "Geez, he really is one of those Spec Ops guys."

"Right." The captain thumbed his belt. "You're on deck. What's your plan?"

Z smirked. "Watch and learn, boys. Watch and learn." Then he strode across the street toward the bank's entrance.

"What the hell's he doing?" one officer said to another.

Z tuned them out as he reached the other side of the street and stepped up onto the sidewalk. The glass door to the bank lay right ahead of him, the awning above it providing some shade. Through the glass, he could make out the forms of multiple people inside lying on the floor.

When he got to the door, a thick man in a ski mask stepped into view on the other side. He kicked open the door, causing a breath of wind to blow past Z.

"You with the police?" he growled.

"No," Z said.

The robber unloaded the shotgun into Z's chest, blasting him backward onto the sidewalk.

He died.

(Five Seconds Earlier)

"You with the police?" the robber growled.

"Yes," Z said.

The robber pulled the trigger again, and the shotgun blast plowed him backward to the sidewalk.

He died.

(Five Seconds Earlier)

"You with the police?" the robber growled.

Hm, Z thought. Maybe this wasn't a yes or no answer.

"My name's Z. What's yours—"

The robber fired the shotgun.

He died.

(Ten Seconds Earlier)

"You with the police?" the robber growled.

Z threw his hands up. "What would it take for you not to shoot me?"

"We said for no police to come close." The robber gripped his shotgun.

"I'm not with the police—I'm…a mediator."

The robber jabbed the air with the shotgun. "A what?"

"A person who helps two sides reach an agreement."

The robber thought about it for a moment. Then his eyes

shot wide inside the ski mask's eye holes. "You mean you're a fucking negotiator?"

Wrong answer, Germ said.

The robber pulled the trigger.

He died.

(Fifteen Seconds Earlier)

"You with the police?" the robber growled.

Z kept walking toward the robber standing in the bank's entrance. "I want you to understand that I tried to do this civilly. I really did."

Seeing that Z wasn't going to stop, the robber fired his shotgun.

Z dodged to the side, then stepped in quick. He knocked the shotgun barrel upward with his arm before the robber fired again. The blast tore a hole in the bank's awning. Sunlight punched downward. Z followed up with a two-finger jab to the side of the robber's neck, catching the man as he slumped.

Turning, he stripped the shotgun from the man's hands and threw him out into the street. Before the man had even come to a rolling stop, Z swiveled back and entered the bank, keeping low.

Immediately he saw the four adult hostages off to the side lying facedown on the floor with their hands over their necks. He didn't see the child hostages, which was why he was here in the first place. Ahead of him was the teller's counter.

"The hell was that?" one of the two remaining robbers yelled from behind the counter.

"The cops!" the second one screamed as he locked in on Z and fired. The blast decimated a promotional sign in the lobby. Z meanwhile rolled behind the cover of a freestanding countertop containing deposit slips.

Z cupped a hand over his mouth to amplify his voice. "No one has to get hurt."

A shotgun blast answered him.

"That said, I would prefer that I get to hurt someone," Z muttered. To his pocket, he said, "Germ, scope out their position."

As shotgun blasts rang out, Germ hopped out of Z's pocket and skipped along the polished floor on tiny tentacles. A woman lying on the floor with her hands over her head saw Germ and passed out. Z wasn't worried. She'd never believe she'd seen a tiny black octopus during a bank robbery. "It was a hallucination brought on by stress," her psychiatrist would probably say.

To keep the robbers occupied, Z angled his shotgun around his cover and fired a warning shot up at the ceiling. The two robbers continued to fire at his position.

The robbers are wearing backpacks stuffed with cash.

"Did they hurt anyone back there?" Z called.

No. The three bank employees are safe and on the floor.

"You see the three kids?" Z yelled.

"Who the fuck is he talking to?" one of the robbers said.

"Doesn't matter. We gotta go!"

The three kids are back here too, Germ said.

Z needed to make his move now. He rose from cover and aimed at the counter, but the two robbers were already heading out the back door.

Oh well, they wouldn't get far. There were police officers out back.

Z vaulted over the teller counter as the robbers threw open the back door, two of the kids held out before them like hostages. They'd left the third child, a young boy, inside the back door.

The roar of a dump truck thundered outside the back of the building. There was a *crunch* of metal and shouting. A round of shooting ensued.

"The hell..." Z approached the child left behind by the back door and made sure he was okay. The boy nodded, and Z waved for him to find his parent out in the lobby. Then he edged up to the back door.

When he threw it open, the two robbers were climbing into a dump truck and pulling in the two children, a girl and a boy, after them. Z raised his shotgun, but the dump truck noisily shifted gears and roared off.

There was a police car stationed behind the bank, and it was missing most of its rear bumper after the dump truck rammed it.

Two officers were on the ground, and a third checked their wounds, which didn't seem too bad. Z sprinted over to the car and hopped inside through the window. The key was in the ignition so he started the car and took off after the truck.

CHAPTER FORTY-ONE

Z whipped the police car around the back of the building and out onto the street to pursue the robbers' getaway dump truck.

There was no way he could've seen that coming. On the other Earths, the getaway driver never even attempted to pick up the three robbers inside because of all the police cars. Good ol' Earth-D, switching things up on him…

He took one hand off the steering wheel and beat it against his forehead, taking his eyes off the street for a moment.

"Oh shit!" He swerved, nearly striking an officer who had jumped in front of the vehicle. Then Z realized it was Marshall. He was screaming obscenities at him.

Z smirked. "Officer, can I give you a ride?"

Marshall tore open the passenger door and climbed inside. Z floored it before Marshall could close the door. The forward motion threw Marshall back in his seat.

"What the hell are you doing?" he spat.

Z replied matter-of-factly, "Pursuing the bank robbers. We have to get the hostages to safety."

Marshall's eyes were livid. "I mean, barging your way into the bank like that! I put my reputation on the line. There weren't supposed to be any shots fired."

Z blew through a red light and turned a street corner, gaining on the dump truck. Traffic had backed up ahead of them. They'd be stopping soon. "I never promised there wouldn't be shots. I promised the hostages wouldn't get a scratch. I didn't kill that robber—I knocked him out and threw him into the street for you guys to arrest and shit."

Marshall held onto his seat and exhaled loudly. "I am so getting fired for this."

"Relax. We'll get the bad guys and save the hostages. You have my word."

"Why do I get the feeling that your word is shit?"

Z braked as they approached the traffic jam up ahead. "You're turning into a big potty mouth." Of course, if it wasn't Z, it would be another asshole that toughened Marshall up. Z didn't mind giving back some of the shit his dad had given to him over the years as he was growing up.

"I will kill you if the hostages get even a scrape."

"Duly noted, Officer Peet. Now, look alive."

The dump truck's brake lights flashed red as it approached the backed-up traffic. Then the truck's doors were thrown open, and one of the two robbers and the driver hopped out, pointing pistols back at the police car.

"Oh shit!" Marshall shouted, ducking inside the car.

Meanwhile, Z threw his door open and knelt behind it like a shield as he raised his pistol.

He waited for his opening and then peeked around the cover and pulled the trigger. His shot winged the getaway driver, who dropped his gun and clutched his bleeding upper arm.

"Get the driver." Z sprinted toward the dump truck. He had to duck behind a blue metal postal drop box when the robbers fired at him. "I'll get the hostages."

Marshall prepared to exit the car, then ducked back inside when another round struck the vehicle. "You're crazy!"

The two bank robbers were squeezing their way through the backed-up traffic toward the sidewalk. Each had a kid held out before them, and their gun aimed back at Z.

"They're going to get away," Marshall called as he finally managed to exit the police car.

"Not on my watch. Secure the driver."

As Marshall approached the injured getaway driver, he shouted, "Hands in the air!"

The man looked at him and snarled. Then he dove for his dropped gun. Marshall holstered his firearm and tackled the man before he could reach it. He kicked the dropped gun out of the way. "You're under arrest, asshole."

Z turned his attention away from Marshall and the driver and focused on the two robbers with their human shields. They were on the sidewalk now and backing toward a tattoo shop. When they were inside the shop, Z broke from cover and dashed through the traffic and up onto the sidewalk toward the store's glass-windowed façade.

Bullets spat out at him, shattering the glass storefront. Z threw himself into a sideways barrel roll onto the sidewalk. He raised his pistol as he came out of it, but he couldn't see anyone through the open storefront.

He clambered to his feet, rushed up to the doorway, and peeked inside. A stunned tattoo artist stood frozen, leaning over a pudgy man on his side who was getting a heart tattooed on his ass cheek.

"Ew. Really?" Z said. There was no unseeing that sight. He

flipped his gaze over the cramped interior containing two tattoo chairs, a cash register on a desk, and some vertical mirrors with tattoo designs taped to them. There was no sign of the two robbers and their two child hostages. "Next time, bud, go with a dragon tat."

The stunned tattoo artist pointed toward the back of the store. Z nodded and ran down a short hall. A back door closed as Z reached it. He checked his gun. He was getting those kids back safely, that was for sure. He needed to right this in the timeline so the butterfly effect would travel on and right an even bigger wrong. It would mean the world to him if he could fix that big mistake.

He drew a deep breath and threw his shoulder against the door.

One of the robbers was standing to the side and shoved his pistol against Z's face and pulled the trigger.

He died.

(Five Seconds Earlier)

Z drew a deep breath, preparing to throw his shoulder against the door.

Instead, he twisted the knob and kicked it open with his boot. The gunman waiting outside edged forward with his gun, expecting to confront Z.

This time, Z stayed inside the doorway. When the robber's outstretched arm appeared in front of him, Z pistol-whipped the man's wrist. He cried out in agony and dropped his weapon. From the *crunching* sound the bone had made and the anguish in the man's cry, Z had broken his wrist.

"Guess you won't shoot anyone soon, asshole." Z slammed the butt of his pistol against the robber's nose. Even though the man was wearing a ski mask, some blood splatted and dripped through the dark fabric as he fell backward, clutching his face.

Z flicked his gaze around as the sole remaining robber ran around a street corner, herding the two kids in front of him. Z quickly drew a zip tie from his jacket and secured the injured robber's wrists behind his back to a sturdy pipe. Then Z two-finger jabbed the robber in the side of the neck so he sat there limply for the police to find.

Rising, he took off toward where the last robber took the two kids.

Around the corner, he came to a roped-off straight section of road. There was nowhere for the robber to hide that way.

He crossed the street and faced a tall chain-link fence with barbed wire on the top. The ground on the other side was flat bare earth. Mounds of dirt and gravel lay heaped up in sections, and heavy equipment and bulldozers sat beside reams of metal I-beams and stacks of concrete blocks. A construction site. The perfect place for someone to hide.

Z quickly scanned through the chain-link fence for the robber and the two kids. He didn't see them. Also, he didn't see a gate or a way through the fence. Maybe the robber wasn't in the construction site.

He was about to turn around when he heard a boy shout, "Help me!"

Z followed the boy's voice around the side of a parked work truck and found the boy hostage huddled up on the ground. The robber was nowhere in sight.

Z dropped beside the kid. He laid a hand on his quivering shoulder. "Are you all right?"

"I-I-I, he still has my sister!"

The girl hostage.

Trying to keep his voice as soft as possible, Z said, "Did the bad man let you go?"

The boy jerked his head sideways. "Amy whispered to me to run when she gave the sign."

"The sign?"

Nodding, the boy gave a weak smile. "She bit the man's hand, and he started shouting bad words. Then Amy told me to run. I ran. But…I didn't want to leave her behind…" The boy looked like he was about to cry.

Z patted his head. He might be an arrogant asshole, but he knew how to talk to kids. If there was any type of person he hated more than those who hurt or kidnapped women, it was those who did the same to children.

This last robber was going to pay.

"Look, kid, I'll get her back. I promise."

The boy's eyes shimmered as he looked up at Z. "Thank you, sir."

Z smirked. "Now stay here and stay safe. The police will be here shortly." He scanned the street and the worksite on the other side of the tall fence. "Do you know which way they went?"

The boy bobbed his head. He pointed a little farther down the fence where there was a vertical slit in the chain links.

Z nodded his appreciation. This asshole was going down.

CHAPTER FORTY-TWO

Ouch! Germ blurted.

Z shimmied through the vertical slit in the chain-link fence. He glanced down at where a piece of cut fencing had further torn his jeans. A small black stain was beginning to spread through his pants. "Sorry."

You're gonna miss me if I die.

It was odd to think of the tiny black octopus as being capable of dying. He was, after all, created from a highly mutated form of the same time virus that had infected Z. How could such an entity die?

He knew from experience though that Germ could bleed, and if something could bleed, that meant it could die. "I wouldn't miss you," Z said. "I'd find myself another sidekick. Maybe Alice."

Words hurt, you know.

Z winced. Now on the other side of the chain-link fence, he surveyed the construction site, searching for where the last robber had taken the girl hostage. "I'm joking, you know."

Germ hopped up from Z's pocket and scampered up onto his shoulder. He moved much slower than usual. Shit, how much blood or ooze had the little guy lost?

When Germ reached Z's shoulder, he pinched Z's ear with a suction-cupped tentacle. *I know.* He smirked. *I am irreplaceable.*

"You're something, all right." He'd taught Germ well.

Z bent to the ground. Multiple boot prints in the dry dirt drew his attention—evidence of a work crew being here recently. He searched for a fresher trail that would signify the robber and girl's footprints.

Crouching, he widened his search radius. Instead of looking for the boot prints of the robber, he inspected the dirt for a child-sized shoeprint.

He found it.

"Hey Germ, can you use your binocular eyes and see where this goes?"

On his shoulder, Germ's black beady eyes elongated and tracked the girl's shoeprints away from their position.

Start running. I will direct you.

Trusting Germ, Z ran through the construction site. He passed several large portable generators and a tall boom crane. Then he skirted a massive hole excavated for a basement to the side. Up ahead was a partially constructed, wide multi-story building, its outer and interior walls formed in intervals by vertical two-by-fours like a maze. Darkness extruded from inside where the sun didn't shine.

"He had to go in there, didn't he?"

Germ bobbed his tiny octopus head.

"Shit. Okay, I might need your night vision for this."

Z is afraid of the dark. Z is afraid of the dark, Germ chanted.

"Am not, you little asshole." He stopped outside the wall of spaced-out timbers. The inside floor was concrete, and Z could make out buckets of tools and nails littered throughout the dim interior. He saw several metal wheelbarrows as well.

"Don't come any closer!" The words came from inside the dark, partially constructed building. "I have a hostage."

Z spat a chunk of spit off to the side as an intimidation tactic to show the robber that he was calm and in control. "What's your play? Shoot the hostage?" He whistled. "If you think the cops are after you now, how about when you have a dead body on your hands—a dead child."

"Shut up."

"I don't know your story, but you were robbing a bank so you're probably a desperate man. Desperate men make stupid mistakes. Kidnapping a child? That's scraping the bottom of the bucket. That's an all-time low that I can't abide."

"I said shut up! I did what I had to. None, none of this is going according to plan. How'd you even get past our sentry at the bank's door? He was a trained, disgruntled Marine—a big man."

"One word." Z thought back to how he'd dodged the shotgun blast and incapacitated the robber in the bank's doorway before tossing him out into the street. "Practice."

"Practice? The fuck? You must have barged right up to the front door like you'd rehearsed it or something."

Z's presence was unnerving the man. Time to crank up the intensity and force a reaction.

The robber continued, "You like a Navy SEAL or something—"

"How long," Z interrupted, "do you think the money in your backpack is gonna last you on the run?"

"Fuck you."

"The way I see it, you're running low on options."

"I have a hostage—"

"You and I both know you're not going to kill her."

"I will if I have—"

"You're not that dumb," Z said.

"You need to take it easy—"

Z darted inside the building. With the ability to Repeat the situation if he died, one way or another he'd make it work.

"You're insane!" the robber yelled.

"A little." To Germ, he said, "Where's he at?"

Gun at your three o'clock.

Z ducked behind the cover of a wheelbarrow as a gunshot rang out. The bullet deflected off the wheelbarrow's rim. The robber had the advantage here because he was looking out toward Z, whose body cast a silhouette against the sunshine outside, whereas the robber and his hostage were holed up in the dark.

The robber fired again, solidly striking the wheelbarrow this time.

"I can see in the dark, you know," Z said.

"You're bluffing."

Z whispered to Germ, "You think you can flush him out of cover? Maybe do the 'octopus inkjet on the face' trick while I rush in and get the girl to safety?"

Germ flinched. *I am still wounded from the fence poking me through your jeans. The gunman is fifteen and a half yards away, and I am so little...*

"All right, all right. It was only an idea." He wiped his mouth on the back of his hand. "Sorry for the fence getting you like that. I should've been more careful."

You are trying to right a wrong and save the girl. I understand.

"Who the hell are you talking to?" the robber called.

"My little friend." Z rose from behind the wheelbarrow with his gun extended.

The robber fired, striking Z in the throat. Z fell backward, clutching his torn-open trachea.

Not wanting to wait until he bled out or choked to death, Z turned his gun on himself and pulled the trigger.

He died.

(Ten Seconds Earlier)

"Who the hell are you talking to?" the robber called.

"My little friend. Now I'm giving you to the count of ten to surrender."

There was a pause. "Or what?"

"Then I'm going to barge right up to you like I did to your friend in the bank doorway."

"You're nuts—"

"One, two, three…"

No movement, Germ said, scanning the dark interior.

"…six, seven, eight…"

He is running now, with the girl held out in front of him.

Z tucked his head and charged with a war cry.

"The hell!" The robber shifted on his feet somewhere in the darkness up ahead.

In the dim light, Z could make out the shape of a metal sink up ahead. Then he saw the muzzle flash from the robber's gun, and there was a searing pain in Z's chest.

He fell in a sideways sprawl.

He died.

. . .

(Five Seconds Earlier)

Z tucked his head and charged with a war cry.

This time, instead of staying on a straight course, he diverted to the side so the metal sink covered him. The robber fired at him but missed.

Z broke from cover, seeing a vertical hot water tank.

Too late. The robber had already pulled the trigger.

Z's skull exploded from the perfectly lined up headshot.

He died.

(Five Seconds Earlier)

Z broke from the cover of the metal sink and made a beeline for the hot water tank. The robber fired but missed.

Z peeked out from behind the vertical appliance. The robber fired, striking Z in the head yet again.

He died.

(Five Seconds Earlier)

Z crouched behind the water heater tank. The robber must be positioned backward to him, not more than five yards away, waiting for him to make a move. That meant he effectively had Z pinned down for the moment.

Z needed a distraction.

The girl is fighting back, Germ said. *I think she is...trying to bite him.*

"Ow!" the robber blurted, shuffle-stepping to maintain his balance while gripping the girl out in front of him with one hand and pointing his pistol behind him.

Z saw his chance. Up ahead was a row of vertical two-by-fours forming a partial interior wall. It wasn't as dark here, and he could see better now.

Z sprinted toward the robber, the partial wall between them. The robber fired and missed, disoriented by Z's form darting behind the wooden slats.

This is it, Z thought. *Takedown...*

Pivoting hard on the balls of his feet, he threw his shoulder to the side and crashed into the two-by-four wall. The wood beams splintered upon impact, throwing shards outward in a thunderclap cloud of dust.

When Z's shoulder struck the fleeing robber, the girl flew from his arms, landing in front of him lithe as a cat. Beside her, a paint can sat on the concrete floor, its top open and serving as a holder for a screwdriver.

Despite their conjoined tumble to the floor, the robber somehow managed to slip away from Z and rise to his feet. He pointed the pistol down at Z's head. "Any last words?"

Z eyed the girl standing behind the robber. Then he flicked his eyes back to the ski mask staring down at him. "Yeah. Kick the paint can!"

The girl did. The screwdriver tumbled out as the container flew toward the robber and struck him in the back of the head.

"She shoots; she scores." Z smirked as he stepped in and delivered a finishing two-finger jab to the man's neck. The robber crumpled to the concrete.

"Nice shot, kid."

"How did you know I played soccer?" the girl asked softly.

"Your shoes. My daughter has some like them. She plays soccer too."

The girl grinned. "I'm sure she's a good player. Maybe I can practice with her?"

"Eh, she lives far away."

She squinted up at him. "Like, another country?"

He wasn't about to explain that his daughter lived on a parallel Earth. "Something like that." After crouching and zip-tying the man's hands behind his back, he stood and laid a hand on her shoulder. "Now, how about we get you back to your brother?"

CHAPTER FORTY-THREE

Marshall met Z as he exited the partially constructed building. "You are the biggest goddamn headache I've ever had!"

"Hey now, language. There's a child present here." Z glanced down at the girl standing by his side. She giggled.

Marshall's face turned red. "All the stunts you've pulled this morning…I'm going to be fired for sure."

Z leaned up against one of the exterior two by fours. "You'll be fine. Both hostages are good—not a scrape on them as promised—and all three robbers are incapacitated. I even tied two of them up for you."

"But you—"

"You should thank me. I've wrapped up this case with a neat little bow on top."

Marshall grabbed his head in both hands. "The paperwork, though…"

Z thought about that aspect. How much property damage had there been after Marshall had talked the police captain into letting him take charge of things?

A lot.

Then there was the whole explaining who Z was to the police captain after he disappeared from the scene now.

"About that…" Z lifted his head at the sound of rushing footsteps. He turned. Several news reporters with accompanying camera crews had spotted Marshall and were quickening their pace toward him. Z stepped back into the shadows of the partially constructed building.

"Go with the nice policeman," Z told the girl. "Despite his foul language, he's a nice guy."

The girl giggled and waved at Z, then Z backstepped farther into the shadows.

Marshall glared at him. "You're not sticking around? How the hell—heck—am I supposed to explain all this to the captain?"

Z shrugged. "You'll think of something." He watched from the shadows as the reporters thrust microphones in front of Marshall's face.

Noon was only half an hour away now. Z stopped by one of his weapons caches for supplies and made a call from a phone booth. He didn't expect the call to pay off, but he was about to go up against two super robots and wasn't going to turn down backup in case it did arrive. He put the odds at fifty-fifty.

As he strolled through Central Park, his hands in his pockets, Z reflected on the beauty of the park. Here in a city of millions of people was a sanctuary of green grass and trees and even a lake and reservoir. There was so much life here. And Nunez wanted to end it all by unleashing the time virus? Why?

On one side of the sidewalk he was walking on, children

were playing tag. On the other, a young couple was walking hand in hand, licking ice cream cones and chatting.

Z stopped and closed his eyes. Dogs barked playfully from up ahead, and behind him came the sound of someone playing the guitar. A warm breeze blew the tantalizing aroma of hotdogs and sauerkraut to his nose.

"Move it, asshole!"

As he opened his eyes, a man on a bike passed him on the sidewalk, flipping him off as he went by.

How rude, Germ said.

Z shrugged. "See any sign of Nunez's robots anywhere?"

Not yet. Germ had flattened himself inside Z's pants pocket so that only his eyes protruded from the top.

"We are a bit early," Z muttered.

Central Park was a big place, and he'd wanted to scope it out ahead of time to look for suspicious activity. He'd seen nothing out of the ordinary—no old robot dudes wearing tuxedos and black sunglasses.

For a moment, he wondered if Alice had lied to him about the Central Park time bomb threat, but he quickly dismissed the notion. He wanted to meet up with her again. There was something about her that he found alluring. Maybe it was those long legs, but perhaps it was something deeper. He wasn't lying to Germ earlier. He'd felt a connection with her—

"Nice warm hot dogs! Get yer hot dogs while they're hot."

Z started at the sound of the hot dog vendor's voice beside him.

"How about it, sir? Hot dog? I know you're hungry."

He knew the hot dog man shouldn't have caught him off-guard. He needed to be more focused for when the robots showed up. One way to stay focused was with food.

Since this Earth didn't have donuts...

"I'll take one dog and a bottle of Coke." Z turned to the vendor and reached inside his jacket. "You got change for a hundred?"

Earth food is so un-nutritious, Germ said a couple of moments later as Z bit into the hot dog.

Z nodded at the ground. "Oh, go eat some grass, you turd."

I am not a turd.

"It's an expression."

A stupid expression. Humans have the dumbest sayings.

Z sipped his Coke. "What can I say? We're a dumb species at times."

Got that right.

He surveyed the park from left to right, still seeing no sign of Nunez's robots. He would start a new lap around the park and see if he could spot them. The bike that jerk had almost run him over with earlier seemed like a good idea now. Maybe he could find the man and offer him a stack of hundred-dollar bills for it.

He chuckled at the idea.

As he started back on the sidewalk path through the park, he glanced down at Germ's beady eyes peeking out of his pocket. "How did you ever develop such keen eyes and ears?"

I am hyper-evolved. Having once been suspended in a state of exponential evolution, I have lived the equivalent of millions of years. I have told you this.

Z ate his hot dog while he walked. "Right, millions of years. Hell. I doubt humanity will survive that long."

You got that right, partner. Hot dogs and donuts will be the death of you all.

Z nearly choked on the laughter that escaped him. It felt good to laugh. Especially when he was about to confront two killer robots intent on releasing a bioweapon into Central

Park, thus endangering the entire multiverse if the time virus contained within was allowed to hyper evolve, as had happened with Germ.

The thing Z kept turning over in his head was why Nunez would try this all over again. Was it desperation? If so, why? Was he sick or dying, maybe?

How was this Earth's version of Nunez involved? Why had Nunez had his robot kidnap his younger self? Was he intending on somehow manipulating some of the time virus in the bioweapon to infect his younger self so he could go back in time?

He shook his head. Nah. That probably wasn't right.

Something was niggling at him, though.

"Alice's cover story about Mel Phoenix going missing. I guess her name was Mel Garcia? For that matter, why the hell was Earth-D's Eduardo Nunez named Ray Garcia? There are too many unanswered questions. Regardless, Old Nunez gave Alice that cover story to entice me. Why did Nunez tell her to give me that particular story?"

He thought of the answer at the same time as Germ.

Perhaps he is trying to save his wife, who went missing in the 1980s.

It made sense.

"Something happened to Old Nunez's wife on Earth-Z. Ever since, Old Nunez has been trying to find a way to go back in time or reverse time so he can prevent his wife from disappearing."

Yes.

Z slapped a hand to his forehead. He should have realized that Mel was Old Nunez's missing wife ever since he was looking at their photos in Ray's house while Marshall had been talking with him in the kitchen.

"So Old Nunez traveled to Earth-D because its timeline is about forty years behind Earth-Z. Nunez can't warp backward in time, but he can hop to parallel Earths in real-time. That's why he came to this Earth. He wanted to try to stop this Earth's version of his wife from dying. Or going missing or whatever happened to her." He scratched his chin. "I guess he failed."

From his pocket, Germ blinked up at him.

"You think that might be what Nunez is trying to do? You think that's what this whole mess is all about? And another thing. How has he been keeping tabs on me?"

Why don't you ask him yourself?

"Huh? What do you mean—"

Then Z saw him.

Nunez. Five yards away. Standing under a tree with the reservoir behind him. He wore a tan Panama hat and a smile directed right at Z.

CHAPTER FORTY-FOUR

"I've been expecting you," Eduardo Nunez said.

Z set his jaw as his fists clenched. "I'll be honest with you. I wasn't expecting you."

"Wouldn't have been a surprise if you did." Nunez folded his hands behind his back. He stood with a straight back, and his chin thrust outward like a great man in profile before an artist.

"Why did you want to surprise me?"

"So we could talk."

Z flexed his fingers at his side. "Talk?"

Nunez rolled his eyes. "Talk. Chat. Speak. Palaver. When two people exchange words—"

"I know what talking is, asshole."

At Z's raised voice, a jogger veered around Z, and a mother cupped her hands over her child's ears and hurried away.

Nunez gestured for Z to come closer. Behind him, the reservoir's surface shimmered peacefully in the sunlight.

"You're not afraid of me?" Z asked gravely.

"Why would you want to hurt me when we could both benefit from this conversation?"

Z was starting to see red. Here was the man who had ruined his life. Here. In the flesh. Right in front of him. Part of him wanted to reach out and strangle the older man.

Instead, he drew a deep, calming breath. "How could I be interested in anything you say?"

Nunez eyed Z closely. "You and I have something in common. We both lost our wives. You, to the multiverse as a consequence of traveling back in time in your capsule, thus becoming an extraneous person outside the multiversal time-line. And me…" Nunez lifted his tan hat from his head and examined it before placing it back on his head. "I never found out what happened to my wife."

Z made a fist. "We may each have a tragic life story, but I am nothing like you."

"So you say. Let me pose a question to you. What is it you want in this life more dearly than anything?"

Z scratched his chin.

"Please," Nunez said. "You've lost so much. Tell me what it is you'd like most to regain."

"Well…"

Nunez waved for him to continue.

"There is one thing."

"Go on. Go on."

"I lost it in my college days."

"Okay," Nunez said, a bit unsure.

Your virginity? Germ asked.

"An old vinyl record titled *Fuck You.*" He moved threateningly close to Nunez, who looked unworried.

"Go ahead. Kill me if you think it will make you feel better. It won't."

Z scoffed. "And here I thought you were going to say you could give me my greatest wish, turn everything back the way it was before the time virus infected me."

Now it was Nunez's time to scoff. "Oh, I can't do that. But I can give you true death if release is what you desire."

Z stared at the man. "I'm a Repeater. You can do that?"

"At the moment, no. If I put my resources toward it, I have no doubt I can figure it out."

He folded his arms. "With me out of the picture, that would give you free rein to do whatever you want. I would never allow that."

The older man sighed. "You've lost everything. You don't belong anywhere. You're a broken man."

"Am not."

"Without your space and time capsule, you're stranded on an Earth that doesn't have donuts."

Z grunted.

"Plus, you were played like a fiddle by Miss Alice and left behind like a tumbling wad of trash."

"That's not how we parted ways—"

Nunez's eyes bulged in their sockets as he quickly stepped close and grabbed Z by the jacket collar. "You can never be with your wife again. You shouldn't even exist in the multiversal timeline."

Z knocked Nunez's hands from his jacket and shoved the older man to the grass. "I've made my peace with that. It's in the past. I'm living a new life as a new man."

"You're an abomination. A piece of shit in a world that doesn't want you."

Z growled. "At least I'm a piece of shit who's trying to atone for his actions."

On his hands and knees, Nunez wiped his mouth with the

back of his hand. "I've been watching you for some time. Hopping to other Earths. 'Righting wrongs.'" He paused for dramatic effect. "You can fix a million wrongs. You're still a monster."

"Takes one to know one."

After picking himself up, Nunez touched his chest. "Me?"

"You're going to kill hundreds when you detonate the time bomb."

"No, I won't. I've done the calculations. I'll kill thousands."

"Why? You're crazier than I thought if you think it'll bring your wife back."

Nunez sneered at Z. "I don't think that. It's a diversion meant to keep you busy while I finish tinkering with your space and time capsule. That's the only way I can go back in time and stop my wife from disappearing."

"You'd kill thousands of people to save your wife?"

Nunez set his jaw harder than any stone. "I'd kill them all. If that's what it took."

Z laughed. "You're batshit crazy. Delirious. Hell, I thought I was bad trying to start World War III. You're skipping straight to the apocalypse."

"The world doesn't know my pain."

"Oh, boo-hoo. We both lost our wives. Sure, we have that in common. I'm smart enough to know when I can't or shouldn't do something."

Nunez spat. "That's where you're wrong. You don't have my dedication. I would never give up on my wife. Never."

Z scoffed. "What do you think your wife would say if she saw you now? You think she would want to be with you after what you said?"

Nunez ground his teeth together. "I'm an old man. I'm running out of time. I can't keep hopping to other Earths." He shook his head. "No matter. I knew you wouldn't be able to see things my way."

"Germ, why don't you attack this man's face? I'm tired of listening to him."

Germ peeked out from Z's pocket and hopped down to the grass.

Nunez's expression softened. "Germ. Oh, sweet little Germ."

"The fuck?" Z muttered. He shook his head. "Germ, get the bastard. Ink his mouth so he can't talk anymore."

The tiny black octopus swayed in the grass atop his tentacles.

"Germ. You hear me? Go get—"

"He hears you, all right," Nunez said. "He's done listening to you. He's mine now. Always has been."

"Uh, no, he's not. Germ, go get him—"

"You treat little Germ like he's a pet. When you should be treating him like the royalty he is."

"Germ," Z said. "What's going on?"

Germ glanced back at Z. *I can't move...Nunez is controlling me...somehow.*

"Germ," Nunez said. Germ twisted his head back at Nunez. "You and I can achieve great things together."

"This is ridiculous," Z said. "Fight it."

"I will not treat you like a pet because," Nunez said, "I am your father. I created you. I know you. I've been watching Z's movements through your eyes."

Germ quivered. *Nooo...*

"No way..." Z said, horror dawning on him. "Wait. That's how you've been keeping tabs on me?"

"You were never going to beat me," Nunez said. "Germ, come to me."

Z knelt by Germ and reached out. "Don't listen to that asshole. We're partners."

Germ opened his tiny mouth wide and chomped down on Z's hand.

"Hey—oww!" Suddenly Z's world began to wobble like he'd been poisoned or something. The color of the grass and sky and reservoir faded in and out as if being adjusted by a dial. He was barely aware of Nunez stepping up to him and kicking. Z's head jerked to the side with the impact. He spat out blood.

"And you. You think of Marshall as your father, but I'm your real father. I created Repeaters. I created the time virus. And I am going to get my wife back."

Z saw stars. What the hell had Germ done to him? "You could have...asked Buzz and me for help. Instead of destroying the world."

"Like either of you would've believed me. I'm on my own. Just me and now Germ. Goodbye."

Z threw up a hand, fighting against the disorientation. "Wait. Your wife. Why did you have Alice hire me to investigate her disappearance?"

"Isn't it obvious? Everyone loves a good mystery. It certainly kept your mind off me for a time, didn't it? Besides, a small part of me thought that maybe you could solve it. Not that you could. I've already studied all the clues—"

"You're wrong." Z stabbed the air with his finger. The wooziness was starting to wear off. He drew a deep breath. The colors of his environment were starting to revert to normal, and the world was no longer moving. "I'll solve your wife's case whether you want me to or not."

"Will you now?"

"Yes." Z's wooziness was almost gone. He pushed himself

up and rose to his feet. "Now, how about you hand Germ back, leave this Earth, and crawl back to whatever hole you've been hiding in."

"You're a fool. You think you have leverage here." Nunez shook his head sadly. "May God have pity on you. Because I won't." Nunez snapped his fingers and nodded past Z.

Z spun. Standing at each side of him were the two tuxedoed robots.

CHAPTER FORTY-FIVE

Found them, Z thought.

Their faces and tuxes were new and unmarred. They stood tall and powerful, like buffed-out older men with a mind to kill. One of them was holding the metal canister containing the bioweapon. An LCD timer on it showed three minutes.

After a nod from Nunez, the robot initiated the bomb's timer.

"This is a modified time virus," Nunez said. "It moves much slower than the version on Earth-Z."

Z glared at Nunez, holding Germ on his palm. "Why would you risk this again?"

Nunez backed away from the scene. "I've learned from my mistakes and made changes to the virus. Plus, what do I have to live for if it does go astray?"

Z wanted to kill Nunez, but one of the robots lunged for him. He rolled to the side. Nunez was going to get away. "You asshole! Your wife would never want you to do this—"

A robot's fist crashed into Z's mouth, and he staggered sideways in the grass. He spat out some blood.

"A three-minute fuse for your three minutes of Repeating," Nunez called. "Have fun."

Z considered killing himself and warping back three minutes right now, but he didn't like having the two robots in the picture. Previously, whenever he warped in their presence, they seemed to be able to anticipate his moves. If anything, warping with them present made them stronger against him.

First, one robot threw a punch, then the other. Z dodged both as well as a kick. Since they wore the appearance of older men in black tuxes and sunglasses, their movements seemed perversely young and fluid. Still, they were robots—not men—and they had a bioweapon set to go off in less than three minutes.

Stepping in fast, Z landed a jab to the abdomen of one robot, but it had no effect.

He attempted to kick one of their ankles out from under it when the other one circled and grabbed him by the shoulders. The robot shoved him forcefully back to the ground and held him in place by his upper arms. Then the other robot leaned over him and began to pummel his face until it was black and blue and bleeding through cuts all over it.

Suddenly, they released him. He rolled over and picked himself up. He wiped the blood on his jacket sleeve. "What's wrong? You boys getting tired?"

"We want a real fight," one tuxedoed robot rasped.

The other one said, "You are a pathetic combatant."

"Oh?" Z rushed forward, feinted, and succeeded in slamming his palm into the abdomen of one robot while tripping it with a foot behind its ankle. The robot tumbled backward. Then the second robot swung at Z with a strike that probably would've disintegrated his shoulder had it connected. Z evaded and kicked the second robot behind the knee.

The robot shrugged off the attack and raised its leg, kicking in a vicious arc at face level. The heel of the robot's dress shoe clipped Z's chin, opening up a thin gash that leaked blood.

With a smile, the robot said, "Now that is better."

The first robot, having regained its footing, tackled Z from the side, landing on top of him in the grass and pinning Z's arms to his sides while the second robot proceeded to beat the shit out of his face again.

Z's vision blurred. As he gazed out at the park, he didn't see anyone in the nearby area. They must've run off at the first sign of a fight. Or maybe they'd gone to call for help. But for who? The man with the face scar or the two older gents he was fighting?

Fuck. Where's Germ when I need him?

If the tiny octopus was here, he could launch himself at the robots' faces and ink-jet them so they couldn't see for a short time.

Atop him, the second robot continued to strike.

Then, like the first time, the robots stepped away and allowed him to rise to his feet. He was much slower this time, and the world was shaky before him. For a moment, he saw double so that it appeared he was facing four tuxedoed robots. Then the figures converged, and he was fighting two again.

"You are weak," one of them rasped.

"This is too easy."

Enraged, Z threw himself forward. If Germ were here, he probably would've reminded Z of some important aspect or notion, maybe provided a bit of philosophical advice. He wasn't here, though. Z put everything he had into his next attack on these sharp-dressed robotic assholes.

He feinted to the left and struck out with his right fist. The first robot caught it, met Z's eyes, and twisted Z's hand until his wrist snapped.

Z clenched his jaw shut as a grunt of anguish escaped his lungs. The next thing he knew, one of the robots held him from behind. Its vice grip fingers dug into his upper arms while the other robot stood in front of him, jabbing him repeatedly in the gut.

He doubled over, puking into the grass.

This wasn't good. It wasn't going according to plan at all.

When coming to Central Park, he'd hoped to be able to get the jump on the robots, maybe take them out quietly one by one if he was lucky. Instead, Nunez and the two robots had surprised him, and now they were alternating between beating him up and letting him have a chance to fight back. They purposely weren't killing him. They were…playing with him.

His torso jerked with the impact of another fist to the gut, and he dry heaved to the side. As he brought his vision back to the front, he saw the red LED countdown of the time bomb slung over one of the robot's shoulders. He watched as it ticked down from thirty seconds to twenty-nine seconds.

"You assholes—"

Another fist pounded into his gut.

They were waiting for the three-minute timer to tick down. So he couldn't warp back to before they'd set it. He had to warp back in time. If they wouldn't kill him, he'd have to do the job himself.

Without Germ here, he felt so alone.

The robot sent yet another blow to his abdomen. He

allowed his body to hang limply in the robot's grip behind him.

"Has the weakling had enough?" the robot behind him sneered, still gripping him tightly.

The one in front of Z kicked him tentatively across the jaw as if checking if he was still alive. Keeping his body and jaw relaxed, Z allowed his body to absorb the attack.

The robot gripping him from behind released him, dumping him to the grass.

Z wasted no time in drawing his pistol from inside his jacket and turning its barrel upward.

He pulled the trigger.

He died.

(Three Minutes Earlier)

"A three-minute fuse for your three minutes of Repeating," Nunez called. "Have fun."

Z had warped back as far as he could and was only able to go back to the setting of the bomb's stop clock. The robots had done a good job of keeping his mind off the time bomb and fighting them.

While keeping the robots in his periphery, Z turned to Nunez. "This isn't going to work, you know."

Nunez only smiled, petting Germ's head as he held the black octopus in his palm. "We shall see. My robots are quite formidable."

There was movement in front of him, and Z turned back to the robots as they both rushed toward him. He raised his hands to defend against them, but one of them had already lifted him off the ground while the second one reached inside his jacket.

Reached inside for his gun…

The bastards know I've got a gun from my last Repeat.

But how?

Z kicked the second robot's hands away from his jacket and drew the gun himself. Tilting its barrel upward, he fired twice point-blank into the head of the robot who was holding him. The robot dropped him, and Z landed on his feet. He fired upward at the second robot, striking it once in the head. Both robots stepped back a couple of steps and recalibrated or whatever they had to do after being shot in the head.

From around him in the park, people began to scream and cry out. The first time around, he hadn't fired his gun until near the end of the three minutes. Now he'd fired it within the first fifteen seconds, and people were fleeing, as they should be.

"How did you know I had a gun?" Z didn't expect the robots to answer.

The robots shook their heads to clear them. They still seemed a bit stunned. Z's gunshots had destroyed both of their sunglasses, but one of them still wore half a frame over a glowing red eye.

Both of the robots turned their head one way to reveal the futuristic gold earpiece in their ears. "The nanotechnology in them," one of the robots rasped, "can remember your warps."

The other robot continued. "It informs us what happened before your warp so we can react accordingly."

Well…fuck.

These robots couldn't warp back in time, but they didn't need to if they could read Z's future movements. Nunez's earpiece technology effectively neutralized Z's warping powers in a fight.

It wouldn't have been an issue if he was fighting humans

wearing the earpieces. Humans could die. A pair of indestructible robots wearing the earpieces was a different story altogether.

Z suddenly remembered that he had one of the gold earpieces in his jacket. Alice had given it to him. It probably had the same ability as theirs, but it wouldn't do him any good. He needed some other edge.

The robots stepped forward and rolled their shoulders and heads in preparation for battle.

"You cannot win against us," one of them said.

"You should probably run away," said the other.

Z had to admit that he wasn't in a good position. But he couldn't run away.

So what could he do?

He was getting ready to rush forward to fight them again when a clear voice boomed behind him.

"Hey, you. Yeah, I'm talking to you two robot assholes."

The two robots turned to face the new arrival. So did Z. It seemed the last-minute call he'd made before coming to the park for backup had paid off.

Marshall stood there, the sunlight glinting off the outstretched police revolver in his hands and the silver badge on his chest.

"Maybe nobody told you two motherfuckers, but killer robots aren't welcome in my goddamned city."

CHAPTER FORTY-SIX

Standing there in his police blues, Marshall glared at the two robots. Z couldn't help but be impressed.

"What took you so long?" Z asked.

Still keeping his revolver aimed at the robots, Marshall shrugged. "Took a while at the bank scene and the construction site once you disappeared."

Z smirked. "I'm guessing they didn't fire you."

Marshall paused. "They promoted me to day shift. Then I got your message to meet you at Central Park but to come alone. I was able to slip away since I'm technically off the clock. Now, what's the situation?"

The two robots exchanged glances and rushed toward Z and Marshall. As if reading Z's mind, Marshall moved away from him so they put the robots between them.

Z called, "Here's the situation. Two indestructible robots. Don't waste your ammo shooting them." He ducked as his robot swiped at his head. "Your robot is carrying a bioweapon set to blow in about two minutes."

Marshall evaded a particularly nasty punch from his robot. "That's not good."

"No, it's not."

Z and Marshall stepped to the side as they danced around the robots' attacks. They soon found themselves back-to-back, facing their respective robot. Since Z had shot them in the head earlier, the robots were moving a little slower than usual.

"What's the damage of said bioweapon?" Marshall called.

Z ducked a blow and threw a kick into his robot's gut. It barely fazed the robot. "A time virus that will consume all life forms it touches as it expands outward."

"Well, fuck me."

"Pretty much."

"First killer robots. Now time bombs? What next?"

Z smirked as he tagged Marshall on the shoulder, and they switched robots. "I'm from the future. A parallel Earth with a timeline sixty years ahead of this Earth's."

"Sure you are." Marshall ducked behind his robot and kicked it in the ass with minimal effect. "Now, how about we get to the part where we kill these bastards and disarm the time bomb."

"Good idea," Z said. "You make it sound so easy."

Marshall stepped back in time to receive only a glancing blow to the shoulder instead of a full frontal punch. "It's a good thing I trust you. Mostly. You said they're indestructible. You got a plan?"

Z did. With a second person to use as a distraction, it might work. "Yeah, but you're not gonna like it or believe it." Z raised his gun and shot his robot in the head, then pivoted around it so he was next to Marshall. He shot Marshall's robot in the head and whispered the plan in Marshall's ear.

"Why the hell are you whispering?"

"So they can't hear. See, when I die and warp back, they know what I did before I warped."

Marshall swallowed, for the first time looking like he might be out of his league on this mission. "What did you say?"

Z dug the gold earpiece from his jacket and inserted it into Marshall's ear. "I'm saying that I'm probably going to have to die for this plan to work."

Marshall scoffed. "You're crazier than a squirrel in a nut shop—"

His robot jumped in front of him, its fingers straight out like a knife. It drove its hand into Marshall's chest and pulled them out lightning-quick.

Marshall sagged to the ground. There was a gaping hole in his chest, and the robot held Marshall's still-beating heart.

Z growled. "You bastards."

"Two can play at this game," the robot with the time bomb sneered. "You cannot win."

"We'll see." Z turned his gun on himself and pulled the trigger.

He died.

(Ten Seconds Earlier)

"The fuck is going on?" Marshall said. "This earpiece told me I get my heart torn out of my chest by this robot—"

Z evaded a blow from his robot. "Then don't let it happen again." He was glad the earpiece worked as the robots had described. He'd had his doubts. Now that he knew it worked, it effectively meant that he could have a human sidekick who could "remember" his warps, a big aid in any fight where he might have to die and warp.

Marshall frowned. "What? That isn't possible. I didn't die. You can't un-die—"

Marshall's robot quickly stepped in and plunged its hand into Marshall's chest, ripping out his still-beating heart. Marshall dropped to the ground, his face ashen.

"You died again," Z complained. He ducked a particularly vicious punch. "Gotta be quicker, Dad."

He turned the gun on himself and pulled the trigger.

He died.

(Five Seconds Earlier)

"Get out of the way!" Z yelled. "Move!"

Marshall sidestepped as his robot jabbed its straight-fingered hand forward like a knife at the spot where Marshall had been standing.

"This damned earpiece says I've died two times now. Had my heart ripped out—"

"It's true," Z said. "I saw it happen both times."

"But how—"

"Long story. Now, look. Remember the plan?" Z saw Marshall's eyes flick toward the reservoir about twenty yards away. "These robots are going to throw everything they've got at us." He ducked out of the way of a kick and found himself shoulder-to-shoulder with Marshall. "We have one chance at this before they wise up to our plan. You ready?"

Marshall nodded.

"Now!" Z shouted.

He and Marshall raised their firearms and fired at the

robots' heads, being careful that each shot was good first and wouldn't go into the park where it could strike a civilian.

When Marshall had expended all his ammo and Z had one round left in the chamber, he angled his head toward the reservoir and beckoned Marshall to follow him.

"We shot them in the face," Marshall huffed from right behind Z. "I can't believe that didn't kill them."

"Believe it. 'Cause they're robots. We have to get this right, or they'll know what we tried. Then they won't fall for it again, and we're screwed."

"I hope to hell this works," Marshall said. "Because we're out of ammo."

"All part of the plan." Z sucked in a breath. "Their guard will be down because they'll think we're defenseless." He still had one round left in his chamber, their backup plan in case he had to kill himself and warp back.

As he ran, he threw a glance over his shoulder at the two robots regaining their composure after the head shots. They loped after him and Marshall. He hoped the plan would work. It should work. Right? Germ would know, but he wasn't here.

He and Marshall neared the water's edge.

The footfalls of the two tuxedoed robots swished through the grass behind them. Z and Marshall turned to face their fast-approaching attackers.

Now it was time for their "last stand."

"For New York!" Z roared.

"New York!" Marshall yelled.

The robots, it seemed, still didn't suspect Z's plan. They barreled onward, stopping before reaching Z and Marshall. They drew back their fists to strike.

Z and Marshall evaded the blows meant for them and spun, grabbing their respective robot and throwing them into the water, using the robots' momentum against them. Z also succeeded in stripping the time bomb from his robot's shoulder.

The robots fell into the reservoir with a twin splash.

A moment later, the robots resurfaced. "Hah. We do not short circuit in water like weaker models of robots."

The other robot gave a curving grin.

Z grinned. "Oh, I'm not counting on the water short-circuiting you."

He pulled a taser device from inside his jacket. He'd retrieved it from his weapons cache before coming to the park. Alice using one on him in the motel had given him the idea. This wasn't a futuristic taser. It was a taser from this time, back before they had more safety features. It was bulky and looked lethal. Z leveled it at one of the robots and pulled the trigger. The two prongs shot off, embedding in the robot's ruined forehead. Would it work on a humanoid robot?

Smoke issued first from the tuxedoed robot Z had struck with the taser, then the second one started to smoke. Their red eyes began to dim.

Marshall slapped Z on the shoulder. "Well, I'll be damned…"

Z didn't feel like celebrating yet. In their damaged and disoriented state, he might be able to get some information from them before they were toast.

"What is Nunez's plan?"

"Not going…to tell you…" the first robot said.

"Against…protocol…" said the second.

"Tell me," Z demanded.

The robots' red eyes dimmed even further.

"Use space and time capsule…travel to the outdoor concert…to before wife went missing…"

Z basically already knew that. Nunez had already told him that. He needed to ask better questions. "Why did Nunez give the thugs at the warehouse the bomb only to have you steal it back?"

"They were…expendable. Wanted to deploy the weapon… in the streets…Central Park better target…they would not listen."

Made sense.

"Why did Nunez kidnap his younger self?"

One of the robots' heads was jerking and twisting erratically. The smoke was worse now. "If wife still lives on this Earth…wants to kill younger version of himself…assume the younger version of himself through temporal displacement…"

Shit. As crazy as it sounded, that could work. This had happened to his mother, Carolyn. If an older version of oneself hopped to a parallel Earth with a younger version of them, the universe's natural order would convert them into their younger self if that younger self died or was already dead. They would then literally be the age they should be on that Earth's timeline.

Z decided to keep asking questions for as long as he could. "Why is the younger Nunez on this Earth named Ray Garcia?"

"Nunez's real name…on all Earths…changed it after… police suspected him of wife's murder…"

That would explain why Buzz couldn't find much information on Nunez before the man rose to fame for his scientific exploits after his wife had died.

Now it was million-dollar question time. Z stepped closer to the reservoir, being careful with his footing. "Where is Nunez going? Where is the space and time capsule?"

The two robots were making *zzzzt!* sounds now. "He is…he is…"

The red lights in both of the robots' eyes blanked out to nothing.

"Fuck," Z said. He should've asked that question first. What was he thinking?

Marshall nudged his arm. "Uh, Z."

Z turned. "What?"

Marshall was pointing at the time bomb in Z's hands. Its timer read 0:17.

Z flipped over the metal canister in his hands and retrieved his combat knife from his boot. He found a metal cover on the back and pried it off with the knife. Inside the canister was a housing containing two wires, one green and one red.

Marshall gulped. "You feeling lucky?"

With a smirk, Z cut the green wire.

There was a moment of silence followed by a shrill *beep*. Then gas began to filter out through both ends of the canister.

"Dammit," Z said.

Already the grass beneath his feet was starting to shrivel up and turn to dust. Beside him, Marshall's skin began to wrinkle and decay before his very eyes. Z himself was immune to the time virus.

Marshall made a choking sound. "What the…"

Z turned the knife on himself and punched it through his heart.

He died.

(Forty Seconds Earlier)

Z warped back far enough so that the two robots were in the water but were still functioning. He needed to find out where Nunez was holed up before he cut the correct wire this time.

"Where is Nunez going?" Z demanded.

Meanwhile, Marshall was frowning at the words spoken into his ear through his earpiece.

The two short-circuiting robots made jerking motions in the water. "Cannot answer…at this time…cannot answer…"

"What the hell?" Z muttered. "Answer me. Where is Nunez going? Where is the space and time capsule?"

"Remote override activated…remote override activated…"

Dammit. Nunez must've been alerted to Z's warp and shut his robots down remotely.

Suddenly, Marshall blurted, "Don't cut the green wire!"

Z continued to stare at the robots. "Come on. Answer me."

"Don't cut the green wire!" Marshall repeated. "It'll arm the bomb—"

"I know, I know." Z focused his attention on the water. "Come on, you stupid robots, answer me!"

The two robots' red eyes went dark.

"Shit." Z drew a deep breath and ground his teeth.

"The bomb," Marshall said.

Z drew another deep breath and relaxed his jaw. Then he flipped the bomb over in his hands and opened the back cover with his combat knife. He unceremoniously cut the red wire and the timer blacked out.

They'd succeeded in preventing the bomb from going off and killing billions of people.

CHAPTER FORTY-SEVEN

Z whistled as he walked down the sidewalk to try to calm his mind. It sometimes worked.

This time it didn't. It only reminded him of Germ and how the tiny black octopus would occasionally whistle in his mind. Annoying as hell, but he missed the little guy. What was Nunez doing to Germ right now? Experimenting on him?

As Z passed some people on the sidewalk, he disregarded their odd looks and stares. Some of them wrinkled their noses as he passed. Yeah, he smelled and looked like shit. He got it. Also, he didn't care.

He mentally replayed what had happened back at the park. Nunez surprising him. Siccing his attack robots on him, equipped with futuristic earpieces that could remember when Repeaters warped back in time and relay to the wearer what had happened.

He recalled the scene before he left where Marshall had asked Z what the hell he was going to do with the two very human-looking robots that were now dead and floating in the Central Park reservoir. Z suggested they drag the robots out of the water, but then he'd noticed that something odd was happening to the bodies. They were…melting.

First, the robots' human-like skin dissolved. Then the plastic-like bones underneath started to disintegrate in the water. Z and Marshall had stood by and watched in disgusted awe throughout the whole process.

A minute later, nothing remained of the two tuxedoed robots except for a floating pair of tuxedos. It was more than a little creepy.

Z had scratched his chin. "Must've been a self-destruct mechanism if they ever 'died' so no one could re-engineer their technology."

Marshall hadn't known what to say. For all he'd witnessed and experienced that day, he was holding together quite well.

"Eh, no body, no crime," Z said. "Right?"

Marshall had only nodded.

Then Z took Alice's earpiece back from Marshall, tucked it in his jacket's inside pocket, and smacked Marshall on the back. "Good job today, Pops. I'm proud of ya." He didn't know if Marshall had heard him or not. The man had still been trying to wrap his head around everything. "Congrats on the promotion. You deserve it."

He'd left Central Park then.

Now Z was wandering alone down the streets of New York, trying to figure out his next move.

As he walked, Nunez's words kept eating at him. He didn't know why they bothered him. They shouldn't. They were stupid words.

Maybe they were true words.

Germ was gone. His wife was gone. His old life and home were gone. Maybe Nunez was right. Maybe he was broken.

Perhaps the world didn't need him, and he didn't belong anywhere.

If Germ were here, he'd know how to make him feel better. *How about you start a fistfight over a game of billiards. Or go to a strip club. Or get a Big Mac.*

The little octopus knew him all too well. His thoughts went to Alice, and he wondered how she was faring. Maybe if he could track her down, he could let her know that he'd killed those two robots and ask if she wanted to grab dinner. Together they could talk about how fucked up life was.

She was gone too.

What was the point of continuing? This Earth didn't even have any donuts.

Damn. He'd never felt this low. Fucking Nunez and his words and time manipulation schemes. The one good thing was that he'd prevented the bioweapon from being detonated at Central Park. He wasn't completely useless…

"Oh, Mimi! Please come down. I'm so scared and don't want you to get hurt."

"The hell…" Z muttered, glancing over at an attractive middle-aged woman in a pink dress. She was wearing pink high heels and pink lipstick and had her blonde hair done up in a fancy twist.

After appraising her bare legs, Z walked over to the woman. "What seems to be the problem, ma'am?"

The lady in pink was on the verge of tears. She could barely speak as she looked up and pointed at a tree off the sidewalk in a grassy clearing. "M-my cat. Mimi. Stuck."

Z followed her gaze up to the tree's leaves. A white short-haired cat perched on a tree limb eight feet above the ground. The cat sat there licking its paws. It meowed pleasantly down at Z.

"Oh, the poor dear must be...sc-scared out of her mind," the lady said.

Z put a hand gently on her shoulder, and she stiffened. He removed his hand. "Let me help. I'll climb up and get her for you."

Her eyes lit up. "You. You w-would?"

He beamed. "These days, helping people is my sole existence in life."

She nodded slowly as if this were some foreign concept she couldn't possibly understand in a thousand years.

At least she was hot. Z inspected the tree's trunk and grabbed hold. His body was still a bit exhausted from tangling with the two robots in Central Park, but renewed energy coursed through him with this new opportunity to help out someone in need. It was like a sign from the fates telling him to push on. Not that he believed in all that fate crap.

As he shinnied up to the tree branch the cat was sitting on, he heard the murmuring of a gathering crowd below. Germ would probably have something witty to say about that if he was here. But he wasn't.

When he was high enough, Z tested the tree limb with some of his weight to see if it would support him. It seemed like it would. It was a strong branch.

With his arms and legs hugging the limb, he inched along it, getting closer and closer to the cat.

A bystander gasped from the grassy earth below. "He's going to make it!"

Damn right I am, Z thought. He pulled himself another inch closer to the cat and held out his hand. "Here, Mimi. Here, Mimi."

The cat licked her paw and meowed at him. No surprise, she was wearing a pink collar.

"Come here, little Mimi," he cooed. The tone felt all wrong to him, contrasting with his tough-guy masculinity, but he'd do pretty much anything for a woman in need. "Here, kitty, kitty…"

"OMG, he's a frickin' cat whisperer," a college-age girl whispered from below.

"It's like watching a nature documentary," said a college-age boy standing next to her.

How many people are watching me? Z wondered as he pulled himself another inch along the limb toward the white cat.

Suddenly there was a soft *cracking* sound beneath him.

"Oh shit—"

The limb he was straddling gave way with a loud *snap*, and he let go of it, blindly reaching for the cat as he fell.

He hit the ground.

He didn't die.

He groaned.

Considering the pain in his knees and hip and elbows, he kind of wished he had. But his body was still in one piece, nothing felt broken, and luckily all of the bystanders had been standing far enough away that they didn't get hit by the tree branch.

Everyone was silent as Z sat up. In his hands, kept safe from the fall, was Mimi. The cat meowed.

"He did it!" someone said, and at least twenty people began to clap.

Mimi meowed again and leapt up into the pink lady's arms.

Z grinned. He was starting to feel pretty good about himself. Slowly, he picked himself up off the ground and patted the dirt from his torn and sweaty clothes. Quickly, he tested all his joints to make sure his body still worked.

It did.

The pink lady made googly eyes at her cat and gripped her close to her chest.

Z wished he was the cat.

A crossing guard stepped up to Z and shook his hand. "Sir, you're a hero."

"Thanks?"

The lady in pink stepped up to him. "Oh, thank you so much. How can I ever repay you?"

Z thought about it. She was quite an attractive woman. "Dinner? Tonight?"

She eyed him as if he was a five-day-old can of opened tuna.

"What?" Z said.

"I'm married."

Z scratched the back of his head. He blinked. "So…that's a no?"

With a scoff, the woman gripped her cat tight to her chest and spun, her high heels *clicking* as she strode away.

"Shit, that was unexpected," the crossing guard said.

Z agreed, wondering what quip Germ would've come back with had he been there. It probably would've been a real humdinger.

Damnit, Z thought, *I'm like that cat. Stuck in a tree not knowing what to do. Well, I'm not going to let Nunez bust my balls. I'll find a way to get my buddy back and stop that bastard once and for all…*

His stomach growled.

"But first, food."

CHAPTER FORTY-EIGHT

Beer. Z forgot how good it tasted.

He set down his glass and took another bite of his burger as he glanced up at the big boxy TVs mounted above the sports bar. Each one had the Euro Cup on, and it was a close game. When he finished the last sip of his beer, he raised a finger for the bartender to come over.

This wasn't a bar Z ever frequented on any of the Earths. It was one of his dad's favorite bars on Earth-Z so it seemed like a good enough idea. So had the first beer. And the second. And the third.

"Dude," the bartender said, a hipster guy with a long beard. Apparently, the eighties had hipsters too. "Maybe you should lay off the brew?"

Z grinned, starting to feel the effects of the alcohol. "And here I was about to order another burger."

"You've already had two."

"I've burned a lot of calories today."

When the bartender looked at him, Z said, "Yeah…I'll take a water." He planned to stop by the new *Paper Warriors* office after this and would prefer to be sober when he used the printing press to talk to Buzz.

Buzz. Buzz*ed*. Heh heh.

The bartender smacked the bar top. "One water coming right up."

A hand fell on Z's shoulder, and he started. He spun with one arm raised defensively, the other drawn back and ready to two-finger jab whoever it was.

Z grinned. "My man Marshall!" He threw a hand on Marshall's shoulder. "Of all the gin joints in all the world…"

"Cut the shit," Marshall said. "I'm too exhausted. This is my favorite bar."

Maybe fate was a thing.

On the TV screen, a goalie barely managed to stop a ball. Z cheered. Then he patted the stool next to him. "I'm glad you came. Take a seat."

Marshall glanced up at the TV screen and shook his head. "Had I known soccer was on, and you would be here, I would've picked a different place."

"Very funny. Why didn't you go home?"

Marshall looked at him. "If you'd been an accomplice to a double robot homicide, died several times, learned that time travel is real, and helped defuse a bomb, would you have gone home?"

Z shrugged.

"I mean, what the hell was I supposed to tell my wife when she asked how work was?"

Z picked at a piece of burger in his teeth. "Um, I don't know. Lie? Hey, you did get promoted to the day shift today so at least you don't have to go in at midnight tonight. You can sleep."

The bartender came back with Z's water.

Marshall ordered a whiskey and Coke. "Make it a double." He turned to Z. "I don't think I'm going to get any sleep for a while."

"Yeah, probably not. Get a burger. They're really good."

"I know." Marshall ordered a burger when the bartender came back. "What did you do before you came here?"

"I saved a cat."

"I don't know if that's a joke or not."

Z was closely watching the game. It went to a commercial break.

Marshall sighed with relief.

"What?" Z said.

"Soccer. Never cared for it much."

"I know," Z said.

Marshall scratched his head. "What do you mean, you know?"

"Oh, um, you have that look about you, like you don't like soccer."

"Really?"

The bartender set Marshall's whiskey and Coke down, and Marshall sipped it. "Now that hits the spot."

Z had an idea. He caught Marshall's eye. "Hey, let me tell you about this memory I have of my dad. He wasn't a soccer fan either. Said it was a 'pansy ass sport' that only Europeans play. Which is bullshit because soccer is huge in South America too. But that's beside the point."

Marshall shrugged.

Z sipped his water and began again. "When I was little, I saw some kids playing soccer at a park. It looked fun. I asked my dad about soccer, and he explained the rules. Well, not the rules—he didn't know shit about soccer. But he explained all the delicate footwork required and the stamina and the precision necessary for scoring goals."

Marshall crossed his arms. "Yeah, it probably does require a lot of athleticism."

Z continued. "My dad wanted me to play a 'real man's sport' when I was growing up. He wanted me to play tackle football. I played soccer despite him. He went to all my games that he could fit around his work schedule, although I'm not sure he ever understood or enjoyed the sport. I wish he had. Maybe we could've bonded over it."

"Sorry to hear that," Marshall said when it was clear that Z had finished speaking about the memory. He unfolded his arms. "Maybe you should've told him how you felt. He probably wouldn't have been as hard on you as you think."

Z scoffed. "You don't know my dad…" He smirked. He was talking to his dad—well, a parallel Earth-version of him. "Yeah, maybe I should've." He sipped more water. "You know what, that felt good to get off my chest."

Marshall sipped his whiskey and Coke. "Got anything else to spill while you've got my ear?"

Germ immediately came to Z's mind. "Maybe. But you wouldn't want to hear."

"Try me."

Ordinarily, Z wouldn't have opened up any further. It must've been the alcohol. "What the hell. Fine. I recently lost my sidekick. He was…a good guy. I can't help but feel like I let him down."

Leaning on the bar top on his elbows, Marshall said, "What happened to him? He die?"

"I honestly don't know. I don't think so. My nemesis took him."

"Your nemesis…" Marshall scratched his forehead. "Don't take this the wrong way, but I think you should drink some more water."

"My nemesis is the one who sent those two tuxedoed robots after me and burned down my office."

Marshall bit his lip. He nodded.

"I have faith I'll find him soon. I'm going to track down some leads after I leave here. Still, I'm running out of time. Once I find and confront my nemesis, well, there's a chance that things won't go the way I want them to."

Marshall frowned. "You trying to rope me into another last stand against some killer robots?"

Z waved it off. "Nope. I guess what I'm saying is that this is goodbye. Just in case."

"I'm not going to read about you in the papers in a few days, am I?"

"I don't think so. If I fail, I don't think there'll be any more papers anywhere."

Marshall bobbed his head. "Riiight."

Z smirked. "You know, you've grown into quite the asshole since you've met me."

"I've also moved up the ladder at the workforce since I met you too. Guess that evens things out." Marshall chuckled. "On the day shift, I feel like I can help more people."

"I'm glad for you. Really. I am." Z glanced up at the soccer match on the tv screen. "You get that dent fixed in your car yet?"

"The dent you put in it? Not yet. But I know a guy. The money you gave me should cover it all. You sure it's not dirty money?"

"I think so."

"You think so? What do you mean you think—"

The front door to the bar slammed open, and a man and a woman wearing ski masks entered with pistols raised in front of them. They locked the door behind them.

"This is a holdup!" the man said.

The woman racked her pistol. "No funny business and no one gets hurt."

"Seriously?" Z muttered to himself. "Two robberies in one day?"

Marshall turned incredulously to him. "Did you know about this?"

"No. You got a gun on you?"

Shaking his head, Marshall said, "I'm off duty. You?"

Z had his pistol in his jacket. It still had only one round in the chamber since he'd warped back at the reservoir after killing himself. He nodded. "Only one bullet."

"I don't need a gun…" Marshall pushed himself up from the barstool and turned to the man and woman robber duo. "I'm Officer Marshall Peet. You don't want to do this. Put down the guns."

The robbers turned to each other.

"Shit," the woman said.

The man turned his gun in Marshall's direction. The barrel wavered. "I ain't going back!" He pulled the trigger.

Marshall fell to the floor, bleeding from a chest wound.

Z hopped off his stool and dropped to the floor beside him. Marshall was already dead.

"Shouldn't have done that," Z said with fire in his eyes as he stared up at them. He drew his combat knife from his boot and stood.

Both of the robbers started firing.

Z fell backward and sprawled out upon the floor, his outstretched hand almost touching Marshall's hand, kind of like in Michelangelo's *The Creation of Adam.*

He died.

CHAPTER FORTY-NINE

(One Minute Earlier)

"On the day shift, I feel like I can help more people," Marshall said.

Z shushed Marshall.

"Don't you shush me."

Z spoke in a whisper. "Stay cool. Two robbers are about to hit this place."

"Huh? Oh, shit. Let me guess. Has this happened before?"

"Yes."

The front door slammed open and a man and woman wearing ski masks entered the bar, handguns raised before them. They locked the door behind them.

"This is a holdup!" the man said.

The woman racked her pistol. "No funny business and no one gets hurt."

Z and Marshall, a few others on bar stools, and everyone out in the dining area swiveled to face the robbers. "You got a plan?" Marshall whispered.

Z and Marshall were sitting at the bar right beside the cash registers. For the two robbers to get any money, they'd have to walk up right next to them and either hop over the counter or demand that the bartender get the cash for them.

With the robbers so close to them, Z and Marshall would probably have a good opportunity to take them down without anyone getting hurt.

The male robber shouted, "Everyone put your hands on the table in front of you where we can see them."

Z and Marshall slowly complied. From the corners of his eyes, Z watched as the two robbers circled the dining area, showing off their guns and ordering everyone to stay seated and to keep their hands on the tabletop in front of them.

"Plan? I usually like to try to talk things out first," Z said.

Marshall watched the robbers in his peripheral vision. "Does that usually work?"

"Not usually. But that means I get to use my fists the next time around."

"The next time around?"

"After I die and warp back."

Marshall grabbed his head and groaned.

"Hey, you two!" The woman angled her pistol at the bar. "You saying something?"

The man fired his gun once into the ceiling. "No talking means no talking!"

Patrons gasped and cried out at the gunshot. A scant amount of dust dribbled from the ceiling where the bullet had penetrated.

The ski-masked man grunted and spun to face all the patrons in the dining area. "The rules are simple. Shut the hell up. Bartender gives us money. We leave. No one gets hurt. Simple." While still sighting down his pistol, the robber nodded at his accomplice. "Honey, watch the bartender. He might have a shotgun or something behind the bar."

"Good idea, babe." The woman sidled up toward the bar until she was standing next to Z's stool. She jabbed the pistol in the air at the bartender across the bar from her. "No funny business, okay?"

Z cocked his head over at her. "How much money you guys need? I have some in my jacket—"

"Shut the fuck up!" she screamed, thrusting her pistol's muzzle against Z's forehead.

Enough of this shit. Z had finished talking. Time to do things his way.

Meeting the woman's wild eyes to distract her, Z threw a hand up and latched onto her gun hand's wrist. Before she could utter a word, Z had stood, twisted her arm behind her back, and was holding her body out in front of him like a shield. He easily stripped the pistol from her hand and held it to her temple.

At that moment, the ski-masked man turned and saw what Z had done. The man's eyes clouded with rage as he gripped his handgun. "Let her go!"

There was no way the man would try to shoot Z—he might hit the woman.

Suddenly the woman stomped on Z's foot and back-kicked him in the crotch. As Z released her and doubled over, the ski-masked man pumped him with bullets.

He died.

(Three Minutes Earlier)

Z silently excused himself to Marshall and went outside.

He easily picked the lock on Marshall's red coupe and found two pairs of handcuffs in the glove box.

He walked back into the bar and set the two pairs of cuffs on top of the bar.

Marshall eyed him closely. The bartender, who was wiping a glass out behind the counter, said with a raised eyebrow, "No funny business in here, okay?"

"It's okay, I'm a cop," Marshall said. He turned to Z. "What the hell is going on? Are those mine—"

Z clapped a hand on Marshall's shoulder. He eyed the bartender too. "In a few moments, a pair of robbers are going to come through the front door. They'll have handguns, but they won't use them as long as everyone does what they say."

Z turned to go.

"Wait a minute," Marshall said. "How do you know that?"

"Remember what happened at Central Park with the robots?"

Marshall groaned. "Not again…"

This time Marshall didn't have the golden earpiece in his ear so he wouldn't remember anything if Z had to warp back. The earpiece was in Z's jacket.

"Your friend is a strange one," the bartender said to Marshall.

Marshall turned back to Z, who had started walking off toward the bar's kitchen and bathrooms. "Hey, where you going?"

Z didn't look back or stop walking. "To take a shit."

The bartender stopped wiping his glass.

Z made his way to the bathroom and stepped inside. As the door closed behind him, he heard the two robbers enter the bar.

Perfect timing, he said to himself, imitating Germ's voice.

Someone had to provide the little guy's inner monologue in his absence.

There was a squeak in front of Z, and a toilet stall opened. A man with bloodshot eyes stepped out into the bathroom.

Z waved him back in the stall. "You should probably stay in there." He hooked a thumb toward the bathroom door. "Couple of robbers. A few more minutes and everything should be good."

"O-kay?" The man returned to the stall and closed the door.

Z stepped up to the bathroom sink and leaned toward the mirror. Not only did he need a shower, but he also needed a shave.

Outside, the robber duo barked demands.

Z hoped Marshall had the sense to hide the handcuffs in his pocket or at least on his lap under the bar. He turned on the sink faucet and splashed water on his face. Then he toweled it off.

A gunshot rang out in the bar as the male robber fired into the ceiling. "No talking!"

Z straightened his jacket and gave himself a final look over in the mirror. *Okay, showtime...*

He threw open the bathroom door and strolled out into the bar with his hands in his pockets while he whistled a tune.

The two robbers standing beside his empty stool were both training their guns on the bartender standing behind the cash register. They both swiveled their guns Z's way.

"Freeze, motherfucker!" the male robber said.

"Yeah!" said the female robber.

"Wanna see a magic trick?" Z picking up two empty glasses from the bar top. As he did so, he made eye contact with Marshall, sitting behind the two robbers.

"No fucking funny business," the ski-masked man said.

Z nodded at Marshall and tossed the two glasses at the robbers.

The pair uttered obscenities as they raised their hands to try to intercept or deflect the projectiles.

"What the—"

"Shit—"

As Z rushed toward them, he saw that Marshall was sneaking up on the male robber so Z angled toward the female one.

Marshall grabbed the man's gun arm and wrestled with the gun. Z meanwhile reached for the woman's gun. The two glasses shattered on the floor.

In the struggle, the male robber managed to discharge his gun once, but the bullet struck the floor. A minute later, Z and Marshall had their respective robber pressed up against the bar, their wrists held out behind them. Marshall handed a pair of cuffs to Z and together, they handcuffed the two robbers.

"I've called 9-1-1," the bartender said.

Z gave him a thumbs-up.

A sudden cheer went up throughout the bar, and at first, Z thought it was for the show he and Marshall had put on. Then he realized one of the soccer teams on the TVs had scored a goal.

"All right." Z grinned.

Marshall glanced up and saw the soccer team celebrating. The TV showed an instant replay of the goal.

Marshall turned to Z. "You know, I think I changed my mind. Soccer ain't half bad."

"It's why I taught my daughter the sport," Z said.

"Hmm." Marshall was thinking something over. "If I have kids someday—"

"You will," Z said.

"—maybe I'll see if they want to play it. Teach them it's okay to follow their dreams."

With a satisfied grin, Z patted both robbers on the shoulder and Marshall's as well. "Well, hoss, you got this?"

Z slapped some cash on the counter for his burgers and beer and backed toward the back entrance.

Marshall was indignant. "Hey, now, where the hell do you think you're going?"

Z waved at his face. "The news cameras don't like my face. They like yours, though." He winked. "Take the win."

"But—"

"Go home and talk to your wife. Maybe not tell her *every-thing*, okay? And get some sleep."

Marshall raised a hand. A police siren sounded outside the front entrance. "Come back here, you asshole…"

Z was already gone, smirking as he exited the building.

CHAPTER FIFTY

Z stifled a yawn. Exhaustion was beating at his eyelids, and he wanted nothing better than to return to the new *Paper Warriors* office and crash on the floor.

While walking along the sidewalk, he passed a tourist wearing a shirt that said *I heart NY. The City that Never Sleeps.*

"I feel like the *man* that never sleeps," Z muttered. Yes. Sleep was calling his name.

Then he stopped suddenly. He had an idea.

A man in a business suit bumped into him from behind. "Move it along, asshole," he whined.

Z disregarded the man and turned. There was someplace else he needed to go before returning to the *Paper Warriors* office.

If he was ever going to get Germ back, it would help to have some form of leverage against Nunez. What was it that Nunez wanted most?

His wife. Mel.

Nunez's short-circuiting robots in Central Park had confirmed his plan. If Z didn't stop the mad doctor before he figured out how to pilot the space and time capsule, he was going to time jump back on this Earth before his wife disappeared at the outdoor concert.

Z couldn't let that happen. Once Nunez disappeared from this current timeline, he would be beyond Z's stopping. Nunez had already proved to be a threat to the entire multiverse's existence.

So he knew what he had to do to get an audience with Nunez.

He had to solve Mel's case. He had to find out what had happened to her.

The only place he could think to go to look for clues was her home. Or, her and Ray Garcia's home, Ray being this Earth's younger Nunez...

He smacked the side of his head to stop it from hurting. Too much thinking. Since he didn't have Germ to converse with to pass the time, he whistled the rest of the way to the Garcia residence.

Yellow police tape barricaded the house's front door. He could've cut the tape and picked the lock, but instead, he snuck around to the back door and picked that lock. He gave the house's interior a quick once-over, searching the bedroom and the trashed office room where he and Marshall had made their last stand against one of Nunez's robots. He even checked the bathrooms.

Nothing.

Nothing but destruction and bullet holes courtesy of Nunez's robot, Z, Marshall, and the police the first time Z had been here back when the robot had kidnapped Ray, the younger Nunez.

Another yawn overtook him, and he considered hanging it up and walking to the *Paper Warriors* office to catch some shut-eye. However, this was his best chance at picking up a new lead. He returned to the dining room and inspected the picture frames he'd seen the first time he was here.

Younger Nunez and his wife looked so happy.

Z was about to leave when he turned back and picked up one of the frames. In the photograph, Young Nunez and his wife were standing at Niagara Falls.

Of all the photos, Mel looked the happiest in this one. On a hunch, Z turned the picture over and pried out the frame's backing with his combat knife. The back of the photo contained some writing. It was slanted and delicate and looked like a woman's hand had written it.

The most beautiful place on the planet. Our spot. -Mel

She'd drawn a cute little heart around the words "Our spot."

Z pondered this. It could mean something. Probably not.

Mel had last been seen sometime during the nighttime outdoor concert. That was a fact. Z's gut was telling him that no one had kidnaped Mel. What if something had happened at the event and she'd driven or paid a taxi to go somewhere else? Why wouldn't she have told anyone else? Her friends. Her husband. Anyone.

Z wished he had Germ to bounce ideas off.

The idea that she was headed toward Niagara Falls when she disappeared didn't seem that plausible. Still, when he got back to the printing press, he'd send a message to Buzz to check for disappearances in the Niagara Falls area. Surely Nunez's wife hadn't gone to Niagara Falls at night. That was at least a six-hour drive. Then again, maybe she had, and along the way, something had happened to her.

He yawned again. He put the frame back together and set it down.

It was time to go.

On the way to the news office, another idea worked its way into Z's head, and he made an unplanned stop at a tattoo parlor.

A lean man with a green mohawk and a tattoo sleeve of skulls greeted him. "What can I do ya for?"

Z explained his situation and the tattoo artist instructed him to sit in a leather swivel chair. Z took off his dirty jacket and stripped off his sweaty muscle shirt. Then he sat and lifted his arms.

The tattoo artist inspected Z's ink job under each arm. When he finished, he stood and scratched the back of his head. "You didn't…pay much for these tattoos, I hope?"

Z maintained a bit of pride in his voice. "Did them myself."

"They're so…" The man was thumbing his chin while observing them like an artist at an easel. "Crude."

"I like crude."

The tattoo artist nodded as if he understood now. "I sense they have important meaning to you."

"Yeah, they're a list of wrongs I plan to right on different Earths. I've almost finished with this Earth. Can't wait to see if the butterfly effect pays off down the line."

"Uh-huh."

Z yawned again. "Sorry. Like I said, can you strike through the items I tell you to? They're in code so only I can read them."

After lifting his eyes from the boxes and strings of letters and numbers under both Z's arms, the tattoo artist nodded.

"Right on, man. I'll go get my equipment ready. And something to clean off your skin."

Z winced as he realized he should've taken a shower first before getting an ink job done. "Sure."

Before the tattoo artist left to go, he made a slight face. "It's not official store policy, but can I please see that you have the means to pay for this job before I begin?"

With a smirk, Z reached for his jacket and pulled out some hundred-dollar bills from inside. "Will this work?"

"I'll be right back."

While Z waited, he mentally reviewed the wrongs he'd righted on Earth-D so far. He'd prevented a man from being late to his court hearing so he kept joint custody of his daughter—the girl who'd dropped her ice cream.

He'd stopped a semi from hitting another man while he was changing a tire on the side of the highway. The man lived and continued to work at the airport where he was a TSA agent.

Then he'd taught a defenseless young kid at a playground how to fight back against bullies so that he grew up empowered instead of becoming an even worse bully himself one day.

Z had a couple more minor wrongs to right in Earth-D's timeline, but he'd worry about them after he stopped Nunez and got Germ back. Once he had the space and time capsule back in his possession, he'd be able to jump forward in time to see if the butterfly effect had worked on a multiversal scale or only on Earth-D.

He wasn't holding his breath, but it would feel damn good if it worked out the way he hoped.

The tattoo artist came back and wiped Z's skin clean with a soapy rag.

When he was clean to the artist's liking, Z pointed out the line items to strike out so he knew they were already complete. So many worlds, so many things to fix. He was tired of thinking.

He was plain tired.

He fell asleep in the tattoo artist's chair.

When the artist woke him, Z shook off his sleep. He rubbed his eyes and paid the artist, who accepted the money graciously.

"Lemme know what you think, man. Hopefully, I did it justice."

Z yawned, stretching as he did so in the leather chair. Then he drew a deep breath and looked down at the artist's handiwork. The items he had requested now had a line drawn through them, but that wasn't what he was looking for.

On his waistline, right above his left jeans pocket, was a fresh new tattoo. It was a little black octopus with cute beady eyes.

A tear glazed Z's eye and he blinked that shit away.

He turned to the tattoo artist. "It's perfect."

CHAPTER FIFTY-ONE

The smell of fresh paint smacked Z's nostrils when he entered the new *Paper Warriors* news office. Whew. With fumes that strong, he wasn't sure he'd be able to sleep in here let alone type out messages to Buzz on the printing press.

He fanned the air in front of his nose. "Someone plug in some goddamn fans in here."

The tallest newsman turned away from the wall he was currently painting a bright orange. He saluted Z. "Aye, aye, big man. On it! I'll go buy some."

The newsman proceeded out the door but stopped and stuck his head back in. He offered Z a cheesy grin. "You have any more money, by chance?"

Z dug into his jacket pocket and handed the man a hundred-dollar bill.

"Gee, thanks, you're the best, big man!"

Z scratched at his stubbly chin. "I'm not that big."

The middle newsman approached Z from behind. "You could bench press all three of us."

"Yeah, but—"

"Do you like the furniture?" The shortest newsman wiped the sweat from his forehead as he crossed the office to Z.

"Huh? Oh…" Z's eyes landed on the plush leather couch in the small office. A glass coffee table sat before it. "Wow." He imagined himself lying down on it and passing out for a couple of days.

"We want this place to be comfortable to news reporters and eyewitnesses who stop by the office," the shortest newsman said.

"Oh, it looks comfortable."

As Z made his way toward the couch, the middle newsman said, "What do you think of the new color scheme?"

Z stopped in front of the couch and surveyed the once-pink, now-orange walls. "It's…cheerful."

The middle newsman beamed. "We could all use some cheer right now, couldn't we?"

"Yeah," Z said absentmindedly and let himself fall backward into the couch. It felt like…

Heaven.

He was asleep as soon as his eyelids closed.

The shortest newsman grunted as he set a flower pot on the glass table in front of the couch. "A gentleman by the name of Eduardo Nunez sent a newspaper through the printing press while you were away."

Z jolted upright on the couch.

"You know him?" the newsman asked.

Fuck. What did Nunez want? Z stood and trotted back to the printing press, disregarding the aches and exhaustion seeping through his body.

"Yeah," he called over his shoulder. "He's a major asshole."

With a quick-beating heart, he reached the printing press

and plucked up the sole newspaper resting on it. It contained only a single headline on the front page:

I KNOW WHAT YOU DID TO MY ROBOTS. -DR. EDUARDO NUNEZ

Z scoffed. So Nunez had resorted to printing press threats?

"So what did you do to his robots?" the middle newsman said from right behind Z.

Z started. "Geez. Shit. Don't you guys make a sound when you move? And do you have any concept of personal space?"

The newsman frowned and took a step backward. "Sorry." He looked bashfully at Z. "So what did you do to his robots?"

"I killed them."

"Oh."

Z thought about sitting back on the couch but figured he might as well compose a message to Buzz first. After yawning, he thought about what he wanted to send. He settled on,

I killed those two tuxedoed robots. Turns out, they weren't indestructible after all. Nunez captured Germ. Long story. Got to get him back. Running out of time. Need a big win.

Nunez threatened me. I need something to use against him. Need to locate his wife. I have an idea. A long shot. Can you search for disappearances in the Niagara Falls area? If I can track her down, I think I can stop Nunez. -Z

Z hit the "Send" button, and a green light flashed on the printing press.

Buzz would probably be fast with his reply when he saw the message come through. In the meantime, Z sat on the floor and rested against the machine's metal struts to take a nap. When he leaned his head back, he struck it on the hard surface.

"Ow." He twisted his head and inspected the metal. He still couldn't believe it had survived the fire at the old *Paper Warriors* office. Not only had it been undamaged by the blaze, but it had also fallen from the second floor to the ground floor without suffering any damage to its frame.

What had Germ said about the printing press? Something about being made of a strong futuristic metal alloy or something.

All Z knew was that it had raised a bump on the back of his head. That would sure be a joy to sleep on...

Instead of sleeping in a sitting position, he lay on the floor on his side and used his hands as a pillow. Then he was snoring.

The *clicking*, stuttering vibrations of the printing press beside him awakened him. He sat up and wiped the drool from his mouth.

It was cold inside the office. He rubbed the chill from his arms. Why was it so cold? He blinked, and all three newsmen were standing over the printing press, peering in awe at the newspaper currently being printed.

Z rose, seeing box fans stationed throughout the news office, circulating fresh paint fumes toward the open front door. The gentle hum of all their spinning blades was oddly comforting.

These guys are fast. He waited for the printing press to spit out the completed paper. When it finished, he scooped the paper up, some of the ink smudging under his thumb and fingers.

He scanned the front-page story.

BUDDY, YOU WERE RIGHT!

At least, I think. I searched for disappearances around Niagara Falls. Didn't find any disappearances. But a woman's body was found immediately downriver, trapped under a rock. Due to bloating, fish nibbling, and decomposition, the body was filed as unidentified—sad stuff. If it was her, I can see why Nunez wouldn't have looked that far away for it. That's a long way from NYC. My predictive algorithms say that it's quite possible that it's her.

See page B11 for the exact coordinates of the location. Her body should still be in the water—it won't be discovered until another couple of days by some tourists. Think that's enough to get Nunez's attention?

You're welcome.

Be careful and good luck.

-B

P.S.: Forget chasing women. I have a new sexbot with your name on it back at the labs I'd like you to try. Her name is Terra, and her models are flying off the shelves.

Z nearly choked on his laughter. Oh, Buzz and his sexbots. While he kept assuring Z that his robots were getting better with each new product line, Z had never had any use for a sexbot. Wasn't that kind of like cheating if you were single? It was if you were married. Which he wasn't anymore.

Ugh. He didn't want to think about women right now. He needed more sleep.

First, he arranged one last message on the printing press

and adjusted the dials to send it to the device that Nunez's newspaper had come from. It contained only a headline.

HEY NUNEZ, I KNOW WHERE YOUR WIFE IS.

Z didn't know where Nunez was, but he didn't need to. This message should bring Nunez to him.

Satisfied, Z punched the "Send" button and collapsed on the heavenly couch.

A scraping sound awoke him. When he opened his eyes, he had to shield them with his hand because of the sunlight streaming through the windows. They were no longer tinted.

There was another scraping sound. It came from the shortest newsman trying to pilot a dolly containing a file cabinet across the news office's floor. He wasn't strong enough, and the dolly kept reverting to its vertical resting position.

With a chuckle, Z rose and went over to the man. "Here. Let me." Z applied his body weight to the dolly's handles and tilted the file cabinet backward. "Where you want it?"

The newsman directed him over to a set of three desks with a pristine typewriter resting on each.

"Wow." Z surveyed the rest of the office. "More office furniture. You guys have been busy. I like what you've done with the place."

"Aw, thanks."

Z started. The other two newsmen were standing right over his shoulder.

"Seriously. You guys need to stop sneaking up on me. Gonna have to get you all a bell to wear around your necks."

"Does that mean you're going to stay for a while?" the tallest newsman asked.

At first, Z didn't understand what the man meant by that. Then he remembered that before this trip, he rarely spent much time on Earth-D. The newsmen were used to him showing up out of the blue whenever a mission called for him to be there. He always hopped to the next Earth as soon as the Earth-D mission was over.

Things were different now. Now he didn't have a space and time capsule to Earth hop. He didn't tell the newsmen that, though. Instead, he scratched the back of his head. "Eh, I'm not sure. I might."

"Please stay."

"We don't want you to leave."

"How can we sweeten the pot for you to stay?"

Z looked at them. He was a bit stunned that they liked him that much considering how crudely he treated them at times. "I'll admit. This Earth is growing on me. It needs donuts, though. Tell you what, you get donuts on this Earth, and I'll never leave it."

The three newsmen stared reverently at Z and saluted. "Challenge accepted," they said as one.

Good luck, Z thought.

Then a bell jingled from the front of the office. Z squinted at the bright sun as a stunning woman with long legs and gold French-braided hair strutted inside. She wore a tight black miniskirt and blouse that accentuated her every curve.

"Wowza," Z said.

"It's our first customer!" said the tallest newsman.

The middle newsman stood upright and put on his biggest smile. "Hello."

"How can we help you?" the smallest newsman said cheerfully.

The woman strode past the newsmen, stopping directly before Z.

Z grinned. "Well, hello beautiful—"

The woman's hand shot to his throat. He grunted as she suspended him off the floor a few inches.

"Eduardo Nunez formally requests your presence."

CHAPTER FIFTY-TWO

"Let me guess," Z gasped, impressed by her strength and fighting for breath as he glanced down at the woman's cleavage. "You're a robot."

The woman sneered. "You are smarter than you look."

Z smirked, and she applied greater pressure. "Ouch." He tried to pull her iron grip off his throat. The toes of his boots didn't even scrape the floor. "Can you please let me down now?"

She pouted. "But I like being on top."

Z sucked in a partial breath. "Technically, I'm the one who's on top here."

"Very well." The robot woman powerfully flung Z forward and released her grip on him. His body soared through the air until it struck the side of the filing cabinet, leaving a dent in it.

As he tried to stand, the woman strode his way.

"Please don't kill our friend," the tallest newsman whimpered.

"She's so strong!" the second newsman gasped.

The shortest newsman clapped his hands to his cheeks. "My filing cabinet."

None of the pleas stopped the robot woman. She continued up to Z, who was clambering to his feet. When she reached him, she stopped and sent a swift kick to his jaw. He staggered sideways, and she caught him by the hair. Bending him backward, she pressed her moist lips to his ear.

"Nunez says that you better not be playing with him."

Z grunted. "You're the only one playing with me—"

Jerking him forward a few steps, she kicked out with her other leg, connecting with his side. He doubled over. "You like it rough, don't you," Z said.

She licked her lips. "Oh, you have no idea." She spun and kicked him again across the jaw. A mixture of blood and saliva dribbled out and splatted on the clean floor.

Z grimaced. "Hey, you guys polished the floor while I was sleeping too—"

The robot woman gripped his hair again, hard, and tugged him closer. She kicked him in the crotch and grabbed the back of his jacket. Pivoting on her heel, she swung Z like a shotput. He soared through the air yet again, landing atop the glass coffee table in front of the couch. It shattered under his weight.

"The table!" the tallest newsman cried.

"Son of a bitch," Z groaned as he tried to rise to his hands and knees. Glass shards bit into his palms and knees, and he had gashes on his forehead and chin. He spat out a couple of chunks of glass. Then she was on him again.

He felt her weight on him as she sat upon his back and wrapped the crook of her elbow around his neck. She reeled him back against her warm chest, which felt nice, considering the circumstances. He had to remind himself that she was a robot and not a real woman.

Tucking his elbow in close, he jammed it back into her side.

She laughed.

She choked off his air supply again.

"What do you want?" he gasped.

She eased up ever so slightly so that he could at least suck in a partial breath. Her words came as a whisper. "Do you really know where Nunez's wife is? Or is this some trick?"

"I know. I know."

She reapplied pressure to his throat while squeezing him backward against her. "You wouldn't lie to me, would you?"

She was gripping him so tightly that he couldn't respond. She eased up a bit.

"Lady, I don't even know your name."

"Terra. My name is Terra."

Terra. Of course. Buzz's sexbot. He should've known Nunez would've gotten his hands on another model of Buzz's robots after Z destroyed the two tuxedoed robots. At least this robot was prettier to look at.

"Well, Terra," Z drew in a half breath, "tell Nunez that I'm not playing."

She didn't re-tighten her chokehold this time. "If you know where she is, then tell me."

"Lean closer."

She did.

Z grinned at the advantage this afforded him. "Nunez's wife is…" He repositioned himself to have more leverage and succeeded in using a judo move to throw her over his shoulder to the floor.

She was back on her feet in an instant. Z was ready with his combat knife unsheathed from his boot.

Her eyes played over the blade's gleaming edge.

"Violence!" one of the newsmen shouted.

Terra licked her lips.

"Tell Nunez," Z picked himself up and carefully climbed out of the broken coffee table frame, "that I will only tell him. In person."

She laughed. "Are you negotiating? With me?"

Z put on some bravado. "What can I say? Women find me hard to deal with."

She licked her lips again. "You are an amusing human. Very well. When do you want to meet?"

Z was making this up as he went along. He knew that at any time, Nunez could figure out how to work the space and time capsule. At the same time, Z needed some rest, especially after this beating he was taking.

And with a new "indestructible" robot in the mix, Z needed to figure out a way to even out the odds if it came to another fight—which it probably would. The "taser in the water" trick wasn't going to work again.

"I'm waiting," Terra said.

"Tell him to meet me tomorrow at noon at Caleb's Ice Cream Emporium two blocks from here. And tell him I'm done dealing with his bullshit antics."

Terra smiled, which was as dangerous as it was seductive. "Why tomorrow? Why not now? Are you playing a trick?"

"No. Tell Nunez. Tomorrow at noon. Caleb's Ice Cream Emporium."

She studied him for a time. "I will. But first. A parting kiss."

She dashed toward Z, and he raised his knife. It cut

through her arm, but she didn't bleed, and it didn't stop her final attack. One hand gripped the wrist of his hand holding the knife, and her other grabbed his crotch. She lifted him above her head like a spear or harpoon and hurled him at the couch.

The couch's fabric tore as Z's knife cut through it. Z's forward momentum toppled the couch backward. His body barrel-rolled until he lay sprawled out next to the wall with a roaring box fan blowing cool air on his bleeding face.

She stepped up to him, pried the protective grating from the front of the box fan, and grabbed his hair. She acted like she was going to shove his head against the blades. Z wasn't scared. He would warp back if he died.

Terra sighed delightedly. "What is this I see?"

While still gripping Z's hair and holding him in place slightly up off the floor, she reached down and drew out a stack of hundred-dollar bills from inside his jacket. Then she let Z fall back to the floor.

Ever so slowly, she took the band off the currency stack and started to flip through the bills.

The tallest newsman held up a fist. "Hey, that's not your money!"

She flashed him an evil smile. "It's not yours either now." Then she kicked the box fan backward so its exposed blades were facing upward. She let the money drop into the blades, which cut them up and shot them back into the air like confetti.

"Nooo!" one of the newsmen said.

Terra lifted Z by his grimy shirt collar, reached inside his jacket, and found another stack of bills. She searched again, but there was no more money to be found. This time she used her teeth to bite the band off the money stack before unceremoniously dropping it over the blades as well. The air grew rich with money.

Terra waited for the green cloud to dissipate a bit before stepping over to the orange wall. She swiped a finger across it and stared at the wet paint on her finger. "Orange. Such a cheerful color." Then she flicked her French braid and strode out of the news office.

The tallest newsman was standing with his fingernails in his mouth. "Guys, that was fierce."

"The couch!" the middle one said.

Shreds of paper money rained down upon the office.

The shortest one began to sob. "The money."

Lying on the floor next to the wall, Z felt like a dump truck had hit him.

A dump truck named Terra.

He tried to pick himself up, but his body sagged back down to the floor. The box fan spinning near his head sounded like a wind turbine. He tried to pick himself up again. For the second time, he fell flat on his face. He spat out some money shreds that had gotten in his mouth.

"Guys. Can someone help me up? I don't think I can stand."

CHAPTER FIFTY-THREE

Z had suffered some terrible defeats over the years. Never had he had his ass handed to him so badly.

If not for the three newsmen's help, he wouldn't have been able to sit upright after Nunez's robot Terra left.

One of his eyes was almost swollen shut. He'd need some ice for that later.

He sat atop the ruined couch for a couple of hours. The newsmen brought him some coffee and scones from next door. Finally, he was ready to stand.

As they helped him up, the tallest newsman said, "Maybe you'd feel better if you took a hot shower?"

Z scoffed. "If only I knew a place where I could get one."

The middle newsman made a face. "You can take a shower in the office's bathroom."

"What?" Z winced from the pain of raising his eyebrows. "You guys put in a shower while I was sleeping on the couch?"

The shortest newsman pointed at an unassuming door at the back of the room.

"I thought that was a closet." Z drew a deep breath. It hurt his chest a bit. "If you guys are messing with me…"

———

Nearly an hour later, the bathroom door opened and steam billowed out into the news office. A clean and refreshed Z exited the bathroom with nothing but a towel wrapped around his lower half, stepping through the fog like a rock star at a concert.

He immediately gathered the waiting three newsmen around him and tousled their hair. "I love you guys."

They all grinned. "We love you too."

Z tensed. "Um…like a brother, right?"

The tallest brother held up a finger and shushed him. "Let's enjoy this moment."

After the "moment" had passed, Z eased himself to the floor and began to stretch out his torn and beaten muscles. One of the newsmen brought him an ice pack to hold against his swollen eye. Then the three newsmen sat on the floor and started stretching along with Z.

The middle newsman said, "Is this the part where we discuss how we take our revenge upon the Mean Girl?" He rubbed his hands together excitedly, then strained as he reached his fingertips toward his toes.

"How?" The shortest newsman hung his head, his knees folded outward like a pretzel. "Oh wait, we could write a nasty news article about her. The pen is mightier than the sword."

The tallest newsman hid his face in his hands. "She destroyed all Z's money. We're penniless."

"Look, boys," Z said. "I appreciate your concern, but this is my problem. Besides, Nunez is too dangerous."

Even still, Z needed allies and supplies if he was to stand a chance against Nunez when he met him at noon tomorrow.

The tallest newsman huffed in a determined breath and met Z's eyes. "We discussed it while you were taking that extremely long hot shower." He exchanged glances with the other two newsmen. "We're committed to helping you fight the Mean Girl and the evil Eduardo Nunez. Whatever you did to his robots, I'm sure they deserved it."

Z chuckled. This was unexpected. "I don't want to get you guys involved—"

"Save it." The middle newsman held up a palm. "We're family. We're helping."

"You got a plan?" the shortest newsman said.

Z hedged. "The beginnings of a plan, yeah." He had to be ready for the meeting tomorrow, and that entailed some preparation. He had some good ideas, but he couldn't complete everything by himself, especially in his injured state. With a determined grin, he appraised them sitting around him. "With your help…it might work."

He sighed. Then he leaned in and told them his working plan.

When he finished, the three newsmen were silent for a moment. They shot furtive glances at the printing press and back at Z. "We don't have any money," the tallest newsman finally said.

Z's dirty clothes lay in a heap next to him on the floor. Z smirked as he reached into his tattered jacket, unzipped a hidden compartment, and pulled out a small stack of hundred-dollar bills.

The newsmen gasped.

"My secret stash. It's not much, but it should be enough…"

Z caught a whiff of his days' old sweat wafting up from his

jacket and the rest of his dirty clothes. "But first, do one of you want to run my clothes to the laundromat?"

The middle newsman scratched his chin. "Why don't you buy a new set of clothes?"

"Because these torn-up clothes remind me of everything Nunez has thrown against me and everything I've overcome so far. A man needs reminders of what he's accomplished, or he loses sight of his goals. I'll get some new clothes when I've finished Nunez."

Straining with the effort, he leaned forward and held out his hand. "Team, on three."

The three newsmen excitedly placed their hands on top of Z's. "One, two, three…"

"Team!" they all shouted.

It brought a smile to Z's face. Once they finished with preparations and he could rest up for the remainder of the day, he'd be ready for his showdown with Nunez tomorrow at noon.

———

The sun beat down upon the umbrella-covered tables and patio outside Caleb's Ice Cream Emporium. It was nearly noon the next day, and Z was sitting at a table, in full alert mode, scanning the crowd for any sign of Nunez and Terra. After he and the newsmen had made their final preparations the day before, Z didn't feel so exhausted now. His eye wasn't swollen shut anymore either.

He was ready.

At noon exactly, a woman wearing jeans, a t-shirt, and a ball cap low over her face sat at Z's table across from him. When she tilted her face up at him, he saw that it was Terra.

Z shook his head. "Woman, you know the deal we had. Either Nunez shows, or I don't talk."

Two more women wearing jeans, t-shirts, and ball caps sat at the table to either side of Z, their thighs sandwiching him in so he couldn't get out. When he saw their identical faces, he scoffed. "There are three of you?"

The three Terras gathered around him at the table sharpened their gazes on him. "Place your hands flat on top of the table," the lead Terra ordered.

"Why?" Z asked. "You going to frisk me?"

The Terra to his left whispered predatorily, "Not yet."

Z sighed, then set his palms on top of the table. "Great. Not only did Nunez not show, he sent three of his newest killer robots to…what? Knock me out and drag me away in daylight?"

He glanced out at all the umbrella-covered tables and the people chattering and laughing at them, blissfully unaware of Z and his three robot captors.

The Terra across from him licked her lips. "We could. None of these humans here could stop us. Not even the police. We are stronger than them. Bullets do not hurt us."

Z didn't doubt it. He had a bad taste in his mouth. "Serves me right for thinking Nunez would come. Here I am, not pulling any tricks as I said, and he pulls the biggest one of them all…"

He let his words trail off as another person sat at the table, this time next to the Terra across from Z.

Eduardo Nunez.

He wore his tan Panama hat and a white lab coat over an academic button-up shirt and slacks.

"Well, I'll be damned," Z said. "You showed up."

Nunez didn't say anything.

With his palms still on the tabletop, Z angled his head at the three Terras. "Aren't you a bit old for these ladies?"

Nunez didn't laugh. "They are my private bodyguards. Nothing more. I am still committed to my wife, unlike you."

Z smacked the table with both palms. "Asshole, you don't know what I gave up so my family could be happy and move on without me."

"That's right." Nunez sneered. "You gave up."

"Fuck you." Z seethed. He fought to regain his composure. "We didn't meet here to insult each other as much as I enjoy calling you an asshole, you asshole. You very old asshole."

Now Nunez fumed. One of the three Terra robots placed a hand on the man's shoulder, and he calmed a bit. "Very well. Down to business. You have one and only one shot at leaving here of your own free will. If it turns out this is some ploy, my Terras will render you unconscious and transport you to a secure facility. You'll spend the rest of your pathetic life there, strapped to an operating table in an induced coma and being fed by an IV line."

Z folded his hands in front of him. "I see you've thought this out."

"You wouldn't escape this time," Nunez said. "Why hire humans when their superior robotic counterparts are more capable."

Z repositioned his ass on his seat. "Your last robots turned out to be not so capable."

Nunez leaned over the table, his fingers on its surface like claws. "Where. Is. My. Wife."

"I'm guessing you're not having any luck with starting the space and time capsule?"

Nunez's lips quivered.

The Terra sitting to Z's immediate right formed her

fingers together and applied pressure with her fingertips against Z's skin, right over his kidney.

Z laughed it off, then the Terra sitting to his left did the same to his left kidney. "What's to stop me from killing you?" Z asked.

"Do you think I'm stupid? If you kill me, the Terras will kill you. Then you'll warp back in time, they'll remember your warp via their earpieces, and I'll know this was a waste of my time. Then they'll transport you to the holding facility."

"Okay. Okay," Z said calmly.

"Now, where is my wife?"

"Unfortunately, your wife is dead." Z watched for a reaction from Nunez but didn't receive one. Z wouldn't have wanted to believe it either if someone had told him that one of his loved ones was dead.

"I'm not sure what happened exactly. But I have the coordinates of her location." He cleared his throat. "I'll even share it with you if your two Terras will kindly remove their fingers from over my kidneys."

Silence. The Terras kept their fingertips over his sides.

"I can take you there," Z said. "You have to trust me."

"Sounds like desperation," Nunez said. "You could be lying."

"I want to help you."

"Help me?"

"Also, I want Germ in exchange for finding your wife."

Nunez laughed. "I figured that's what this was about."

"I know where your wife is."

Leaning forward, Nunez said, "Do you think I'm stupid?"

"You have me outnumbered. What do you have to lose?" Z opened his jacket. "Here, take all my weapons. Hell, take my jacket. This isn't a trick. We may be enemies, and I'm not looking forward to a long car ride with you, but I want to help you find out what happened to your wife in exchange for Germ."

Nunez's face tightened. "Search him."

The Terras sitting to either side of Z frisked him as inconspicuously as they could without raising suspicion from any of the surrounding tables. Then they turned to Nunez. "He has a gun in his jacket and a knife in his boot," one of them said.

Finally, Nunez nodded with a sigh. "Take his gun. His knife doesn't worry me." He rose, straightened his shirt, and held a hand out to Z, who accepted the handshake.

"Very well. I don't have to trust you. I'll figure out how to operate the space and time capsule. First I must find out what happened to my wife and if I do, you can have Germ back. Follow me."

Z walked through the maze of umbrella-covered tables to a large park, surrounded by the three Terras. A helicopter awaited them in a grassy clearing.

"Riding in style," Z said. "Nice."

CHAPTER FIFTY-FOUR

"After you," one of the Terras said from behind him.

Z was more than a bit surprised when he stepped up to the helicopter and found another two Terras already waiting inside and yet another Terra sitting in the cockpit. That made a total of six Terras, and they were all dressed identically. Jeans, t-shirt, ball cap.

Z turned to Nunez. "Did Buzz give you a discount for buying in bulk?"

Nunez didn't look amused. He must have hopped to another Earth, purchased the Terras under the guise of some faceless corporation, then jumped back to Earth-D.

One of the Terras gave Z a hard shove to the shoulder, and he climbed inside the chopper. The two Terras already inside motioned for him to sit between them.

"Never have I had so many stunning women in my life," Z said and took his seat.

Nunez climbed aboard and sat across from Z. A short time later the helicopter lifted off and they were on the way.

Z scratched his clean-shaven chin as he eyed Nunez. He'd

shaved back at the *Paper Warriors* bathroom. "If I could ask, how do you hop to other Earths?"

Nunez dug a small flat metal item from his pocket. It looked like a very complicated TV remote. "My greatest invention as of yet. I call it an Earth hopper. Once I discover the frequencies to new Earths, I can program it to open a portal there." He smiled wickedly. "Don't get any ideas of trying to steal and use it. It's keyed to my DNA—only I can use it."

"Of course." Z bobbed his head as the Terra pilot banked the helicopter. A few minutes later he said, "Where's Germ?"

Nunez angled his head toward the pilot. Z leaned forward for a view. Germ sat on the Terra pilot's lap. The little black octopus twisted around and raised one tentacle at Z, formed it into a human fist, and flipped Z the bird.

Z feigned indignation. "Ouch."

Nunez made me do it, Germ said. *He is still controlling me.*

"How?" Z said.

Germ blinked. *The metal remote. It forges a command between him and me. With it, he can order me to do anything. I am sorry.*

Nunez grabbed Z by the shoulder and eased him back into his seat.

Z closed his eyes. "Nothing to be sorry about."

He faked sleep the rest of the flight, now and then mentally reviewing and updating the plan in his head.

The helicopter touched down downstream of Niagara Falls on the New York side of the Canadian border. From there it would be a short walk through the grass and a small forest to

Buzz's coordinates at the base of the falls to a part not usually accessible by tourists.

Two of the Terras and the Terra pilot stayed with the helicopter. Before they started walking, the three other Terras and Nunez grabbed pistols and spare magazines from the helicopter. They tucked the guns into the smalls of their backs, and one of the Terras tucked Z's pistol into her pants as well.

Then, surrounded by the three Terras, Z followed Nunez across the grass and into the woods. Germ perched atop Nunez's shoulder as Nunez consulted the metal remote in his palm which indicated the way to the coordinates.

"What can't that device do?" Z asked.

Nunez didn't answer.

They exited the forest and walked over some more grass. The falls loomed in the distance. The closer they got to it, the louder the pounding water grew until it became difficult to hear each other.

There weren't any tourists down here. Nunez led them toward the misty spray at the base of the falls, which formed a thick fog.

Z caught Nunez's attention. "The most beautiful place on the planet, right?"

"Mel thought so. I always thought it was only water."

Z could barely hear Nunez's words over the water's roar. "A cold analysis."

Nunez considered this, then called over his shoulder. "I'm a scientist. I study things. But Mel...she opened my heart a little."

"You have a heart?" Z said.

Nice one, Germ said.

They followed the metal remote's indications past a

section of spaced out large limestone rocks that dominated the area to an area of deep water at the base of Niagara Falls—well, one of the falls. Three separate waterfalls comprised Niagara Falls, Z knew.

Nunez suspended his hand over the embankment toward the deep choppy water. The metal remote indicated that they'd arrived.

Fog engulfed Nunez as he faced Z. "She is down there?"

Z nodded. "You bring a pair of swimming trunks?"

"I tire of your jokes."

Z turned to the Terras with a smirk. "Looks like one of you is going to have to get wet. My human body is too inferior and weak to dive to the bottom."

The Terras all gave him dirty looks. Nunez pointed at the Terra carrying Z's pistol and nodded at the roiling water.

Z thought she might strip off some of her clothes before getting wet, but she set the weapons on the grass with her ball cap and dove in.

Nunez cleared his throat. "I can't help but realize I'm down a bodyguard now."

Z shrugged. "You worried I might try something?"

"No. I only need one Terra to incapacitate you."

Z turned in a slow circle and surveyed the falls behind them. The fog hid them from any tourists who might be around farther up. He whistled. "I can see why this place was so important to your wife."

"Shut up," Nunez snapped. "You know nothing of my wife."

"I know she loved you. You claim to have loved her. But she ran away from you."

"That's not what happened!"

Knowing it would unnerve Nunez further, Z kept his

voice calm. "That's what the facts say. Why else would she leave an outdoor concert at night without telling you and come out to this place, a six-hour drive away?"

"I...I don't know, but it doesn't involve me—"

Z stood his ground as the fog rolled past them. "You were a college professor at the time. Maybe you were focusing too much on your academics instead of her?"

"I wasn't!" Nunez lurched forward and punched Z in the jaw. Judging by Nunez's gasp of pain, Z thought Nunez had probably hurt himself more than him. It took practice and skill to throw a proper punch.

Z shook off the blow and leaned forward over the bank, peering at the tumultuous water. He clucked his tongue. "Terra has been down there an awfully long time..."

"She's a robot. She doesn't need to breathe."

"For a robot that doesn't need to breathe, she sure liked to talk a lot when she was beating me up and trashing my new office."

Nunez shook his head. "You and those three newsmen are pathetic."

"At least they're something. It's more than you've got."

Nunez held his tongue and glanced down into the water. For the first time, he started to look nervous.

Finally, the Terra that had gone in broke the water's surface. With her wet hair plastered to the back of her neck, she glanced up at Nunez. "There is a female body down there beneath a rock. But I need help to free it."

Nunez considered this as the fog continued to roll past them. Then he nodded at a second Terra to join her. After she set her ball cap and pistol in the grass next to the others, she dove in as well, leaving Z, Nunez, and the remaining Terra standing and eyeing each other.

The dry Terra glared at Z. "Don't even think about trying anything."

"Try anything?" Z shoved his hands into his pockets. "Never." He stared at her.

After a time, she said, "What is wrong with you?"

"Oh. Nothing." He continued to stare at her.

The Terra felt at her cheeks. "Do I have something on my face?"

Z shook his head. "I was about to suggest that you jump in the water too. I've never judged a robot wet t-shirt contest before."

That sounds like a stupid contest, Germ said from Nunez's shoulder. Terra scowled.

Z chuckled. "You'd have to be a human male to get that."

"You're a pig." Nunez stepped through the fog to peer down into the water.

"You're still an asshole," Z muttered.

Germ snickered.

Nunez suddenly called, "I see them. Terra, come here." The scientist glanced at Germ on his shoulder. "Watch Z. If he tries something to undermine me, poison him with your neurotoxin."

Germ shuddered.

"You must obey me. I am your creator. I control you."

Z didn't see the metal remote in Nunez's hand so he must've already slipped it into his pocket. That would certainly make it a little trickier to get it and use it to free Germ, especially when the remote only responded to Nunez's DNA.

Germ hopped off Nunez's shoulder and plopped onto the grass.

Sorry Z, but I have to obey him.

Meanwhile, the two wet Terras breached the water's surface, fighting to keep upright amid the crashing water. They held something in their arms. Z didn't have a good view, but it looked like long-submerged human remains.

Nunez gasped. "Mel? Could that possibly be you?"

CHAPTER FIFTY-FIVE

"Germ," Z said. "I know Nunez has control over your actions. But he's going to double-cross me once the Terras climb out with that woman's body."

That 'woman's' body? You mean, 'Nunez's wife's' body?

In a whisper, Z said, "Look, I don't know if it's his wife or not. It was reported as a Jane Doe."

But you said it was...

"I had to make a move. I had to get Nunez away from the space and time capsule before he figured out how to use it. Do you know where it is?"

Yes. The tiny black octopus regarded him. *I cannot tell you. Nunez forbids it.*

"Well, I un-forbid it."

You do understand that now I have to tell Nunez that this is all an elaborate trick, right?

"You little shit. It might be his wife. I don't know. Buzz's algorithms say it's highly probable."

Germ shook his tiny octopus head as he tried to decide

what to do. Nunez and the dry Terra were leaning out over the water now.

Z raised his shirt a few inches. "Check out my new tattoo. Like it?"

Germ's eyes elongated into binoculars and locked in on the tiny black octopus tattoo on Z's waistline above his pants pocket. *Is that supposed to be me?*

Z smirked. "You bet, buddy. Pretty good, huh?"

Germ hesitated. *I must confess, it does not look as shitty as the rest of your hand-drawn tattoos.*

"That's because I didn't do it. I paid a professional to ink it for me."

Germ's tiny blob-ish form stood stock still as his eyes reverted back to their normal cute beady form. Z had never seen Germ look so deep in thought.

I...really like it.

Suddenly, Germ quivered like Jell-O. *Oh, Z, I miss our banter! Nunez is too serious and mopey.*

Z watched as Nunez and the dry Terra eased some human remains onto the grass beside the stack of ball caps and handguns. Z was running out of time until he outgrew his usefulness to Nunez. "Believe it or not, I went through a mopey phase myself after you were gone."

How did you get out of your slump?

"I saved a cat."

How strange.

"Will you help me?"

I cannot go against Nunez's orders. He controls me with that metal remote.

"Yeah, I get that. But I can't walk up and reach into Nunez's pocket. A Terra would be on me before I could pull my hand out. Can you get it for me?"

No. He would construe that as a trick. He ordered me to poison you with my neurotoxin if you try any tricks.

An idea hit him, but he was no futuristic technology expert. Either it would work or it wouldn't.

Z held up both palms peaceably. "I see. But I 'promise' that I only want to look at the metal remote. I don't want to push any buttons."

Germ leapt up onto Z's forearm and pressed a tentacle to his wrist artery. *You promise not to press any buttons? I will know if you are lying.*

"Promise," Z said earnestly, meaning it. A glance through the fog revealed Nunez kneeling over the remains that the two Terras had brought up.

Germ's octopus head twitched. *No heartbeat stutter to suggest a lie. I know the tenor of your voice well enough to know that you are telling the truth.*

"So you can get me that metal remote, right?"

Germ winked at him.

Just then, twin splashes broke the water. The two Terras climbed out onto land and stood at either side of Nunez and the human remains in the grass. Water fell in big drops from their soaked clothing.

Below them, Nunez reached down and unclasped a silver necklace from the remains. He held it to his heart and closed his eyes.

"It's her."

Even Z gave Nunez a moment of silence.

At last, Nunez cleared his throat and opened his eyes which were red and watery. "I can't believe you're gone, Mel."

The waterfall muffled his words.

He held the silver necklace to his chest and bowed his head. "Why did you come here? How?"

When he sniffled, the dry Terra patted his shoulder. Nunez continued, "Although I don't know what happened to you, at least I finally know where you are."

"You're welcome," Z called.

The dry Terra glared at Z. "What do you want us to do with the warper?"

Still clutching the silver necklace, Nunez thought contemplatively for a few moments before piercing Z with a fiery gaze.

"Subdue him."

By "subdue him," what Nunez meant was to capture him and knock him out so they could put him in a coma at a long-term storage facility.

That meant game over for Z.

The three Terras stood staring at him, two of them dripping. They did look good in wet t-shirts. He'd have to compliment Buzz's latest design the next time he was at a printing press.

Before they could rush him, Z pointed at the wet Terra on the right. "You win."

"Huh?" the Terra said, and the other two squinted their eyes in unison for an instant.

An instant was all Z needed. "Germ! The remote!"

Germ launched himself like a slingshot onto Nunez's hip. From there, he whipped a tentacle down into Nunez's pants pocket.

"Give me that back!" Nunez roared as he reached for Germ. Germ had already hopped off Nunez's hip and cocked the tentacle back like a baseball pitcher's arm. He tossed the small device to Z, who caught it and promptly threw it against a nearby rock, where he stomped it under his boot tread. The metal frame didn't suffer too much damage, but the buttons and internal mechanisms under them *crunched*.

Nunez shot to his feet. "No!"

I'm free! Germ shouted.

"Get my gun," Z called over the roar of the falls.

But bullets do not faze these robots...

Z grunted. "Less questioning, more doing."

Nunez waved both arms emphatically at Z. "Get him!"

The three Terras charged at Z while Germ skipped to the stack of guns by the water.

When the Terras reached him, Z already had his combat knife in his hands. Now all he needed was to buy enough time for Germ to bring him his pistol so he could use it against them.

The two wet Terras swung at him with fists that would knock him out cold—they knew how to throw a proper punch. Z sidestepped and hacked out with the combat knife to no effect. These robots didn't bleed, and their plastic bones resisted conventional metal. When they rounded on him again, he sliced through t-shirt and jeans and felt very much like the scarred villain of a slasher film.

As if reading Z's mind, Germ said, *This is like that horror movie we watched the other night, but the tropes are all mixed up.*

The dry Terra jump-kicked Z, sending him sprawling backward in the grass. Through her legs, Z saw Germ trying to pick his way across the grass, but the two wet Terras were eyeing him and blocking his passage. If Germ tried to lob the gun to him, the Terras would intercept it. It was much heavier than the remote had been.

I cannot get through, Germ said.

"What's your play here?" Nunez called above the water's roar. His white lab coat billowed with a draft coming off the water. "You already know that bullets can't stop my robots."

"Watch and learn." Z rolled on the grass to avoid a punch from the dry Terra. He came to his hands and knees and called to Germ, "Can't you get around them?"

These robots are too fast.

Z grumbled, "Excuses." He focused on the dry Terra in front of him, and when she kicked at him, he grabbed her outstretched leg and rose to his feet, shoving her to the side when she was off-balance.

"Get him!" the Terra yelled as Z ran past her.

Ahead of him, the two wet Terras stood with their backs to him, focusing on Germ out in front of them. Z charged ahead, intent on tackling through them. Right before he reached them, they spun and reached out for him with their fingers bent like claws.

Z dove between them, crashing against their thighs as their fingers raked his back, tearing his jacket.

You are in desperate need of new clothing, Germ said.

Z's chest struck the ground, and he lifted his head and made eye contact with Germ. "Throw me my gun!"

Germ tossed it, and Z caught it. He rolled over onto his back as the two wet Terras were descending on him with clawing hands. Z racked the pistol and fired once into the nearest robot's head.

CHAPTER FIFTY-SIX

Time seemed to stop as the gunshot boomed above the roar of Niagara Falls.

A hole appeared in the robot's forehead, and for a moment, Z could see right through it to the sky above. Then smoke started to issue from that Terra's head, and she toppled over into the grass.

"What is this?" Nunez cried, crouched near his wife's remains.

The other wet Terra threw her arms up defensively and took a step backward. Z fired again, the bullet striking her forearm and punching a hole straight through it. She turned and bolted. Z fired again as she fled toward the water, striking her in the leg. Tiny sparks spat from both holes as she dove for the pile of guns by the water.

Incoming. Germ launched himself at Z.

Z caught him and hit the grass. Gunfire chewed up the ground all around him.

"You killed our sister!" the wet Terra with the gun shouted.

After reloading, she tossed a gun to the dry Terra. Nunez had his gun out now too.

"You're robots!" Z scrambled behind a large limestone rock.

He only had one magazine of special bullets in his pistol. He had to conserve his ammo.

"How is this possible?" Nunez said.

Z chuckled. "Your robots are made out of some hard shit. I had to find something harder."

Nunez fired at Z's rock, and the two Terras fired as well. "Impossible," Nunez spat. "What material did you use?"

"Melted down one of the printing press's metal struts. Well, a friend of a friend did and cast them into bullets yesterday evening. Picked them up this morning."

"That's why you wanted to meet today…" Nunez's words trailed off.

"Yeah. Because I figured you'd double-cross me even if I did help you find your wife—which you did." He shook his head. "Conducting your business like that…not good for the reputation."

Nunez cursed and fired again even though the rock protected Z. If Z did die, he'd warp back. Z could feel the tables turning.

"I cannot believe my wife died here," Nunez said. "Why would she have come here?"

Peeking around the rock, Z saw motion as one of the Terras approached. He snaked his arm around the rock and fired. He blew another hole into the injured Terra, this time in her belly. There were no internal organs to wound on the robot, but she retreated to the dry Terra and Nunez all the same.

"I don't know," Z called. "But I can take the space and time capsule back and find out."

Nunez fired until his gun was empty. He inserted a new magazine. "All is not lost. I will keep searching for an Earth with a timeline that is farther back and stop Mel from coming out here…"

"How?" Z yelled. "I broke your Earth hopper device."

Nunez roared.

"I think it's time you hung this schtick up," Z said. "You're getting forgetful."

"I hate you. I hate you!" Nunez's voice was harsh and shrill. Several more bullets smashed into the rock Z was hiding behind.

Z peeked around and hunkered back down when the Terras unleashed a barrage of bullets. "You know," he replied, "I could say the same thing about you. My life wouldn't be messed up if you hadn't created the time virus."

Then I wouldn't have been born. Germ clung to Z's shoulder.

"True enough," Z said. "Maybe there's a plan to the grand scheme of life."

Uh, speaking of plans. You do have one, right? They kind of have us pinned down in case you haven't noticed.

Z peeked over the rock and fired at one of the Terras but missed. He cursed as he took cover again. "As a matter of fact, I have noticed!"

Germ hopped to the rock and peered around it. *The Terras are coming.*

Z edged out and fired at the far left Terra, blasting a chunk of the robot's shoulder away. He fired again, striking the Terra on the right in the heart. It didn't stop her.

Suddenly Germ blurted, *The Terras are coming. The Terras are coming!*

"I know—"

No, behind us.

Turning, Z saw the two Terras from the helicopter running his way. They leveled rifles at him.

"Shit." Z dove to the side and rolled as rifle fire ate at his previous position against the rock.

So you don't have a plan. Germ cartwheeled through the grass beside him as gunfire spat through the thin rolling fog.

Z raised his pistol and fired at one of the helicopter Terras, but she managed to roll out of the way. The other Terra fired, the bullet opening a gash on the side of Z's upper arm. He grunted and fired, hitting her in the chest, and she opened fire again.

Z scrambled to his feet and threw himself forward to the cover of another limestone rock.

They are surrounding us, Germ said. *I do not think you have a plan.*

"I do. I called in reinforcements before I started this mission, but I don't know where the hell they are."

You called Marshall? Germ said hopefully.

Z grunted, threw himself back against the rock, and fired in front of him at the two Terras and Nunez.

"No. He's on day shift now."

Really? Good for him—he deserves it. Germ squeaked as a bullet struck the earth right beside him.

Z knew the situation was hopeless. Even with his special robot-killing ammo, they had him outnumbered. If they succeeded in killing him, they would remember everything before the warp, canceling out his advantage of foreknowledge, making this situation harder to escape successfully with each successive warp.

If his reinforcement didn't show up ASAP, he and Germ were screwed.

Germ flattened himself against Z's side to escape the bullets closing in on their position. *Who did you call then?*

"Hey, robo-bitches!" a woman's voice yelled over the pounding of the falls and the gunfire.

For a moment, the shooting stopped, and a figure in blue darted through the fog. Then Alice rose and fired twice in quick succession, taking out one of the helicopter Terras with a head shot.

Alice? You called Alice? Germ chirped.

Z rose and fired at the other helicopter Terra to cover Alice, who darted toward him. "Yeah, tracked her down yesterday. Wasn't easy."

Germ waved at Alice as she ducked behind the next closest rock. *I like her. Good choice.*

"Stop them!" Nunez called from behind Z and pistol shots smacked into the ground around Z.

Cursing, Z vaulted over the rock and dove behind Alice's rock. "What took you so long?" Z said.

Alice peeked around their cover and fired. "You owe me big time." She was wearing dark jeans, a blue blouse, and a fanny pack.

"Oh?" Z said. "I thought killing robots would be payment enough."

She scoffed. "You're a bastard, you know?"

Z traded gunfire over the rock with Nunez. "I know. You're not the first one to say that."

She ejected a magazine and slammed another one into her pistol. "Not surprising. Hey, you finally got a shower. Clothes still look like shit."

"You're looking good too," Z said. "Making me hot how well you handle a gun like that."

"I grew up in a rough neighborhood." She turned to him, their faces almost touching. "You going to shoot or what?"

Smirking, Z returned fire. As he fired his last round, Nunez retreated around them toward the helicopter.

"Shit. You got any extra magazines?"

Alice slid him a couple of magazines from the fanny pack she was wearing.

Z nodded his thanks and loaded one. "It's good that gunsmith contact of yours was able to cast these bullets last night on such short notice."

She shrugged. "The money was right."

"That money was all I had." Z rose and fired at the retreating robots and Nunez.

"Yeah, yeah, a real sob story," Alice said. "Is anyone going to tell me what's up with that little black octopus on your shoulder?"

"His name is Germ. Sentient bioweapon from the future. He's a nice guy."

"Um. Right."

Tell her I like her hair.

"No, you pervert."

"Excuse me?" Alice said.

"Germ says he likes your hair."

Alice smirked. "Tell him I think he's cute."

Tell her I say thanks.

"He says thanks. Aren't you a bit weirded out?"

Alice stood and returned fire with a Terra that was covering Nunez's retreat. "I find out that killer robots from the future are real. Then I find out that the man the robots are trying to kill has an octopus sidekick...I believe it. I'm a *Paper Warriors* girl, remember?"

Z grinned, standing so they were shoulder-to-shoulder. This woman was perfect for him. "Let's go get Nunez. We can't let him escape."

CHAPTER FIFTY-SEVEN

Before they chased after Nunez and his Terra robots, Z dug the gold earpiece out of his boot and handed it to Alice. "Put this back in your ear."

"Uhh, no fucking way. That was in your shoe."

Z started running after Nunez and the Terras. "Yeah, because I knew they would frisk me."

Alice caught up to Z and pulled ahead of him a bit. Up ahead of them, Nunez and the Terras were approaching the section of woods. "Still not putting it in my ear."

"You need to put it in your ear."

I now see what you mean about women being so stubborn, Germ said thoughtfully.

"Why?" Alice asked.

Z was keeping up with her now even though his fatigued and beaten body demanded rest. He caught her eyes as they ran. "In case I have to die and warp back in time, I need you to wear it so you'll remember what happened."

"Are you serious?" She laughed. "That sounds ridiculous."

Z huffed in a breath as he ran. "Oh, so you'll believe a tiny octopus on my shoulder but me warping back in time when I die is too much?"

"I can *see* the black octopus."

"Just put the damn earpiece in your ear, Ms. 'I Read Alternative Science Magazines.'"

She made a disgusted sound and put the earpiece in her ear. "Fine. But if I get some unidentified ear fungus…"

"Get down!" Z threw himself in front of Alice and shoved her to the ground as one of the Terras sprang out from a patch of tall grass and fired. The bullet missed Alice's head, but it pierced Z's chest.

Z collapsed with a *thud*.

Alice's eyes widened as she crawled to his side. "Z!" She placed a hand on his shoulder to steady him. Her hand was warm.

"Fuck, that ain't good," Z breathed.

Germ picked himself out of the grass and took a quick look at Z's injury. *Yikes…*

Shock painted Alice's face as she leaned over him. "Where'd you get hit?"

Z tried to suck in a breath, but something wasn't right. "Lung shot," he managed. A bit of pink foam dribbled from his mouth.

"Shit. Fuck." Alice grabbed her hair in both hands.

Germ hopped onto Z's chest and inspected the wound. *Yep, that's terminal.*

Z looked up at Alice. "Don't look. Okay?"

Before she could protest, he pressed the muzzle of his gun under his jaw and pulled the trigger.

He died.

. . .

(Thirty Seconds Earlier)

"Fine. But if I get some unidentified ear fungus—"

Alice froze in her tracks and trained her pistol on the patch of tall grass the Terra robot had jumped out of before the warp.

"You shot my friend!" she yelled as she pulled the trigger.

The Terra clambered out of the grass to the side, narrowly missing Alice's robot-killing ammunition hitting her. The robot fled after Nunez. Alice fired a few more times, striking the robot twice but not in the head.

Then Alice turned, faced Z, and threw her hands on his shoulders, surprise gripping her face when she saw that he was unscathed.

"But you..." She patted his chest where the gunshot wound had been before the warp. It wasn't there.

Then she reached up and touched him under the chin. "Then you..."

No hole there either.

She groaned. "What's going on? Have I lost it?"

With a grin, Z gently gripped her wrists. "I died. I warped back." He watched her nod uneasily.

"But you died."

"I'm not crazy. You're not crazy. Everyone's happy. Except Nunez," he added. "That asshole is going down."

She looked at him. "Wait. So you're a Repeater?"

"How do you know..."

She pressed a finger to his lips. "I read about them in the *Paper Warriors* newspaper. I thought it was a made-up story, but now that I know it's true..." She lowered her hands to his thigh. "I'd be lying if I said I wasn't turned on right now."

"Um." Reluctantly, Z removed her hand from him and gestured at where Nunez was heading into the trees. The helicopter was waiting on the other side of the woods. "Later. We have to move."

Alice winked. "Let's get him."

I really do like her, Germ said as they started running again.

"Me too, buddy. Me too."

***

They made it to the forest without any more Terras popping out at them. Even though the Terra robots were wearing the gold earpieces, Z now had an advantage over them because Alice had one too.

Together, they sprinted through the wooded section. Still no Terras.

As they neared the clearing on the other side of the woods, the helicopter's rotors started up.

"He's going to get away," Alice said.

They came to the tree line, and two Terras started firing at them from twenty yards away in the grass. The helicopter was another twenty yards away, the downdraft from its rotors flattening the grass around it.

Z and Alice ducked back into the cover of the trees.

"No, he's not getting away." Z touched her arm and met her eyes. "You skirt around and get the pilot while I take on the rest."

She rolled her eyes. "Such a macho man." She smirked. "I like it."

Z felt an attraction like magnetism drawing them together, and he shook his head to clear it. "Not counting the pilot, there are three robots left. Plus Nunez. Be ready in case I have to warp. Now go!"

She nodded.

The two Terras continued to fire at the tree line. When there was a lull in the gunfire, Z leaned out and noted the robots' positions. He pulled back, avoiding taking a round to the head, then leaned out and took out the robot on the left with a head shot.

Nice shot, Germ said.

Z's head exploded as the second Terra shot him.

He died.

(Ten Seconds Earlier)

Z knew the two Terras' positions, but this time when he leaned out, they knew his, and they shot him before he could aim.

He fell to the ground, staring up at the tree leaves above.

He died.

(Five Seconds Earlier)

You got this, Germ said.

Warping back against these Terras was a nightmare. It was those damn gold earpieces. If he managed to kill both Terras, the mission was as good as done.

He peeked out from behind the tree and got shot in the head.

He hadn't seen either of the two Terras. So who had shot him?

He died.

(Five Seconds Earlier)

Sniper. In the helicopter, Germ said. The tiny black octopus was on the ground, peering out around the tree with his binocular eyes.

"Sniper?" Z said.

The third Terra is in the helicopter with Nunez. She is looking at our position through the scope of a sniper rifle.

Great. So not only did Z have two unaccounted Terras somewhere out in front of him, but he also had to contend with a killer robot with a sniper rifle?

He sneaked a peek beyond the tree. The helicopter was about forty yards away. Its side door was thrown open, but the inside was all shadows. He couldn't see the sniper Terra or Nunez.

He pulled back barely in time as a rifle bullet blew a chunk out of the tree he was hiding behind.

To the left! Germ blurted.

Z threw himself to the ground and tilted his pistol up at a Terra sneaking toward him through the woods.

Shit, they're in the woods... Z thought as he pulled the trigger.

He watched as the bullet found the robot's head. She fell sideways against a tree trunk and backward against the ground.

"One down," he muttered.

Behind you! Germ said.

Still on the ground, Z swiveled as fast as he could, but he knew he wasn't going to be quick enough to take out the second Terra before she took him out. He was going to have to Repeat...

A single gunshot sounded, but Z didn't feel any pain.

Then the Terra robot collapsed to her knees with a hole in her head. Alice was standing behind her with her pistol leveled at the robot.

She smirked and tapped her gold earpiece. "You must either love dying, or you suck at this *Mission: Impossible* thing." She dashed up to him and offered her hand to help him up.

Z accepted and patted off the dirt from his pants. "Shit. What would I do without you?"

Alice cocked her hip. "Probably die a lot more."

From outside the woods, the sound of the helicopter's engines intensified. It was about to lift off. They shared a glance.

"There's a sniper inside," Z said. "I'll draw her fire while you take out the pilot."

"I've been thinking..." Alice nodded at her pistol. "We're shooting bullets made of the hardest material known to science."

"Your point?" Z said.

"We shoot through the helicopter's siding."

Z paused and studied his gun. "Yeah, well. All right, then let's go!"

With a war cry, he stepped out from the tree line and opened fire on the helicopter's body. Alice stepped out as well, screaming and firing at the helicopter's cockpit.

The helicopter lifted a few inches off the ground.

"Keep firing!" Z yelled. He waited for a sniper rifle bullet to pierce him, but it never came. The helicopter kept ascending.

He and Alice were shoulder-to-shoulder now, firing at the helicopter as they took slow, careful strides ever closer to it.

It is working. It is working! Germ said.

Sunlight punched into the helicopter through all the bullet holes littering its metal hull. It was about ten feet off the ground when the aircraft's engines groaned, and its nose tilted downward.

Both Z's and Alice's pistols *clicked* empty. They were out of ammo. Z held up an arm and started to back up along with Alice.

That's when he noticed the stream of fuel running along the helicopter's metal body.

Z grimaced. "Oh shit. Must've hit the fuel tank. Get back!"

He and Alice turned and ran.

Behind them, the helicopter nose-dived into the grassy clearing with a ground-shattering *whump*. It exploded in a ball of flame, and the rotor tore free, screaming as it sliced through the air.

Z turned to look at it. "You've got to be shitting m—"

The spinning helicopter rotor sheared him in half.

He died.

(Twenty Seconds Earlier)

"Watch out for the fuel tank!" Alice yelled as they fired at the helicopter.

Alice catches on fast, Germ said.

Z shook his head as he continued to plug away at the helicopter. "What are the chances that the fucking rotor would hit me?"

Alice smirked. "Guess you're a lucky guy."

The helicopter slowly started to descend.

"I'm something, all right. You sure you want to hang around me?"

"My life was starting to get a little boring."

Ahead of them, the helicopter touched back down on the earth, flat this time, on its runners. Z's and Alice's guns *clicked* empty.

"Let's finish this," Z said, and Alice nodded. She handed him a magazine from her fanny pack and inserted the last one into her pistol.

Z made his way toward the helicopter's open side door as Alice went around to check on the Terra pilot.

He immediately saw the sniper Terra slumped forward in the helicopter, holes lining her body. Sparks shot up from them along with some tendrils of smoke. The robot lifted her head and glared up at Z. He finished her off, then climbed inside.

Nunez was sitting up against the far wall, pinpricks of sunlight piercing him through the holes in the metal siding. The scientist coughed, but his eyes were closed.

Z edged up to him, noting the pistol resting on Nunez's lap. Blood stained Nunez's white lab coat from multiple holes in his chest.

"How bad is it?" Z asked.

Germ inspected Nunez's wounds from atop Z's shoulder. *Not good. He doesn't have long to live.*

Just then, Nunez's eyes shot open. They focused on Z, and Nunez laughed. It was a harsh chuckle. "You did it. You beat me."

"Yeah. I guess so."

Nunez coughed again. "How does it feel?"

Z thought about it. "I don't feel any different." He moved closer to Nunez, and the doctor gripped the gun in his lap and raised it.

"Don't come any closer."

"You're an asshole. You get that, right?"

From outside the helicopter came the sound of repeated pistol shots. Z hoped it was Alice shooting the pilot, but he couldn't be certain.

Another cough wracked Nunez's body. "I guess this is goodbye?"

Z tilted his head from side to side. "I could warp back and find a way to take out the helicopter without killing you."

"You would do that?"

Z rolled his shoulders. He kept his pistol trained on Nunez's chest. Maybe he was a fool for saying what he was about to say, but he felt like a different man now than when he first came to this Earth. Maybe he was even growing as a person.

"I know what it's like to be driven mad by something. Your time virus killed a lot of people. There could also be a lot of good still inside you. Depends on you."

Nunez rested his pistol on his lap. "This must be a trick."

Z hesitated. Part of him wanted to blow this asshole away for all he'd done to him. Still, Z had received a second chance. He'd offer the same to Nunez. "No trick. You want a shot at redemption or not?"

Nunez thought about it for a few breaths. When he spoke, his words came in a wheeze. "My old bones are beyond saving."

Then, his face tightening with the effort, Nunez aimed his gun at Z.

Z beat him to the trigger pull. Three gunshots later, Nunez had three more holes in his chest. The pistol dropped from Nunez's hand.

Z edged up next to Nunez and gripped his wrist. "I'll find out what happened to your wife. And stop it...if I can."

"You would do that for me?" Nunez wheezed.

"Not for you. For me."

With pained but grateful eyes, Nunez nodded. Then his head hung forward in death.

A scuffle sounded from behind him, and Z spun, his gun at the ready.

It was Alice.

He climbed out of the helicopter, and she threw her arms around him.

"Is it done?"

"It's done."

"Thank God."

When they finally pulled apart from each other, there was an awkward pause.

Alice played with a strand of her hair. "That was pretty intense."

"Yeah."

"All those killer robots. And guns. Don't forget the exploding helicopter. Plus all those times you died and warped back..."

There was another pause.

"So what now?" Alice asked.

Z rubbed a sore spot on his hip. "You feel like jumping back in time?"

Her eyes widened. "You're serious?"

He nodded. "I'm going to figure out what happened to Nunez's wife. Germ knows the location of the space and time capsule. We'll need to go back to the *Paper Warriors* office first so I can plot out all the variables."

Alice grinned. "Time travel? Sign me up."

When Z returned to the *Paper Warriors* office, he didn't initially see the newsmen. But he heard them.

Clack, clack, clack, ding.

He spotted them at the back of the room, *clacking* away on

their new typewriters. Fortunately, they hadn't been damaged during the Terra fight here.

When they didn't get up to greet him, Z cleared his throat.

The tallest newsman stole a glance up at him and went back to his typewriter. "We're working on an important story. Got to pay the bills. No time to talk."

Alice stepped inside the news office and whistled. "Nice. New office smell." She put her hands on her hips. "You could use a new couch, though."

"It is new," Z flatly stated as he made his way back to the printing press.

He needed to let Buzz know that all was right in the world again, or rather, worlds. He composed the following headline.

Multiverse Is Safe Again. Nunez, Gone.

He punched the "Send" button and waited for the flashing green light.

Then he grabbed a pencil and a piece of paper and started to make some calculations for the time jump back to the night Mel had disappeared at the outdoor concert. He'd promised to solve her case, and he was going to keep his word.

The thought of using the space and time capsule again excited him, but not as much as usual because his body was tired and sore.

After the last few days of abuse, he could use some more rest before time jumping with Alice. When he finished his calculations, he stumbled toward the couch and let himself fall onto it, ruined or not.

"Ahh," he grunted and closed his eyes.

The couch shifted as Alice sat next to him. He cracked an eye open. "You're still here?"

She scoffed. "You know what the best part of this office is?"

Z closed his eye again as he tried to relax. "What?"

"It's right next door to a coffee shop."

Z thought it was only a statement so he didn't say anything, just sat back and sank into the couch. When Alice smacked his arm, he started.

"I said, it's right next door to a coffee shop."

"So?" Z was a bit perturbed now.

Germ tapped Z on the arm. *I think the woman is requesting for you to buy her a coffee. I believe this is called a date.*

Z sat upright and eyed the little black octopus. "Holy shit. You've finally figured out human women."

I guess you haven't.

Z turned to Alice. "Next, I guess you're going to suggest you escort me to a clothing store to buy a new wardrobe…"

She batted her eyelashes at him.

"But these clothes are so comfortable. And airy—"

She pressed herself against him and kissed him on the lips, and he pulled her to him. His body was sore and tired but oh well. He kissed her, and they ran their hands over each other's bodies.

Eventually, Alice glanced over at the newsmen and back at Z. "There doesn't happen to be someplace a bit more private in here…a bathroom, maybe?"

Z pointed toward the back of the office. "Even has a shower in it."

"I could use a shower. How about you?"

He grinned. They climbed off the couch and headed back there.

Sitting at their new desks, the newsmen didn't look up once the whole time Z and Alice had been on the couch. They kept *clacking* away at their story.

CHAPTER FIFTY-NINE

Z and Alice followed Germ's directions to the space and time capsule. It was resting in the back room of an empty science lab Nunez owned, with a sheet draped over it.

Z grabbed the sheet and ripped it off in a dramatic fashion. "Baby, I'm back," he said.

Alice groaned. "Ugh. You talk to it?"

"This capsule and I have been together for a long time. We've shared some experiences."

"O-kay. Hey, are you sure traveling in this won't mess me up since I'm not a Repeater?"

Z shrugged. "Not more than you already are."

She punched him. "I'm serious. I've never been in a time machine before."

"Eh, you'll be fine." Z opened the glass lid. "Look how I turned out."

Throwing back her hair, Alice said, "That's what I'm afraid of."

Z motioned her into the back seat of the two-person space

and time capsule and watched as she fitted her seatbelt harness.

"Is this necessary?"

Z climbed into the pilot's seat and closed the lid. "Probably not but I'd suggest you wear it."

I do not think you are making her feel at ease, Germ said.

"This isn't going to kill me, is it?" Alice asked.

Z flipped some switches. "Not unless I miscalculated the landing coordinates."

"Has that ever happened?"

"First time for everything," Z said.

"We're good, right? No misgivings about me after I set you up and betrayed you to Nunez…"

Z punched up the controls and inputted the variables he'd calculated back at the *Paper Warriors* office. "Water under the bridge, babe. Ready?"

She nodded. "But first—"

Z initiated the launch sequence and the space and time capsule started to vibrate.

A few moments later, darkness replaced the science lab's fluorescent lighting. Stars twinkled high above in the sky, visible through the capsule's glass lid.

"Wow," Alice said. "They're so beautiful. Where are we?"

Z powered down the capsule and popped the lid. He got out and helped Alice climb out. They were in a field in the middle of nowhere.

"Upstate New York. Half a mile outside the outdoor concert venue."

Alice's eyes were wide. "You mean, we traveled back in time?"

"Yeah." He started walking in the direction of a big hill with a glow of light behind it—the venue.

Alice hurried to keep up with him. "I don't hear any music."

"Concert hasn't started yet. We want to get there before Mel does and disappears."

Alice glanced back at the space and time capsule. "How come we had to park so far away?"

"So no one would discover the space and time capsule and try to tinker with it."

"Oh."

"Now, are we going to play twenty questions or are we going to stop a woman from dying at Niagara Falls?"

They walked in silence until they crested the hill. At the bottom of it was a lit-up constructed stage with an awning over it. Beyond it, sprawled out for over half a mile, were hundreds of blankets lying on the grass. People chatted and ate from picnic baskets or food bought from vendors off to the side. Everyone looked so happy.

"So how do we find Mel?" Alice asked.

Z looked at her. "We keep walking."

Z and Alice split up, checking a different side, walking up and down the grassy aisles, and stepping over blankets. There were so many people. And it was dark.

While the stage lighting was pretty spectacular, the rest of the place was dark so people could look up and enjoy the stars.

Z thought it would be nice to lie down on the grass under the stars with Alice and listen to the music. Maybe another time. He was starting to think they should've arrived sooner so they would have more time to look for Mel.

They'd made their way about halfway down the rows of people when an announcer came over the loudspeaker and introduced all the bands that would be playing that night. Then the national anthem began to play.

Z held his hand over his heart as he and Alice continued to search. Some of the eventgoers gave them dirty looks and nodded for them to get out of the way.

Yep, should've gotten here earlier.

The national anthem wrapped up, and the first band began to play acoustic folk music.

I see her! Germ said.

Germ was the one with the good night vision so it was no surprise that he was the one to find her. Z called Alice to him, and they proceeded to the cluster of blankets Germ had indicated.

Mel looked as pretty as in the framed photos at the Garcia residence. Petite, cheery, and she was wearing a pink sun hat, although she seemed a little anxious. She was sitting on a blanket next to some other people her age, nibbling on her fingernails. By the carefree way they were talking to each other, they all must have been her friends.

Z was about to approach her from the center aisle when Alice grabbed his arm. "No offense, but that sexy face scar might scare her. Let me talk to her instead?"

Z thought about it.

"Besides," Alice said. "I'm the one who got you roped into this investigation in the first place. It's only fitting that I get her to trust us so we can figure out what happened and stop it."

Z nodded. He watched as one of Mel's friends held up a Polaroid camera, turned it around, and took a photo of themselves. The concertgoers behind and around Mel's group cried out in annoyance at the bright flash.

An eighties selfie, Z thought. *Nice.*

That was probably the photo that Alice gave him when he took this case. Nunez must have given it to her.

Alice stepped up to the group of friends and crouched by Mel. The two women had a brief whispered conversation and glanced up at Z. He smiled and waved, and Alice and Mel stood. Z guided them off to the side where they could talk privately and not be in anyone's way.

Mel looked at Z for a moment. "This lady says you're some kind of…psychic?"

Germ snickered from inside Z's pocket.

"Um, well…sort of," Z said.

Mel swallowed. "Then you saw something about my future?"

"Sort of."

"Something good?" Mel looked hopeful.

Z shook his head.

"Oh." Mel's eyes fell to the ground. Then she started to cry.

Z was trying to figure out what to do when Alice went up to Mel and comforted her.

"It doesn't have to turn out bad, though," Z added.

Mel sniffled and wiped her nose. Alice pulled a white handkerchief from her pocket and handed it to her.

"That's not laced with a knockout solution, is it?" Z joked.

Mel didn't hear him, but Alice did.

Probably shouldn't have said that, Germ said.

Judging by the glare Alice sent him, the little octopus was right.

Mel gave Z a teary-eyed look. "It's about my baby, isn't it."

"Baby?" Z scratched his head. "You don't have a baby."

Mel blew her nose in the handkerchief. "Not yet. But…" She pointed at her belly. "I found out today. Took a test before the concert…I didn't even want to come here, but I was too afraid to tell my husband. He's so busy with his work, and I don't want to tell my friends because they're having a good time, but I can't have a good time because my mind is on the baby and…"

Z put a hand on her arm. "It's going to be okay. Really, it is."

His words comforted her, and she started to relax. "Really?"

"My um, vision isn't about your baby. It's about…" Z tried to think of how to word it. "Were you thinking about leaving the concert early? Going someplace else?"

Mel swallowed and nodded.

Z continued. "Somewhere with water?"

Mel started crying again. She blew her nose and nodded.

"Niagara Falls, maybe?"

Wide-eyed, she nodded again. "I know it sounds crazy— it's so far away—but Niagara Falls is my safe place. It's the most beautiful place on the planet to me."

Z took her hand in his. "So you were going to drive out to the falls right now?"

"Y-yes. I was going to get a taxi—there's a bunch of them parked along the road for after the event. Is that a bad idea?"

Drawing a deep breath, Z confirmed, "A very bad idea."

At least now he knew how Mel's pink sun hat got to the barn not far from here. It must've blown off when she was in the taxi or when she was walking to the taxi.

"What happens?" Mel's eyes were blurry with tears. "You've seen the future. You have to tell me what happens."

He recalled the sight of the Terras lifting her bloated

remains from the water beneath the falls. He recalled the sight of Old Nunez kneeling over her.

He couldn't tell her. Not that.

"You uh, have an accident on the way."

Mel put a hand over her mouth. "Oh dear. What, what should I do?"

"Honestly," Z said. "I think the best thing for you to do is to go home to your husband. Tell him about the baby. He'll be ecstatic. He may be an asshole, but he's a good man—as long as you're in his life."

"Um. Okay?"

"Maybe be very, very careful if you ever go back to Niagara Falls? Never step out where you might fall."

Mel nodded.

"Good," Z said. "I'll go out to the road and grab a taxi for you."

Mel dabbed at her wet eyes. "Thank you, oh thank you."

Alice nodded at Z to let him know that he'd done a good job.

Z turned to go toward the road. As he walked, he spoke his thoughts to Germ. "So Nunez trying to find a way to go back in time, creating the time virus, infecting me, and thus sending me on a crazed spree. All this was due to a terrible accident? A woman scared by finding out she was pregnant and going to her happy place—Niagara Falls. By herself. In the dark. Then slipping on a rock and drowning…"

He dropped his head as he walked. "That's depressing."

Yep, Germ said.

"Think of the impact that one person has…"

Yep, Germ said.

Z walked the rest of the way in silence. He'd solved the

case. By saving Mel, he'd given the young Nunez of this Earth the gift of being able to spend the rest of his life with his wife.

"And they lived happily ever after…" Z muttered.

CHAPTER SIXTY

Three months later

"So this is Earth-Z? Where you're from? It's so different…"

Z and Alice were strolling hand-in-hand along the sidewalk. "Yeah," Z said.

It had been a while since he'd been to this Earth. He didn't belong there anymore. But there was something he had to check on.

They were silent for a while as they walked. Alice was taking in the new sights. Although they were still in New York, the year was 2035, and fashion trends were much different than in the 1980s. Also, cars looked different, and all the flashing signs and storefronts were new.

Finally, Alice spoke. "I can't believe I'm in the future. On a parallel Earth." She smiled like a kid in a candy store. "This is so crazy!"

Some passersby flashed her odd looks behind their futuristic-looking sunglasses.

Z grinned apologetically. "It's okay, everyone. I'm walking ol' Alice back to the looney bin."

Alice punched his arm.

He laughed.

"Where are you taking me?" she asked.

"You'll see. You'll see."

I'm so excited! Germ's tiny black eyes peered out of Z's pants pocket. *I hope it worked on this Earth.*

"Me too, buddy. Me too."

It was late afternoon, and the sun would be going down in a couple of hours. It was the perfect time to catch a soccer game.

When Alice stopped and looked into an electronics storefront, Z tugged her after him. "We're almost there."

A few minutes later, they came to a park with a couple of soccer fields and metal bleachers. Several teams of little girls were out on the fields practicing drills while the scoreboards counted down until match time. The bleachers were packed full of parents and other supporters.

Z kept to the back of the park and made his way to the field he was interested in seeing. From his position standing in the shade under a tree, he had a perfect view of the girls practicing on the field and the metal stands on the opposite side. The shade meant that no one in the bleachers would be able to see him. The scoreboard said ten minutes until kickoff.

Alice stepped up beside him. "Do you know one of these girls?"

Z grunted. Alice understood not to press him so she gave him some space.

Z watched his daughter send a pass at the halfway line.

She has good technique, Germ said.

Z nodded. "Who do you think taught her?" He watched his daughter practice for a few more minutes before turning his gaze to the bleachers across the field. He saw his wife sitting in the stands…

But the seat next to her was empty.

"Shit," he muttered. Maybe it hadn't worked. But it had on all the other Earths. What the hell was going on?

The girls continued to practice while Z and Alice stood in the shade of the tree. Eventually, the two coaches gathered the girls to the sidelines, and they huddled up.

Z looked back at the bleachers. There was still an empty seat next to his wife. The younger version of himself was nowhere in sight.

He shook his head sadly. "I righted all the wrongs… It worked on all the other Earths so why not on my home Earth?"

Germ extended a tentacle from Z's pocket and patted him on the arm. *Cheer up. Maybe this wrong, for some cosmic reason unknown to us, cannot be righted on Earth-Z. But think of all those other Earths where your younger self did make it to this match.*

"Well, yeah, but this is my home Earth. This is the one that counts, to me at least."

He sighed. Missing his daughter's first soccer match was his life's biggest regret. It wasn't because he was off saving the world at the time. In those days, in addition to running missions with his team, he was still employed part-time at the grossly understaffed CIA. Those days, he worked late every night because of casefile overload. To sum up, he was too busy doing paperwork to see his daughter play soccer—the lamest excuse ever for a superhero such as himself.

That's why, with help from Buzz's supercomputer algorithms, he'd made a list of wrongs he needed to right, to reduce his workload and enable him to leave work on time on this day.

Over the past three months, Z had righted the wrongs on all the known parallel Earths so none of the younger versions of himself would miss his daughter's first soccer match.

Not every wrong he'd righted had to deal with this day. There were plenty of instances where he'd been an asshole to a stranger on the street, and he went back and fixed it.

He'd saved Earth-Z for last because it was his home Earth and it meant the most to him. It had worked on all the other Earths he'd tried it on.

So why hadn't it worked on Earth-Z?

Among the wrongs he'd righted on each of the Earths was the father who killed himself because he missed his court case. The man was a top CIA analyst who continued to work and became a legend, solving some of the cases making up Younger Z's backlogged caseload.

The man who got sideswiped and killed by a semi on the highway ended up catching a drug dealer at the airport where he worked security. The drug dealer who, being in prison, didn't kill a young police detective on the street who eventually cracked a major case and solved some gang connections Z was working on, thus reducing his caseload further.

As for the bullied little boy at the playground, he never grew into a huge bully himself—a mob boss—cutting a few more of Z's cases.

It was through Z's manipulations of the timeline on each Earth that he'd successfully cut down his younger version's caseload and allowed him to come to this match and spend more time with his family in general. It also righted some of the random shittiness that was life.

He stared down at the ground. Maybe Germ was right. Maybe the universe or fate or whatever didn't want him to right his biggest wrong on his home Earth. Perhaps it was cosmic punishment.

"It's about to start," Alice said.

Z looked up in time to see the opening kickoff. His daughter's team had won the coin toss, and his daughter was preparing to kick. Z felt a tear forming in his eye. He was so proud of her.

In the stands—look! Germ shouted.

Z glanced across the soccer field at the metal bleachers. The younger version of himself had taken the seat next to his wife. After kissing her, he turned to watch the game, his face glowing with pride.

You did it! It worked! Germ cheered.

"Well, I'll be damned," Z muttered. "It worked. It actually worked." Tears bubbled up from both eyes, and he let them fall in fat rivulets down his cheeks.

After the match, Z and Alice got some ice cream together, and they headed back to where Z had parked the space and time capsule.

Alice looked up at him as Z opened the glass lid. "I would hate to take you away from your home. Are you sure you want to go back to Earth-D?"

Z sighed. "Yeah. The newsmen will be ecstatic when I tell them about this feat." He threw an arm around her shoulders. "We can throw a big party at the office."

She poked him in the abs. "You're a big softie. You know that?"

"Shut up." He kissed her long and slow. Then they both got in the capsule. He closed the glass lid and punched the coordinates and date and time into the center console. The space and time capsule began to vibrate. Then it was gone.

When the vibrating stopped, Z opened the glass lid and prepared to climb out into the small office he'd constructed inside the new *Paper Warriors* office so he could have some privacy. Before he got out, though, Alice pulled him back in.

"We don't have to leave yet. We could celebrate in here first."

Z flicked his gaze between Alice and the interior of the space and time capsule. "In my baby?"

She batted her eyelashes. "Here I thought I was your baby."

Z closed the lid and climbed into the back seat with Alice.

Humans, Germ said as he watched. *Such interesting creatures...*

When they finally emerged from Z's office, Alice made a beeline for the bathroom to straighten her messy hair. Z was about to follow her when the tallest newsman shouted, "He's back! Guys, he's back!"

"Um, hi?" Z said.

The three newsmen rushed up to him, beaming.

"Something happen while I was away?" Z asked. "You guys sure look happy."

They grabbed Z's hand. "Come on. Follow us!"

Z allowed them to drag him after them. He glanced back at Alice standing outside the bathroom, giving him a curious shrug.

They guided him outside onto the sidewalk, and Z raised a hand to fend against the bright sunlight. "Guys, where are you taking me?"

"You'll see in a moment," the middle newsman said breathlessly.

The newsmen turned and led Z into the building next door to the news office. The smell of coffee perked Z up.

"Guys, I can get coffee anytime. What's this about—"

He stopped.

There, on the order board was the bolded food item: Donuts.

His gaze shot throughout the room at all the patrons smiling and dipping donuts into their coffees. One of the coffee shop's employees was even eating one behind the cash register. She waved for Z to come up to the counter.

"B-but how? What happened? Am I dreaming?"

The shortest newsman beamed up at him. "We wrote and published that article you had an idea for. You know, the Great Donut Conspiracy."

"It worked!" the tallest newsman said.

Germ grinned and crossed two tentacles across his chest.

"Guys," Z said. "I'm so happy I could die."

AUTHOR NOTES RAMY VANCE
NOVEMBER 23, 2021

I hate reading children's books.

I hate it.

I don't care how hungry that damn caterpillar is nor do I give a crap what the Gruffalo's struggles are … and if I have to act surprised for about one more damn pop-up, I'm going to scream. *Oh look – an airplane.* Ahhh!

I know, I know – as a writer, I should love reading kid's books. Bedtime stories should be something I relish to do. But I don't.

It surprised me…surprised my wife even more – she thought I'd be into it for sure. I think she kind of feels duped, like I tricked her somehow. But if I didn't know I'd be like this, can I really be blamed? Depends on who you ask, apparently.

Irrespective of the marital strife, I'd love to get to the root of the issue. I guess it ultimately stems from the fact that most children's books don't have vampires.

There! I said it.

So, in an effort to find age-appropriate vampire novels for

my kid (he's 6), I did a deep dive into the children's book section and I discover 3 gems.

1 – The ABCs of DnD: Wow – what a great book. It's kind of like a player's handbook for kids, explaining the basics. It's companion book: 1, 2, 3, DnD is also great and the conversations my son and I have about DnD is awesome. (We talk about liches, a lot. Come to think of it, that's probably why the big bad in Dark Gate Angels' is a lich.) I've already got him creating a character: a forty-seven-foot-tall robot... not quite on trope for DnD, but close enough.

2 – Last Kids on Earth: It's a bit mature for a six-year-old and my wife would prefer I read more kid friendly stuff. But reading a light-hearted story about a bunch of kids surviving a zombie apocalypse isn't he worse thing in the world. We all have to pick our battles and wife didn't pick this one. Besides, I'm training my kid how to write early.

3 – Rocks in Your Pocket: Not DnD related. No zombies, vampires or werewolves, either. Still, *Rocks in Your Pocket* is awesome. It's about a family of farmers who need to fill their pockets with rocks, lest they are blown off their mountain-home by heavy winds. It's a sweet, sentimental story that causes me to tear up every time I read it. I love it. My son loves it. And my daughter just looks at me confused as to why dad is crying.

I guess there are some books I can tolerate, and as they grow, I'm sure to find more and more. Who knows – this might become an Author Notes thing: Shit Ramy Will Read to His Kids. But with these gems and few others, bedtime is no longer a chore, but something I actually look forward to...

Now if I can only convince my 18-month-old that pop-up books suck, I'll be set.

Thank you for not only reading this story but these author notes as well.

Ok, I have to admit here that our youngest child turned twenty-two this year, so I have no right to talk about children's books.

However… *(you knew there would be a "however," right?*

Here are a few cool titles I'd like to suggest (none are very kid-friendly, though.)

Title: *ABCs for Little Fighters* starting with "A is for Axe."

Title: *ABCs for Little Shopkeepers,* starting with "A is for Amethyst."

Title: *Double-Tap Dirk Learns to Go for the Shins.*

Title: *Dark Magic for Six-Year-Olds,* followed by *Black Magic for Nine-Year-Olds.*

Title: *How to Start the Apocalypse without Getting Grounded.*

Title: *Why Asmodeus Was Simply Misunderstood* for preteens.

Title: *How to Pick Pockets* for kids in the Thieves Guild.

Title: *Why Chaotic Neutral is a Good Alignment for You.*

I am jealous that Ramy wasn't my dad. Well, maybe not my dad, but perhaps my weird but really cool uncle?

My coolest uncle when I was young was my Uncle Tom. He was the guilty party who got me started on the Intellivision video game system back in, like, 1979 (or maybe 80.)

I was on a family trip to Oklahoma (from Houston, TX. It felt like it took forever), and he had it hooked up in my grandparents' room. I stole whatever time I could and played it.

I had a video-game habit (very much like a drug habit) from then until my middle child, Jacob, kicked my ass when he was, like, eight years old. We were playing Starcraft, and once he did that, I hung up my proverbial mouse and went and played real adult games like…Stock Market.

It would have been less expensive to continue playing video games. However, I probably would not have continued to pursue building my own company had I not been so hugely embarrassed by my incredibly young son.

He might have been as old as ten, but I doubt he was much older than that.

These are my ruminations, thinking about Ramy's author notes. I hope they brought at least a small smile to your face as we continue creating mayhem in stories and characters you (hopefully) care about.

Have a good week or weekend. Talk to you in the next story!

Ad Aeternitatem,

Michael Anderle

Other Middang3ard Books

Never Split The Party (01)
Late To the Party (02)
It's My Party (03)
Blue Hell And Alien Fire (04)

Death Of An Author: A Middang3ard Novella

Dark Gate Angels
Dark Gate Angels (01)
Shades of Death (02)
The Allies of Death (03)
The Deadliness of Light (04)

Dragon Approved
The First Human Rider (01)
Ascent to the Nest (02)
Defense of the Nest (03)

Nest Under Siege (04)
First Mission (05)
The Descent (06)
Sacrifices (07)
Love and Aliens (08)
An Alien Affair (09)
Dragons in Space (10)
The Beginning of the End (11)
Death of the Mind (12)
Boundless (13)

Other Books by Ramy Vance

Mortality Bites Series
Keep Evolving Series